THE RESTLESS BOOKS EDITION OF *THE BOY*
WAS GENEROUSLY SPONSORED BY HOWARD GREENE

THE BOY

MARCUS MALTE

THE BOY

TRANSLATED FROM THE FRENCH BY
EMMA RAMADAN AND TOM ROBERGE

RESTLESS BOOKS

BROOKLYN, NEW YORK

Cet ouvrage a bénéficié du soutien des Programmes d'aide à la publication de l'Institut français

This work received the French Voices Award for excellence in publication and
translation. French Voices is a program created and funded by the French Embassy in
the United States and FACE Foundation (French American Cultural Exchange)

French Voices Logo designed by Serge Bloch

This project is supported in part by the National Endowment for the Arts.

First Restless Books paperback edition March 2019

Paperback ISBN: 9781632061713

Library of Congress Control Number: 2018948541

Cover design by Richard Ljoenes
Set in Garibaldi by Tetragon, London
Printed in Canada

1 3 5 7 9 10 8 6 4 2

Restless Books, Inc.
232 3rd Street, Suite A101
Brooklyn, NY 11215

www.restlessbooks.org
publisher@restlessbooks.org

CONTENTS

PREFACE

Reading *The Swiss Family Robinson* recently with my eight-year-old son, I came across a passage—amid the ardent shelter-building, tropical-plant identification, animal-shooting, and campfire cookery of the novel's first chapters—where our narrator, William, expresses the fear that his family's new home might be inhabited by savages. The author's (and translator's) use of the word seemed to require explanation, or context; I asked my son if he knew what it meant.

"I think he means wild animals," he said. "Beasts."

I explained, with some discomfort, that the author was actually referring to people, indigenous to the island, who likely lived as hunters and gatherers, employing technology that had been used for thousands of years, and practicing forms of religion, storytelling, dance, dress, and music-making that would have been unfamiliar, and perhaps even frightening, to Europeans. I explained that the word originated with the Latin *silva*, meaning *wood*, and *silvatica*, out of the woods; from this came the French *sauvage*, and finally our English *savage*, with its attendant fear of the unknown, of what might lurk in forests, fierce and untameable and possibly intending to do us harm. But why would a *person* be called a savage, my son still wanted to know; and what made the Swiss family fear them? Underneath his question I sensed another: What is it that makes us recognize one another as human? And what does it mean to be human in the first place?

This subject was much on my own mind because I'd been reading the book you now hold in your hands: Marcus Malte's brilliant and disturbing novel *The Boy*, which poses the same question in a different way. Using a trope familiar to literature, one that has long fascinated

ix

and perplexed us—from Romulus and Remus abandoned by their mother and nursed by a she-wolf, to the tale of Victor of Aveyron, the eighteenth-century French boy who was discovered after more than a decade on his own in the wild—Malte envisions a man-child, newly orphaned at fourteen, who has lived all his life in the isolated wilds of southern France, with only his nonverbal mother for company; the story opens in the first decade of the twentieth century, on the verge of one of the greatest upheavals of Western history. Notably, the point of view belongs not to some curious observer but—as in T. C. Boyle's "Wild Child," or Karen Russell's "St. Lucy's Home for Girls Raised by Wolves"—to the feral child himself, nameless and languageless. As we inhabit him, as we experience his journey into the populated world, there is no way to perceive him as *other*, only as a version of ourselves, at times compassionate, at times violent, always curious, always seeking comfort and love, a balm for what's been irrevocably lost. Moving from wilderness to village, from village to town, and from town to city, this extraordinary character perceives, and thereby reveals, the strangeness of the twentieth-century world.

To see every element of our lives (and yes, these are *our* lives, with only minor differences)—the things we eat, the way we behave towards animals, the way we house and clothe ourselves, the way we worship, speak, make music, treat our children, medicate ourselves, perform the act of love, and wage war—through the eyes of someone to whom all of this is new, constitutes a reevaluation of everything we take for granted. In what ways are we ridiculous, or compassionate, or divine? In what ways are we beastly? Mona Ozouf, president of the Prix Femina jury that awarded its 2016 honor to *The Boy*, called it, in my imperfect translation, "a novel about, among other things, the ensavagement of human beings by war, which reminds us that barbarism camps on the borders of the civilized world."

Marcus Malte himself, speculating in an interview about his reasons for choosing the book's historical setting, said this: "Until now,

I'd always located my novels in our own time; I'd described the contemporary world exhaustively, especially its faults, so maybe I'd arrived at a time when this world, our world, weighed on me too much—when I needed to get away from it, at least in my fiction." But isn't the story of human ensavagement the story of every time? And isn't the question of what is barbaric or savage in so-called civilization one we have to face in every era? In our own moment, when acts of racial violence and xenophobia have become the stuff of daily news, don't we need, more than ever, to be reminded of the value of wordless communication, of immersion in nature, of loving touch, of music-making, of empathy, of literature read aloud by one person to another—as well as of the fact that certain wounds, inflicted deeply enough, can never heal?

The book you're about to read shines a fierce and necessary light on our world. Read it patiently, if you can—a challenge at times, considering the wild and unexpected turns it takes, and the pleasures that lie around every corner—and discover, or re-discover, what it means to be a member of the human tribe.

JULIE ORRINGER
1/15/19

For Frédérique, waiting for the gold.

THE BOY

EVEN THE INVISIBLE and the immaterial have a name, but he does not. At least, it's not written anywhere, not in any registry or on any kind of official certificate. Not buried in a cleric's record book in some parish. His real name. His original family name. Perhaps he never had one. Later, over the course of the story, a woman, who will be for him a sister, lover, and mother, will give him her own, to which she will append, *en homage*, the first name of a celebrated musician whom she cherished more than anyone. He will also bear a nom de guerre, assigned to him by the military along with his regulation killer's uniform. Thus love and its opposite will have each baptized him in their own fashion. But all of that is gone now. Those aliases destined to disappear in the wake of that woman and that war and the entire bygone world to which they belonged. Who will remember it?

Though hard to believe, the only evidence of his existence that remains is this.

1908

DAY HAS NOT YET BROKEN and the first sight on the distant moor is a strange silhouette with two heads and eight limbs, half of which seem to be immobile. Thicker than night itself and maneuvering transparently behind a veil of darkness. We squint at the apparition. Should we trust our eyes? We wonder. We doubt. At this hour people are sleeping, in the cities, in the villages, elsewhere. Here, there is nothing and no one. If the moon appears it only illuminates a landscape of scrubland, raw and desolate. Uncharted territory. Who goes there? Or what? We don't know. We scrutinize the bizarre shadow, with heightened attention, to try to assimilate it to some known and categorized species. There are hardly any that fit the bill. To what order does it belong? What is its nature? We ask ourselves. We follow it with our gaze. We see it advance, hunched over, spine deformed by an enormous protuberance, its pace slow and somewhat mechanical in its regularity. We guess. We feel that there is something in that gait that arises from both despair and obstinacy. Like a giant tortoise standing upright on its hind legs. A mythic beetle the size of a young bear. We're vaguely worried. We chase away these thoughts. But they return. For after reflecting on the various species of local wildlife, in vain, we are indeed forced to give way to monsters. Real ones. Legends and myths come to mind. We summon the bestiary of primitive, archaic, imaginary, phantasmagorical creatures. We draw on the sources of our oldest fears, our deepest dread. We shudder.

And while our mind teems and torments itself, over there the hunchbacked silhouette continues to move, step by step, along a path that has never been marked.

We draw nearer to one another. Our eyes have sharpened, now capable of discerning. Suddenly they split the entity in two. Two distinct bodies. One straddling the other like those clowns playing at jousting to enliven the fairgrounds—if a tournament ever took place it's over, the rivals have all disappeared, victors or vanquished, we don't know.

And so they are two.

The mystery surrounding the nature of the apparition is cleared up, but curiously we are not reassured. We do not breathe any easier. To the contrary.

There are two of them but who are they?

What are they?

What are they doing?

Where are they going?

We keep asking ourselves questions.

The one acting as a horse has the stature of a fourteen-year-old boy. Straight and stern. Ribs, muscles, tendons jut out, just under the skin. And covering it are indistinct pieces of fabric, an assortment of clothing that looks like it's been taken off the back of a scarecrow. He walks without shoes, the soles of his feet are like bark. Like cork oak. His hair flows over his shoulders and forehead like a clump of seaweed. He is drenched with sweat, he glistens, having just now emerged, it seems, from the primordial waters. Sweat salts his eyelids as he moves, and then drips down, following the path of his tears. A drop sometimes gets caught on the young sprout of fluff that hems his upper lip. His eyes are black, blacker than the depths of time, and in them are pulsing memories of the first star.

It's the child.

The one on his back looks nothing like a knight except perhaps for her somber face. A woman. What's left of a woman. The relics. From beneath the rags, pieces of arm are visible, pieces of leg, flesh that seems to flee the heaps of rags like straw from an old doll. She does not weigh very much but it's an almost dead weight. Shunting about

4

with each turn. Her head rests between the boy's shoulder blades. Her eyes are closed. She has a sallow complexion, the withered skin of crabapples fallen from the tree. She looks sixty. She's not even thirty.

It's the mother.

From time to time the boy takes a break. His jaw clenches. He inhales, exhales forcefully from his nose, we hear the air whistle. We think we can also hear his heart beating but it's only an illusion. The seconds pass, and he stays like this, immobile, attentive, apparently indifferent to the tremors that spread in short, spasmodic waves along his thighs. His knees tremble but do not buckle. His torso is bent beneath his charge. His eyes shoot into the night. He probes, in search of landmarks that only he is able to extract from the shadows. He has only taken this path once before but that suffices. He remembers the details. The thickness of a bush or the slope of a tree trunk or the contours of a boulder: what the average person is ill-equipped to notice, he grasps and retains. Even the most minuscule detail. In the tunnels of his brain there are alcoves where a thousand linden leaves accumulate, only the ribs differentiating them from each other. And a thousand plane leaves, a thousand oak leaves. There are pockets full of pebbles that distinguish themselves from each other based solely on the subtle variations of the glimmer that each gives off in the midday sun. The boy retains all that. In a sky saturated with stars he could point to the precise location where one of them is suddenly missing. It is without a doubt his only treasure.

The woman on his back has not moved. She is suspended in a sort of sack made from goatskin and leather and rope. Crude work done by her own hand in anticipation of this event as soon as she was certain it would arise. Her limbs hang over the boy's sides. Before setting off again, a final pull on the strap that crosses his chest in order to ease the tension. The leather is embedded in his skin, leaving a groove, violet like a fresh scar. Time will erase it. Now the boy has his bearings, he recognizes his guideposts, he is back on his path. Not without gnawing anguish, we watch the two of them grow distant and then dissolve once again into the black that gave rise to them earlier. Towards what destination? To what end? Deep down, we don't really care to know, but we catch ourselves hoping that they'll reach it.

It's the child carrying the mother.

SEA, SHE HAD SAID TO HIM. Sea. Sea. Several times. She had squeezed his arm, looking him straight in the eyes as she always did when she wanted to be sure that he had understood. Useless precaution: he understood everything and right away. But sometimes he cheated and delayed the moment he confirmed his understanding with a nod of the head because he loved to feel her hand and her gaze on him. But that was rare.

They had crouched on the shore and she pointed her finger towards the immensity spread before them. That day, the sky and the water had been the same gray and yet couldn't consummate their union until far away, very far, at the extreme edge of the horizon. The boy had been alarmed. He had seen puddles and ponds before, but never this. Puddles and ponds can be crossed. Puddles and ponds are dead water, while here he felt the presence of a force that was eminently alive, a phenomenal power painstakingly restrained beneath the surface and capable of liberating itself at any moment. In its muffled, incessant rumble, he perceived a threat. Its acrid and heavy fragrances filled his lungs, reached all the way to his heart. And then there was the whitish foam that dribbled onto the sand.

The mother had stayed there for a long time with her gaze on the open sea. In her eyes shone a flame that the boy did not recognize. Which he would have liked to light himself or at least gather it in the palm of his hands to protect it from the wind and from everything. That new glow astonished him. What did she see there that set her soul ablaze?

The boy had never heard of boats, nor voyages, nor continents.

7

That had been perhaps two months earlier. Sea, the woman had repeated one last time before getting up, and this time he hastened to show her his full and complete understanding, to reassure her, to please her. To preserve the flame. Which had, despite everything, disappeared, as though blown out, as soon as they had turned their backs. The dull curtain that normally covered the mother's eyes had fallen again. Was it his fault? What more could he have done? No one could respond to his questions because he couldn't express them.

They had returned to their home.

That day she was the one who had guided him. Leading the way. She was already very weak. The sickness had already taken hold of her. She breathed with the sound of sleet and sometimes coughed to the point of vomiting. But her legs still carried her, she could still move around on her own. Slowly. He who yesterday had to trot to follow her was now forced to check his speed so as not to run into her. He respectfully kept her in his line of sight, at a length of four or five steps. Really observing her, he noticed that she had shrunk. It wasn't just a feeling. Over the course of the weeks, the mother's body had stunted, hunched, shriveled—her size had truly diminished. The effect of the illness, already. It was clear, a hole had opened in her, in the center of her, a drain through which her own life was gradually emptying.

Nevertheless she walked. She moved. Without hesitating about which direction to take. The route, apparently, was no secret to her. Had she taken it that often? Some mornings the boy woke up alone. The mother was not in her bed, she was not in the hut, nor was she in the garden. He searched for her, in the rather vast domain that was familiar to him, his playing and hunting grounds, his entire universe. She was not there. The boy would return to the hut, sit on the ground at the threshold, and spend the next few hours waiting. Sentinel. Lookout. More solitary than ever. Sea, sea: was that where she had gone? She would leave without warning. The boy never imagined that the absence could be permanent. He would wait. Most of the time, night arrived before her return. As light as they were, he would hear her footsteps long before perceiving her shape, crowned by a lunar halo. He had not left his post. The mother explained nothing. She would pass in front of him to enter their lair, not addressing a word to him, nor a caress, but a simple look, neutral, as she passed, and leaving in her wake her odor of humus and sweat, of saltpeter and ash, which were on those nights mingled with—yes, it's true—foreign aromas, more distant, more musky stenches, which the boy detected without being able to identify.

Sea, she had said to him.

HE'S BEEN WALKING for four hours now. The mother on his back, in accordance with her final wish. He doesn't know how to keep track of the yards and miles traveled. He's thirsty. By the time he'd thought of the goatskin, it was too late to turn around. The air was heavy, charged, for a long time he thought a storm would erupt. Along the route, two meager flashes cracked the sky, that's all. The clouds withered away. The rain won't fall. It hasn't fallen for weeks, there's barely any hope of finding anything to quench your thirst at the bottom of a rut or in the hollow of a rock. Everything has been drunk. The boy is condemned to water himself from his own spring: he regularly licks the edges of his lips in order to lose nothing of the clear salty broth that his body generates from the heat and the effort.

Is the woman thirsty too? She doesn't say so. She is no longer in any shape to do so. She burns. Her blood burns. Her bones burn, down to the marrow. Her innards are shriveled like pieces of cured meat. Fever consumes and mummifies her. She doesn't have the least drop to exude. A thin layer of dried saliva cements her mouth, seals her lips. She no longer groans. She no longer coughs. She no longer spits. The boy thinks she's asleep. She's lost consciousness. The only tiny difference between sleep and death is the frail trickle of air that filters through her nostrils. The boy feels it at the base of his neck. It's as fine as falling ash.

Now he traverses a zone of cracked earth where thistle and glasswort grow. Sprinkled here and there a thick carpet of sea purslane into which his feet sink. From time to time a lone umbrella pine. He walks for another three quarters of an hour before suddenly coming

10

to a halt. Nose to the wind like a deer on alert. Among the array of odors there is one that stands out: iodine. His pulse accelerates. He gets moving again.

And soon he hears it. It rumbles quietly at his approach. And when he discovers it, it's already occupying his entire field of vision, unfurled in all its mass, in all its immoderation, to the far reaches of the known world. Its skin undulates and fluctuates, stands up in certain places. Ink-black but inexplicably gleaming beneath the moonless sky.

This time the boy is not afraid. What he feels is joy and relief. He stands still on a small sort of dune and inflates his lungs and extends his arm towards the horizon. To show or to offer.

Sea.

The woman on his back does not raise her head. She does not open her eyes. She remains silent.

Absorbed in his satisfaction, the boy did not notice that the breath at his neck had cut off. A few minutes, a few steps earlier. The woman's heart has stopped beating. It won't beat again.

His mother is dead, it's as simple as that. This time the two of them are not on the same shore.

The boy still does not know.

Like a camel he bends a knee and positions himself delicately on his backside. He unties the strap around his waist, passes the one that binds his torso over his head. As soon as it's detached, his burden topples backward and slumps over without any resistance. The boy is surprised. He turns around. He remains on all fours for a moment, examining the inert body. He can distinguish nothing of the woman other than the pale stain of her face. An ancient page of parchment on which are inscribed the sufferings and the miseries of her existence. For those that know how to read it. That night, even more than on previous nights, she looks minuscule. Floating in her rags. If not for the scars on her flesh one might mistake her for her son's daughter. She has certainly already begun her conversion.

The boy reaches out with his hand and touches her shoulder. He applies timid pressure with the tips of his fingers. Then he grasps the end of her chin and gently shakes it. The mother does not wake up. The boy withdraws his hand.

He stays there, immobile, staring at her. All joy is gone. Something else takes its place in his stomach. And there is also a sort of ringing that vibrates his eardrums and gradually drowns out the rush of the surf. These are phenomena he is not familiar with. He has seen dead birds. Dead lizards. Dead field mice. A number of dead insects. He has broken the necks of chickens and rabbits, he has crushed toads and vipers. They were stretched on the ground at his feet and had stopped moving and the boy had been perfectly aware that they would not get up again. But that was nothing like this. Back then, nothing had happened in his ears or in the bottom of his gut. Numerous times he had had the chance to observe the metamorphosis of these dead creatures. The decomposed or desiccated cadavers, or more often three-fourths devoured by an infinity of vultures, foxes, crows, ants, flies, maggots, all taking their meager but indispensable pittance. And finally, the earth itself.

Is it his fault?

The boy embraces the surrounding space with his gaze. Each thorn of the compass rose. Then he raises his eyes to the sky. There are no stars. Not a single one. There is nothing. Suddenly his mouth opens wide as if to welcome the rain water but it's air, it's air he's searching for, which he snatches greedily as though he might suffocate, while in the same moment spasms run through him, hiccups, dry sobs from his depths that rattle his ribcage.

The outburst doesn't last. When his breathing is regular again the boy gently straightens the lifeless body. He sits down. With one hand he struggles to prop up the back and the head that sways at the end of the long neck. He rubs his other hand over the thigh in order to remove the grains of sand, then brings it towards the woman's face.

He places his fingers on an eyelid (the skin fine like tissue paper) and lifts it cautiously. He leans over to see. There is no gleam. No flame. There is nothing. The boy removes his fingers, and the eyelid falls closed again.

Was there something more he could have done?

He hesitates. Indecisive. Once more he glances through the darkness, inland, in the direction he came from, then in the opposite direction, towards the vast, moving, liquid plain, towards the invisible shores where the waves are born. The extremities of the world. Nothing surges from one or the other to bring him aid or advice. He hadn't been expecting it. In truth he isn't thinking of anything.

After a moment he positions himself behind the woman. He props her up against his back to serve as her support. She leans on him, face turned towards the horizon. As promised.

The boy has folded his knees against his chest. He squeezes his arms around them. The sweat has started to dry on his skin and he's almost cold. His pulse pounds with a slow cadence. His vision is blurred. We must keep in mind that never in the course of his short existence has he heard the word "mother." Nor the word "mom." Never was a nursery rhyme told to him, a lullaby sung, that might have incorporated one of these terms and revealed to him if not the exact significance, then at least the secret essence.

Never.

The boy cannot objectively know what he has just lost. Which does not stop him from feeling the absence of it in even the tiniest atom of his being.

STRETCHED ON HIS STOMACH, his mouth stuck in the sand; the day sneaks up on him. He'd slept in a bottomless slumber. It's the light that extracts him from it, raining down, a flood, dense. Before even opening his eyes, he props himself up on his elbows and lifts his head. He grimaces. Sand crunches between his molars. He sits up and wipes his lips, then his chin, his nose, his cheeks rough with a salt crust. He rids himself of this fake beard grown during the night. He scrapes his teeth with his tongue and spits.

Up above the clouds have deserted him. The sun blanches the blue of the sky, already approaching midday. A golden rain pecks at the surface of the water: there are a myriad dazzling drops, a constellation of fireflies and will-o'-the-wisps in broad daylight. It's beautiful. The boy succeeds in keeping his eyelids open and the magic is reflected in the mirrors of his pupils. The spectacle enchants him. He likes things that shine. Using his hands as a visor, he protects his eyes. Avoids letting them drift to the corpse slouched against his leg.

Seeing them both like this, it's impossible not to think of shipwrecked sailors the day after a storm. Only one survivor among them.

The sea is calm this morning. It washes ashore lazily, twenty feet from the boy. But it's not the sea.

It's actually a lagoon. The biggest in Europe, thirty-five miles long and nearly as wide, but a lagoon all the same, enclosed, and of quite modest size compared to the oceans. A vast fishbowl. It's the Étang de Berre. Connected to the Mediterranean by the umbilical cord of the Canal de Caronte.

The woman had been unaware of this detail. When she came here to sit on the shore she'd thought she was facing infinity. Sea: that's what she'd called it all her life. And in her head she had been embarking on the great, the true. The path we take without any hope of return. The one that opens onto the field of the possible, that transports us to unmarked territories where we can begin, begin again, erase everything that was so badly written and finally start writing what should have been. And so each time it had produced the miracle of the small flicker that lit up her eyes and her soul.

But it wasn't the sea. Just a sample, a substitute, just a miniature reproduction. We make do with dreams. Whatever the body of water was, it never had the scope that she had imagined. She departed carrying that illusion with her. Mystified from start to finish. No matter, it's often the ideas we have of things that count more than the things themselves.

The boy gets up. Sparks still crackle before his eyes. He approaches the edge of the foam. Stops. Lets the waves lap at his feet. The cold surprises him, he had been expecting something warm. His toes recoil and dig into the loose ground. It's a pleasant sensation. He starts walking again while behind him his footprints are already vanishing. He sinks himself into the water. When it comes up to his knees he stops again and stands motionless for a long moment. Then he splashes his face. He wets his hair. The water cascades over his shoulders and down his neck. All that water, there is all that water, cold, clear, within reach, as far as the eye can see, and then he's thirsty.

For a second he stares at the palm of his hand that he holds open in front of him. Glistening and wet. He laps at it once with his tongue. The taste is briny. Then he leans over the surface as if over a water trough and gulps a full mouthful, rises while puffing up his cheeks, and spurts everything out again in a geyser. The bitterness remains, lining his palate.

Turning towards the shore he sees a couple of seagulls busy examining the corpse of the mother. Doctors of rotten meat. They stomp around with bent necks, serious expressions, icy eyes, before suddenly jabbing into the heap of rags with their beaks. The boy starts to run. He waves his arms, claws at the air, a scowl appears on his lips from which escapes a sort of hissing or yowling that certain snakes and angry cats make.

The birds flee at his approach. Trotting first with dainty steps, wings spread, like old incensed Carmelite nuns raising their shoulders. But that's not enough for him. The boy chases after them until they're forced to take flight. And for a long time after he pursues them with his gaze. They are nothing more than gulls, then sparrows, then blurred gnats in the azure, while he is still there, stationed, arms extended in their direction with his fingertips hooked like talons that seem to cling to the sky.

If he knew of God he would pray for Him to curse them.

After that he turns back towards the woman. He loads her onto his back and takes off again.

NIGHT HAD ALREADY FALLEN when he crossed the threshold of the hut. He looks like an old man when he appears. His own ancestor. Each step pains him. Each movement. In the shadows he approaches his mother's bed, prepares to sit down on it, but his strength abandons him and he falls heavily on his behind. The weight of his load causes him to fall backwards. He needs an infinite amount of time to unhook the harness. One strap has cut into the flesh above his chest, a bit of blood has pooled there.

He pulls the covers over the dead woman then stands back up. His legs are seized by tremors that he tries to stop by clutching at his thighs. After a minute he suppresses them and goes back out again.

Outside he crosses what one could call the courtyard. Moving with very short strides as if his ankles were chained together, by obligation as much as by prudence, knowing that at this point of exhaustion, when he is utterly spent, the earth can at any moment open beneath his feet and swallow him. He does not want to fall before having something to drink. Numerous times on the return he had been tempted to leave his path to go off in search of a spring; he resisted out of fear of getting lost before his mission was complete. His gums are green from all the stems he chewed and sucked on to extract sap. So it might be the courtyard he's crossing but it's a vast desert, with an oasis on the other side.

Next to each other are a basin and a dented enameled-tin pitcher. The basin is empty. The boy lifts the pitcher with both hands and brings the rim to his mouth. His neck extends. He doesn't drink, he swallows. The first mouthful nearly suffocates him. The water spurts out of his nostrils. He coughs. The dry cough is the only noise in the night. In the distance, his echo answers him like a series of muffled detonations, an exchange of gunfire.

He catches his breath. Then, once again, he lifts the pitcher and forces himself to drink parsimoniously. A mouthful, then another, then another. Once his thirst is slaked, he lets out an enormous burp.

We find him a bit later on all fours in a sort of enclosure that houses the chicken coop. He searches around. He's woken up the poultry, as evidenced by the cackling concert that accompanies him. The boy doesn't care. He extends his arm and gropes around at the bottom of the large slatted racks, feels, with his fingertips, the thin straw bedding that is sometimes decorated with red feathers or wisps of down as soft as silk, pushes the birds when necessary, without consideration or concern for their cries of fright or rage. He knows the places the laying hens like, the illusory hiding places where they shelter the fruits of their love.

A few steps away he finds a rabbit hutch, but it's been empty since the end of winter.

He withdraws. He has unearthed two eggs that he brings beneath his nose and sniffs, crouching in the middle of the courtyard. He sets one at his feet and lifts the other above his face. Head tilted back, mouth open. He breaks the shell and separates it into two with his thumbs. The viscous substance flows over his tongue, spreads into his throat. He lets it drip until the last drop. He licks the inside of the shell then throws it to the ground. Then he picks up the second egg and begins again.

With his wrist he wipes away the slimy traces that follow the curve of his chin. He diligently sucks his ten fingers. He will go drink again at the pitcher but no more than three mouthfuls this time. Then he returns to the hut, his stomach preceding him, looking like a swollen goatskin with the liquid sloshing around with each step.

For a long time the boy's eyes remain open. Lying down on his straw mattress in the darkness. For a long time the surface of the water continues to glisten in his eyes. Or something else, but what?

It's the sound of the waves that puts him to sleep. It's the calm and regular breathing of the sea that he makes his own.

HE KNOWS THAT THERE ARE other men on earth, but he has no idea how many. If someone told him that this year the population is estimated at one billion seven hundred and forty million, he wouldn't understand what they were talking about. If someone said to him that there are more men and women in the world than there are starlings in the December sky, he would burst out laughing with his booming laugh—sadly, so rare.

Surprises are in store for him in the future.

For his part, so far, he has had confirmation of five. Five specimens of the human species whose existence he has been able to verify visually. His mother not included. Three of them were poachers busy setting traps and snares. The fourth was a strange solitary figure, hooded, walking, who looked like a monk. Perhaps a pilgrim. Perhaps a penitent gone astray from his own Stations of the Cross. The boy had observed them from too far away to make out their features. Only the fifth and last had come less than thirty feet away. A peddler, he too had certainly been lost to have wound up there. Long before seeing him they had heard the tintinnabulation of his gear. The man had come right up to them. He had stopped in front of the hut and shouted two big yoo-hoos to signal his presence. The boy had shuddered at the sound of that voice, the first man's voice he had heard. He and the mother had been sitting in the middle of a mulberry tree ten feet above the ground, watching the peddler through the foliage. The man was carrying a wicker basket on his back that he could have fit inside of, and his offspring with him. It was filled with fabric and lace and other articles of haberdashery and a full hardware store and a small library composed of books and almanacs and images ranging from the pious to the licentious and an array of products of first and last necessity. The boy twisted his neck to peer into that bric-a-brac, fascinated by those objects, most of which he could not imagine any use for. Hiding on her branch the mother had surveyed the actions and gestures of this intruder who looked like the Grand Duke. She had armed herself with a short, hard wooden log that habitually served as her club for beating rabbits or garter snakes to death.

The peddler remained standing for a moment in the courtyard. A drooping, fuzzy mustache decorated his emaciated face. Sweat traced a large dark path around his neck, like the mark of a yoke. He slowly turned his gaze from side to side, circumspect, or perhaps deep down vexed that his coming hadn't been as anticipated as the prophet's. The mother had squeezed her club a bit harder when she saw him head towards the entrance of the hut. The man stopped on the threshold and called out again, and because his call rang once more without response, he risked his head inside and the shadow coldly decapitated him. From the tree above, they saw nothing more than a wicker basket on legs. Then the peddler backed into the light again. Once more he did one or two spins to survey the surroundings. No one. Last peddler in a phantom hamlet. His eyes lingered longer than necessary on the chicken coop. Lingered on the vegetable garden. A godsend? No doubt he weighed the pros and cons. He scratched his cheek and his resurgent beard rasped under his black nails. Who knows whether it was honesty or some superstitious fear that led him, in the end, to continue on his way without taking anything. He left with his full wicker basket and his spiel stuck in his throat. Long after losing sight of him they could hear his gear jangling in the distance like the little bell of a lost sheep. They didn't leave their hiding place until the silence was complete. Then the boy jumped from his branch, he hurried into the courtyard and leaned over the footprints the man had left and he touched each one with his fingertips. After which he'd remained standing, sniffing the air until all the unfamiliar scents had disappeared.

THE PEDDLER NEVER CAME BACK. Not him nor anyone else. The boy has had no other contact with civilization since then. What do men do when they aren't walking around with their houses on their backs? He has no idea. He has no idea of the rest of the world and it's reciprocal: the mother was the only person on earth to know of his existence and the mother is dead.

He spends the morning building a pyre. That's what she had told him to do. He breaks branches. In the surrounding trees he chooses low thin branches and hangs on them until they cede to his weight. He carries or drags them into the courtyard and assembles them into a large bed frame. On top he piles a mattress of kindling that he gathers from here and there and brings back in entire bundles. He does all of this without haste. Without enthusiasm. In addition to his limbs that still suffer from the efforts made over the last few days, his heart is heavy. That's where the pain is sharpest. More so than the day before. More so with each passing hour.

Sometimes he interrupts his labors to go back inside the hut. During the brief seconds that it takes his eyes to acclimate to the darkness he cannot help imagining that the mother will have woken up, or else that she will have completely and simply disappeared. It's stronger than him. The thought forms unbeknownst to him, it rises and swells and breaks the surface of his consciousness like a bubble of gas, then immediately bursts: the frail body is still lying curled up on the bed where he'd left it. The more insane the hope, the more immense the disappointment. In those moments, the boy takes the time to measure his solitude and his deprivation. His throat tightens, his eyelids swell.

22

He goes back outside and the light of day pierces through his tears, diffuse and hazy as though from behind a stained-glass window.

To the bed of branches and kindling he adds a soft quilt of straw, of leaves, of twigs and pine needles that he scatters and mixes together. All he can amass from the area that's relatively dry. When he decides that he's finished, the pyre is as high as his knees.

He drinks. He runs water over his hands and face. Then he is once again in the hut where he sits on the mattress, thighs squeezed to his chest, as though the temperature had dropped. And he is actually cold, but doesn't think to cover himself. For a few long minutes he remains immobile. The only thing that moves and rustles here are the flies. The odor of the dead body overwhelms all the rest.

He's lived here from the day he was born to today. His home. His refuge. This is the kingdom of which he is henceforth the only ruler and the only subject. See what there is of it: almost nothing.

Beneath the dry stone arch hangs a foxtail that was once supple and soft and which is now gray and rough, half lacquered in a residue of suet and dust. At the bottom of a nook there are two pairs of mittens and two pairs of socks and one pair of muffs cut from rabbit skins, from hare skins. An even cruder fabrication in the form of a cap: a collection of scraps of fur of unknown origin supposed to form a sort of chef's hat that the inbred child of the last servant of the last tsar of all the Russians might have worn. The blankets and the rug are vestiges of six successive goats that the mother and the son had owned. Brave beasts. They had kept some of them for up to several months, sometimes a full year. The boy liked nothing more than to lie on the ground beneath their udders and drink the warm milk from the very source. And then when the mother decided it was time, she would raise a large flat stone up high and drop the twenty-pound weight onto the animal's skull. It made it easier to cut its throat. Nothing went to waste. They ate the heart and the liver and the feast of fresh meat lasted a full week. They dried the rest. The boy helped. He was allowed to keep the horns, which he used to draw suns in the mud. And flowers, birds. The mother had taught him that he had to get rid of the bones and last offal by burning them because otherwise they risked attracting predators. That's what she told him he had to do for her, too.

Who else if not him?

The boy gets up. He takes the woman in his arms and takes her through the doorway. He crosses the courtyard. He carries her like a dozing fiancée, and he places her on the bed of branches and leaves. The wood barely creaks beneath her weight.

Now his eyes are dry, his vision clear. His hands don't tremble when he strikes the match. It takes two for the fire to catch. He blows on the flames as they grow. When the first plumes arise, he reaches his hand through the smoke and touches his mother's forehead. He knows that it's the last time. He'd dug through the ashes and seen what remained of the bones of goats: nothing could have better taught him what it means to return to dust. No form of farewell occurs to him other than this brief, reverent touch. He has no other sort of eulogy, no other prayer. When the heat is too intense, he withdraws his hand.

It's a beautiful blaze. At the height of their intensity, the flames reach twice the height of the hut. The odor stings his nose, tightens his throat. The boy takes his place in the shade of the mulberry tree. He listens to the crackling of the wood in the teeth of the fire. The whistling and sputtering. He watches the thick column of smoke that breaks apart as it climbs, diffuses, disintegrates, and ends by creating many thin clouds that drift in the azure before vanishing for good, as light and evanescent as reluctant kisses. The boy follows them with his gaze. He doesn't have the least notion of the soul, and yet something opens a little bit deep inside him, something that questions and disarms him.

At dusk the pyre is reduced to a nice hearth fire. Far to the west another fire is visible, the glimmers of the setting sun responding to those of the flames in the courtyard. It's the hour when she used to start talking—and indeed in the low rumbling of the blaze the boy thinks he hears her voice. That would happen sometimes: without any warning she would suddenly open her mouth and words would pour out from between her lips. A steady stream, a monotone litany but oh so precious for the boy. He would drop everything to drink it in. The words escaped him, the meaning, but not the sound. The mother didn't look at him. It wasn't him she was addressing. Not any more on this night than the nights before. She was perhaps talking to herself. Or else to a deceased parent, brother, sister, friend, a confidant with whom she might have been having a conversation outside of the typical realms of space and time. As though there were beings very close by that no one could detect. She never seemed to wait for her interlocutor's response.

Perhaps she simply wanted to hear a voice.

The boy would have loved for this to last the entire night, but on these occasions, like today, the surge would cut off suddenly in the middle of a sentence and then the silence would crash into his eardrums like a gong and only the waves would continue to vibrate for a long time.

In the deep night there is nothing more than a thick carpet of embers that the Milky Way, spread above, seems to reflect perfectly on a cosmic scale. The last plumes have dissipated, revealing a limpid and clear sky tarnished by stars. Not one star is missing, but we wouldn't swear that there aren't any new ones, as legends suggest.

On Earth, all voices are quiet. The boy leaves his shelter. In the vegetable garden, he searches for a type of rake whose claw looks like that of a bird of prey. He goes back to what remains of the pyre. With slow and diligent movements he spreads the still-warm ashes into the center of the courtyard. Then he covers them with a layer of dirt. Then he rakes some more until the surface of the ground is perfectly flat and even all over, and when he's finished he stands back up, and he stays standing there beneath the celestial arch armed with his rake, contemplating the finished work.

It was what she had told him to do.

But she hadn't told him what to do after.

EVERY MAN LEAVES HIS CHILDHOOD behind him one day. He won't find it again. Only a few very old or very crazy men benefit, sometimes, from a second chance. The others, when they quit this world, what precious thing do they have to take with them?

The boy leaves on the night of his sixth day of mourning. He doesn't decide to, it just happens. It's obvious and necessary.

It had rained the day before. Finally. A brief and violent shower, enough to transform the courtyard into a thick magma, a somber deluge that mixed the earth and the ashes and the burnt flesh together irrevocably. As if it were the essential mission of the rain, which stopped immediately after. A wind from the north cleared the sky, the sun resumed its reign, and between the two elements it didn't take more than twenty-four hours for the ground to dry and the crust to solidify. And under that rug hides the dust of the past. Mineral memory regenerates itself. The boy treads on this new stratum that bears no traces of anything, only the marks he leaves in that very moment.

He frees the chickens and goes.

Whether it be here or somewhere else, everything that he sees he will have never seen before. A round and yellow moon lights up his path. Its pale gleam softens the shadows, dulls the terror that's brooding in his stomach. At random, he sets off north. The North Star pinned straight in front of him at forty-five degrees above the horizon: the only fixed point in the vast whirlpool, and illuminating the night for our eyes with light from four centuries earlier, from a time when Columbus's fleets had not yet set out, when the New World had not yet discovered Christ.

26

He walks from dusk to dawn, he sleeps during the hottest part of the day: at first the boy keeps this rhythm. And then the moon diminishes and its brightness declines. And then he becomes bold. On the fourth day it's not yet noon when he wakes up and starts on his way.

He has crossed the frontiers of his domain. In these unknown territories where he ventures he could just as easily be the hunter as the prey. He advances with his senses on alert. The enemy is all the more frightening because he knows nothing about it. He doesn't know what he should be afraid of. Each noise, each silence is gauged in the moment for the threat it might pose. Each movement tracked in his field of vision. In reality, it's instinct more than judgment that steers the boy. It determines his behavior, incites him to stop, to crouch, to wait or to flee. In the shadow of the next thicket breathes perhaps the creature that will devour him.

As for his own food, it doesn't fall from the sky. He has to unearth it. Gather it. Collect it. He knows most of the berries, but they're not yet in season. He knows the plants and the roots. He picks and peels and gnaws the young buds of hogweed and coltsfoot. Chickweed stems. Tubers of burdock. He stockpiles amaranth leaves which he shoves into the shapeless sack that hangs from his hip and which still holds the jumble of goatskin and matches and three inches of candle in addition to a snare, a knife with a chipped blade, an onion, and a handful of fava beans and another of chickpeas dug up from the abandoned vegetable garden. These are his only provisions.

When fortune smiles on him he kneels like a believer in front of an altar of cep mushrooms. Of chanterelles. Peels away the black ears of Judas mushrooms that flank the dead trunks. His lips, his teeth reddened sometimes with the blood of early blackberries and strawberries.

On a plot spotted with gorse he notices a funny brown bird the size of a partridge and manages to get less than three feet from it before the bird scurries away on its feet and further on takes flight in a heavy and inelegant beating of wings. The boy searches for the nest and finds it in a dip in the ground but the nest is empty. He places a trap at the opening of the hole and keeps watch for an entire half-day, lying on his stomach behind a juniper tree, but the bird doesn't come back. He thinks of the chickens abandoned in the courtyard. He curses them.

He eats the beans.

He eats the onion.

He dips the chickpeas in the water of a small brook to soften them. Then he sucks on them one by one, lets them melt on his tongue like sweets.

At all times and in all places his hunger is with him; it feeds on nothing and yet grows in his chest, weakens him.

His fate perhaps lies in the stagnant waters of a small pond. He happens upon it one night. He sees the pink and the orange of the sky reflected in it. But it's a broken mirror, its surface as though riddled by bullets from the compulsive and incessant plungings of a number of frogs gathered in this area to celebrate some unknown event. There are a hundred or more. Plunk. Plunk. Plunk. Plunk. God bless this furious fête. They are for the boy's taking. And take he does, first with his bare hands and then with the help of an improvised net made from the infamous rag he wears as a shirt. It takes some time, but when he withdraws the dripping fabric from the water for the final time the pond has been scraped clean of its amphibians.

Exhausted, the boy collapses onto his back. He inhales. The night is over at this point. The surface of the pond spreads, as black and opaque as a blanket of oil, one star shining in it. A shroud of silence gently falls again.

The decapitated frogs lie in the grass where he's thrown them, each barely bigger than a tree frog and all together forming a single half-demolished burial mound, a cairn of flesh and nerves. Some are still dying. Some have moved more than a yard away after their decapitation, crawling, trailing, exaggerating a macabre and grotesque pantomime or suddenly shaking with terrible convulsions and bounding wildly, executing extravagant, fanciful paths in the air, with neither balance nor coordination, spasmic, subjected to new laws of physics, to iconoclastic rules and equations issued from the brain of a drunk or mad scientist, or maybe a cruel clown.

The boy gets up. He prepares a fire. In the light of the flames he skins his prizes one by one until deep into the night. Then he lines them up in a rosary on the longest branch he can find. While they cook he rinses his dusty fingers in the pond. The aroma of the roasted meat makes him salivate.

He eats the frogs. Everything he's able to swallow. He sucks on the bones, small as fish bones, and spits them back into the flames perfectly polished and immaculate. He wraps the leftovers in his wet shirt and shoves them in the sack for later. Then he lies down, curled up in a ball near the embers, belly swollen and deliciously painful, and he closes his eyes and sleeps as the day breaks.

HE EATS THE FROGS dusted with rosemary flowers.

He eats the frogs sprinkled with savory.

He eats the frogs rubbed with sage leaves.

He saves the last bone of the last skeleton and places it in his matchbox as a kind of talisman.

On the summer solstice he enters into a valley of rockrose. It's one of those moments when he lets his guard down and is awestruck. So great is the beauty of the world and so small is he, he could never contain it. He crosses this river of shrubs, his arms deployed like wings, feeling the softness of their fuzz as he passes, caressing the corolla of the pink and mauve petals, in a gesture that is simultaneously a hello and a goodbye, for these ephemeral flowers that bloom at dawn will die when the night returns, their entire reign carried out in this single ellipsis. Is this why, as he crosses, the boy's initial rapture is tainted with melancholy and then with genuine sorrow? The sad pollen reaped. Having arrived on the other shore, his vision is now obscured. He prefers not to turn back. Perhaps he's thinking of the extinguished flame in the eyes of the mother. Not only do beauty and harmony not last nor win out, but their appearances are so brief that the memories of their arrival persist and emphasize their absence, making the void they leave behind all the more dizzying.

The month of July starts with a torrent. The rain falls for four days and four nights without stop. The boy flounders, drenched, the entire first day without finding shelter. His feet suctioned by the red mud with each step. At night he sees the gray and bare rise of a hill and takes refuge in a cavity carved halfway up the incline of its side. It's a recess in the rock. Just enough room to crouch inside. Just enough to keep dry, a limestone canopy above his head. He remains cloistered here for the three days and the three nights that follow, between the walls of stone and the bars of rain and anyone who saw him would have inevitably thought of the last resident of an abandoned zoo or the former representative of an animal species forgotten in the hold of the biblical ark.

But there is no one to see him.

After the deluge, summer explodes. A thousand suns in one. Terebinth trees sparkle, euphorbias shoot up, clematis and madders bloom and everywhere on the trees and bushes fruits and berries ripen. When it's brightest, the boy marches with a hand acting as a visor on his forehead and in the other a boxwood staff that he hits against the ground in front of him like a blind man in order to warn off snakes. Far from any path. Far from any known road forged by anyone of his species. Pioneer of these lands, it seems. If there were predecessors, they're dead, they've been in exile for so long that even the memory of their existence has been erased. He roams uncultivated lands. Empty plateaus. Deserted valleys. Jungles dense with arbutus and cork oaks. Entire acres covered with sarsaparilla and rampant ivy that he trips over. From woods to scrubland. From steppe to a forest. He explores. He surveys. Internalizes odors like a sable or muskrat. Beast among beasts. Circumscribing his journey, all that matters is rest, food, and water.

On a riverbank he plays by splashing the swarms of tiny grasshoppers around his feet, those mischievous and Lilliputian escorts. In a field of lavender he floats on a flying carpet woven by a swarm of blue butterflies. He always makes sure to urinate on the domes of anthills so he can watch the hordes of panicked workers file out. These are the pleasures offered to him that he accepts.

He is three-quarters naked, his skin cooked and tanned.

He eats figs.

He eats prunes.

He eats gooseberries.

He eats almonds.

One clear night he searches the burrow of a marauding polecat and exhumes from its reserves the remains of a baby rabbit.

He eats the baby rabbit.

Three days later, he eats the fresh meat of two young hares that he snares in quick succession, using some string. They don't weigh more than two pounds each but both times his heart soars. He lifts them by the ears and brandishes them at arm's length like trophies—the young hares rolling their eyes and kicking the void, strangely silent.

He eats one. Then the other.

There are no more matches. He now has to collect tinder or something like it and then scrape the blade of his knife against flint in the hope of creating a flame. A precious miracle.

He catches a wild rabbit, so big and so combative that he has to clobber it with his stick before he can grab it.

He eats the rabbit. He saves the pelt and at night he places it against his cheek, caresses it with his lips before falling asleep.

The cicadas sing starting at nightfall and into his dreams.

One morning he follows the course of a stream and soon the stream becomes a river and the boy wades into the flowing water and at noon he rushes with it through a breach made in the middle of a gigantic rock massif. He walks over pebbles laminated by a current a hundred thousand millennia old. The water is clear and freezing, it climbs to his ankles, to his calves, to his chest sometimes when the walls of the canyon narrow, and then the boy is short of breath and still he continues to advance with his mouth wide open, carrying his sack above his head to keep it dry. When he lifts his eyes he sees nothing but a blue crack in the ceiling: that's the entirety of his sky, the part granted to the light by the shadows.

He floats through these gorges for perhaps five or six miles. The gulch sometimes narrowing, flanked by steep inclines, untouched and white as snow, sometimes widened and tiered where there are colonies of boxwood trees, elderberry trees, ivy. He passes through a strait made of fallen rocks, he cascades between enormous blocks of stone that seem to have fallen straight from a distant galaxy during the era of total chaos.

At three in the afternoon he comes to a stop in a cove on a shore of gray sand. Here is where the sea reigned long ago. Today the restrained course of the river forms an almost-round basin, a dwarf lagoon three feet deep and fifteen or twenty feet across. A stretch of pebbles precedes the thin sandy beach, then the slope gently rises over a lush cliffside before summiting a hundred and fifty feet above in a wall of rock, once again as abrupt and bare as a rampart.

Darkness comes quickly. Already in the shadow of the banks, the water is tinted a deep and cold green. The boy lies on his back in the last puddle of sunlight. His skin and his rags start to dry. He surrenders. Drops of golden light cling to his eyelashes. Then he closes his eyes, and we wonder whether he might rest here for eternity.

HE STAYS THERE FOR A WEEK.

He bathes. He jumps into the swimming hole from the precipice of the rocks and lets himself glide on his back. He likes the splashes, the geysers, all the pearls he throws in the air, the color of honey or pure crystal depending on the hour and hue of the sky. He likes the sound they make when they crash back down.

He naps in the warmth of the sand.

After a morning of patience and effort he extracts a brown trout a half-arm long from the water. He throws it onto the riverbank where it lands with the sound of a wet cloth. In the open air it suffocates little by little. He watches it without moving for as long as it takes to die.

He eats the trout.

A bit further upstream he builds a dam. Picking up, transporting, adjusting pebble after pebble, stone after stone, meticulously. Perhaps it's a serious enterprise. Perhaps he really does intend to disrupt the course of the river. He's still working when the moon comes out. He can no longer feel his hands nor his feet. The construction is higher than his hips and yet the water continues to flow, its rush barely slowed.

What he does, he undoes the next day, stone after stone, pebble after pebble, meticulously.

Often at nightfall he's crouched in front of a small basin of stagnant water puddled in a rock. Contemplating his reflection in this mirror for several minutes. A piercing look, without blinking, until he manages to separate himself, detach himself from himself, make himself into a perfect stranger: friend or enemy, it doesn't matter as long as it's someone else. As long as there are two of them.

Night at the top of the canyon is cut into a narrow ribbon of sky in which only fragments of constellations can be discerned. Ursa Major and Leo and Canis Minor and Delphinus and the entire stellar menagerie march by in incomplete formations and so the boy, before drifting off to sleep, witnesses the inexorable carousel of time.

On the last day, in a nook of the cliff six feet off the ground, he discovers the entrance to a cave concealed by a thick blanket of ivy. It's a sanctuary where the sun has never been let in. The boy sacrifices the stump of candle he still has to explore it. On the wall of the vestibule are etchings whose contours he traces with the tip of his index finger: an arc, a spiral, obscure symbols, perhaps incarnate spirits, hybrid divinities born of a cosmogonic cult, anthropomorphic animals, whose depictions bear a slight resemblance to the portrait the puddle reflects back to him when he gazes into it at night.

Crawling through a half-collapsed tunnel where, four millennia earlier, men had settled in preparation for eternal slumber. An entire burrowing wildlife preceded him here. The earth already dug, patiently desecrated. Vestiges come to the surface. In the space of an hour he discovers three vertebrae, a tibia, a kneecap, two femur heads, a heel bone, twelve phalanges, half a lower jawbone, and eighteen teeth that he lines up carefully, in rows, like pieces on a chessboard. He also excavates shards of a vase covered in a limestone coating. A spear tip in blond flint. Six oblong and translucent aragonite pearls. A physical anthology.

All sorts of offerings here, objects of lithic industry, ceramics, jewels, funerary pendants and finery that the revered dead were generously endowed with. In addition to the tears spilled at their bedside—those tears that nothing fossilizes.

The boy scratches at the ground again in the glow of the candle. Scratches with his fingers, with his nails, a miserable archeologist on his knees in front of his elongated shadow in the archway. Might it be his own roots that he's searching for underneath? His own origin.

35

Who knows if the second kneecap he unearths might have belonged to one of his distant antecedents? It might be a link on the chain that runs from the beginning to this day and beyond. The lineage, the great forbears, the fathers of our fathers to the sons of our sons, all born from the same seed. Who knows if one of these dead buried here might be his ancestor?

Of course they were. Inevitably.

His last discovery is an ivory die that's not quite twenty-five centuries old.

The wax is running out. The boy has to leave before the darkness encloses him more completely than the slab of a tomb. He keeps the spear tip and a few shells. He keeps the pearls that he rubs and wets with his saliva. He also takes the eagle's talon and the die, his loot joining the frog bone in the matchbox.

Then he re-enters the first cavern and in the last quivers of candlelight he starts to engrave a fish in the rock. An outline of a trout among the other petroglyphs. His testament and his contribution.

THAT YEAR, THE AUSTRO-HUNGARIAN EMPIRE annexes Bosnia-Herzegovina.

That year, the Congo Free State, the private property of Léopold II, King of Belgium, becomes a Belgian colony, the monarch having ceded the territory to his country.

In Paris, the King's Camelots distribute the first copies of *L'Action Française*, a paper that was anti-Semitic, anti-protestant, anti-masonic, anti-communist, anti-democratic, and anti-parliamentary, edited by Charles Marie Photius Maurras, a deaf provincial writer and champion of integral nationalism.

Charles Maurras would be elected to the Académie Française thirty years later, by a vote of twenty to twelve.

That year, the Metro's no. 4 line, connecting Porte de Clignancourt to Châtelet, was put in service, its facilities and operation turned over to the Paris Metropolitan Railway, which had been founded by Baron Édouard Louis Joseph Empain, a man associated with Schneider du Creusot's institutions.

Croquignol, Filochard, and Ribouldingue, a trio of small-time scam artists, collectively known as "Les Pieds Nickelés," make their first appearance in the magazine *L'Épatant*.

That year, the French Football Federation refuses to stand with the English Football Association for the simple reason that the latter had authorized the establishment of professional football.

In the streets of London, tens of thousands of women rally in support of the suffrage movement, demanding the right to vote, which they would be granted twenty years later.

That year, Charles Joseph Bonaparte, grand-nephew of Napoléon Bonaparte and Attorney General of the United States, founded the Bureau of Investigation, the first iteration of what would become the Federal Bureau of Investigation, and which at the time consisted of fewer than ten agents.

In Valparaíso, Chile, Salvador Allende Gossens is born.

In Seine-et-Oise, in the communes of Vigneux, Draveil, and Villeneuve-Saint-Georges, sandpit workers launch a strike that will last one hundred days and leave six dead and hundreds injured by the blades and bullets of the gendarmes and dragoons sent there by Georges Clemenceau, called the Tiger, a radical socialist, Minister of the Interior, and President of the Council, who would go on to arrest and imprison all of the main leaders of the General Confederation of Labor.

Georges Clemenceau would be unanimously elected to the Académie Française in 1918.

That year, in Detroit, Michigan, General Motors, the world's largest automobile manufacturer, is founded.

That year, in Detroit, Michigan, the Ford Motor Company inaugurates the mass production and consumption of automobiles with the brand new Ford Model T, fresh from the factory, and the first of fifteen million subsequent sales across the decades and the continents.

Henry Ford, its inventor, would be decorated, thirty years later, with the Grand Cross of the Order of the German Eagle in recognition of his moral and financial support of the Third Reich, and cited as a role model by of one of his most fervent admirers in a book entitled *Mein Kampf*.

That year, Gideons International places bibles in hotel rooms for the first time.

That year, *Cannabis indica* cigarettes are sold in all of the best pharmacies in France, with Indian hemp, an anti-spasmodic and anti-asthmatic, having been recognized as highly effective in the battle against respiratory diseases.

In Lucerne, Switzerland, the meeting of the International Association for Labor Legislation prohibits children under the age of fourteen from working night shifts for industrial jobs.

A three-year-old boy, named Puyi, becomes emperor of China.

In the ring, Jack Johnson sends Tommy Burns to the mat and becomes the first African American boxing world champion in the prestigious heavyweight division; the police interrupt the fight in the fourteenth round to prevent cameras from recording the black man delivering the knockout blow to the white man.

Wilbur Wright, in his Flyer, beats the double world record for the furthest and longest-lasting flight by gliding seventy-six and a half miles in two hours, twenty minutes, and twenty-three seconds.

The members of the Académie Française, consulted in order to find a name for these new flying machines, propose: "aéroplane," "aéro," "philair," "auto-planeuse," "aérion." Clément Ader, an engineer, continues to champion the term "avion."

That year, an enormous ball of fire explodes in the sky above the Stony Tunguska River in central Siberia, creating a shockwave later estimated to have been several hundred times more powerful than the bomb that would be dropped on Hiroshima, devastating an area of forest greater than twelve miles across, uprooting and killing tens of millions of trees, and decimating entire herds of reindeer, without leaving the slightest trace of impact, nor one bit of debris. Asteroid? Comet? Something else? The nature of that cosmic object remains a mystery. To this day, we still do not know.

ON A WINDY DAY he discovers the horse and the wheel.

It starts as a trembling in the ground beneath his feet, enough to make him stop short. He steps into the meager shade of an olive tree. On alert. The mistral blows through the foliage and whistles in his ears, its powerful and frigid current drowning out all other sounds. Yet the boy thinks he hears, suddenly, a roll of thunder in the distance. He looks up reflexively but there's nothing between the branches except blue—blue, limitless and faultless. In the time it takes to lower his gaze, the din grows twice as loud, the trembling of the earth morphs into a quaking and the boy's chest expands, tightens, while inside his heartbeat swells and hastens, then stops altogether when, out of nowhere, in a halo of golden dust, emerges the most extraordinary creature he has ever seen.

For anyone else it would have been an everyday occurrence, a yoked pair of horses pulling a carriage at full gallop, but to the boy's innocent eye it's a fantastic and monstrous and magnificent sight, one that will feed his dreams, as well as his nightmares, for a long time. It was as if he had come across a winged chariot or a dragon.

The team passes thirty steps from his nose. The closest horse turns its head in passing, the wind and the speed tousles the long tuft of hair growing on its forehead and reveals its eyeball and the boy is struck by the dark lightning gaze the animal shoots at him. Like the other horse in the pair, it's one of those Camargue horses that traditionally roams wild and free in the marshes. One of the oldest breeds, born in the sea spray, they say, the source of its silver coat.

It doesn't last more than a few seconds, but the thunder and lather and lightning are phenomena that the boy will not forget.

The team disappears. Only he and the wind remain. He still hasn't moved. Dumbstruck with ecstasy. Until he's brought back to reality by a lukewarm stream of urine flowing down his legs.

He breaks away from the tree trunk and leaves the shade and hurries over to the two thin furrows that the wheels of the carriage left behind. He scrutinizes the horizon, but for as far as he can see, there is nothing. He raises his nose and sniffs, but the mistral has cleaned the air, chased away the dust and the residue of the dust and even the odor of the horses. Nevertheless, full of fresh fervor, he darts off to follow the team.

Another era has begun. Of course there was the wheel, of course there was the horse, fabulous animal, but the boy's greatest discovery concerns only himself. Because it's here, today, at this hour—God only knows why—that he suddenly becomes aware that he belongs to this particular realm that he cannot yet define but which is none other than humanity.

He is human.

For him it's a revelation. Or rather it's an abrupt confirmation of an inkling that until now has been dormant, too vague, too weak to illuminate. But now the darkness collapses and the light floods in.

From now on he wants to see. He wants to know. He wants to understand. He will no longer keep his distance, as his mother had previously decided, for reasons known only to her, as his own instincts had subsequently perpetuated. From now on he wants to follow paths other than those of reptiles and quadrupeds. He wants to rub shoulders with his fellow man. From this day forward he will no longer reject their company, he'll even seek it out himself, and this won't change until the twilight of his life when undoubtedly he will have understood what they are and what he is and will have deemed it appropriate to detach himself from them, and he will once again seek out the solitude that is, in the end, the only certainty and the sole truth upon which humanity can depend.

Might as well say it now: he will never see the carriage and its pair of silver horses again.

IN THE WEEKS THAT FOLLOW, he skirts the edges of villages. Hamlets. Farms. He approaches in stages. He stands at the edges of properties, identifies a thicket or more often a leafy tree in which to perch like a sailor in a crow's nest, where he can see without being seen. A spy on his own behalf. Bestowed with the chameleon's gift of camouflage. From his post he watches, and he listens. He observes. He absorbs. So many new things, objects and beings, attitudes, voices, all these discoveries that continue to surprise and enchant him and then those that trouble him, plunge him into the depths of confusion. Indeed how strange certain rites he witnesses seem to him. But they know, he doesn't: there must be a reason.

He observes, and he imitates. At night, once everyone has retired to their quarters, he makes an effort to reproduce the gestures, the facial expressions, he replays the scenes he watched play out. In his open-air theater, he rehearses. He is the fat man with the pipe: soft, twisted lip, sucking on a cane pipe as he imagines he's puffing impeccable rings of smoke, he meanders, his large belly preceding him, beneath the indifferent eyes of swallows that crisscross the sky above his head. He's the grandpa, the old man who is placed on a bench under the lime tree and forgotten about for long periods of time, who ruminates, bobs his head. Leaning on an imaginary cane, he gets up and drags his carcass, crippled by rheumatism, to the doorstep of an invisible house. One time. Two times. Ten times before he gets tired of it. He goes back over the images he's collected. Remembers his models. Brings them back to life. Perfects their profiles. Mimics. Wriggles his lips, bares his teeth, raises his eyebrows, knits them, squints his eyes slyly, and then quickly opens them wide in an expression of utter stupefaction. He imitates the young girl who hops on one leg, and her little sister who applauds and their crystalline laughter, which he propels towards the setting sun, piercing the crickets' litany with its splendor. Everything he finds he chews like tobacco. He spits out the bitter juice, swallowing his disgust. He crumbles a dried oak leaf in his fingers and stuffs a pinch in his nostril as if it were tobacco snuff. He sneezes until he nearly ruptures his sinuses. In his mind, the bells ring, and he immediately makes the sign of the cross, one time, two times, ten times in a row, with his left hand, with his right hand, afraid to mix up the movements because that's undoubtedly one of the habits that most escapes his comprehension. What purpose does it serve? What is its significance? He wracks his brain but doesn't understand. Nevertheless, he commits to practicing it without protest. Because this is how humans live.

They know, he doesn't.

Sometimes he goes back there at night. Takes advantage of the darkness to get as close as possible. Sneaks into back alleys and yards, walks alongside buildings. He needs to touch. He puts the palms of his hands flat against the stones of the houses. He presses his cheek against them. He presses his ear against them, as though he might hear them, the people inside, as if he might feel their breath, their pulse, mold to them. Penetrate their shell if he can't penetrate their hearts. Soon. Soon, perhaps.

But his presence doesn't always go unnoticed. The animals in the stable smell him. There's a rustling. A hoof nervously scrapes at the ground. A sudden bark and his blood freezes. A shutter flies open, a voice cries out: What is that? Who's there? In his panic he stumbles, then leaps up and rushes out and his bare feet carry him towards the depths of the night.

In a place called Les Roches-Blanches he had the time, before running away, to catch sight of the metallic gleam of a rifle visible through an open window, immediately followed by an explosion that surely disrupted the order of the planets, and he heard strange lead bees whistling past his ears.

For these honest people nothing good can happen at this late hour, only three types of scourge: thieves, phantoms, or the devil in one of his countless disguises.

An array of legends dating from this time period originate with him. Rumors are born and spread across the country. And among the carnival of monsters on display on these summer nights, the ancestral figure of the werewolf predominates. People swear they've seen the hideous beast on the prowl. They attest to his hairy body, his gigantic size, his clawed fingers, his eyes as yellow as the fires of hell, his eyes as red as glowing embers. They dread the full moon. Women pray, put their fate in the Lord's hands. Their husbands worry just as much but remain silent, they purse their lips and prepare the buckshot and leave the rifle hanging next to the bed. People relieve their bladders in makeshift chamber pots to avoid crossing the yard, exposed. Lying in the dark, everyone is on the alert. They scrutinize the slightest sounds. They weigh the silence. They sense his presence. He's coming. He's approaching. He's here. Jesus, Mary, and Joseph. The proof is that the dogs sense him, too. People say the dogs are acting crazy. They hide, retreat, trembling, in the most remote corner of the house, or else they're enraged and bare their teeth and pull on their leads, strangling themselves. The pitiful dogs that bark or howl at death.

They speak of sacrifices. They speak of hunting.

Of course the boy has no idea of the trouble he's sowing. The tales develop unbeknownst to him. And in an ironic twist of fate, the more he strives to join his peers, the more they deny him his place in humanity.

His steps have carried him south. In mid-August he finds himself less than seven miles, as the crows flies, from his point of departure. He's spent the past three days in an abandoned kiln. It's surrounded by scrubland. The kiln hasn't been fired in ages, but the structure is intact, undamaged. A model of dry-stone masonry. The building has been placed under the protection not of the Virgin Mary but of a gecko, who guards the entrance, immobile, immutable, like a bas-relief carved into the stone over the door. Small black-and-gold scorpions sleep between the slabs, waiting for nightfall.

The boy sleeps, too. He nodded off nestled in the kiln after returning from one of his expeditions. When he emerges from his siesta it's six in the evening. His body is coated from head to toe in a layer of sweat. He drinks. Afterward he puts the goatskin in his satchel, which he closes again and slips over his shoulder, then he stands up and leaves.

Hardly has he crossed the threshold when he confronts a double-barrel rifle pointed at his forehead. Two dark orifices, so close they make him squint—and chill him immediately.

The man holding it is approximately his size. He has a three-day beard and hair the color of copper, unless it's the rays of the setting sun inflicting these reddish reflections. A dead hare hangs from his belt, one eye open and glassy. A streak of dried blood drips from the animal's ear and tarnishes its fur.

The boy doesn't move. He looks at the rifle and he looks at the dead hare and he remembers the terrible noise that had exploded in the dead of night and that had almost done the same in his skull. He looks at the man. And the man returns his gaze. He stares at the boy with eyes that are in this moment more black than blue.

"WHAT'S THAT?" the little girl asks.

"Mind your own business," says her mother.

"A vagabond," says her father.

"I'd say he looks like one of those Romany," says Eugène.

"A bad omen," Eugénie chirps.

"What's a Romany?" the little girl asks.

"Nothing much," says her father.

"Plague and cholera," Eugénie chirps.

"Wasn't there a circus that just passed through the area?"

"Not that I know of."

"Is it a guy or a girl?" old Blaise asks. "I can't see too well from here."

"Doesn't matter, he's not hiding much. How long has it been since you saw a woman, Blaise? Do you remember what they look like, at least?"

"Shut up, Eugène," Eugénie chirps.

"Well, what is he saying?" Napoléon asks.

"Nothing," says the little girl's father.

"You asked him?"

"No."

"Maybe he doesn't understand our language," Marie-Aimée suggests in her gentle voice.

"A foreigner, you mean?"

"It's happening everywhere," says the little girl's mother. "In town, last month, we even saw some arriving from the colonies."

"Darkies, you mean?"

"A whole family from the looks of it."

"We're being invaded."

"The eighth plague," Eugénie chirps. "'They cover the surface of the entire earth and the earth descends into darkness . . .'"

"You speak French?" Eugène bellows.

"'. . . They devour all the plants of the earth and all the fruit in the trees . . .'"

"Why are you all yelling like that?" Napoléon says, "He's not deaf."

"We dunno that, could be."

"Is he really going to eat all the fruit?" the little girl asks.

"I think you're scaring him with your loud voices," Marie-Aimée suggests in her gentle voice.

"I bet he's escaped," Pierre says.

"Escaped?"

"The kid might be right," says Eugène. "Now that you mention it, he sure do look like someone on the run."

"On the run?"

"On the run from what?" asks the little girl's father.

"How should I know? From prison. From slavery. It don't matter. Maybe even a nut house, why not?"

"He don't seem crazy."

"He don't seem all there, neither."

"Maybe he's like Kazoo?" old Honorine says.

"We don't need two of 'em."

"This one doesn't slobber," says the little girl's mother. "At least he's got that going for him."

"Where'd you find him, Lucien?" Napoléon asks.

"In the kiln in Borel. He was sleeping inside."

"He was sleeping? In the kiln?"

"Yeah. I nabbed him when he woke up."

"What were you doing messing around over there?" says Eugène.

"I can go wherever I like, can't I?"

"Yeah, yeah. I was just asking."

"I was tracking this creature, see."

"Guess you didn't miss the poor bastard."

"Eugène," Eugénie chirps.

"What creature?" old Blaise asks. "What creature is he talking about? I can't see nothing from here."

"A hare," old Honorine says. "A beauty."

"You need to get glasses, Blaise. Soon you won't be able to see your nose to blow it."

"If he was sleeping in the kiln, he must not have a home," Marie-Aimée suggests in her gentle voice. "He must be a poor orphan who was chased away, or got lost."

"Are we going to eat him?" the little girl asks.

"Eat him?" says her mother. "What are you going on about now?"

"The hare, are we going to eat him?" the little girl says.

IT'S A HAMLET. Four farms, four families, thirteen inhabitants total, of which eleven form a half-circle facing him in this moment. Missing is someone named Joseph and his son Louis-Paul, whom they call Kazoo.

The man who led him here with the tip of his rifle does indeed have red hair no matter the hour of day or night. He's a fox-man. He exudes a strong odor of spices that sting the boy's nostrils. When they arrived, they'd stopped at a small clearing at the intersection of the buildings. A sort of public square. It was a little past seven in the evening. The man didn't call for anyone, he simply stayed there, his rifle wedged in his armpit, with a sly and satisfied expression, as if he were waiting for the arrival of a photographer meant to immortalize his exploit. They waited two or three long minutes, then one by one the doors opened, and people came out one by one onto the thresholds of their houses. For a moment they observed the boy from a distance, then they converged towards the center of the square and they stopped five or six feet away and it wasn't until after another long minute that the little girl was the first to open her mouth and say: What's that?

Since then, they've been deliberating.

The boy watches them through the sticky locks of hair that trickle over his forehead. His eyes dart back and forth, following whoever speaks. He listens. Words aren't his strong point. He concentrates on the timbre and the intonations. He perceives suspicion, hostility, compassion, indifference. There are those who speak with their tongues and those who speak with their hearts; he is capable of distinguishing them. It's strange, perhaps, but he's no longer afraid.

The fox-man had relieved the boy of his sack as soon as he'd stepped out of the kiln. He searched the contents en route. He kept it with him, hanging from his shoulder. And now he brandishes it towards the sky, shows it to everyone as if it were the scalp of their worst enemy. But he is given no glory. He hands the sack to his wife, who opens it and examines it herself before passing it to her neighbor, and so on. The boy watches his possessions pass from hand to hand. Each person roots through it, each person unearths something. The knife, the goatskin, the matchbox, the pieces of flint. The young woman with the soft voice refuses to touch it. She bats her eyelashes, which are long. Her gestures float in the air. She's the butterfly-woman. With a look she dissuades her brother, Napoléon, too, who sighs but gives in and passes the sack along without opening it. The little girl wrests it from his fingers. She tips it upside down at once, empties it, then crouches in front of the objects spread over the ground, and from among them she chooses the matchbox and brings it to her ear and shakes. Then she opens the box and turns it over too with a rapid movement of the wrist. The pearls fall. The eagle's talon. The shells. The ivory die. All the offerings to the dead. Everyone watches them fall.

"What is that?" asks old Honorine.

She wrinkles her long and pointed nose in which bristle four white hairs. She's the shrew-woman.

"Let's have a look," Eugène says.

He leans over and picks up a few pearls, which he places in his palm and examines the way he examines seeds to determine their maturity. He shrugs his shoulders.

"Trinkets," he says. "I bet they ain't worth a nail's head."

"What isn't worth a nail's head?" asks old Blaise.

"Your peepers," laughs Eugène.

He lets the pearls run through the funnel of his fist then rubs his hands as if to dust them off. And then everyone loses interest in the treasure. Except the little girl. Except her little brother, Victor, a toddler of eleven months carried in his mother's arms. He wriggles and groans for his mother to set him free. And as soon as she places him on the ground, he drags himself on his knees, on his stomach, he crawls towards his sister. He's the worm-child.

"Well," says Eugène. "We still dunno what the hell to do with him."

"Maybe we'd better get the gendarmes," says Pierre.

"Jesus, Mary, and Joseph," Eugénie chirps.

"The gendarmes? Why the gendarmes?" asks old Honorine. "Until proved otherwise, he ain't done nothing wrong."

"He was in the kiln in Borel," says Pierre.

"That's a crime?"

"And he was hidin'. And if he was hidin', it's cause he ain't want to be found."

"Again with your escapee story," says the mother of the little girl.

"You'll see I'm right. And don't come cryin' to me when you do."

"This boy is free," says Marie-Aimée. "It's not up to us to decide his fate."

"That's true," says Napoléon. "He gets to have a say after all."

"Well, he just gotta say it then," says Eugène. "He been quiet as a carp."

"Maybe he's looking for work," says old Honorine.

"Work?"

"He doesn't have a lot of meat on him, but he seems sturdy."

"So what?"

"We could always use a hand."

"Another hand means another mouth," says the father of the little girl. "I don't have the means."

"What's in his trap?" asks old Blaise.

"Huh?"

"The lil guy, what's he got stuck in his throat? I can't see from here."

"Good God, he's as red as a cow's tit," says Eugène.

"Victor?" says his mother.

"Don't swear, Eugène," Eugénie chirps.

"Looks like he's choking," says Napoléon.

"Victor!" cries the mother.

The worm-child has indeed changed color. He's seated with his legs spread, his chest bent forward as though trying to do gymnastics. His mouth is gaping open and the sound that escapes from it is like a bronchitic wheeze. His mother grabs hold of him, tilts his forehead back, and sticks a finger down his throat, then another, as far down as she can.

"For Christ's sake, what have you done this time?"

This invective is addressed at her daughter.

"I didn't do nothin'," the little girl whimpers. "It wasn't me, he did it on his own."

"Be quiet," says her mother.

She pulls back her fingers. They're glossy. She lifts the child and turns him upside down and shakes him like a sack of flour.

"Spit. Spit it out now, good heavens."

She's a very angular woman. Built out of squares. Tall and flat and broad-shouldered. Taller and wider than her husband. She's the mantis-woman.

"Hit 'im on the back," says Eugène. "Gotta get it out."

"I didn't do nothin' at all," repeats the little girl.

"Be quiet," repeats her mother. "We'll just see if you done nothin'. I'll do somethin' to you, in any case, you can count on that."

And as she wedges the toddler beneath her arm and starts to deal him a series of great smacks between the shoulder blades, the little girl's face wrinkles, creases, then transforms entirely into a hideous grimace that looks like the mask of an old angry man, and soon tears seep from the slits of her eyelids and snot from the holes of her nose.

Her name is Blanche. She's eight years old. An uglier child would be hard to come by. Her enormous, disproportionate eyes are set on opposite sides of her face. She has at least three chins and the skinny thighs and bulging stomach of a frog. She is the toad-child.

53

She and the toddler are the only young people in the hamlet—Kazoo doesn't count: his age means nothing. Blanche and her brother Victor represent the future. And for now a good part of that future is obstructed.

"Hit," says Eugène. "Go on, don't be afraid to really do it."

"She'll end up breaking him, she will," says old Honorine.

"What did I tell you," says Pierre. "Only been here an hour and already bad things are happening."

"The plague and cholera," chirps Eugénie.

"Worse," says Eugène.

The mother continues to pummel the child, who is struggling like a suckling pig about to be sacrificed, his legs pedaling in the air, his stubby pink thighs with their folds and their bulges.

The boy observes the scene. He thinks of the mother knocking out the goats. He wonders if they're going to kill the worm-child, if they're going to cut him up and eat his liver. He's never been hit. Each of the mantis-woman's blows provokes a brief contraction deep down in his stomach.

And then suddenly the child belches. From his mouth spews a sticky white slop: phlegm, lumps of milk curds. And drowned inside, the ivory die from the second Iron Age. Two thousand five hundred years of history.

"Good," says the mother.

She hits him again but nothing else comes out. The child hiccups. He coughs. Then he gobbles a large gulp of air which he expels just as quickly in a shriek of anger and fright and relief. His tears soon rival those of his sister.

"Bugle's unblocked," says Eugène.

When he laughs, the pink flabby skin of his goiter trembles. He's the turkey-man.

The group exhales. The mother sets the toddler upright again, his chin ornamented with a filament of saliva. She wedges him into the crook of her arm, then she bends and extends her other arm like a compass needle and brings it down through the air and gives the crouching little girl a smack that knocks her onto her butt.

The boy's eyelids close at the sound of the smack. When he opens them again he sees the little girl sprawled on the floor, inert, her dress hiked up on her pale skin: he thinks she's dead. He feels a tingling, a slight burning on his own cheek.

"That was your fault," says the mother. "Who told you to dump everything out? Now you gather it up, and quick, don't make me give you another."

Then before the boy's eyes the dead girl stands up and does as she's told. Tears blur her vision. Her nose runs but she doesn't think to wipe it. She gathers the boy's modest possessions and shoves them in his sack. He follows each of her movements and so he sees her make disappear one of the translucent aragonite pearls, which is nothing but a drop of daylight, along with one of the black shale pearls, its counterpart, taken from the source of shadows. The little girl holds them in her fist then slides them surreptitiously into a pocket between the folds of her dress, all without ever stopping her crying. Then she closes the sack again.

She forgets the playing die fashioned by the men of the second Iron Age—but who among those men could have imagined when they made it that it would end up stuck in a puddle of vomit, regurgitated by a worm-child twenty-five centuries later?

She forgets the frog bone, which is lost somewhere in the dust and won't be found again.

What is precious in this world?

What is sacred?

They know, he does not.

Both of the boy's cheeks burn now, and the burning gets stronger.

"Here comes Joseph," says old Honorine.

ALL THEIR HEADS TURN at the same time. All eyes look in the direction of the sun, which is plummeting behind one of the buildings and far beyond in order to illuminate the Indies and the Americas and other parts of the earth that none of them has ever conquered nor even visited, nor will they ever do so.

The boy looks too. What he sees are two vertical shadows and their lank reflections on the ground paving the way. The one called Joseph walks with an even stride. He's big. He's straight. Head covered with a smooth mane of hair, white like the feathers of a swan. He's holding a small sickle in his right hand. On his pelvis is a cloth pouch as worn as the boy's sack. It contains herbs and plants whose secret virtues so few of them know. Fewer still are those who know how to extract their essences and combine them just so. The one they call Kazoo is walking a step behind in a very personal choreography, improvised or in any case impossible to anticipate, even by him. A ballet of grace and chaos. He is as tall as his father. He is handsome, the kind of beauty reserved for young gods and cursed poets. He smiles. Small bubbles hatch from the corners of his lips. He keeps a hand raised horizontally in front of him, completely flat, on the back of which is a splendid insect that could have been fashioned by a goldsmith. It's a beetle with amber and emerald wings and chiseled mandibles like the crown of any self-respecting imperial dynasty. And just as dead as the first of the Chinese emperors, as devoid of life as the brooch once pinned to the heart of his concubine. But that's a notion that Kazoo's mind cannot comprehend. He doesn't take his eyes off the insect, waiting for it to move, for it to walk, for it to tickle his skin. He sometimes encourages it with a slight movement of his fingernail, which he does more through camaraderie than through impatience, because time is another of those laws that Kazoo has been free from since birth. He burbles. He seems happy.

Gradually the assembly moves aside. The half-circle is cut down the middle, creating a breach, a passage at the edge of which Joseph comes to a halt. His shadow traces a perfect line between his feet and the boy's. There is no sound. The toddler has stopped bawling and his sister has stopped whimpering. And suddenly there is the feeling that what has taken place up till now was only a simulacrum of a trial, a comedy in which meager extras were permitted to assume roles too big for them. But no one is playing anymore. The judge has arrived. Perhaps Justice itself.

The boy stares at the silhouette planted opposite him, tall and straight as a totem. The man has just appeared and yet it's as though he's always been there, in his place, between the earth and the sky. He's the oak-man. His roots are deep, his branches countless. He has seen the seasons pass. He has seen the centuries pass. His limbs have served as refuge to flocks of birds just as often as they have as gallows for the condemned.

Kazoo joins them in his turn. At the end of his pirouettes and arabesques he stops moving, his two feet on the ground but still in a state of suspense, still in the precarious balance of a tightrope walker on a thread. His gaze wanders over the assembly, glances at the familiar faces, then comes to rest on the boy. Immediately his smile grows wider, revealing his teeth and those that are missing. Kazoo starts moving again, joyfully balancing his limbs, forgetting the presence of the beetle for the moment, his insect companion, which slides and drops and rejoins the miserable cemetery in which already lie the bones of dead frogs and the die of destiny and entire dynasties of Chinese emperors. For Kazoo there is no border: he crosses the semicircle without hesitating and penetrates what is, to his eyes, perhaps a clearing or an ice floe, who knows?

Seeing him approach with such great strides, the boy stiffens. He starts to recoil but Kazoo is already on him, he throws himself to his knees and wraps his arms around the boy and nestles his cheek into the crook of his chest and squeezes him tight, tight, tight. The boy raises his hands. He doesn't dare move. He feels the breath of the giant on his skin. He feels his drool, the drool of a faithful dog, which overflows his mouth and flows in a long shining string like holy water on the foreheads of the baptized. This is a show of love, the purest and the most complete there is, the boy feels it. It's something that shouldn't be forgotten.

It's a beautiful summer night. Kazoo closes his eyes. Apart from his burbling, a profound silence reigns over the hamlet, over the surrounding fields, over the hills, over the vines and the olive groves. It seems that everything has been said and the sentence pronounced.

HE WILL STAY WITH THIS COMMUNITY for nearly six months. All the universe is there. If he had the intention of discovering or at least of better defining what his place was, what role was allocated to him, then it must be said that his place and his role strongly resemble, at least in these beginning stages, that of a farm laborer, a servant. And in that description, isn't it the word "laborer" that takes priority? Three decades later, somewhere in the confines of the Amazonian jungle, an old *índio*, discerning and disillusioned, will tell him, in essence, the following: Your people (and by that he means all of humanity besides the few tribes neighboring his own), your people is made up of only laborers and masters, a large number of laborers and a small handful of masters, an infinite number of servants, he will insist, for one sole master in the end, each servant aspiring with all his heart and all his soul to become a master in his turn, but each master being in reality the servant to another master even more important than him, and that applies also to your gods, who serve, without a doubt, the designs of a power that is far superior to them, and not at all good and charitable, but malevolent, evil, you only have to open your eyes to be convinced, you only have to see what is imposed on you, what you endure, what you accept, you only have to watch yourself act and watch yourself live, it's staring you right in the face, your gods are servants just like everyone else, no more or less, so much so that if we add it all up there are thousands, millions of servants for this sole master, the supreme master, in all likelihood cruel, in all likelihood delirious, so much so that we must assume that he subjects himself to his own cruelty, to his own folly, which is to say that he is essentially his own servant. But how can we break free of this? the old índio will ask. How can your people, the people you belong to, he will say to the boy, recover their freedom? Killing the master will not turn you into free men. Eliminating the master will not permit you to eliminate the servants that you are. Why? Because another will immediately take his place, and another after him, and another again. Endlessly. The cycle will continue and the droves of workers will continue. Because what makes a servant is not his master, what makes a servant is his desire to become a master. That and nothing else. To kill the master would be useless, then, what has to be done is to kill, to eradicate the desire to be a master. That ambition, that desire, that need, you have to deliver yourself from it. It's the only solution. But it doesn't appear to me, he concludes, that your people are close to reaching that point, nor even that they're close to envisioning it. This is what an old discerning and disillusioned índio will say to him many years later. A speech supported by many experiences, initiated by his agreeing, out of curiosity, to leave his dear forest and his giant palm trees and his golden tamarinds for the first and last time to follow a team of British ethnologists who will end up bringing him to London and to Cambridge and to Edinburgh and to various capitals of Europe and the United States and into cities of lesser importance, where he will have had the occasion to meet our greatest leaders and our greatest sorcerers and lesser leaders and less famous sorcerers and a retinue of charlatans and mobs of poor people and the sickly and what he would not be able to describe as anything other than savages, and even though his journeys will have lasted not more than a year, it will have been amply sufficient for him to dismantle the machinery and understand the functioning of our civilization and form an opinion about it from which will arise the sentiments about our people that, to be frank, will oscillate between scorn, disgust, and compassion. A speech that the boy will listen to avidly until the end, but on which, however, he will not have the possibility to meditate, having been spoken to in one of those aboriginal dialects that is absolutely unintelligible to him. Will that be why the old Native American, at the end of his long speech, will suddenly stray from his disillusioned tone to burst into an enormous fit of laughter? As if he had just played a good trick on the boy. As if all that was nothing but a joke, a farce, one more gag in the great tragic and grotesque comedy of life. And his extravagant laugh will even incite the macaws hiding in the canopy to take flight and the shrunken human head the size of a grapefruit hanging around his neck to twitch back and forth.

But we're not at that point.

The boy harvests. He threshes. He wields the pitchfork and the hoe and the flail and the whetstone stone and all the tools that a farm-hand must master. The method of his learning is always the same: he observes, he imitates. He has his willingness and courage at his advantage. No task scares him, never does he balk at a duty, and on some nights if they didn't stop him he would probably continue to toil under the starlight until he collapsed.

It's that he has no more time to lose. Now it's out of the question to lay down at every turn and contemplate the sky and let the clouds tell their slow and silent movement to him. He has abandoned the beetle races. He has stopped drawing suns. He disdains the rain made of feathers, those mini storms, those fluffy fireworks unleashed by blowing onto the head of a dandelion. The boy doesn't play anymore. Trifles, frivolities: he leaves all that to Kazoo, the imbecile, to Victor, the worm-child. He digs. He weeds and plows. He makes himself useful. His thirst for learning is immense and intensified tenfold by an even greater thirst for recognition. Not so much for what he does but for who he is, for what he aspires to be: one of them.

In addition to his drive and his ardor, in addition to his malleability, he has another advantage, a not negligible one, of not asking for any compensation. He doesn't rent himself out. He doesn't sell himself. He gives himself.

They share him.

AT FIRST HE SLEEPS in Joseph's hay barn, in the attic. In the stable below is a pair of oxen and an ageless mule with coarse hair. Joseph used to own a Percheron that weighed almost a ton but it died and none of its successors have measured up. He once had sixteen hundred sheep and eight shepherds and twelve sheepdogs, including the descendant of a border collie imported directly from Scotland—the first and only ever seen in the country to this day. As the herd migrated across the plain, people would hear it in the surrounding areas and know either that summer had begun or that summer had ended. That was during his glory days. Joseph Antoine Félicien Peyre would survey his domain in a long fox coat, a fedora propped on his head and decorated with a shiny bluish grouse's feather. A get-up that no one would have thought to mock, for the field mouse wouldn't dare laugh at the eagle that holds it in its talons. At that time everything here belonged to Monsieur Joseph: the entire hamlet, the buildings and the land, each stone, each tree, each grain of wheat, each drop of rain or sweat. Among the three other families populating these places there isn't a man who wasn't at one time his serf, and if not his then his father's.

But all that was hanging by a thread and that thread was love. Who would have imagined?

Joseph had gone to Mexico in 1862 with the French Expeditionary Corps, and when he returned five years later he brought back with him neither glory nor injury, but a young wife with doe eyes and the allure of a jaguar. He was twenty-six, she was twenty. She was from Oaxaca, Zapotec blood running through her veins. When she wasn't around, the locals called her "the Indian" and admired her for her exotic beauty and her magic powers, which they simultaneously sought and feared. Justifiably, perhaps. She sometimes appeared without anyone having seen or heard her approach. She wasn't there and the next second she was, right in front of them, in the middle of a field or between two rows of plants. After their initial shock, their first instinct was to remove their hats. A sign of respect. Or allegiance. She herself went bare-headed, her cascade of jet-black hair split into two braids like two plaited leather whips, or else done up in a thick but elegant woven bun, in which was pinned, depending on the seasons and her mood, either a cornflower, an *aphyllanthes*, a rockrose, a local species of cardamine, or any flower whose radiance and color emphasized the beauty of the specimen that supported it even more. Old Blaise was convinced he had seen the Indian frolicking about in the river one gentle night in spring, dressed only in a veil of moonlight. Unfortunately, even the much younger old Blaise was already incredibly short-sighted, and no one could trust what his eyes told him. Whether it was true or false, he held on to that vision forever, kept it deep in his defective retinas as well as in a separate compartment of his heart, and it would be the inspiration for his most feverish dreams and his most delicious torments.

That was the woman that Joseph loved. My God how much he loved her. He didn't know it was possible to love so much. He alone understood her language. She had taught it to him. She had taught him the songs of her childhood. She had revealed the words used to invoke the god of rain and the god of light to him. Cocijo. Coquihani. He was ready to believe everything so long as it was she who affirmed it. He no longer looked at the sky in the same way. Joseph loved his wife more than anyone and was amazed, every day, that she could love him back. What did he have to offer her? What riches? His land, his farms, his animals, his people: that was for her. The crops and the harvests. The wine from the vineyard. Everything. But still so little. Almost nothing. He found the kingdom he put at her feet to be quite meager. To him, no empire seemed worthy.

Their love lasted two decades without diminishing. It seemed eternal. Then the Indian died giving birth to that child, to that son that she had promised him, and that he was no longer waiting for. She was forty, he was forty-six. Nothing could save her. Not the gods, nor the priests, nor the experience of Honorine, nor the science of the doctor that Joseph went looking for in town and whom he had wrested from his bed and brought by night at a great gallop atop the Percheron. They could save the child, not the mother. After twenty-eight hours of torture she had turned to look at Joseph and put her last reserves of strength into a frail smile for him, in a slow batting of eyelashes, and then she let go.

The Zapotecs are the people of clouds: she went to rejoin them.

Joseph had howled. Joseph had cried. Joseph had wanted to kill the doctor. He had wanted to kill the child, that atrocious purple thing emerged from the beloved stomach who had sucked up all the air, who had devoured it as viciously as a tumor. Joseph had wanted to kill himself.

The day had barely risen when he picked up the still-warm body of his beloved. They had seen him leave, march straight ahead, carrying her in his arms as on their wedding night. No one had tried to stop him.

One week later he came back. Alone. They never knew where he had gone nor what he had done. If he had given his love a grave—and that's something everyone wanted to believe—he'd kept the location secret all these years. It was clear to everyone, at first glance, that it was not the same man who had returned.

During his absence, Honorine had looked after the newborn. She thought he wouldn't survive, that he would pass away before the next full moon. From an old woven basket she used to transport logs, she had made a bassinet. The child had survived. His nanny had been a dwarf sheep; no human woman in the area at that time had been able to lactate. Honorine boiled the animal's milk, soaked a handkerchief in it, and then patiently squeezed it between the infant's lips. It reminded her of a nearly dead blackbird she had found a half-century earlier. She had taken care of it and fed it, she had saved it, then the bird flew away. Each morning and each night for almost a year, she had waited at her window for it to come back to see her, but it never did. Fifty years later her heart still skipped a beat every time she saw a blackbird in the sky.

When he returned, Joseph had stood in front of the basket for a long time staring at the child. His son. He hadn't said a word. At first, Honorine had been relieved to find him at her door, but gradually she started to hope that he would leave again just as he had come: alone. The child was not sleeping. His eyes were small amethyst marbles that seemed to stare at the man above him. His father. He didn't cry. He rarely cried. He was already burbling. When Joseph had finally grabbed the basket to take it, Honorine thought she saw a set of wings flapping through the room. She had remained glued to her chair. I call him Louis-Paul, she murmured, the only thing she had the strength to do before Joseph had crossed the threshold. She wasn't sure he had heard her.

After the death of his wife, Joseph Antoine Félicien Peyre had lost his possessions and his riches. He had burned his fox coat. He had sold his herd. He had kept, for himself and the child, one of the farms of the hamlet and one acre of land. The rest he had distributed. He had given it all away to other families. The families had suddenly found themselves owners of the roofs that sheltered them and the lands they cultivated. The letters validated it, the notarized seals attested to it, and these peasants held the paperwork between their thick fingers and stared at it all with incredulous, skeptical, wary eyes. Most of them didn't know how to read. He had to convince them. It's written here. The proof of their emancipation. The former employees now possessed as much if not more than their former boss. There was no more Monsieur Joseph. Joseph the master had been transformed into Joseph the monk, or something close to it. The inhabitants of the hamlet had taken a long time to get used to their new status. And despite everything, they had never been able to—they still couldn't—consider Joseph their equal. Somewhere, deeply anchored, exists the sentiment that they are his eternal debtors. There remains the fear that everything that had been given to them could be taken away overnight. And it's this fear that makes Joseph their clear superior: having lost the love of his life, he has nothing more to lose. Nothing more can be taken away from him.

THUS THE OAK-MAN and the cloud-woman had given birth to a river-child who became a flood-child. Likewise the fox-man and the mantis-woman had given birth to the toad-child and the worm-child. It's a strange thing. It's one of the trickiest ideas for the boy to grasp: ancestry and lineage. Siblings. Blood lines. Difficult to sort out for someone who has no idea of their existence, or only vague notions.

He has not yet thought of his own origin. He does not know that he came from his mother's stomach. (Like in every good, cruel tale, she had given birth alone in the moonlight, however she had not cut the umbilical cord with her teeth but with that same little knife with the now-chipped blade that the boy still carries in his sack.) He is there. He was always there. Before him the world didn't exist. He has no memory of being fed by the maternal breast and if some-one were to remind him, he would wrinkle his nostrils and spit on the ground in disgust. Mother, son, what does that mean? Was he attached to that woman because he was of her flesh or simply because she was the only being that he had spent time with? Because they had shared the cold and hunger and hours of silence watching the rain fall in the gray rectangular entrance of their hut? Because they had shared the almost-nothing that they had possessed? Would he have felt the same sentiment for a she-wolf, for a female bear that had taken him into her cave?

The boy has also not asked himself about his father because he doesn't know that life is made from two. He has no idea about the reproductive act. He has seen rabbits straddle each other and roosters straddle hens but how to establish a relationship of cause and effect between these brief epileptic convulsions and the miracle of creation? He has no father and isn't looking for one.

In the community of the hamlet he observes individuals and the little clans. Those who eat at the same table, sleep beneath the same roof. He doesn't belong to any group. He goes from one to another depending on the work to be done, like a sort of day laborer. Joseph asks nothing, but between the three other families there are agreements in place, more or less tacit, to share the boy equally. His hours, his arms. One day he clears the stones from an abandoned field for the Janicots, the next he plows soil for the Siffres, the next he harvests alongside the Tonellis. Those who profit from his services take care of his pittance. The seventh day is that of the Lord. They give thanks to Him or at least respect His rest. That's another thing the boy has no way of understanding: Sunday means nothing to him. Nor Monday nor Thursday. He knows the rising and setting of the sun, the light and the darkness, the seasons, he feels deep down inside of him when the first frost is coming or when the revived sap starts to flow, but he cannot understand that all of that was weighed, measured, rationalized, that all these phenomena were the object of astronomic and infinitesimal calculations, and it's impossible for him to imagine that scholars thought to dissect time, to divide it, to fraction it and assign each of its parcels, no matter how tiny, a name or a number, a symbol destined for clocks and calendars. Divide it for what reason? To better control it?

And it was the same for everything. They had, beneath their eyes, the book of God, the work of Nature, the work of Great Chance, and they reduced it to mathematical formulas. Who needed to know? The magician does not reveal his tricks. You see, my boy, the sun is not the sun, the clouds are not clouds, a rainbow is not a rainbow. They are only chemical combinations. Don't laugh, it's not a joke. The air that you breathe is a combination. You are a combination. A few black holes hidden in the most distant galaxies only barely manage to escape their equations. But they will end up succumbing to them. Tomorrow the immemorial cosmogony will be entirely contained in the pages of an almanac.

How could he comprehend all of that?

They know, not him.

Only Kazoo is free of many of these conventions. He is not completely free, certainly, but his cage is of another size. Sunday, like every other day, he goes to see the boy. The affection that he has for him has not diminished. It is blind and without boundaries, without expectations, without even the idea of reciprocity. It's a gift. The flood-child has the body of a man, the soul of something else. Of an elf perhaps. Of a sylph. He accompanies the boy everywhere, not like a rigid, disciplined shadow but like a puppy, always gravitating around his master, picking up every odor, exploring every path, curious to rediscover the world at every moment, but who always comes back, thrilled to share the fruits of his investigations: flowers, insects (dead or alive), moltings and shells, husks, hulls, pebbles. One day a garter snake is rolled around his wrist; the boy thinks it's a viper and throws it violently to the ground and crushes it under his powerful heel.

At first this permanent presence bothers him. It makes him uncomfortable, vaguely worries him. After all, Kazoo is three heads taller than him and who can predict his next move? But little by little he gets used to it, and above all he perceives that the one of them who's in control is not the one people think.

One day he escapes Kazoo's attention and perches on a branch in a plane tree. He observes Kazoo, below, turning and spinning, looking for him, frantic, distraught, stupid, panic widening his pupils that usually shine with that joy that nothing seems able to corrupt. He sees him scamper from one side to the other, rear back, return, take off again, in a kind of arrhythmic and solitary crisscross. It's the dance of the fly trapped under glass. It's the course of the flood-child who smashes against the rock. His soft burbles evolve into a mournful hooting. The boy doesn't move, doesn't show himself, lets it play out, not without pleasure, the pathetic spectacle he watches, dedicated to him. Though they may be invisible, there are strings, and he's the one pulling them. And when finally he deigns to jump from his hiding place and show himself, he receives, not without pleasure, the exuberant caresses poured out for him, and the joy rediscovered in the bright eyes of the flood-child, and the gratitude that splashes over him.

One day, one day when he wants to do his business without a witness, he pushes Kazoo with great force. In vain. He picks up a large stone. He threatens him. Then throws it. He is skilled at this game; he can hit a sparrow on its perch thirty feet away, or one out of three times if it's in flight. The stone hits his chest then falls at the feet of the imbecile, who lowers his eyes and contemplates it a moment, as if it were a meteorite fallen from the sky. Then he forgets and starts walking towards the boy once again. He has to try five times, launch five projectiles for Kazoo to stop advancing. While the boy relieves himself out of his view, the tall silhouette of Kazoo remains planted alone in the middle of a field like a scarecrow. He waits. He turns his neck and looks around him as if he didn't know the area, as if he were wondering which of the planets he had landed on.

And the next day the boy throws a stone again, this time without a reason. To see. He aims at Kazoo's head. His brow line splits. Kazoo staggers but remains standing. The boy draws closer. He feels neither fear nor remorse. He's drawn blood, a narrow rivulet along Kazoo's cheek. The boy runs two fingers over it, slowly, leaving two diagonal and purple streaks on his skin, signs that the Indian might have interpreted had she been alive. The boy considers the tips of his fingers for a moment, then brings them to his mouth and takes communion.

Because at this stage and among all the inhabitants, the flood-child is still the one most likely to understand him. The creature whose nature is closest to his own. And often when he sits against a tree trunk to eat a bit of bread and cheese, he lets the giant lie at his side and place his head on his thighs and gently drool on him.

ABOUT TWO MONTHS after his arrival he is overtaken by an illness that dissociates his body from his mind. His body refuses to move. Each effort he makes to get up sinks him down even further. His teeth chatter. Sweat inundates him in waves and soaks his sheets. And while he lies there, heavy, paralyzed, his mind escapes him. He floats. He wanders in places that his memory doesn't recognize, if it ever knew them in the first place.

He's crossing a river, a river made of time that he cannot evaluate. Days and nights blend together. Darkness reigns. From time to time an uncertain gleam pierces through the shield of his eyelids: maybe it's a lighthouse, maybe the lantern of a captain standing in a small boat, waiting to take him down one of the tributaries towards hell. But it's not he who decides, he goes groaning wherever the current takes him. Barely is he aware of a hand pulling him to the surface a few times when he sinks below, that catches him and brings him back to the air and makes him drink a bitter beverage that trickles down his throat from a strange sort of cup.

When he finally comes ashore, everything is changed. He blinks his eyes, opens them. The first thing he sees is a negro sorcerer in a terrifying mask of black ebony and red vermillion. Then his eyes adjust and the sorcerer becomes the image of a firefly marching on the bed sheet a few inches from his nose. Which is no less strange. All this: the insect, the sheet, the quilt, the narrow bed he's resting on. The shadows that sway imperceptibly on the walls like palm trees in the absence of wind. The odors.

His mind and his body start to come back together. He turns his head. On the bedside table burns a tall and thin candle surrounded by various objects: a fragment of quartz, a long rusted nail, the molting of a cicada, four crimson petals, the shell of a quail egg, a bit of golden ribbon. If it's not an altar, it certainly looks like one. A bit further towards the center of the room is a chopping block two feet tall and nearly three in diameter, cut from an oak tree. And on top, six candles, thick and short, congealed in their own wax. Their flames heat up a kind of incense burner supporting a small metal tripod, in which faded leaves are infused in a liquid mixture. A vapor, thinner than that of incense fumes, rises from the container. The boy follows it with his gaze. And through this filter he sees the face of a woman who stares back at him with her large black eyes. He trembles. His fingers tighten over the sheet. He closes his eyelids for a moment then reopens them. She is still there. She is beautiful. A thin smile stretches over her lips. Two long plaited braids flow over her shoulders and her forehead is surrounded with a tiara made of flowers. She holds in her hand a scepter fashioned from a corn stalk.

It still takes another few seconds for the boy to accept that she is not of flesh. It's sheepskin, with hair and eyes of the same material. It's a tapestry, suspended by two strings from a ceiling joist. A representation. An icon. The boy stares at it for a long moment. He guesses, he senses that this is not an ordinary being, but he has never encountered a queen nor a goddess, and with the modest vocabulary he has collected he can find no word to define her. He's happy she's there. Her presence does him good. She soothes him. But suddenly the face transforms and now it's his mother that he sees. The exact image of his mother. When she would fix her eyes on him. When, even more rarely, she would put her hand on his shoulder or his arm. And he feels, he can actually feel at that moment, the contact of maternal fingers on his skin, and then his throat tightens, and tears overflow his eyes.

There's nothing he can do to hold them back. The boy knows that. It's one of the first truths, one of the first lessons. Soon the image of his mother fades: the eyes, the hand, the fingers, everything. Only the idol remains. And the boy's tears continue to run along his temples, forming a tiny salty lake in the auricle of his ear.

One of the walls is pierced with a window, barely larger than an arrow slit. Outside it's daytime. A pale autumnal light stripes the closed shutter. That's all he needs. He is now incredibly thirsty for the sky. For air on his face and earth beneath the soles of his feet. He wants to drink the rain. Drink the sun. He wants to run as the swifts fly.

Then he hears the door handle turning. The panel slides open and a willowy silhouette sidles into the room. Kazoo. He moves towards the bed. He's wearing a white shirt that must have been buttoned by a sleepy or mischievous blind man. He stops at the boy's bedside, leans over, extends his neck. Dressed like this one could just as easily take him for the nurse in an asylum doing his rounds or, instead, for one of the patients, escaped from his minders. When he sees that the boy is awake a large smile lights up his face. He takes little hops, between a kick and the leap of a mountain goat, then runs off, scampering about. A minute later he comes back. His fist is closed, brandished in front of him. He kneels at the foot of the bed, extends his arm over the sheet, presenting his fist to the boy. He unfolds his fingers. His hand opens like petals at daybreak, revealing, in the crook of his palm, two minuscule down feathers. Kazoo brings them to his mouth and breathes on them gently: in this light wind the feathers quiver, ruffle, and it's the absolute truth to say that nothing more enchanting has ever happened in all of eternity.

The boy watches the feathers. Then he watches the perfection that is the face of the flood-child and the ardent fire in his eyes. It's this memory of him—his features, this fire, this moment—that he will keep and which will resurge sometimes, without warning, from time to time.

Joseph, the father, enters the room in his turn. He stops next to the chopping block and stares at the boy in silence. Then he goes to the narrow window and opens it and pushes back the shutters and closes the window again. Beneath this brief current of air the candle flames contort and the canvas sways softly, like a sign at the entrance to an inn. The brightness is too strong for the boy. He squeezes his eyes. When he manages to open them again he finds the oak-man standing next to the bed, close to his son, who is still on his knees. Joseph seems even more immense because the ceiling is low, his white mane of hair gleaming like permanent snow at the summit of his head. Once more he remains silent for a moment, observing the boy. Then his voice descends from the heights.

"Día de los Muertos," he says.

He nods his chin.

"Today is the Day of the Dead. You can think of it as the day of your second birth."

That's all he says.

Then Kazoo gets up. One at a time, delicately, he gathers the feathers from his palm and places them on the bedside table with the other offerings.

FOR A WEEK STRAIGHT he stays in the bedroom, docile, and continues to submit to the diet that Joseph concocts for him. Remedies he makes himself, that Joseph takes from his jars or else goes to gather at the very source, up in the hills. Willow, plantain, gentian, black elderberry. The boy swallows and inhales the potions, the concoctions, the elixirs. He chews the raw roots that still taste like the dirt they were pulled from. He tolerates the burning weight on his chest without batting an eye. He sleeps a lot, a deep, peaceful slumber. For always, at every hour, someone watches over him: La Diosa Centeotl. She is the idol, the sovereign from the canvas. Joseph identified her. Goddess of corn. Her gaze is a haven and the boy abandons himself to it. Never has anyone devoted so much attention to him.

The morning of the eighth day Joseph blows out all the candles. It would seem that it's over. It would seem also that it's just beginning. Kazoo arrives with his arms laden with a heap of clothing that he places on the blanket. These are the clothes he wore when he was twelve. A complete set: underwear, undershirt, shirt, pants, sweater, and wool stockings, as well as a sheepskin vest. Kazoo lifts each article of clothing with a grand gesture, like an illusionist pulling scarves from a top hat. Then he slips away for a short moment and reappears more burbly than ever, holding a pair of thick leather work boots that he knocks together as if the legendary pied piper had swapped his flute for cymbals and dragged in his wake not a procession of rats but a circus show.

The boy sits up, on his backside. He stares at these peasant rags, which are the greatest luxury he can imagine. Then he looks towards the oak-man, eyes wide open, expressing both the desire to understand and the fear of allowing himself to be deceived.

Joseph nods his head.

"Get dressed," he says.

Ten minutes later a new avatar crosses the threshold and enters the daylight. A pastoral prince. A mannequin in its Sunday best. He moves cautiously. His legs are stiff. They look, truthfully, like they are not his legs but stilts, and those of a stranger on top of it. They don't belong to him. They carry him while he lowers his head and watches them, one, then the other, astonished, dumbstruck with each stride. The heavy shoes are two or three sizes too big.

The boy stops in the middle of the square, already out of breath. Wisps of steam escape his mouth and his nose. He reels a bit, as though inebriated. It's the pleasure and the effort. It's the cold air that intoxicates him and the morning light, though veiled, parsimonious. But the drunkenness is exquisite. And to add to his vertigo he lifts his head and turns it towards the East, where behind the haze he sees the vast platinum disc. He closes his eyes and his nostrils dilate and he breathes deep into his lungs, as if he wanted to gobble all the air between him and the horizon.

Kazoo stops darting around and imitates him.

Behind them Joseph surveys from the doorway. On his lips a wide smile that evokes La Diosa Centeotl.

The boy will not go back to sleeping in the hay barn. He remains here, under this roof. The low and somber room which was probably a former pigsty becomes his bedroom. He also acquires a place at the table. That night he sups with his hosts. He sits opposite Kazoo and the two of them flank Joseph, who presides. They eat as if it were completely natural, the only noises the silverware and swallowing. Joseph doesn't talk much. When he talks it's through parables that he delivers in a deep voice, without inflection, staring straight ahead at something that isn't there but elsewhere, in another realm of time.

And the boy listens. Though the meaning of these words still often remains impenetrable to him, their somber melody nevertheless goes straight to his heart. It penetrates his heart, fills it, nourishes it, and his heart becomes so full and so big that the boy is often forced to expand his chest with a deep breath. Is it simply the sonorous flow that has this effect on him? The rhythm? The vibrations? He has felt a similar sensation before: when at dusk he would come upon his mother in her solitary conversations. He would feel it once again, later, thanks to a particular melody emerging from the bell of an oboe. But what? What is it exactly? No one knows. And may it remain a mystery. The indecipherable and the indescribable. No one should ever know the source of the emotions that enthrall us to the beauty of a song, a story, a verse.

After supper he helps clean up.

He goes to bed early.

La Diosa Centeotl is not the only one to keep watch. Before leaving, the Indian had taken care to place the entire house under high protection. In the main room reigns the Princess Donaji, her tapestry portrait appended to the wall opposite the chimney. And on the chimney is the clumsily made statuette of a quetzal. And another of a jaguar on the side table. And that of a *coati* on the dresser. The sacred faun of the Sierra Madre del Sur. Scattered here and there, there are also a dozen hand-painted pebbles that resemble tiny leatherback turtles, like amulets, and bobbles suspended on the bread basket, and garlands made from the acorns of oak trees and the teeth of impaled rabbits on the stove pipe. Above Joseph's bed, which was the nuptial bed, radiates the soft and luminous face of the Virgin of Solitude—Virgen de la Soledad—with her gold tiara and a pearl on her forehead. (*Faith may abandon us*, says Joseph, *solitude remains*.) In Louis-Paul's bedroom, sitting on a lectern, a fabulous, distressed leather codex, ordered in times of happiness from the greatest artisan bookbinder of the region. During the nine months of her pregnancy, just as others knit tiny wardrobes in anticipation of the child about to be born, the Indian set about filling the book with drawings and paintings, with glyphs and symbols, the still-blank pages of the creation destined for her offspring. She had finished it the day before she gave birth, which was also the day she died. No one, not even Joseph, can decipher it. Perhaps it is indeed filled with tales of births and deaths, of struggles and marriages, of conquests, of victories, of defeats, of betrayals, of miracles: the adventures of the only heroes that we have ever known, gods and men. But perhaps not. The book was bequeathed to Kazoo, who would never learn even the first letter of his name, and yet often he consults these pages, plunges himself into them, is absorbed, as if in this complex language, invented for him alone, intelligible to him alone, the secret laws that govern the world—past, present, and future—were revealed.

WINTER SETS IN.

On Christmas night the boy has the distinct honor of taking part in the manger scene. A living recreation of the Nativity. Eugénie, the Janicot matriarch, instituted this practice. Eugénie Janicot barely tolerates her neighbors, but she loves God, which is not incompatible, it seems, and even more common than one might think.

The viper-woman has given birth three times. Two girls to start, who had rushed to grow up so they could marry boys in another town, where they just as quickly went to live. Eugénie Janicot had placed a lot of hope in her last-born. A male, finally. During his first few months, and even his first years, she had seen the child walk on water numerous times. In dreams and in visions. Even though she knew that it was sinful pride, she couldn't rid herself of the idea that the fruit of her loins had been chosen, among all others, to be the new Messiah. The worthy successor of the Other. And if her son was the Chosen One, she, the mother, was too, effectively. On nights of great exultation she fancied herself a virgin again, convinced that her husband Eugène had had nothing to do with the conception of the child, that she had found herself pregnant solely by the grace of the Almighty.

The first time Eugénie had submitted the idea of the Nativity to her neighbors, she had expected more reticence on their part. She insisted that the entire hamlet participate. That each of the inhabitants be an actor—but also, most importantly, that they consider themselves privileged spectators, the dazzled witnesses of the arrival of her divine child. Apparently her faith and her fervor had guided her to the right words to convince them. Or else entertainment was so rare that no one wanted to be deprived of any. Everyone agreed to take part in the play.

Thus Pierre Janicot, praised by his mother, had been the baby Jesus for the first five years of his existence. At that point you would need a hypertrophied imagination to see a newborn in place of that strapping, fifty-pound lad whose limbs overflowed the crib. On the sixth year the crib had ceded under the weight of Christ at the critical moment, when the Magi came to honor him. Eugénie had almost fainted. She had felt, at first, an immense shame, but then very quickly another sentiment, one far less charitable: hatred. She would forever refuse to admit it to herself, but at that precise moment, seeing him sprawled there flat on his back, she had hated her child with her entire being. And she had to own up to the obvious: he certainly was his father's son.

Over time it became necessary to adjust the cast's size to the growth curve of the population, but the grand tradition was solidly established, and no one would have thought to question its evolution.

Once more they are preparing for the coming of the Savior. Outside it's pitch black. The troupe assembles in the Siffres' barn. Lanterns and oil lamps are placed at strategic locations, as determined by Eugénie. She might not be the Virgin Mary anymore, but she is still the great priestess, the uncontested master of ceremonies. She picks everyone's part. She henceforth reserves that of the narrator for herself. Off to the side, stiff as an altar candle, she recites. She tells the story. She intones or she sings.

As is customary, all the inhabitants have been requisitioned except Joseph, who has declined the invitation since the death of his wife. But Joseph is represented by his ox and his mule. The ox plays the ox and the mule plays the donkey, and these are certainly the most faithful interpretations of the lot.

The boy helps with the final preparations. Decked out in a shapeless red bonnet that will be his only accessory. His first time participating, it would be wrong to pretend that he grasps the nature of what has to happen, but he knows his part nonetheless. It is simple and concise. They assigned him a role that might have been destined for Kazoo: that of the Exalted One. Because it's a Nativity that is at the same time mysterious and pastoral, a mixture of Provence and Judea, biblical characters and those typical to the village. In the afternoon the viper-woman had him rehearse. All he had to do, at her signal, was walk towards the cradle and raise his arms high, displaying a large smile in order to manifest the ecstatic joy that overtakes him when Christ is born. He understood that.

As for Kazoo, he's been assigned to the grindstone. Experience has shown that this is the only way to keep him from encroaching on Mary's turf. He is the Grinder. He is given the sharpening tool along with some old blades that are no longer usable, and for the only time that year and to his great pleasure, he is allowed to sharpen as much as he likes.

Midnight approaches. Silence falls. But hearts beat faster, stronger. Because now we are in the Holy Land.

"A very long time ago . . ." Eugénie begins.

But as soon as she opens her mouth, Kazoo starts the grindstone. The axle squeals, the metal screeches against the sandstone. Like the chirping of monstrous crickets in the arid hills of Galilee.

"A very long time ago," Eugénie begins again, raising her voice, "in the small town of Nazareth, lived Mary."

From the stall that serves as backstage, Marie-Aimée advances. She has reclaimed the torch of her virginity. She walks with delicate steps, batting her eyelashes.

"Mary was at home," recites Eugénie, "when suddenly an angel appeared."

And now Pierre emerges from the shadow. The former Jesus, deposed, relegated to the meager rank of messenger. He is dressed in a chasuble made from a sheet, from which his worn boots peek out. We can tell the road to get here was long and difficult.

Pierre clears his throat, he spits in the straw and says:

"Greetings Mary, full of grace. I am Gabriel and God has entrusted me with a message for you."

He doesn't speak, he grumbles; his words are drowned out by Kazoo's grindstone.

Marie-Aimée kneels at his feet.

"You have been chosen for a great duty," says Pierre. "You will bring the son of the Heavenly Father into the world."

"We can't hear nothin'," complains old Blaise backstage. Lucien, at his side, nods his chin.

"Don't you know the story by now?"

"Mary didn't understand," Eugénie recites. "She reminded the angel that she had not yet known any man. But the angel, in order to prove that what he had said was true, announced a wonderful surprise: her cousin Elizabeth, despite her old age, was expecting a son."

Old Honorine comes out in her turn, holding her laboring stomach made from a sack filled with hay, which shifts beneath her dress with each step. She adores this role; it revives sensations in her that have been dead for an eternity.

"My heart is full of joy," Marie-Aimée says, holding her arms wide.

The donkey wriggles his behind.

Kazoo takes up his second blade and old Honorine withdraws to go give birth to John the Baptist.

The boy soaks up every word. His eyes dart between the characters and the narrator. He stands at the ready, watching for the signal agreed upon for his intervention.

Joseph arrives. The Carpenter. As it happens he looks like Napoléon, Marie-Aimée's twin brother. We see him turning around, conspicuously rubbing his goatee with a worried look.

"Joseph was worried," Eugénie recites. "He and Mary had not yet lived under the same roof and he was embarrassed that she was expecting a child. But the angel reassured him by telling him the child had been engendered by God. And the angel added: 'You will give him his name.'"

"You will call him Jesus," says Pierre.

"Jesus," repeats Eugénie.

"He'll deliver his people from all their sins," says Pierre, "and his reign will have no end."

"His reign will be eternal," repeats Eugénie.

Napoléon places a hand on his heart.

"Then Joseph was filled with happiness," recites Eugénie, "and he wed Mary, to take care of her and the coming child."

And while the brother and the sister move towards each other and embrace, there are knowing looks exchanged all around. For there have been murmurs for a long time now that the love between these two is more than that of siblings. That they get up to mischief at night under their roof. That this Mary has been blessed more than just the one time, and that this Napoléon doesn't need any angel to find his way to heaven.

Pierre turns back towards the rear of the barn, dragging his feet. This is not yet the end of his degradation: in the next scene he must swap his archangel costume for the animal skin of a modest shepherd.

"The spouses," recites Eugénie, "soon head for the city of Bethlehem. When they arrive, no one will give them shelter. They take refuge in a cave."

She punctuates these words with a slight movement of her hand, as if to indicate to the couple the paltry conditions reserved for them.

The signal. That's how the boy interprets this gesture. Immediately he starts to wobble, shielded by his red bonnet and conscious that everyone's heads, at once, turn in his direction. At that moment he seems to be the central character of the drama. Everything rests on his shoulders. Despite this burden he continues to advance, bravely, to the designated spot, between the ox and the donkey. Then he turns around and lifts his arms to the sky, as high as he can, and he smiles baring all his teeth from above the empty cradle.

There follows a moment of mute consternation during which the metallic chirps of the crickets seem to double in intensity.

"What's happening?" asks old Blaise.

No one responds.

Joseph and Mary look at the Exalted One with a stupefied expression. Then they look at each other. Then they look at Eugénie, who herself casts an evil eye at the boy, filled with venom. Why? she asks herself. Why is the Heavenly Father inflicting her with such trials, after everything she's done for Him? Why?

She closes her eyes, exhales deeply.

So be it.

"The time," she continues, "the time had come for Mary to give birth."

With these words Marie-Aimée shudders, looks down at her stomach, for a second really believing her water had broken. Then she understands, relieved, and heads into a shadowy corner, where Gabrielle is waiting for her, not a female archangel but Victor's mother, the worm-child, whom she carries in her arms.

He's the new Messiah.

Marie-Aimée takes the toddler. He's chewing on a candy cane that they made sure to give him so that he would keep quiet. He already has it all over him. The mouth, chin, hands of Jesus shine with saliva that's sticky like syrup.

Mary puts the child in the cradle.

"The Lord was born," recites Eugénie, hands joined. "Hallelujah!"

"Hallelujah!" repeats the chorus.

And each person can finally legitimately join in the joy of the Exalted One.

"Are we on?" asks old Blaise.

"Not yet," says Lucien. "First the shepherds."

85

There they are. Pierre, formerly the son of God, recently an archangel, now a poor shepherd, accompanied by the little girl Blanche. Both of them armed with a long gnarled staff.

"The shepherds," recites Eugénie, "hurry to Bethlehem to meet Joseph and Mary and the child lying in the cradle."

They walk, they walk, it's a long road and fatigue overwhelms them. When they arrive they lean, in their turn, over the cradle, and what the little girl sees in reality is not Jesus but only the candy cane that he has in his mouth. She covets it. She drools, too, from envy.

The boy still has his arms in the air. He doesn't dare move, since no one told him exactly for how long he had to hold this pose.

Kazoo starts on his third blade.

"After that," recites Eugénie, "the wise men, come from the East, arrive in Judea, guided by the star."

Lucien elbows old Blaise, he starts on the road, Eugène follows, and soon the three of them stride into the barn in a procession of iconoclast Bedouins. Blaise is Melchior, older than Herod, head encircled by an itchy mauve turban. Lucien put walnut resin on his face in order to represent the black Balthazar, though his red hair still escapes from the handkerchief that acts as his keffiyeh, and more than a king of Africa it calls to mind a chimney sweep. As for Eugène, he remains Eugène no matter his outfit, and it's probably the most ludicrous Caspar that has ever existed in all of Christianity.

"The wise men recognize the child King," recites Eugénie, "and they offer him presents of gold, frankincense, and myrrh."

Eugène bestows the first gift, bowing and putting down his parcel and rewarding, once more, the son of God with a few goochy-goos and tickles in the folds of his neck, where the syrup has now oozed like a string of molasses. After which he promptly slips away in order to don a new costume and a new role to match. Lucien takes his place. When it's Blaise's turn his bad vision betrays him yet again: he bangs into the cradle and almost topples it over. As a result, the candy cane slides from the toddler's hands and drops to the ground in the straw. This godsend is too perfect for the little girl, who drops her shepherd's staff and throws herself on the candy and shoves it into her mouth, straw included. Seeing that, Jesus freezes, seized. Then his features contract and divine anger bursts into a powerful bawl.

"Then," recites Eugénie, "they rush from everywhere, people of every nation, to celebrate the birth of Our Lord."

Gabrielle rushes in, wearing the costume of an Arlesian, alerted by the cries of her son. Old Honorine rushes in, having changed into a washerwoman. Eugène rushes in, having transformed into a tambourine player, banging on his tambourine and breathing into a tiny flute, from which he extracts sounds about as melodic as the brakes of a locomotive.

"Hallelujah!" rejoices Eugénie. "Hallelujah!"

The divine child has stood up in his cradle, in tears. Not able to retrieve his possession he manages to grab onto his sister's hair, he pulls on it, and the little girl removes the stick from her mouth in order to let loose her own wailing.

"The entire earth and all its inhabitants bathe in joy and bliss," recites Eugénie. "O joy. O bliss. Hallelujah!"

"Hallelujah!" repeat, in chorus, all those who are not bellowing or crying.

The Arlesian in Bethlehem seizes the opportunity to sneak up to the cradle. She stares at her son for a moment, suspended from his sister's hair, after which she deals her daughter a large smack on the cheek.

"Hallelujah!"

The little girl's wails double. The candy cane escapes from her mouth and falls back to the floor of the barn where Melchior, that old blind bat, crushes it beneath his foot, reducing it to powder.

"Hallelujah!"

Christ bawls even more intensely. His face turns scarlet, like Israeli pomegranates.

"Glory to God, glory to God," sings Eugénie, "glory to God and peace to His beloved mankind."

The blood drains from the boys' arms, which are still raised. A cramp seizes him. His smile of ecstasy mutates, little by little, into a sort of demonic grin.

"Glory to God, glory to God," sings Eugénie.

The donkey brays.

Eugène blows and hammers.

Kazoo starts on his fourth blade and the crickets of Judea are unleashed.

And suddenly, during that grand finale, a ghastly odor arises from the cradle of baby Jesus: so great is his anger that he has soiled his diaper.

The boy wrinkles his nose, thus perfecting his atrocious grimace. And one might say he has finally earned his place among men, for nothing, in that moment, distinguishes him from those around him.

What is there that is precious?

What is there that is sacred?

They know.

1909–1910

AT TWO IN THE AFTERNOON, the snakes came out of their dens and started to slither on their stomachs over the ground, moving as if the flames of hell were licking at the scales at the end of their tails. All kinds, garter snakes and vipers alike. Tracing ephemeral and sinuous grooves over acres and acres of fields, of scrub, of stone—some cover distances of more than fifteen leagues, some perish from exhaustion (their forked tongues still extended, shriveled, their eyes without eyelids glazed over), the majority will never return to their point of departure.

And yet, there was no blaze on the horizon.

At four o'clock new springs emerged from the ground, all over. Small streams no thicker than a finger, black as oil, in reality nothing more than entire colonies of ants flowing from their shelters in uninterrupted tides, carrying their eggs with them.

The worms followed. The woodlice, the mole crickets, beetles, millipedes, earwigs. The burrowing macrofauna including a few creatures, nocturnal and fossorial, that were seeing the light for the first time.

Then we go directly to the eighth plague. Waves of those famous locusts, dear to Eugénie Janicot, unfurled over the hills and the meadows, nevertheless taking the time to devour the fruit or the plants or whatever was there.

At five o'clock the bees deserted their hives, and an entire swath of sky was momentarily darkened by an enormous cloud of undulating contours made up of dozens or hundreds of thousands of hornets, which are soon joined and then swiftly surpassed by squadrons of birds of all sizes and species, flying low and unleashing piercing cries.

Then it's the rats, field mice, voles, shrews.

There was not one dog in the hamlet, Lucien Siffre had killed the last, his own, the previous year, mistaking it for a rabbit, and so all that could be heard from there was a vague echoing concert of barking and howling that exploded in the surrounding areas at seven at night. The din of chickens and geese, however, was loud and clear, permeating the farmland at nearly the same moment.

Then the Janicots' two pigs began to attack each other, and by the time Eugène, with the help of his son Pierre, managed to separate them, one of the animals had an ear half-pulled off.

Even Joseph's old peaceful mule started to stumble around the stable, snorting and rolling its bulging eyes.

There was still neither flame nor smoke in sight.

Many would later say, after the fact, that they had seen it coming. They would explain that the animals' behavior was not the only thing that had seemed bizarre: the weather, too. Heavy, stifling. Premature heat accompanied by sudden storms. Like it was August in May. And the first days of June had been even worse. The oldest would say that they hadn't seen such a thing since the terrible spring of 1853, when it had been so hot that the figs, already overripe, exploded on the trees like grenades.

The boy would say nothing.

It is now nine o'clock. The day persists. A ribbon of clear sky stretches to the hills. The air is transparent. The boy is standing in the courtyard. He shoots worried glances at everything he thinks he sees moving, but in reality everything is immobile. Everything is frozen. Everything is suspended. He listens but everything is silent. The dogs, the hogs, the chickens have gone quiet. Only Kazoo continues to live his life. Kazoo is an oversized insect captured in the jelly of this dusk, wriggling and buzzing.

The boy has changed. He hasn't grown much taller but he's gained mass. His body is thicker, denser. Over the weeks, the temperature soaring, he was forced to remove layer after layer of the precious clothing they had given him. With reticence he had put away the sheepskin jacket, the sweater, the knitwear, the stockings. Today he wears nothing but the shirt and the velvet pants, and the heavy work boots that he wears directly on his feet. His bare feet bathe in the juice of sweat and leather, but he absolutely refuses to take off the shoes. They're now only one size too big for him.

At Easter, Marie-Aimée had cut his hair. He still has a spot on his neck and around the perimeter of his ears that's a little paler, where the sun has not yet had the time to spread its color. He now has a human face.

Kazoo's merry-go-round exasperates him. He wants him to shut up. He is burning to hit him. To bite him. He might do it if it weren't for the presence of Joseph, seated beneath the arbor in the shadows that the Indian used to love to sit under to sort through her herbs and plants. From time to time the boy turns to the man, studies him, searching for an answer. But Joseph's gaze is a bottomless pit.

They went out at night after supper to search for cooler air. They didn't find it. The boy sweats. Something weighs on his chest and crushes him. Seeing nothing, hearing nothing, he tries to smell. His nostrils quiver. No strange odor filters through.

But something is brewing. He knows it, but he doesn't know what.

It's coming.

It's close.

It's here.

IT BEGINS WITH A SOFT RUMBLE coming from the depths of the Earth's crust, and gains strength and breadth as it rises and pierces and shatters everything it passes through, the rock, the silica, the mica, the quartz, and then bursts with a formidable and frightening roar as the last layer of earth cedes and releases.

The thunder is nothing but a muted belch by comparison. We're talking about a thousand thunder claps. It's a hundred thousand horses with lead hooves launched at great speed.

The earth exults.

The boy covers his ears. Then he loses balance and falls on all fours. The ground vibrates and his body with it. His limbs, his jaw. His teeth chatter to the point of breaking. When he lifts his head again, in the foreground of his field of vision is Kazoo, standing, arms raised, torso tilted back, like a sorcerer's apprentice in a trance, like a young visionary preacher praising the sky for the accomplishment of his predictions. Kazoo bounces around, lightly, to the rhythm of the convulsions, as if he had known and been practicing the dance since the dawn of time. Was it his mother, the Indian, who had passed the secrets on to him? Was it our Mother Earth herself? His eyes radiate recognition and wonderment.

Behind him falls a rain of leaves and blossoms from the linden tree. The ancient tree, once aloof, reduced to nothing, less than nothing, a twig, a piece of straw, a weakened wretch in the clutches of this new fist. Great tremors run through its trunk. Its bark splits. Its branches peel away. And further in the distance, in the background, the boy sees the wheat shifting, an entire acre dusted like a massive doormat. The ears of corn bump into each other, producing a sound that is neither wind nor scythe.

He closes his eyes. He lies down. The vibrations echo in his stomach, the waves spread and resound all the way to his bones. Walls everywhere crack, shake, ten-pound stones come loose like teeth, wood cracks, windows explode, inside the dressers sway, roll, topple over, the china cabinet crashes, spilling its contents. Just before dying the boy thinks of La Diosa Centeotl. On the screen of his closed eyelids is inscribed the beautiful face of the goddess, her soft smile, serene, benevolent.

But he doesn't die.

It's finished.

It's done.

It takes him some time to understand that his body is still trembling. It's just a relic: the repercussions of the great tremor, the aftershocks of fear and trauma. Just as the racket in the catacombs of his skull is really nothing more than an echo. His eardrums hum. His ears whistle. Then everything stops.

A cinder-colored haze floats in the air. When it falls back to earth, the world returns to dust and the first star appears in the sky. Nearby, the linden tree still sheds a few last lonely leaves. The boy stands up. His legs wobble. It's the kind of silence that reigns over battlefields, after an attack, before the flies. Kazoo is still standing up but he isn't dancing anymore. Tiny flakes of ash land on him softly, on his eyelashes, on his cheeks, in his mouth: his angel face sprinkled with specks of apocalypse. The boy turns towards the arbor, where Joseph's silhouette can be discerned among the shadows. Perhaps the only thing or person that didn't move. The oak-man. His mind is elsewhere, his heart is elsewhere, for a long time now his mind and his heart have resided up above, with his spouse, the cloud-woman, but his roots are here, holding him down, so deeply buried that it would take much more than an earthquake to pull them up.

Joseph returns the look. In this world, at least, it's the last they'll exchange.

A cry suddenly tears through the silence and makes the boy jump. He recognizes the voice of Lucien Siffre. He waits. He watches. There is no other cry. He crosses the courtyard and goes to see.

The doors of houses open as he passes them and others come out to join him. The small population of the hamlet. They venture outside of their shelters carefully, advancing with wary steps, tense shoulders, the walk of a chicken on alert, and the same round eye jumping around, worried, sometimes towards the sky, which could fall, sometimes towards the earth, which might open up. Old Honorine is in a nightshirt, barefoot. Eugène holds the handle of a straight-razor in his fist. The left side of his face is white with soap, the right, clean-shaven, is red with blood. The trickle seeps from a gash on his cheek and flows down to the hair of his chest, which overflows his sweater. He doesn't seem to be aware. His son Pierre follows him. Napoléon precedes them, marching to scout the situation without letting go of his sister Marie-Aimée's hand. His other hand holds a hurricane lamp with broken glass, which he holds in front of him at arm's length, as if he were preparing to confront much deeper shadows. Without saying so they head towards the Siffres' barn. Or what's left of it.

A pile of rubble. A shapeless heap in front of which already stand three silhouettes, stiff, monolithic, and black in the crepuscular backlighting. Lucien is leaning against the handle of a shovel. His wife Gabrielle is carrying little Victor in his arms. There's Eugénie.

The others join them. They stop at their sides and lower their eyes and let their gazes wander over the ruins. And it's there that they discover in their turn, lying beneath this clutter of beams and planks, the body of little Blanche. Or what's left of it.

Two halves. The torso, the legs. Separated not by magic but by the sharp edge of a slab of sheet metal fallen from the roof. Intestines are everywhere. The guts, the viscera, a mash of waste and undefined, rank offal. A large piece of wood from the framework has also crushed her skull. At the impact an eye shot from its socket. It hangs on by a strand, a nerve, or something else. In the little girl's hand, between her slightly spread fingers, rests an egg, whose shell is intact.

Marie-Aimée turns away. She buries her face against her brother's chest. Spasms run through her. Napoléon uses all his strength to try to overcome the trembling that moves his arm, causing the flame of his lamp to falter. He doesn't want it to go out. He doesn't want that because then, he thinks, they might enter the depths of time and never be able to get out.

Lucien cries. Tears overflow and stream down slowly, like the pool of a fountain. He does nothing to hold them back. He does nothing to dry them. His wife's eyes, however, remain dry. Gabrielle Siffre stares at the ruins without batting an eye. She stares at that thing. It's her daughter. It's her child. She must tell herself, remind herself of this fact. She asks how they're going to collect her without everything disintegrating. She tells herself that the dress is done for, she wouldn't be able to repair it.

Eugénie's lips move noiselessly. Prayers. Always prayers. Jesus, Jesus, Jesus and Our Most Holy Father and the Virgin Mary. Good and merciful God. Rosaries and litanies of prayers. Just yesterday they were celebrating the Nativity. Yesterday the barn was a cradle and today it's a tomb. But no. The opposite. Remember: Didn't Matthew say it? "And then, there was a great earthquake; for an angel of the Lord descended from the sky, came to roll the stone and sit on top of it . . ." Suddenly Eugénie remembers the words of the apostle and then it hits her. It's the sign. It's the confirmation. It's the proof, if they needed one. Jesus is alive! He is here, among us! Eugénie's heart is set on fire, she falls to her knees. What the rest of the group takes for grief is actually the effects of a joy too heavy to carry.

"What is it?" asks old Blaise.

He has just arrived. Disheveled, unkempt. He glances at the rubble, eyelids squinting, using both hands to hold up his pants, his suspenders hanging at his sides.

"What is it?" he repeats.

Then Pierre turns around suddenly.

"It's him!"

The boy jumps. He sees an arm extended and a finger at the end of it, aimed at him. A poison arrow of which he is the target. And the others turn and look at him, too, except for Eugénie, who has been blinded by divine light.

"It's him," says Pierre. "I told you all. I told you all he was nothin' but trouble."

His tone is unmistakable: the boy hears his rage, the notes of an ancient, primitive, hereditary hatred. He perceives the danger it harbors. It's the voice of bile and blood.

"It's his fault. All of this, it's his fault. Don't say I didn't warn you."

His finger vibrates, pointed at his forehead. Without breaking eye contact the boy takes a step back. Pierre takes one forward.

"It's him!"

He retreats, the other advances, outside of this elementary choreography there is no movement. Those around him preside, as on the day of his arrival. The same jurors, the same deliberations, but this time mute. Each deep in his soul and conscience. But what soul? What conscience? Fear, once again, consumes the boy's heart. His pulse races. Now his eyes break from the accusing finger to look around the assembly. The fox-man, the mantis-woman, the turkey-man, the deer-man, the butterfly-woman, the mole-man, the worm-child, the shrew-woman, the viper-woman, the goat-man, the eviscerated toad-child. Except for Joseph and his son Louis-Paul, whom they call Kazoo. Tonight they will not show themselves. There will be no one to intervene on his behalf. In any case the verdict has already been pronounced.

"It's him!"

The boy doesn't retreat. He makes a sudden turn and runs away.

He runs.

"Go back to hell!"

He runs.

He runs.

He runs straight into the night.

The shadows had already absorbed him when old Honorine, seized perhaps by remorse or pity, opens her mouth to call him back. But how could she when she doesn't know his name?

HE WON'T GO BACK.

During the next two days there are five aftershocks of the earth-quake, each one weaker than the last, but each pushing him still further in his flight. He doesn't know what he did wrong. What he did or didn't do to provoke the anger of men and the Earth. He carries his confusion and guilt with him. He walks night and day without stopping, and when suddenly his strength abandons him he collapses on the spot like a puppet with its strings cut, and he remains there on his behind. A witness noticing his mouth hanging open and his dazed expression might assume he was a drunkard sleeping off his wine. But it's fatigue that intoxicates him, and even more so the essence of the sorrow spreading through his heart.

He falls asleep leaning against a stump.

He wakes up four hours later beneath the gaze of a doe. She stands immobile on her fine legs and stares at him with a mother's eyes for her child. The boy barely dares to breathe. This stare touches him. His throat tightens. Tears flow. When he sniffles, the sound sends a shiver down the animal's fur. The doe takes off. A few bounds and a silky rustling and it's as if she were never there. A fern sways in the clearing. The boy squashes his tears, leaving a salty trail on his cheek. Then he stands up and gets going.

And once again it's the solitary paths, the empty fields, the roaming, the open air, the one-on-one with his shadow, the harsh and sublime desolation. Once again it's hunger and hunting.

He travels across two departments. He crosses bridges, rivers. He avoids villages and town squares, goes around them—far enough away for time to do its work and for his fears to subside. He always advances, he proceeds as if the highest point of the world were waiting behind the next hill, the next mountain, as if the horizon line were the edge of the precipice that marks the border with the beyond.

Sometimes he steals from gardens and orchards. Waiting for total darkness before he acts and hurrying to gather or pick, heart racing, forehead covered with sweat as cold as frost. He now understands that this is forbidden. The Earth does not belong to everyone. It's one of the truths that his stay in the hamlet taught him. As senseless as it may seem, the Earth does not belong to each and every person. Nor its fruits. There is not one Land, but lands. (How many such illusions will vanish? How many tacit promises will be renounced?) Now that the boy has been forewarned, he no longer has a claim to innocence.

One night he is chased by a pair of watchdogs and owes his salvation to his agility. Hanging from the branches of a walnut tree while the dogs bark at the foot of the trunk, foaming at the mouth, enraged, ripping the bark with their claws. Dogs without a breed. Degenerate guard dogs. Nearly an hour goes by before they turn around, throats hoarse, and go back towards the void from which they had come.

At Saint-Jean we find him perched at the top of a rocky spur, this time by choice, crouched like an eagle with folded wings. From there he watches the spectacle of the bonfires that burn in the plain. There's a party tonight. People gather. They bang on crates. They feed the pyres and dance, they spin around in sarabands. From a distance what he sees is hardly more than a ballet of moths around a lamp. The gleam of the flames is very far from reaching him, but there is something of that heat that rises up to him and warms him. In the early morning the blaze has gone out but his pupils continue to sparkle.

The summer becomes a furnace. It's noon from dawn to dusk. The grass turns yellow. Everything mineral cooks, and in the hazy halo that is released, mirages multiply. The boy searches for the forest shade.

The damp haven of undergrowth is worth more to him than the blessed coolness of a church. He often walks along riverbeds, his shoes in his hand. There is very little water, it's a miracle if it reaches his ankles.

And it's a miracle of another sort when, in the twists and turns of one of these streams, he happens upon the Ogre of the Carpathian Mountains.

HE IS SEATED IN THE WATER, on a large flat stone. Naked as on his first day. He presides on his throne. He splashes around. The boy is not yet certain that he's truly human since he's never seen a human like this—and never will again.

His head is gigantic. The back of his skull is a vast hemisphere, perfectly clean-shaven and gleaming in the sun like seal skin, while in front his forehead juts out, inclines on a dented slope, before stumbling over the line of his arching brow, which is a cliff, a bony promontory sheltering the caverns of his eyes. His jowls are enormous, prominent, his jaw jutting out impossibly far. Squeezed between these features is a nose the size of a pear, as well as a mouth that's astonishingly delicate and feminine.

Such is his portrait—an undeniably crude silhouette.

When he discovers the boy's presence, he does not seem surprised. His lips stretch from one ear to the other, and that smile illuminates and softens the harsh architecture of his face. By way of a greeting he raises a hand that could prop up the moon.

The boy does not respond. He observes.

The man remains for a moment, plunged in the current. Then he sprays his body and rubs his skin vigorously, he gargles, he spits, finally he stands up.

He is not as tall as one might imagine. Five foot nine at the most. But his chest is almost as wide as he is tall. A buffalo's chest. Bowed legs. He reaches the riverbank and unhooks a piece of white sheet suspended from a bush. It's a sort of rudimentary tunic with three openings for his head and his arms. The man puts it on. The fabric floats, falls to his knees. Thus attired, he turns around and places his hands on his thighs. He looks like an orator preparing to speak in front of a full assembly. But there is no audience besides the boy.

"Hygiene," he says.

The word vibrates in the air.

"Hygiene. Something we neglect too often."

His voice is strong and resounding, as is to be expected. He doesn't need to make an effort for it to reach the boy.

"Have you noticed how people stink? In our country especially. I know what I'm talking about, I've been around the world. Not a world tour, but almost. And in all honesty, I have to say: when it comes to stench, the French are the champions."

He shakes his head as if this statement has upset him. Then he taps his colossal nose with the tip of his index finger.

"I don't know if it's because of this, but I'm very sensitive to it."

He smiles again.

The boy has not moved an inch, his feet glued to the riverbed.

"A bath every week," says the man. "That's the national average. I read that somewhere and I can confirm it, unfortunately. It's the sad reality. Normally it happens on Sunday, before mass. Day of the big clean: we wash our fannies before going to cleanse our souls. The more grime, the more sin. Deep cleaned. By the bath plug and holy water, I absolve you. Ha! Ha!"

His laugh rings out in two brief detonations, scaring a dragonfly buzzing over the dome of his skull.

"And that goes for everyone," he says. "The bourgeois and the rest, don't be fooled. Nice clothes, but you've got to see what's underneath. Personally I think the bourgeois are the worst. No excuse. A tub at home, great luxury—I've seen some that were Chinese porcelain, Carrara marble, from real sultan's palaces—and what do they do with them? Nothing. Those handsome messieurs settle for changing their false collars and their shirt cuffs to keep up appearances. That's their entire washing routine. Shame on them. As for me, I say Sunday's not the only day that counts. What do they think? That God spends the rest of the week holding his nose?"

The question goes unanswered. Although he seems able to discourse on the subject for several more hours, the man is now quiet. He uses his hand as a visor and stares at the boy for a long moment. As one studies a unique specimen. Which of the two is the phenomenon?

"I don't mean to harp," he says, "but what I'm trying to tell you is that since you already have your feet in the water, you'd do well to seize the opportunity and soak the rest of you, too. No matter what day it is. From what I can see, it can't do you any harm . . . Hear me, sonny?"

He points at the river, the flat rock where he was sitting a moment ago.

"It's all yours," he says.

AT NIGHTFALL the two of them are seated around a bivouac fire, eating roasted quail with their hands. Behind the boy is a parked caravan, and on its side in letters of over-embellished gold: *Brabek, the Ogre of the Carpathians*. The gold is faded, same as the caravan. The boy has no idea what an ogre is nor what the Carpathians are, and in any case he doesn't know how to read. The man has to decipher it for him. That's how he had introduced himself: Brabek. There was certain amount of pride in his voice when he pronounced it.

His real name is Ernest Bieule, but the last person to call him that was an old woman who is now, and has been for a long time, dead and buried. This is one of those things he prefers not to remember. If he, her descendant, manages to be remembered by the name that he's forged for himself, it'll be his greatest victory. The vainest and most beautiful.

The third brigand is a bay-colored gelding. An animal that would not be out of place in front of a chariot. Thickset, solid. A curious blond goatee beneath its lip, perhaps in compensation for the loss of its male attributes. Brabek had wrangled it from a horse-dealer after a bet at a swap meet near Meyrueis. Certainly his finest acquisition. The animal is attached to the spoke of a wheel. Not one of its muscles quivers: a bronze statue in the gleam of the sunset.

At this hour the heat has diminished. We hear the sighs of the embers and the murmur of the river that snakes somewhere behind them. From time to time the chirp of a cricket. But what is heard above all is Brabek's voice.

"My great-grandfather fought," he says. "My grandfather fought.

My father fought. I fight. It runs in our veins. What can we do about it? Sometimes I tell myself that the only thing none of us has tried to fight is our own destiny. If I think about it, that might be the only thing . . . But then again, why would anyone do that? Find me one good reason. Do you know a man who hasn't fought in one way or another? Can you name me one? No. Because there isn't one. Not in this world. So, if you have to fight, might as well do it by the rules. That way, you see, you can't say you were cheated."

He's finished his piece. He sucks his fingers and raises four towards the sky.

"Four generations. Who can top that? And if I have a son one day, I bet you anything he'll know how to square up to an opponent before he knows how to walk."

Opposite him the boy desperately tries to scrape the tiniest shreds of flesh from bones no bigger than sewing needles. A scene several millennia old.

"But I won't have a son," says Brabek.

His voice trails off. He looks at the boy above the flames. His eyes are sunk too deeply beneath his brow to discern what type of gleam animates them.

Then suddenly he gets up and skirts the fire pit and plants himself in front of his guest. He's still dressed in his Spartan tunic. He lifts a section to reveal his thigh and says:

"Touch here."

The boy stops chewing. A small mustache of grease glimmers above his lips. He stares at the giant standing before him, tunic hiked up, like the most nightmarish of courtesans. He stares at the piece of bare and hairy flesh presented to him.

"Touch it," Brabek insists.

The boy swallows. He points his index finger then slowly brings it to the thigh. The way one might indicate a deserted island or an unexplored continent on a map of the world.

Brabek lets the fabric fall back down. He leans over and pulls one sleeve up and shows his bicep.

"Touch here."

The boy touches.

"And now touch here," says Brabek, presenting his forehead.

The boy touches.

"So?" demands Brabek.

He closes his fist and gives himself small taps on the head with the ridges of his knuckles.

"There's no harder muscle," he says, "as you can see. Strength is inside. Real strength. Don't go looking elsewhere, it's there. We win battles with our head."

Then he points a finger at the boy.

"Remember that, sonny."

He sits back down, apparently satisfied with his demonstration. But he hasn't finished. Just taking the time to bring a tin cup to his lips and rinse his throat, and then he starts up again.

"I fought Raymond Favre. I fought Émile Poitevin. I fought Louis Deglane, called the Lion of the Carpathians. I fought the Greek Kallikratis and the Bulgarian Letchkov. In 1879, in Vienna, I was co-champion of Europe. Only co-, you say. Would you believe me if I told you that I missed the title because of a pork terrine? A rotten pâté. Nothing more traitorous than the pig. It's unforgivable. I'll spare you the details but that nasty slop destroyed my insides. A devilish bout of diarrhea. Going to fight in these conditions, my asshole tense like a nun taken prisoner by a band of pirates. I'll tell you I spent the last half clenching my butt cheeks like never before. The referee didn't even have time to name me the victor before I was straddling the toilet. It was miserable . . ."

He shakes his heavy head several times. Then he drains his cup and clicks his tongue.

"For the finale, there was nothing to be done. The guy I was facing, he was Danish. Ari Rytkönen. Ari the Barbarian. Blond as the wheat, a long braid down his back. Rumor had it he was the descendant of a great Viking warrior. That his ancestors were capable of walking barefoot over ice floes. That his own mother was impregnated by a polar bear. You know the type? A heap of legends to impress your average Joe. Buffoonery. Inventions pulled out of a hat. Ari did nothing to contradict them. He was right not to. At the time, I was young, I hadn't yet understood that this was exactly what the people liked. Legends, stories that make you shiver. That's what the crowd wants. That's what attracts them. Now I know that . . . Anyway. A good fighter, the Viking. But not better than me. I could have won. But on that day I couldn't defend myself. Barbarian or not, my most formidable adversary was my own gut. At the moment when the battle should have begun, I was still purging my guts. Impossible to show myself in the ring. The judges announced that I'd forfeited. Pretty rough, huh?"

The sun goes down for good in the distance. The vampire bats know this and emerge. The boy watches a couple of smaller bats flit across the fire. He doesn't like them. He remembers one that entered the hut where he used to sleep with his mother during the night. They found it when they woke up, hanging from a beam in its black cape, its face like an evil gnome and its little eyes wide open, fearless. If hell exists, the angels there are bats. The mother had killed it with a bludgeon. She hit it so hard she nearly decapitated it.

"The whole thing repulsed me," says Brabek. "After that, I never ate pork again. And I never fought in a championship bout again."

He shakes his head again.

"After that," he says, "I discovered America."

And he tells story after story while in the stratum above the stars rise again from their ashes.

He recounts how, on a rainy night in the last century, as he was leaving a fight won without contest, a man had suddenly approached him and invited him to climb into a sumptuous carriage pulled by four chestnut palominos adorned with feathers. And how, as he ushered him to the miserable room at the miserable inn where he was staying at the time, this man had described the heavenly destiny that awaited him on the other side of the Atlantic.

He recounts how he had been impressed by the otter fur pelisse the man had been wearing, by his top hat, by his signet ring, by the enormous cigar he chewed, whose odors complement marvelously the subtle fumes of the calfskin covering the benches and doors of the carriage.

The man was American. His accent was thick, but the meaning of his words was easily accessible to anyone who wanted to understand them. The future he proposed could be summed up in two words: glory and fortune. In other words, have your cake and eat it too. Money, he'd said in English. A lot of money. Guaranteed. With a magician's embellishment, the man had produced a business card on which was modestly written: *William C. Harding—Manager*. Modest in content, but the characters seemed to be chiseled in fine gold, and in the same sort of arabesque style that he himself had tried clumsily, many years later, to reproduce on the sides of his own modest caravan.

Who could have resisted that?

Not him.

He recounts his journey. He relives the crossing. Three thousand nautical miles. Not a trace of land, not one hill, not one tree in sight for days and days and nights. The ocean, sonny. That's when you realize how small we really are. That we're nothing. A drop of water in a desert of water. And then one morning the fog slips away from the bow of the ship and all those little lights you see twinkling behind are the lights of paradise. In other words, a great circus.

William C. Harding hadn't lied, he just had a different conception of the celestial.

He practiced the art of make-believe, which he pushed to the point of illusion. Put a crown on the head of a monkey and it becomes a king. Put bells on the crown of a king and he becomes a jester. W. C. Harding, manager, didn't manage fighters, but artists. He didn't organize fights, but performances. Shows, he said. Nuance.

He recounts the tours from one coast to the other, one ocean to another, in that country which is a world unto itself. New York, Boston, Philadelphia, Washington, Baltimore, Cincinnati, Atlanta, Nashville, Springfield, Chicago, Milwaukee, Des Moines, Kansas City, Dallas, Houston, Denver, Salt Lake City, Phoenix, San Diego, Los Angeles, San Francisco, Portland, Seattle. A procession of eighteen carriages and fifty-six people, including twenty artists, a dozen tent mounters, an orchestra of eight musicians, a half-dozen hostesses, three poster-gluers, two touts, two chefs, a dwarf handyman, a costume designer, a horse-keeper, and a bookmaker: the troupe of the Wild World Wrestling Company. This didn't include Sheerpa, the trained black panther who was both mascot and living advertisement.

W. C. Harding thought big. W. C. Harding raked it in.

He recounts the crowds, the sold-out extravaganzas. Four thousand, five thousand spectators each night. Obliged, sometimes, to do matinee performances. The altercations in the queues. Fanatics who set up camp on the site to have a chance of obtaining a ticket. Families who came out in full force, from the newborn to the grandparent. All those people who didn't come to see the sport. Who didn't come to see the fight. No. Who came to see the spectacle. A flesh-and-blood puppet show.

He recounts how, thanks to a pair of sandals and a tin broadsword, he found himself a gladiator again. The French Gladiator, in the language of W. C. How he fought not on a mat nor even in a ring, but in the arenas of antiquity. How sometimes he faced an Indian, sometimes a one-eyed pirate, sometimes a negro slave, sometimes a cruel cannibal pygmy played by the dwarf handyman, sometimes all four at the same time in an orgiastic and unbridled finale, in the middle of which they might sometimes unleash the panther. Why not? Each person had their role and everyone knew the outcome. Everything was written. Everything was rigged. Everything was false. The legends, sonny. The famous tales. We don't give a shit about the noble art, what the public wants is the stuff of dreams, and W. C. Harding was there to give it to them. Or rather to sell it to them. Do the math: four to five thousand suckers a night, a twenty-five cent entry fee, that adds up to some serious money. "In God We Trust" on each coin and each bill. Official stamp. Word of the gospel. The sole religion of America.

He recounts how his moment of glory had lasted two years. How it had abruptly come to an end one morning in Macon county, in Alabama, when someone noticed that Mr. W. C. had actually disappeared, along with the steel strong-box containing the revenue from the tour, as well as the personal savings of a good portion of the employees of Wild World Wrestling. Just like that! Disappeared into the wild. The cake devoured all at once, and the whole troupe dipped in flour, kicked around, ruined. "Fucked," in that shitty, cursed language. That was also written, of course, on the walls, but no one had known how to read it. In God We Trust all you like, but never trust a guy dressed in otter fur; a word of advice.

He recounts how the company had been dismantled in less than a week. Before going their separate ways, the fifty-five swindled members had sold horses and chariots and everything they could sell, and the sum thus gained had been shared equitably among them, including the dwarf, who received a full portion. What went to each didn't amount to much, and this not-much didn't last very long.

He recounts how Sheerpa the panther had been left to starve to death after his master had abandoned him.

He recounts how, in order not to starve to death, he had reached an agreement with the one-eyed pirate and the negro slave to continue to do the only thing that, in the end, they knew how to do: fight. The dwarf joined them and for weeks and months the four of them had scoured the territory lengthwise, widthwise, and across, like a foursome of tattered and stateless mercenaries. Like the last foot soldiers of a battalion decimated over the course of a war that no one would even remember hearing about.

What else could they do?

No more big cities. No more publicity or posters or celebrated arrivals or rushed ticket booths. From then on they stopped in the little towns, some too small to ever appear on a map, and they fought in the mud or in the dust, in the straw or in the hay, one against the other or against some braggart, it didn't matter who, from the meager population of grocers and seed merchants and toothless farmers. No more gladiator, one-eyed pirate, negro slave, pygmy cannibal, no more Roman arenas, no more costumes, no sets, nor the least trace of that bygone splendor. They were just three raggedy tough guys who fought each other, and a pipsqueak who went through the few rows of seats with a hat.

Everything comes to an end, sonny. And it's rarely a happy one.

One by one they had fallen from grace. The former slave had been lynched during a raid by hooded phantoms in the state of Tennessee. The former pirate had drowned trying to cross the waters of the Pocomoke River in the state of Maryland. The former pygmy had been recruited as a cannonball by another traveling circus.

And so at the end of that journey, he had returned to his starting point, alone and without a dollar in his pocket, and forty pounds lighter. New York City. The Big Apple. And that's how, wandering aimlessly on the piers, he had seen the Statue of Liberty disembark in various pieces. And how, day after day, he had seen it reconstituted and erected, watched it grow foot after foot, and how he had cried when, in the end, she had proudly brandished her torch towards the sky and aimed her beautiful and somber gaze above the seas, towards the old Europe where she had been born, and how on that day he had sworn to be worthy of this symbol, to refuse to be a prisoner to that strange land and to that greedy and pitiless people, and how, the following week, he had set off, in total secrecy, for Bordeaux, in the hold of a transatlantic liner. Before leaving, he shot a gob of spit in the face of Manhattan by way of goodbye and even farewell forever. Bye-bye. So long.

And so that adventure came to an end.

The boy sleeps, his chin on his chest. He'd dozed off when things started to go badly, but Brabek pretended not to notice and continued with his story. Now silence falls again. The fire is nothing but embers. Brabek remains seated for a moment, staring at the boy. Then he sighs and gets up and takes him in his arms and carries him to the caravan. At the back of the vehicle is an alcove bed: that's where Brabek sets down his guest. Then he withdraws and closes the door behind him and goes back to sit by the fire.

Nothing is stopping them from tackling the road together.

VEYNES, EYGUIANS, ORPIERRE, Saléon, Le Poët, Trescléoux, Sainte-Colombe, Esparron, Serres, Embrun, Buissard, Crévoux, Arvieux, Saint-Crépin, Les Orres, Rosans, Tallard. They go from place to place. Brabek knows all the dates and all the locations of the fairs and festivals, and he seems to be universally known at each of these events. The result of more than twenty years of practice—not to mention the fact that his face is quite memorable. Connections have been made. He was here yesterday, he comes back today, he'll come back again tomorrow and on and on until an evil wind carries him off for good and we'll be able to confirm with certitude: Brabek is no more. That day will come.

Roybon, Vinay, Biol, Saint-Ismier, La Verpillière. They clear out before dawn. Sleepily sitting side by side on the caravan's bench, bouncing, bobbing their heads. The roof provides a bit of shelter and two lanterns hang from it, though they hardly illuminate anything further than the gelding's hindquarters. The reins are slack in Brabek's fingers. The horse knows where it's going. He too has already come through here and remembers. On the dark paths he follows his own tracks. His step is heavy but not inelegant—his feminine side probably. A name falls from the mouth of the ogre: their next stop.

Châbons, La Tour-du-Pin, Le Gua, Tullins, Échirolles, Pontcharra, Billieu, Crolles. He has the map in his head. He recreates his American experience, on a smaller scale.

Beaurepaire, Voiron, Charavines, Chanas, Bully, Condrieu. They enter towns with the stalls already in place. They're the only thing missing. At first Brabek makes a full round with the caravan, an arm raised and a smile on his lips, as if he were in a parade. Then he stops his chariot in an empty spot and starts a second tour, this time on foot, spreading, as he goes, all that he has, which is to say a lot of heart and a decent amount of spirit. He shakes a hand, gives a hug, shouts to every merchant, compliments one on his well-behaved poultry, makes fun of another for the ridiculous size of his pigs. It's charming or it's funny, and it never stings. He *tutoyer*s the mayor and the county warden. It's a sight to see him push open the door of the café and greet the company and cross the room with large strides to bend over in profound reverence before the matron, lean over the cotton of her apron as one might do over the satin robe of Her Royal Highness. The woman lifts him with a strike of her dishrag. This isn't the first time she's been through this, but her cheeks are blushed, she's ecstatic. The little waitress guffaws. Brabek grabs her around the waist and sweeps her off the floor and spins her around in the air. She cries out and laughs. Everyone laughs. Brabek is an enchanting ogre. Many people believe that the Carpathians are marvelous islands where it rains cider and honey.

Vourles, Marennes, Lentilly, Lucenay, Chassagny, Courzieu, Villechenève. The boy follows. The first few times, it was dizzying. So many people and so much noise all at once. But he quickly habituates himself. He starts to like it. Brabek presents him as his assistant. The gossips whisper that he's his secret bastard son. The perverts whisper worse things, but hardly anyone listens to them. After their warm-up laps the ogre and the boy return to the caravan. The first goes to get changed inside while the latter clears the ground in front, sweeps the plot, and outlines a circle twenty-five feet in diameter, just as Brabek taught him. The combat zone. Everything is ready when the ogre re-emerges. He's wearing tight black trousers and supple shoes with laces that go up to his mid-calf. Standing on the running board, he starts to whip up the crowd. He hails, he shouts, he roars, and during the gathering that follows, he goes down the stairs and enters the circle and prowls around like a wild animal in its cage. He poses. He flexes his muscles. He plays to the gallery. He provokes. He defies. He eyes his target: the brute of the village, the local champion, lumberjack, wheelwright, cooper, carpenter, whoever has a bulging torso and a reputation to defend. Or else the man with a fiancée hanging from his arm, who won't be able to sneak off under the eyes of his beauty. Honor, sonny, is like suspenders, no one wants to find himself with his pants around his ankles. Brabek prods, Brabek titillates. Where are the men? With his thumb he indicates the gelding behind him and insinuates that it's the only male he sees here: no one in the audience seems better endowed . . . Ooooh! He's hit the nail on the head. The women elbow and giggle. Their eyes shine. The messieurs crack wincing smiles. In the end there is always someone who takes up the gauntlet. The strapping man exits the crowd and comes forward, rolling his shoulders, and enters the circle. Shouts fly. They encourage him, they whistle, they applaud while he takes off his jacket and rolls up the sleeves of his shirt.

Anse, Lozanne, Bron, Aveize, Le Perréon. What follows is always the same. A matter of qualitative analysis. There is no finer alchemist than the Ogre of the Carpathians. In less than a minute he's gauged his adversary, measured him up: height, weight, strength, agility, technique, strategy, and the rest. He could, in even less time, make the poor man bite the dust. But what good would that be? Who would find that satisfying? Brabek distills. From the cheap ingredients of a bare-knuckle brawl, he extracts the essence of the moment that is, if not graceful, at least pleasurable. He makes it last. He knows what he can give and what he can take. What he has to concede and what he has to inflict. Play with the nerves, strain them, make them vibrate, release them. Alternate the bravado and the trembling. He also knows when it has to come to an end. Without humiliation. He will win, certainly—he has his own honor and reputation—but only by a hair. So that the other can hold his head high. So that he can imagine he was within a hair's breadth, and that next time, next time . . . It's a matter of respect and commerce. Hurt, no. Delight, yes. People pay for what the ogre supplies, and they get their money's worth. At the end of the day, his wallet has grown heavier in direct proportion to the amount by which these commoners' hearts have lightened.

They pack up again.

Brullioles, Marcy, L'Arbresle. The boy erases the circle on the ground. The fight was ephemeral, as was the joy. Nothing remains of their visit except the impression of a happy but volatile dream, elusive upon waking, and, for some, a few bruises and aching sides.

They leave.

Cogny, Tarare, Châtillon. The caravan takes off, grows distant, escorted by a band of kids screeching to their hearts' content, a half-Sioux tribe fighting a cardboard war. It's Brabek's tribe. All those children that the ogre has not devoured.

And then they leave the town and once again they're alone on their route, the vast horizon, time sluggishly counted off to the gelding's amble.

Villars-les-Dombes, Virieu-le-Grand, Miribel, Sermoyer, Trévoux, Poncin, Ferney-Voltaire, Belley.

They stop at the halfway point. There's no rush. The light is beautiful on these summer nights. Brabek chooses a spot along the waterway. They set up their camp, sprinkle a few stones to outline a fire pit. The boy takes care of the horse. Brabek taught him how. It's not a chore, it's a privilege. Perhaps the moment he most looks forward to. He removes its yoke, he takes off its harness, he brushes, he combs, he cleans, he waters and feeds. It's a joy for him to bury his face in the animal's neck and inhale its odor. It's a joy for Brabek to witness this happiness.

Thoiry Thoissey, Manziat, Saint-Pierre-le-Palud, Dagneux, Ambronay.

They grapple. They embrace. Day breaks and training begins. They constantly talk about the same thing: combat. (Do you know any man, even one, who doesn't have to fight?) The boy wants to know, Brabek teaches him. The rules and the basics, the positions, the holds. Brabek explains and shows him. The art of the cross. The art of the hook. The art of the vine. The art of timing. They practice near the watering hole and we watch, a simulacrum of combat between a student and his master—or should we say, rather, given the proportions, between a frog and a hippopotamus? The art of the takedown. Of rolling. Of the escape. Sometimes Brabek makes a fist and raps the boy's skull three times. Remember. The head, sonny, we win with the head. The art of cunning. Indispensable. The art of throwing. And the most important of all: the art of falling. For that's how, always, each match culminates—Brabek insists on it.

Then the boy washes himself. Lhuis, Seyssel, Fareins, Seillonnaz. Every day of the week—Brabek insists on that, too. Hygiene. For as long as the weather is nice, he does his ablutions in the river or the stream. Later, when cold descends on the earth, he'll bathe in an old oak 50 gallon cask that Brabek salvaged not so long ago from a Pauillac vineyard in the Médoc region, sawing the top third off to convert it into a tub. The cask is hooked beneath the floorboards of the caravan. Each night of autumn and each night of winter, Brabek will unhook it, heat up some water, fill it, sometimes adding an extract of lavender or lilac, and, in turns, the boy and then the ogre will plunge into it, and while the grease and grime detach from them, while their bodies purify, the sky will gradually be unveiled to them, beyond the steam, beyond the mist, stars encrusted in the deep darkness will appear to them by the thousands.

Cormoz, Massieux, Nantua, Argis, Saint-Paul-de-Varax.

But for now it's still nice out. The boy gets out of the shimmering water and lets the air dry his skin. They dine with what they have. Slowly the wheel turns and shadows cover them again. They are now nothing more than two silhouettes around the flames, one loquacious and one mute. During the hours that follow, Brabek opens up: a new episode of his formerly rich and full existence. He retells his story aloud. His own saga. He seems aware that what he once was outweighs anything that he might be. There are unmistakable signs: his reign will come to an end. He doesn't believe in the kingdom of heaven. It's here and now that everything happens. And that's why he requires the presence of a witness, trustee, and heir. Remember, sonny. His life is his masterpiece and the majority of the inheritance that he hopes to leave to him. May the boy conserve not his ashes, but his torch.

Chauffailles, Écuisses, Pierre-de-Bresse, Simandre, Louhans, Vonnas, Perrecy-les-Forges, Dommartin-lès-Cuiseaux.

Deep into the night, Brabek narrates his story. In his telling, the world is vast, the plains immense. And the mountains and hills and vales.

Everywhere a fire burns is their home.

MORE AND MORE OFTEN the boy takes the reins. Brabek taught him how. There isn't much to do but he applies himself. He is proud. Chest straight, staring into the distance, as if he were living lavishly, a princely procession. He invents a unique dialect made of mouth sounds and tongue clicks that only he can decipher. The gelding regally ignores him.

On the outskirts of Cluny, Saône-et-Loire, he passes his first automobile. A bright red Delaunay-Belleville. Six cylinders, forty horsepower. They say it's the preferred vehicle of Tsar Nicholas II—as well as of a man named Jules Bonnot and his gang. This morning the machine is driven by a local baronet who's crazy about engines and wears a protective mask that makes him look like a big fly with bulging eyes. In sum, a sort of two-winged insect riding atop a humming beetle. The boy is lost in awe. Reflexively, he pulls on the reins, the gelding stops. The caravan remains planted on the road and the boy's mouth gapes, as if he were trying to breathe in all of the dust that's already settling again in the wake of the Delaunay. Brabek smiles to himself.

"Machines," he says.

He lets the sound of the cylinders and the horsepower fade and then he adds:

"Man can invent anything. He can create anything, and he can destroy anything. His choice. Man alone has the ball of clay in the palm of his hand. What will he do with it? Have to wait and see . . ."

His smile surfaces, widens—a fissure in the tormented landscape of his face.

"It all depends, of course, on the kind of man whose hand it's in. If he's a scholar. If he's a soldier. And if he's a poet? Of course the result will change, depending. And you?" he says. "What would you do with that clay?"

The boy looks at the ogre's paw hoisted in front of him.

"Don't be afraid to think big," says Brabek. "You can always dream, what's the harm?"

His index finger points skywards.

"I believe that one day, the moon will be our vegetable garden."

The boy raises his eyes. In the sky he sees neither moon nor vegetables, just a thin cluster of clouds in the haze of the horizon.

Sometimes it takes a little while to assimilate.

They take off again.

The route unfurls. The seasons change. Autumn arrives with its lead canopy striped here and there by formations of geese, thrushes, and corncrakes. Everything migrates. The leaves fall and rot. The rain mixes in. The drizzle. There are gray dawns that never end, paths that are nearly impossible to travel for miles. Despite everything, they keep moving. The gelding leaves the mark of its hooves in the soft mud. The wheels sink, create ruts like the rails of an antique train crossing the hinter-hinter-lands, revealing their route. They could be tracked closely from one point to the next.

The moods of the weather sometimes force them to take shelter in a courtyard, barn, or stable. They push bales, tools, and livestock aside. They stack things up. It smells of hay, leather, rock, skin, all of it waterlogged and vaguely rancid and diffused, and then overwhelmed by the powerful odors of manure. Before combat training, the boy rubs Brabek's shoulders and torso with a greasy pomade, a type of unguent that gives off a strong odor of camphor and which offers two further advantages: soothing the ogre's sensitive sense of smell and at the same time making it difficult for his adversary to get a grip on him.

The boy's role has expanded. The assistant is no longer confined to sweeping the area and inscribing the circle, he now also has the duty of trainer, or something like it. Between rounds, he hurries to wipe a wet towel over the face of his champion, massage the back of his neck, his shoulders, his calves. It's impressive. From an old flag that until recently hung from one of the supports on the caravan, Brabek made him a cape. It's the boy's costume. His stage outfit. And more: it's the emblem of his inauguration. Now he is an integral part of the troupe. Official partner to the ogre. Accomplice. Not to mention that it adds a touch of exoticism to the ensemble (sequins, powder on his eyes: relics of lessons from W. C. Harding) and exacerbates the patriotism of his challengers. It doesn't matter if no one knows that the three stripes—blue, red, yellow—represent the faded colors of the modest and defunct principality of Transylvania, all they need to know is that it's a foreign banner, possibly an enemy's, maybe even an invader's: They have to duke it out on principle.

At the end of the fight, the boy stiffens and the victorious ogre lifts him in one fell swoop, carries him outstretched in his arms like a trophy, like that gold belt he'll never wear. (Cursed pork!) It's a new tradition. A type of final parade. They spin and spin inside of the circle. Rotation, revolution. The cape floats, the boy soars. Fifteen years later, he'll have the chance to watch the white stomachs of the albatrosses in the azure sky, and he'll understand.

Winter comes upon them brutally, on the zigzag trails of the Lancier pass, three thousand feet up. Haut-Jura. A shortcut, Brabek had said. It's noon when night collapses onto them. The sky is so low that it hides the roof of the caravan. They have nearly reached the summit. Nearly. Surrounded by a deluge of snow, trapped, besieged. They can't see anything anymore, but there's nothing to see, no path, no crevasse, no summit, no forest of spruces, in an hour everything disappears, everything is smothered and abolished, the shapes and the sounds. A white death. The great immaculate silence.

They shut themselves inside to wait for it to subside. The night brings the kind of blizzard that makes the floorboards vibrate and filters through the tiniest cracks. The temperature drops to five degrees Fahrenheit. The wood-burning stove whistles. The faint flame that it produces hardly heats up anything but its center, and not even that very well. Brabek is lying on his bed. He's not sleeping. He's thinking of the horse outside. After a moment he gets up and wraps himself in his covers and walks out. As colossal as he is, the force of the wind makes him sway. He peers between the shafts, squints through the gusts and the darkness. At first he doesn't see the gelding. Doesn't recognize it. Then he thinks it's dead on its feet. The animal is coated in a thick layer of snow and frost. A snowbank like all the others. The ogre approaches. The animal's eyelids are closed, as if sealed, the beginnings of icicles are stuck to its goatee. Brabek rubs its forehead with the blanket, breathes into its nostrils. Then he tries to untie it but his numbed fingers struggle with the harness buckles. The metal is icy, the leather stiff as bark. He frees the gelding and pulls it forward. The horse shakes the fifteen hundred pounds of his body and the movement makes its frost coating give way with a crack that sounds like glass shattering underfoot. A few minutes later, the boy thinks he's dreaming when he sees the head of the animal burst through the doorway of the caravan. The door is wide open. Blasts of powdery snow enter with it. Whirlwinds, spirals. The curtains fly. The horse keeps moving forward. It gets its neck inside, its shoulders, its withers, but its belly gets wedged in the doorframe. Behind it Brabek pushes, braced against its rump. His bald head reddens with the effort. His ears burn. No one can know the nature of the words that he spits from between his teeth, because the snowstorm wrests them and carries them away. He pushes, he forces. In this moment, the blizzard is his Tartarus and the gelding his boulder. Half inside, half outside, the animal seems to be replaying the act of birth, but in reverse. It's a matter of life and death. Its front legs slide on the floorboards, its horseshoes bang, its flanks scrape the supports. It is, however, advancing, one inch at a time it gains ground, and with one final heave it dives in, its whole body splayed on the floor. From the rear of the caravan the boy watches wide-eyed as the gelding enters. Perhaps he's remembering the silver horse, the first to appear to him, born of the wind and the foam: his legendary unicorn.

"Have to make do, sonny," says Brabek, closing the door again.

They remain cloistered like that, four days and as many nights. The ogre, the gelding, the boy. At best it's an igloo, at worst a padded coffin. The snow is everywhere, like the invisible cottony film that enshrouds certain fantasies. It acts as a buffer, it isolates them and protects them in its way. But it does not nourish them. Their meager provisions run out. With no wood, the stove is dead. Steam comes out of their mouths. Their breaths mix together. They're cold. It takes more than twenty-four hours for the horse to find its bay coat again. The snow coating melts, drop by drop, and forms little puddles at the feet of the animal, which immediately freeze to the ground. Tiny lakes of ice that the boy breaks with strikes from his blade handle. There is a trapdoor in the floorboards that the former owners had installed in case they ever needed a speedy escape from the constabulary: it's through this drain that they relieve themselves.

Over the course of the fourth night, the storm wanes. At dawn it stops. The sun could be the first that's ever risen. It shines on a blank world. A world like an ocean. White. Stormy. A frozen swell. Brabek gives the door a big shove with his shoulder, then he slides out into the light. Standing on the snowy running board, he looks around. Despite the protrusion of his brow, he has to use his hand as a visor so as not to be blinded. He first thinks of paradise. Then hell. Yet it's neither one nor the other and he knows it. After a moment he sighs and lets his hand fall back down. Just yesterday a smile had flourished on his face, but now he's a skeleton of himself. Merely a shadow. Barely. The boy emerges in his turn, blinking his eyelids as if he'd spent a year in a dungeon. He stands at Brabek's side and for several long minutes, they contemplate together, once again. It's not the echoes of Ellis Island. It's not the Promised Land. Brabek turns to face the boy. He places his fingers on the back of the boy's neck, envelops it gently in his palm. He says nothing.

It takes them another day to clear out and another two to get to the end of the pass. They bulldoze over the last part of the slope, keep at it for the final bends of the descent. Apart from melted snow they haven't swallowed anything in nearly a week. When finally they see chimney smoke in the distance, the most affected of the three is not the one you'd think.

WAS IT ONE WINTER TOO MANY?

After the storm, Brabek is not at all the same person. He left one or two things up there in pass that he'll never get back. Things he will never reclaim. Let's call it his compass. Let's call it his grandeur. He's lost his bearings, he's diminishing.

He's grown skinnier, but his body seems heavier to carry. His bones weigh him down. He stoops. His joints swell and seize up. If you'd thought his eye sockets couldn't get any more dug in, you were wrong—his eyes have sunk to the darkest recesses, like young frightened animals cornered at the back of caves, or like old animals, withdrawn there to die.

At night he talks less. His speech withers more quickly. He reserves it, one might say. Saves it. Hoards his saliva and his breath like precious resources, conscious of needing to preserve them for use in his trade and nothing else. Have you ever seen a mute showman? If so, you've seen one dying of hunger. He knows that he can't count on the boy to replace him in that role. So he keeps quiet. He's weary in any case, and yearns for rest.

He goes to bed early. Wakes up in the middle of the night, shivering in his soaked underwear. A buffalo on his own beastly chest. His breath whistles. His bed seems narrower, but the alcove that houses it now the size of an entire galaxy. He searches for stars that aren't there. The night is without light, without beacons. In the morning the boy finds him with his eyes open, looking like an exhausted traveler.

Age? No. It can't be just that. What's afoot is instead more of a change in status. Once an ogre, he's becoming a man again. Once an inferno, he's turning into a flickering candle. A night light.

In Besançon, in Doubs, they treat him like Quasimodo. It's unprecedented. It happens when they arrive in a small café, where they stop to warm up. Though it's true they find themselves in master Hugo's native lands, all the same the word is harsh. The one who said it is leaning over the counter. He's young and thin. A man of letters certainly. Youngest decadent son of a local bigwig. He sweats his provincial sourness and his eight years as a boarder with the Jesuits and the six glasses of absinthe he's just knocked back. (The last, empty, is still in his hand.) There's a short silence. The angel that passes has horns, black wings. The boy looks back and forth between Brabek and the other. He doesn't know what to think. Like most of the locals in the room, he feels uneasy but can't identify why. No one has read the work of the author. Brabek has. Even at the stage he's at, he could still crush the pipsqueak's face against the bar, smash all his teeth, but that's not what he does. He orders two mulled wines. And he hands one of the glasses to the boy and then raises the other, his own, to the insolent man, and his gesture is more of an exoneration than a toast.

"I'll take that as a compliment," he says. "Since, as you know, his ungainly body conceals the purest of souls . . ."

He smiles. Then he drinks, and in the room everyone can breathe normally again, and those who still have some drink join him.

That same night, he responds to questions the boy hasn't asked. He talks about the tolling of the bell. Gargoyles of the cathedral. Appearances. Inside and outside. He talks about ugliness and beauty. He says that he would really like to see the face of this God who allegedly created him in his image. He says that it would have been better for the Father to create a mirror before anything else—don't you agree? . . . All joking aside, sonny, do we have a choice? No. Not about that. He says we shouldn't hope to find equality in everything and for everyone. He says that it's more a matter of chance, or destiny. For some it's heads or tails, for others it's written in the stars above the cradle. For him it was rigged from the beginning. Long before he had a say in it, even before he let out his first howl. He talks about small seeds and semen. He uses scholarly terms like "teratogenic" and "acromegaly." Excessive growth of the extremities. But who are those weasels . . . ? It all comes down to what you have in front of you, sonny. And saying that, he shows him the dome of his enormous skull, he waves his immense hands in the air, he raises, one at a time, his gargantuan feet, which are soaking in a small tub filled with warm water and coarse salt. His Titan limbs. All the attributes of an ogre. He says that it was his lot. His dowry at birth. His fortune and his misfortune. He says that he has to take into consideration the strength that it gave him, the size, the aura, and he has to take just as much of the fear and the disgust and the rejection that it brought. There has been, in this excessiveness, a good amount of suffering and sorrow, and there has been a nearly equal amount of vanity and pride. But with time, he says, it should be noted that the first has been increasing, while the latter has been waning. Who knows why? Who can really identify the causes of a disaster? He says that he feels like his bones are going to pierce his skin. That he has to carry ten times his weight with each stride. That the sky gets higher while he gets shorter, and that, therefore, it doesn't take a genius to deduce that the moon is harder and harder to grab onto. It's simple math, sonny.

Ironically, the celestial body in question pulls away at that moment, hiding behind a cluster of clouds, but they can't see it because they're inside the caravan. A small lamp has been placed on the movable table, it's the only source of light. Brabek breathes. Feet in the basin, elbows on his thighs. The orb of his skull encircled in a golden halo. It's been weeks since he's talked so much. The boy is seated cross-legged on his bed, on the edge of the shadow, staring at him.

The ogre pinches his earlobe between his thumb and index finger. He murmurs to himself, something that doesn't cross the threshold of his lips. And then he sighs, lifts his head.

He talks about the outside. What is visible. The ugliness, in his case. The horrible and the deformed, let's not mince words. But fortunately, it's not everything. What about beauty? Where is it? Where is it hiding? He recalls the creature of Notre-Dame, the monster, the hideous half-beast, and then he evokes the gypsy, the entertainer with onyx eyes. The one that dances. Bewitches. Who reads palms and sometimes diverts paths. She who is the sparkle and the flame and the ember unto herself. The origin and the end. But that's not just in stories, sonny. In life, too. You'll see. Life, at least, has the upside of overflowing its bounty sometimes. It carries. It transports. Love, he's talking about love. And he's talking about fighting, because he can't help himself. Everything is related to it and comes back to it. Fighting and love, and the ways they intersect. Aren't we all just spinning around? Searching for each other? Clutching at each other? Embracing? Isn't there a face-to-face? Isn't there hand-to-hand? So many commonalities, he says, between fighting and love, but there's one big difference: in love, we don't win with our heads, we win with this. And he presents his chest, enormous, and places one of his immense hands on his breast. The heart. He's talking about the heart. He says that this is where it lives, beauty. Inside. This is where it pulses and radiates. He says that it's always astonishing to discover on what vile plots blossom the most radiant flowers. In what squalid boxes nestle the most precious jewels. Think of the rose in the manure. Think of the nugget of pure gold that you have to unearth from slag. He says that these are overused images, done to the point of exhaustion, but which nevertheless express a real truth. The heart, sonny. No muscle more tender. A sponge. It can absorb anything. It can contain everything. And yet, he says, what's even more astonishing is that man passes the majority of his existence hardening and shriveling it.

And with that the moon vanishes again and Brabek looks deep into the boy's eyes and says:

"Maybe that's necessary for survival."

TO PERFORM IN THE FIGHTS, he draws on his reserves. Cunning wins out over brute force. Tactic and technique compensate for his weakness. Experience. There was hope that his vigor would return with spring, fresh blood in his veins, regenerated. There is none of that. March, April, the circle continues to tighten, the adversaries get heavier, and the longer the days, the more the wiggle room narrows. Two or three times he cheats. No one notices but the shame gnaws at his stomach. Victory tastes like bile.

Where is the art? Where is the dignity? The enthusiasm, where did it go?

And then it happens.

He's on his back in Aube. In the courtyard of an inn near Chaource. After all, why not here? It's a beautiful and clear day. The fight lasts less than a minute. Less than half a minute. Time enough to assess the man who enters the circle: a hot-headed bull. Massive, short legs. A breed that he knows like the back of his hand, because he's confronted entire troupes of them. He knows that this man will charge in immediately, straight ahead. And that's exactly what the man does. Less than a quarter of a minute. The time to say oof. Brabek could have dodged. He could have broken his fall. He could have blocked. Maybe. He takes the charge right in his gut and topples backwards. Time enough to see the earth and sky flip. The sun is at its highest point. The other man is already on him, straddling him. He feels a mustache tickle his forehead, he smells an aroma of burnt peat. For the first time in more than thirty-five years, his two shoulders touch the ground. Pinned down. He could have gotten out of it. He could have tried. Perhaps. He doesn't move. A count to three. The bull gets up grunting his triumph, but a far greater weight is lifted from Brabek's chest in that moment. A weight he hadn't suspected. The bell tolls twelve times. He remains splayed on the ground. He stares straight into the sun.

When the boy leans over his face, he discovers a kind of smile he's never seen before. The smile of a Buddha, or a Madonna, that is not aimed at him, that goes right through him.

The smile is still there as they walk along the banks of the Armance. From windmill to windmill. Water flows and wheels turn, paddle after paddle.

It is still there when they stop to bivouac on a clover bed as thick and soft as a Persian rug. There's a small pool nearby. It's just after five o'clock. They unharness the gelding and do what they have to do.

It is still there that night, when Brabek slides naked into the steam bath of the cask. He stays there for a long time. His neck resting on the edge as he watches the night fall.

He has not opened his mouth since they left the inn, but now he opens it to say:

"It's a sacred place."

The boy looks in the direction indicated by the ogre's finger.

"The caravan," says Brabek. "The people it belonged to before me said that a woman is not allowed to give birth in here. We're not allowed to die in it either. For risk of rendering it impure. That's what they said, and they believed it. They believed in those things. In omens and spells. In divine lightning. Why not? To each his symbols . . . What's for sure is that no gypsy will buy a caravan that someone's died in."

In the bushes, a toad starts the concert. They turn their heads towards the pond. They listen. It's a discreet prelude, but still haunting.

"Imagine," says Brabek, "a different story. A story in which the sublime gypsy—what a twist—returns the love of the awful hunchback. They love each other, they get married. And then they take off together on the road, in their dapper caravan. But that's precisely when the problem starts. Because as lovely and dapper as it is, the beauty will never be able to give birth there. And the monster will never be able to die there. For risk of rendering it impure . . ."

He looks at the boy.

"So," he says, "what to do? Do you have a solution?"

He waits for a response. The boy shakes his head.

"No," says Brabek. "I don't either. No one does. Which is why I say that there are some stories that simply cannot be told."

There are two of them now. Then five, ten, a hundred, a full orchestra croaking in the pool.

The water cools down in the cask, his skin wrinkles and withers.

"Travelers," says Brabek. "That's what they call them. But at the end of the day, aren't we all travelers?"

This time he doesn't wait for a response. He stands up, naked and pale and sparkling in the gleam of the flames, and the boy is there to hand him his bathrobe.

It's still there, the smile of the Madonna, or the Buddha, when Brabek goes to lie down in the alcove, when he closes his eyes, when he sleeps.

All night the male toads puff themselves up. They call, they promise. Exalt their love through their song, with the hope that the females will recognize, in their voice, the prince inside.

The boy falls asleep in the early morning.

He wakes up with a start a couple of hours later. His heart is beating wild and fast. The caravan is deserted. Silence reigns. They should have left, they should have been on the road for a while now already, but they're not. He gets up and goes outside. On the threshold the sun's rays hit him right in the face. He looks to his right, towards the pond. A veil of mist ripples on the surface, an iridescent layer of pearly reflection. Nothing else moves. He looks to his left. One hundred yards away stands an old solitary elm tree. He makes out two silhouettes, nearly backlit. One of them is the gelding grazing at the foot of the tree, the other is the ogre, dangling beneath the foliage. There is, in this tableau, a rare peace and harmony. As if each element had finally found its long-awaited place. Perfect composition. Jumping from the running board, the boy shatters the scene. He runs to the elm tree, mouth open, in his throat a cry that doesn't come out. The horse raises its head and observes, still grinding the stalks between its teeth. It curls its lips, a yellowish juice runs over its gums. The boy stops short, five or six steps from Brabek. He looks at his face. Never has he had to lift his eyes so high. The ogre's shadow stretches out infinitely. He used the gelding's lead rein. He must have also used its spine, balancing himself on it to reach the branch. His feet levitate more than six feet off the ground. Brabek is a flying ogre.

Inversely, the boy drops. His legs buckle, he lands on all fours and starts to scratch at the earth with rage, with fury, digging up entire fistfuls of grass and peat and everything that grows there. His tears erupt, his cries burst forth in a roar, guttural, inarticulate, like the wheeze of a wounded animal, making the horse flatten its ears and bristle its fur.

When he stops, the boy is drained. He stays there for a long moment without moving, his forehead on the ground. Then he slowly straightens his torso, uses his sleeve to dry his eyes and the bottom of his face, which is smeared with dirt and mucus. On his knees, he looks at the ogre again. Brabek is wearing his fighting outfit: tight pants, high boots. A butterfly flutters about his head then lands on his eyelid, cleans his eyelashes. Its cerulean wings open and close like a tiny bellows. It's lucky that the crows have not yet come by.

A half-century later a house will be built in this place, embellished with a garden with an elm tree at the center, its pride. A man, whoever he might be, will stand where the boy is standing now. He will watch children playing on a swing hung from the very branch where Brabek hangs this morning. The man, like the children, will have no idea of the fate of the Ogre of the Carpathians, and this is a good thing.

Another hour goes by before the boy brings an end to his prostration. He returns to the caravan and comes back armed with a knife, which he slides between his jaws as he scales the tree. He crawls along the branch and cuts the cord. He isn't strong enough to carry the body nor even to drag it: this task is reserved for the gelding. The boy guides the horse and its burden to the middle of the field. Then, plowing the peat with the sole of his foot, he traces a circle more than seven yards in diameter around the corpse. Then he places the ogre's personal effects on the body. His clothes, his tunic, his sheets. In the caravan he pulls the wooden chest from beneath the bed, a long and flat and heavy chest that had never been opened in front of him. He hesitates a moment, then lifts the lid. The chest is filled with books. Tens, maybe even hundreds. He grazes the covers with his fingertips. Then he grabs the first of the pile and leafs through it cautiously. No images, only symbols. He closes the book and puts it back. With the same tender care he inspects the few objects that make up the inventory of Brabek's riches. Tied together with a beige shoelace is a thin bundle of letters in their unsealed envelopes. He doesn't open them. There's a collection of a dozen medals suspended from a ribbon, on which are silhouettes of fighters in action. There's a pipe made from black wood, its furnace cracked. There's a fan of formerly dazzling colors. Unfolding it he discovers the very realistic design of a young woman leaning forward, her lifted skirt concealing nothing of her pink and chubby behind. That image, along with the sly wink that the demoiselle seems to be throwing at him acrobatically over her shoulder, is the cause for a great distress that he doesn't understand at all, nor does he seek to explain it. He sits there for a good minute examining the fan before refolding it. There's a baptism bracelet engraved with a name. There's an article of newborn clothing in cotton, bordered with lace, unless it's doll clothes. There's a document sealed with a wax stamp that looks like a diploma or a certificate. Finally, there's a rolled-up poster of around two feet by two and a half; he unrolls it. In a close-up at the center of the illustration is a roaring panther, its black face, its white fangs, its yellow eyes. Scattered around and smaller in size are different characters in fighting positions: a pirate wearing an eye patch over his eye, a negro with shackled ankles, a dwarf brandishing a femur longer than his arm. Examining a figure located at the bottom of the poster and representing a man in a toga, a gladiator sword in his hand, the boy is sure he recognizes Brabek's stature and features. In this image he is young and almost handsome, calling into question how much of it is illusion and how much reality.

Once he's done with the inventory, the boy closes the chest and brings it outside to the middle of the circle, then he opens it again and takes out each piece and adds it to the pyre. He leaves the empty chest where it is. The last thing he goes to look for is his own cape, the flag with the colors of the forgotten country of Transylvania, which he unfolds and spreads over the funereal pyre. After that he lights a half-dozen matches and scatters them in various places and blows on them so the fire takes.

That's what his mother had told him he had to do.

While the flames feed and grow he withdraws from the circle.

Today, like yesterday, is a beautiful and clear day.

The boy doesn't wait. He doesn't stay. He harnesses the gelding and climbs on the bench and takes the reins like Brabek taught him, then he clicks his tongue and goes off into the distance with the caravan.

THAT YEAR JAPAN ANNEXES KOREA.

That year French Equatorial Africa is established, grouping together several colonies and extending from the Sahara Desert to the Congo River and from the Atlantic Ocean to the mountains of Darfur, for a total surface area of 1.5 million square miles, or about five times that of France.

That year in Geneva, Switzerland, Luigi Lucheni, an anarchist, is found hanging in his isolated cell. Arrested twelve years earlier for assassinating Sissi, Empress of Austria, he had been condemned to life imprisonment.

In Washington, DC, in the United States, Victor L. Berger is the first member of the socialist party to be elected to Congress.

In Los Angeles, Alice Stebbins Wells is the first woman to become a police officer.

In Chicago, an engineer named Alva J. Fisher develops the first electric washing machine.

In Paris, France, the first illuminated advertising sign makes its appearance thanks to the magic of the neon tube. Its inventor, Georges Claude, chemist and physician, will become an elected member of the Academy of Sciences in 1924. He will also become a member of the Honorary Committee of the Collaboration Group in 1940, and a member of the national advisory board, nominated by Vichy himself, in 1941. Condemned to life imprisonment, he will be freed five years later.

That year, in the 15th arrondissement, marks the inauguration of the great sports arena the Vélodrome d'Hiver, commonly referred to as Vél' d'Hiv'.

That year in Munich, Germany, the first of the "Symphony No. 8" by Gustav Mahler is first performed by eight hundred choir members, one hundred fifty-seven musicians, eight solo vocalists, and conducted by the composer himself.

That year in a *vardo*, in a vacant lot in Liberchies, Belgium, Jean Reinhardt is born, and will soon be given the nickname Django, meaning "I awaken."

That year the Belgian Parliament rejects socialist Émile Vandervelde's proposition that would institute universal suffrage.

In Mexico, a revolution is initiated by Francisco I. Madero and propagated by the guerrillas Emiliano Zapata and José Doroteao Arango Arámbula, better known by his pseudonym Pancho Villa. The three of them will be betrayed and assassinated over the course of next few years.

In England, the Duke of York, George Frederick Ernest Albert, succeeds his father and becomes George V, King of the United Kingdom and Emperor of India. Over the course of the next few years, the power of the British Empire will reach its apogee and King George will reign over nearly a fourth of the population as well as a fourth of the planet's known territories.

In Portugal, the Republic is proclaimed, and King Manuel II is forced into exile.

In Spain, sixty percent of the population is illiterate.

That year the president of the French Republic announces a law for retirement at sixty-five years old. Life expectancy is forty-nine years for men and fifty-two years for women, so the General Workers' Confederation dubs it "retirement for the dead."

That year the law for the abolition of slavery is fully ratified in China.

That year in the United States a report on medical teaching reveals that ninety percent of American medical faculty fall far short from meeting the standards of European faculty. The vast majority of practicing American doctors have received training that is equal parts random and approximate.

That year in the United States the tobacco industry produces nine billion cigarettes.

That year in the United States a federal law is established known as the Mann Act, stipulating the ban on transporting across state lines any woman or girl for the aim of prostitution or debauchery or any other reason contrary to morality, and consequently giving the right to the police to arrest, on simple suspicion or presumption, any man traveling with a person of the opposite sex. The boxer Jack Johnson, the first black heavyweight champion of the world, will also be the first to be convicted under this new law after having been found in his car with a white woman, the jury neglecting to take into account the fact that this woman is, it turns out, his significant other and future spouse.

That year South Africa enacts the South Africa Act, which duly inscribes the principles of racial inequality into law.

That year the Four Nations Tournament becomes the Five Nations Tournament as France joins Ireland, Scotland, Wales, and England at the most prestigious of all rugby competitions. The French team loses its first four matches.

That year the Seine overflows. It's the flood of the century. People move around the streets of the capital in boats. Paris is a lake city. Paris is Venice.

That year a wave of panic swells over the population, people believing the end of the world has arrived when they see an immense fiery arrow surge across the sky. It turns out to be Halley's Comet making its thirty-fourth recorded passage in the vicinity of Earth. As for the end of the world, it will arrive in another form over the course of the next few years.

HE MISSES EVERYTHING, but one thing most of all: words. The ogre's. His stories, his long-winded speeches, his catchphrases and his maxims. (Look, sonny, because one day you won't see anymore. Listen, because one day you won't hear anymore. Smell, touch, taste, embrace, breathe. So that at the very least you'll be able to say, when the time comes, that you have lived the life they're taking away from you.) Even just the sound of his voice.

The nights are long. Darkness struggles to arrive, struggles to leave again. The world gets a bit older each day. During this time, the boy can be seen crouching in front of the fire, his eyes fixed, lost in the flames. Nothing disturbs the silence except the occasional fluttering of insect wings or some other furtive crack, hinting at a nocturnal chase. These are sounds the boy knows, he doesn't raise his eyes. No more than the gelding. But who is there to tell stories? Who deciphers and comments on life for him? No one. Lean closer and you'll see, in the shadow of a mustache that's started to grow in, that his lips are moving. They come to him, words and phrases, full tirades, they remain in his memory, echo, dwell, he repeats them and reformulates them in his fashion—mute, uncertain: a meager approximation. The boy speaks noiselessly and alone.

He questions himself. During this time period, his consciousness emerges, gradually, from the dormant, opaque waters of his tender age. It breaks the surface. But what's troubling is that when it emerges, the light it sees is hardly any less murky than the swamp it's left behind. There are doubts. There are questions, more numerous and pressing and precise. Death? Yes, death is at the center of everything. Death

140

is the siphon, the spiral, the mysterious maelstrom that everything rushes towards. How could it be otherwise? In the space of two years he saw his mother erode, he saw the ogre get devoured—Brabek, big and strong like a mountain, flattened to the ground like nothing more than an overripe fruit. How could he not ask himself questions? In his own way, he wonders whether this is an absolutely unavoidable fate. Whether every person is condemned to die, himself included. To go up in flames and smoke. If the links that bind him to others will be systematically undone, cut. And if this is the case, then to what extent is it his fault (is there always guilt)? And if it isn't his fault, then who decides? Who usurps this right, and why, why? During this time, he starts to grope, his mind launches blindly in search of causes, of reasons and purposes. He asks himself whether, despite everything, there exists, here or elsewhere, a place one can live and remain forever with the people who are dear to one's heart. Whether it be a hut or a solid stone house or a stretch of field on the bank of a river, or even a caravan. It doesn't matter. Something somewhere. A refuge where the hours wouldn't be counted, where nothing could separate those who don't want to be separated. He asks himself, if he were to walk for a long time and cover a fairly great distance, whether he might reach such a place. He asks himself whether this is what, deep down, his mother had tried to indicate to him by pointing her finger towards the horizon. Sea, sea. The opposite shore. What else apart from this perfect asylum could create the gleam that he'd seen in the black of her eyes? But if it really is over there, then how could he get there? He asks himself whether this nexus of life, peaceful and eternal, is only accessible to the one who knows how to walk on water. And if so, how could his mother have known? She had never been there. Brabek, yes. Brabek had gone to the other side of the sea and had come back, and if he had found this place then surely he would have told the boy about it. Surely he would have brought him there, he would have driven them there, the gelding and the boy, rather than hang himself from a branch and crash to the earth like too-ripe fruit. (Look, sonny, because one day you won't see anymore.) It's a time of metamorphosis. Body and soul. Manly hair chases the downy fuzz away, and lucidity tears off the veil of innocence with its sharp talons—and there it is, looking out through the tatters, his sad pallbearer's face. It's inevitable, reliable. Seated at night, staring at the fire, lips moving in a silent drone. During this time, the boy starts to glimpse what it is that constitutes existence: a series of heartbreaks and a few delights.

There are nights when he is wrested from his slumber by the sound of snoring coming from the alcove. He has to get up and grope in the void with his hands to be certain. He knows he didn't dream it. He rarely gets back to sleep on those nights.

He keeps up a few of his adopted habits, like the daily bath—though it's sometimes shortened to a rapid cleanse. Also the departure at dawn, though he no longer has a schedule to respect, nor a precise destination. He doesn't know the dates of the fairs and parades, he doesn't know the names of the cities and villages. What governs his trajectory? Chance. The gelding. A certain star, who knows.

He goes along the fields where people sow, others where people gather or pick. From time to time an old man standing between two furrows lifts his hat to greet him, a little girl waves her arm at his passing. He responds to those signs. He doesn't stop.

He steers west, following the rivers. For days he follows the course of the Orge, then that of the Yvette, often with his nose in the air to identify the nests of gray herons at the tops of the trees. He can climb up to forty feet to steal their eggs. The waters and the riverbanks feed him. He catches crawfish, eels, and little frying fish, thanks to a makeshift trap made from burlap and the remains of a basket.

One afternoon he stops to drink and refill his canteens at the entrance of a wash house. On the hot tiles of the awning, a one-eyed black cat is staring at him. When he leaves, the cat is on the bench of the caravan. The boy tries to chase it away but stops himself. The mouser's haughty stature calls to mind a captain, or a famous pirate, giving an order to the crew to raise the sails. They travel together until the night. They share a meal around the fire. The animal's dark fur blends into the scenery, only its lone eye stands out, gleaming in the night like the exact replica of a miniature moon—but orbiting what? When it's time to go to sleep the cat follows the boy inside the caravan and curls up at his feet. When he gets up it's no longer there. The boy searches for it everywhere, rummages through every corner of the cabin. All the ways out are closed. He never finds it. But he knows he didn't dream it.

Already another summer approaches and it will certainly deliver. Because the universe doesn't care about our misfortunes. Neither our pain nor our torment will stop time. And if nature communes, or even flourishes, over the tombs of our dead, it's because there is no more fertile ground than that of spilled tears and rotting flesh.

It's July 14 and the people of France are preparing to celebrate Bastille Day, officially, for the thirtieth time. Balls are planned. The squares are decorated with emblems and flags. People polish their accordions. The air is light, a perfume of merriment mixes with aromas of alcoholic beverages. The Republic is beautiful. Liberty feels good. No one thinks, yet, of having to protect either, and the price that will eventually be paid is unimaginable. Dance, young people. Dance, while you still have legs. Laugh, while you still have teeth and something besides mud in your mouth.

The gelding's steps have brought them to the outskirts of a village called Toussus-le-Noble. It's the middle of the afternoon. The caravan rolls along a high property wall, behind which, between the chestnut leaves, only the gray slate of a roof is visible. Suddenly there's a sort of banging, and the boy recognizes the sound of a motor of an automobile. A hundred feet in front of him the path curves: he can't see what approaches. But he hears it. It gets louder. The horse stops on its own, its ears are flattened. The boy stares at the mouth of the bend.

He takes a breath and the racket dulls, before starting up again even more intensely. And then he sees the car: a bright yellow double buggy enshrouded by a gauze of dust and fumes. The engine reverberates. The wheels jump off the ground, the sheet-metal rattles. It's traveling in a straight line, but the path is too narrow for two vehicles to pass head on. The car swerves, hugs the wall to its right, and the iron scrapes the stones in a long screeching and sputtering of sparks. In three seconds the distance that separates them vanishes. A large laugh bursts out: it's the whinnying of the panicked gelding, the first time the boy has heard it. The car just misses the horse but crashes into the wheel of the caravan. The axle gives way. Reflexively, the boy tries to stand up and in the shock he topples and falls head first, landing next to the automobile. His head collides with the car's body. The last thing he hears is a man's voice and a name: "Emma!" It comes out as a shout, like a supplication or an injunction. After that the shadows take hold of him.

... His eyes roll back and glisten, his hair whips round,
His head hangs; his blood reddens the yellow battleground ...

She's been playing for more than three hours, if it can really be called playing. She practices. She's persistent. More than a music-lover, she's like a crusader. It's her faith, her war, it's her way of understanding them, and it's what makes her hands move across the keyboard. Her penitence, too. While some crawl on their knees to the Stations of the Cross, she labors on her own path by the strength of her wrists. She hammers. It's possible that she's not fully conscious of any of this, but even under torture she would not admit it.

Windows and blinds are closed. The day falls. A colorless halo of light still floats in the room, and gradually withdraws, like foam on the beach. The heat remains. The humidity. A thin film of sweat covers her arms and her forehead. Her thinnest hairs stick to her temple. One unique, translucent pearl is caught in that tangle of black silk, like a drop of dew on a spider's web in the early morning. Her fingers slip, slide over the ivory keys. The piano is a Gaveau.

... And there's a luckless one, unmoving, nude, and ghastly,
All awash in blood, redder than the maple tree
In the flowering season ...

The metronome's pendulum stopped swinging a long time ago. She hasn't restarted it. She doesn't take her hands off the instrument except to wipe her palms on her thighs, unceremoniously, like a worker or

145

an artisan. Immediately she's back at the assault, claws out, furiously driving them into the beast's gaping mouth, as if to snatch its smile full of teeth that defies her. Her jaws are clenched. The wings of her nose pinch, flare. Sheet music rests on the stand, but she doesn't look at it. The shadows only confuse notes and staves. She has no need for it. What she sees is beyond. What unfurls before her eyes is a galloping horse, carrying on its back a naked man, bleeding, tied in his torment to his mount as they're launched together into a mad dash over the steppes and clouds.

> *. . . He travels in flight, on your wings of fire,*
> *All fields of possibility, all worlds the soul desires . . .*

She sees them, the man, the horse, the rider in despair and the animal exuding steam with its effort, and what she hears first is the caval-cade of words brought forth by the quill of Victor the Magnificent (Hugo again, is it mere coincidence?), the terrible and fantastic ride of Mazeppa.

> *. . . On a stormy night or starry night,*
> *His mane of comets, tangled and bright,*
> *Blazes before the sky . . .*

And Liszt. Liszt, of course. Only Liszt. Because it must be Liszt to reanimate the dead. She attacks the bones and their soul, digs into the tough and the sublime. "Étude d'exécution transcendante n° 4". Directly inspired by the verses of the poet. There are, throughout the entire world, at most forty virtuosos capable of performing the piece. She is not one of them. Not so much due to lack of agility as due to a lack of range: her hands are too small. They're muscular, elegant, but petite. The tiny hands of a little twelve-year-old girl—isn't it true their hands stop growing at that age? She abhors them. From the first bars there are harmonies that require a handspan she simply does not possess. Too great a distance. Liszt, a nasty, egocentric genius. Liszt and his gigantic mitts. A godly music written for the paws of a Titan. What are mere mortals to do? In the past she'd had the opportunity to attend a recital by Rachmaninov, the prince of pianists if there is one. When he came to greet them from the front of the stage, she had been able to observe his hands from up close: double the size of hers. Nature is unfair. Nature is a bitch. And that's not all: from the opening bars, so many pitfalls present themselves, so many traps and obstacles. The poor exhausted horse is constrained to an infernal cadence, he gets carried away, and the soldier's cavalry chases in cascades of octaves, in surges of thirds and fourths, and his suffering intensifies along with the beauty it engenders.

> . . . Who can know, besides the demons and the angels,
> What suffering will follow, what strange jewels
> In its eyes will shine . . .

He may suffer, but she suffers along with him. She must, in order to even attempt to accomplish these prodigious finger acrobatics, importune her muscles, mangle her joints, inflict grueling gymnastics, contortions, extreme extensions. She does it, the devil as her witness. She doesn't spare herself. She works her fingers without rest. She forces herself, she rips her hands apart, nearly tearing her tendons.

For she is the one carrying them, both the beast and the man. With the tips of her fingers. It's up to her to keep them in the race, to maintain their speed, to make the iron shoes sound again and again, along with the victim's tortured gasps, yes, again, again, further, for as long as possible. Even if it means she has to watch the flesh of her fingers bleed. If she yields, the horse will yield. If the cavalier dies, she dies. She drinks from the same chalice as them and only time will tell whether it's elixir or poison.

. . . O how he will be burned by sparks of light,
Alas! and how many cold wings in the night
Will come to strike his face?

The day is no more. Its final traces absorbed by dusk. The contours of the piano vanish in the shadows, and before the pianist's eyes, before the dilated pupils of her fixed gaze, the top of the frame disappears—that flat ridge that had served as her horizon. No more taunting from the gaping mouth. No more teeth. The void is somber as a tomb. It doesn't stop her. She dives in once more. She keeps going. The unknown keeps the pursuit moving. Sweat now shines in a narrow trickle along her neck, down to the hollow of her clavicle. She hurts, in her fingers, in her hands, her wrists, her shoulders. The pain intensifies and radiates. The vise tightens over her muscles. The start of a cramp in her forearm pierces her. The breaking point looms.

She knows she won't manage it. Neither tonight nor later nor ever. The piece is too big for her, a mere mortal, the summit is too high. Out of reach. But knowing that changes nothing. For every pleasure, a price to pay. She gives it her all, as far, as high as she can, and after that to hell with them, her and the man and the beast, all together if necessary. And to hell with all those cursed geniuses, too, the composers and poets.

Is that him, the Evil One, suddenly knocking on the door?

Two clean knocks, behind her.

"Emma!"

She jumps. The horse stumbles.

But it only lasts a second, she picks it back up again immediately. Her hands take hold once more, her fingers rifle around even faster, stronger. The animal takes off again, its four horseshoes thumping the ground.

"Emma, can you hear me?"

She doesn't respond. She continues. It's one of the most arduous

148

passages: rapids, a torrent of triple eighth notes hurtling down between the boulders. The violence of the current carries her. At the end are the falls: they'll either pass or they'll smash.

Two more knocks resound against the wood door. The knob turns, in vain: she'd made sure to lock it.

"Emma, come out of there, please. He's woken up. Do you hear me? He's regained consciousness, Emma. He's opened his eyes."

At these words, her own eyes close. A brusque stream of tears fills them, which she holds back. She squeezes her eyelids.

"Good heavens, open this door, for the last time!"

And then suddenly the horse rears up. She lets go of the keys. The silence explodes. Her hands remain suspended above the keys. Her chest rises. Is it her breathing, her own breath that she hears, or the panting of the animal, or of the cavalier?

"Emma?"

> *At last the end arrives . . . he runs, he flies, he falls,*
> *And rises—king!*

She stands up at once, overturning her seat. A slight vertigo seizes her. She staggers on her feet in the darkness. Then she turns around and hurries to the door. She turns the key and opens it. She gives a feverish, penetrating look to the man standing in the doorway.

"I knew it," she says.

Then she goes past him, runs down the corridor, and rushes down the stairs.

THERE SHE IS. She who bears the name of an abandoned lover, of a heroine who was searching for gold but found lead instead. She is twenty-six years old. She has an ovular face. A plump nose. Full lips that resemble a fruit that has no match in nature, that has yet to be created. Her thick hair undulates, flows free in long brown curls. Her irises are the color of roasted coffee grounds. A dignified portrait of a medallion. Perhaps she had been so perfect that some cruel or jealous artist felt the need to leave his mark: a pale line, a scar that descends from the corner of the eye to the corner of the mouth. Nearly the trajectory of a tear, engraved in her flesh forever.

She stands motionless at the foot of the bed and watches him.

He looks like a poor imitation of Mazeppa, his head wrapped in a crepe bandage that looks like a turban. It's hard to envision him as the future leader of the Cossacks, the dashing warrior, ruthless, who will cut off heads with his sword. Nevertheless, that's what he will do. But at this moment he lies beneath a white sheet with a faded pink trim. He doesn't know what's happened. He sees an interior he doesn't recognize and at the center is this face, this mouth, these eyes. Limbo isn't so far away, he hasn't recovered enough for his mind to understand. He takes the apparition as it comes.

A man is also present in the room. An old man, skeletal and stooped, with limpid eyes. Amédée Théoux. A doctor for fifty years, friend of the family for thirty. He finishes putting his instruments back in a big leather bag he must have had since his first consultation. Then he turns towards the wounded, but it's not to him that he speaks.

"Brain trauma . . . I have to say, this is what worries me the most. Always difficult to evaluate these kinds of lesions, and their risks. Fortunately, this boy seems to have a hard head. The rest too, by the way. Two cracked ribs, broken pinkie finger, a few contusions here and there: the outcome could have been a lot worse . . ."

He observes the young woman from below, out of the corner of his eye. A few seconds go by before she moves forward into the halo of the lamp on the bedside table. The tawny gleam gives her skin the velveteen coat of an apricot, which serves to further contrast the pale stitches that streak her cheek. She leans towards the boy.

"At least I missed the horse!"

She whispers, as if they were in confession, a secret that concerns only her and him.

The other man enters in his turn. Her father. Red, breathless. Behind his spectacles, beneath his heavy eyelids, the gentle eyes of a St. Bernard. He mops his forehead with a handkerchief, opens his mouth to speak, but suddenly a detonation sounds, leaving him speechless. Another follows. Fireworks.

The young woman stands up. She skirts the bed and moves in front of the doctor and goes to the window, while the boy pivots his head softly on the cushion to keep sight of her. What does she still have to offer him? She plunged him into darkness, she wrested him from the darkness, and now?

She opens the two glass panes and pushes on the shutters, carving a large rectangle of night into the bedroom wall.

"Emma . . ." sighs her father into his beard.

The young woman ignores him. With a sidestep she moves away from the frame and does an about-turn, looks at the boy once again. Then she smiles at him. And it's at that precise moment that a rocket flies across the sky. The boy can see it through the window. He sees it climb, with a sharp whistle, up to the firmament. He sees it explode and transform into a vast bouquet that blooms and flowers for an instant in the starlit field, and then just as quickly fades, withers, and falls back down in a fine drizzle of gold.

A series of heartbreaks and a few delights, just as he was promised.

Her name is Emma Van Ecke.

THIS WAS THE TIME when wine was thought to have many virtues, therapeutic and medicinal included. Wine kills bacteria. It's natural. It prolongs life. No better remedy, they say, in case of fever or anemia. They prescribe it to children. Everyone should consume it by the bottle, like mother's milk. Wine, wine, from beginning to end. There are hardly any limits to its praise, or its consumption. In the city cabarets, the masses stupefy themselves with the coarse red, the six-cent slop; in the cafés, the bourgeois spend money on subtler, rarer nectars, numb themselves with more civilized vintages; in the countryside the peasants tear holes in their stomachs with the rotgut juice they make themselves during the harvest. Wine, wine, from high to low, in each stratum of society. Nothing escapes it. It's the common spirit. The sacred union. If there is one thing that acts as a bond in the Republic, it's wine. Because in addition to being a treatment for anything, a cure for everything, wine is a patriotic beverage. We look down on the Germans, those beer-drinkers. We distrust drinkers of water, no matter where they're from. Wine only, only wine. Exquisite elixir of our prodigal land, salt and blood of our beautiful and grand country. Wine, monsieur, is France. To have a drink is to salute the flag. So it's not a question of morals or taste, but simply of duty!

The Van Ecke family is Belgian. Is that why Doctor Théoux allows himself, within their foyer, minor liberties? The potions he administers do not always come from France. For the boy, Madeira wine. A half-glass, morning and night: this is the crux of his treatment.

Officially, the doctor doesn't practice anymore. Gustave Van Ecke and his daughter are his only patients, from June to September only, and free of charge. The girl is never sick but the father experiences ailments typical for his age. The cures that his friend and doctor prescribes range from quinquina wine to kola nut wine, and even include the famous tonic known as Mariani wine, made from coca. Gustave Van Ecke follows every prescription to the letter.

The two men understand each other. Ten years separate them, but death has linked them. One had formerly been entrusted with the impossible mission of saving the other's spouse. Consumption was eating away at her. He had failed. Emma had only been a child then. As much as the trial brought Gustave and Amédée (widowed himself) closer to each other, Amédée cannot, to this day, shake the feeling that the young woman considers him her mother's assassin.

Each day after siesta, the doctor climbs into his buggy and makes a trip to the Van Ecke home to visit the convalescing boy. Pure formality. He takes his pulse, checks the bandage on his head and the splint on his little finger, asks if everything is okay—to which the boy nods his assent—and gives him two satisfied taps on the shoulder. That's good.

Madeira, morning and night. A half-glass.

Emma takes charge of his care. She runs wolf's bane over his scrapes. She changes the dressing. The boy lets her do it. To tell the truth he likes it. When she sits at the edge of the bed, very close, and leans over his head, which they've shaved. He can smell her scent. He can smell the tiny breeze of her breath. Furtively he observes the long scar that follows the soft curve of her cheek. It's a landscape that's unknown to him, that attracts him. He has to restrain himself from following it with his fingers. There are moments when the young woman talks a lot, nonstop, there are moments when she remains silent and then he thinks he can hear his own heartbeat. Strangely, it feels like the memory of a scene that has not yet occurred. A memory, and at the same time a promise.

He will have other wounds, but this one is unique and will remain.

His consultation finished, Doctor Théoux returns to the first floor. Gustave awaits him, anxious, at the foot of the stairs. Like a husband in the hallway of a maternity ward.

"So?"

The old doctor bears a serene expression. He goes down the stairs fluttering his eyelashes like a starlet, a budding actress, while his bony hand, veined with blue, prudently grips the railing.

"He's making progress . . ."

He talks about rest, robustness, solid constitution.

"Has he said a word yet?" asks Gustave. "Has he said his name?"

Amédée pouts his lips, shakes his aged head from left to right.

"Patience, my friend. Patience . . ."

He speaks in a steady, calm tone, of concussions, of amnesia, of aphasia. As though he's explaining a lesson to a schoolchild. These are the possible complications. Possible but not inevitable, far from it. He assures there's no reason for alarm. Nothing irremediable or definitive. It's still too early to assess. He gives Gustave, like the boy, two taps on the shoulder, and concludes:

"Let's give it time . . . What would you say to a quick game, to get our minds off of things?"

Gustave sighs like an ox. The boy's silence is a source of worry. He fears that the shock has cost him the ability to speak. The doctor confirms that from a strictly physiological point of view, no machinery is missing: tongue, palate, larynx, vocal cords, all the gears are in place and functional. But this is not enough to reassure Gustave. The injury might have deep roots. They briefly thought of sending the boy to the hospital for more thorough exams. One look from Emma had sufficed to put an end to the matter.

"He doesn't talk, so what?" she had argued later. "Don't we have to put up with enough foolishness when people speak? In my opinion, my dear Papa, I think many would do well to imitate him. The world would be a better place."

155

His daughter's indifference saddens him. Disarms him, too.

"So how about that quick game?"

Amédée insists. His wet and faded eyes reveal a concupiscent gleam. Gradually he drags Gustave to the living room. They sit in armchairs, facing each other, a low table between them. The doctor has already taken the box out. His own. The set he always brings with him and brandishes with a childish eagerness restrained only by his arthritis. In that moment, Amédée is ten years old in his soul. The pieces that spread over the table are nearly the real age of his arteries. They're made of whale bone and ebony. His uncle, the troublemaker of the family, gave it to him as a gift the day of his Confirmation—emphasizing the gesture with a blasphemous "in domino sancti" pronounced in a merry tone. Dear miscreant, may he rest in peace. Since his Confirmation, the doctor's faith has dulled a bit, but on the other hand his passion for the game has only increased. At this rate, he might just bring it along to heaven—a quick game, Seigneur?

Dominoes.

His candy. His unabashed vice. His guilty pleasure.

Someone less naïve than Gustave Van Ecke might easily have guessed that this playful interlude was the real purpose of the doctor's visit. But Gustave is more generous than naïve. He participates, but his focus leaves something to be desired. Placing his pieces with casual throws, a flick of the wrist, pebbles into a stream. His mind shuts down, while Amédée watches and corrects:

"Excuse me. It appears that that's not a four, here, my friend . . ."

The doctor is less persnickety when he is himself obliged (obliged, yes, that's the term he would use) to substitute a two for a three, a five for a six. This happens sometimes. It's fine. His adversary is completely oblivious.

"It's my fault . . ." sighs Gustave.

"Excuse me?"

"I should never have given in."

Gustave shakes his head, his jowls quiver. His thoughts again turn to the wounded, up above, in the bedroom. To the accident. He ruminates. He reproaches himself for having let Emma drive the car. Nothing would have happened if he had been more firm with her.

Amédée places a piece of bone on the table and leans into the back of his seat, satisfied. He only has two left to put down. He sympathizes:

"Ah, children . . ."

He knows what it's like. He had four. Girls. In theory he still has them. All married and flown the coop. The closest lives in Reims. On the first of every month the doctor receives a postcard depicting, alternately, a view of the cathedral or the statue of Joan of Arc. (The Virgin in armor on her steed, the bronze oxidizing already.) *Loving thoughts* or *Tender kisses* scrawled on the back, in a handwriting he doesn't recognize. Two times a year it's a letter from Fort-Lamy, where the youngest and her husband have escaped to. Lands that far surpass his imagination. The old man would have a hard time listing the names of all his grandchildren. Even their exact number. In the end, the woman he will have lived with for the longest time is his maid, Séraphine. At his service from time immemorial. She keeps his house clean, does his dishes, his groceries, the cooking. Domestic life. The pulse of existence. Up in the morning before him, she prepares his milk; at night she turns the lamps off behind him. There were even a few winter nights when she warmed up his feet. Amédée has often thought of writing her into his will. Let her receive a portion, she deserves it. He seriously considers, but he delays, puts it off for later. Later will be never. When he dies, at the venerable age of 102 years old, Séraphine will be nearly eighty and will have nothing but her eyes to mourn him with. One last time she will scour the house, polish it from top to bottom, so the heirs can reclaim it in an impeccable state. Of the doctor's four daughters, only one will come in time for the funeral. Séraphine will pay the bill for the service out of her own pocket.

Ah, children, children . . . Amédée envies Gustave for having Emma, loving Emma, at his side. His crutch in old age.

"Come on, stop raking yourself over the coals, Gustave. Your heartburn is already bad enough. I'm telling you, the boy is strong. Believe me, soon he'll be on his feet and in good health. Do you still have a six, by chance?"

They play two rounds. Amédée wins the first, always. He wins the second, always—thus depriving himself of the delights of a tiebreaker, but the urge to win is stronger than him. When the last rites have been delivered, he puts the precious pieces away with a melancholic slowness, as one sweeps confetti after a party. His gaze is extinguished. He is his age again.

"Have I told you," says Gustave, "that I published a notice?"

"A notice?"

"In the news. I chose a half-dozen newspapers of every leaning and among the most-read. The result? Nothing! Not a single response to this day. Not the least word."

"Hmm, hmm . . ." says Amédée.

"It's simply incomprehensible."

"And . . . what, exactly, was this notice about?"

"Well, about our wounded, of course!"

"Ah! Of course . . ."

"I gave his description, and one of the caravan and the horse, I gave the day and the hour of the accident. I left our address, too. For more information, please contact us, et cetera. And after all that: nothing. No one came forward. No one wrote."

"Perhaps with a little reward involved . . ." suggests the doctor.

But Gustave doesn't hear the joke. His eardrums reverberate with a worried gnawing.

"He's been here more than a week, Amédée. Can you imagine how worried his family must be?"

"I can, I see the effects on your liver, Gustave. On your weak gall-bladder."

"His parents, his family, put yourself in their place. They don't know where the boy is. They know nothing of his fate."

"What makes you think he has any?"

"Excuse me?"

"Parents, a family. It's entirely possible that he doesn't have any."

Gustave Van Ecke freezes. Eyebrows arched, jaw dropped: the moron in a vaudeville show.

"But . . ."

"You said yourself that no one seems to be worried about his disappearance. And I can confirm that I haven't heard anyone talk about it, in town or in the area. And you know how fast news travels: if someone were after this boy, at this point the entire country would know about it."

"But really . . ."

"On that note, you searched his vehicle, didn't you? Did you unearth any indication that might make one believe the boy was not the sole occupant?"

His moron expression turns sheepish.

"No . . ." confesses Gustave.

"No," repeats the doctor. "So that gives us a certain number of symptoms to take into consideration. What diagnosis can we draw from it? One of three things: either the fellow truly has no one in the world. Sad, certainly, but he wouldn't be the first, nor the last, in these circumstances. Or he's a foreigner. A traveler, come from who knows where. His family is far away, most likely. Unaware of his misadventure, they have no reason to worry. Or finally, a third possibility, and I would lean towards this one: the boy is a gypsy."

"A gypsy?"

"It's also not out of the question that it could be all three at once. But this third option would definitely explain the caravan. It would also explain the lack of any reaction to the announcement that you published, because these people, my friend, do not even know the alphabet. And it would also explain the general silence surrounding this whole affair."

"What do you mean?"

"You know that these gypsies and consorts have a certain reputation: it's appalling. Rightly or wrongly, no one cares for them. When we aren't chasing them away with stones or buckshot, we're suspicious of them. And they know it, too. So it's in their interest to watch their step, to make the least amount of waves possible. To remain invisible, in other words. Come on! Can you imagine one of those simpletons inquiring with the gendarmes because one of theirs is missing? Might as well ask a chicken to complain to a fox!"

"It's unjust," says Gustave.

"Certainly," says Amédée.

"It's shameful."

"Absolutely. But that's the way it is. And I haven't even mentioned their rate of reproduction."

"Their rate of . . . ?"

"Far higher than the average. Another established fact. Statistically and scientifically proven. Studies have been published on the subject. I admit I haven't followed them too closely, but it seems to me that my colleagues are on the verge of proving the existence of a cell that would explain that distinctive characteristic."

"A cell? What cell? I understand absolutely nothing of what you're telling me, Amédée. What on earth are you talking about?"

The old man's bright eyes twinkle. A catlike smile slides between his wrinkles.

"Pardon me," he says. "The jargon of men of letters . . . In reality, it's very simple. We've been able to verify that certain groups of the population have reproduced more and more quickly than others."

"Is that so! Which groups?"

"That's precisely the anomaly. Because they're the groups at the lowest levels. Let's get straight to the point, shall we: it's the poor. Which, we can agree, goes against all logic. In fact, the fewer resources we have, the less, in theory, we should want to have more mouths to feed. While we would expect abstinence in the realm of procreation, or at least moderation, parsimonious activity, it's actually the contrary—abundance and liberality! As senseless as it may be, the poor multiply like flies! Science, naturally, had to study such a phenomenon. Research was done in order to find a rational explanation. And, as I told you, it won't be long in coming, notably with the discovery of that famous cell, a sort of hidden bacteria, which apparently is present in the most destitute. In sum, the microbe of poverty."

"A microbe!"

"Rest assured," says the doctor, "it's hereditary but not contagious. You have it in the blood or you don't. As evidenced by the fact that the pandemic remains limited to the fringe elements of the population. A priori, there's no risk of being contaminated. Unless, of course, there's an unnatural union with someone of inferior breeding. In that case, all bets are off."

The old man sighs with relief.

"You see," he says, "science is marvelous, my dear Gustave, because it explains everything!"

Gustave Van Ecke lets out a grunt. He scowls. He suddenly lifts his sturdy body and begins pacing around the room, pounding the floor, his hands on his back, his forehead down, his step heavy. At certain moments, he resembles a wild boar.

"Far be it from me to denigrate your authority, Amédée, nor that of your colleagues, but I'm having some difficulty accepting this theory, not to mention a few reservations. And even if it were true, I still don't see the connection to our boy."

"The connection," says the doctor, "is the rate of reproduction. The gypsies are one of those groups with an accelerated rate. Good heavens! That's putting it mildly. Their caravans are proof: they're swarming with kids. And, if you want my opinion, all those young scamps are little Hop-O'-My-Thumbs in the making. Do you remember that fairy tale? The parents who don't have anything else to feed their children . . ."

"You mean to say that the gypsies willingly abandon their children?"

"I wouldn't go that far. Abandon them, no. But if it so happens that they lose them somewhere along the way, are they going to move heaven and earth to find them again? One less belly to feed: Is that bad luck or is it providence? After all, a sheep wanders off, but the herd is so big . . ."

"No," says Gustave forcefully. "No. Excuse me, but this is mere speculation. And everything else aside, it's no way to look at the world. If the boy has a family, we have to find them. The only question is: How? I can't exactly go beat a drum in every square in every village!"

He stops short. His arms, suspended in a gesture of helplessness, fall to his sides. His shoulders sink. Silence. He's distraught when he turns back to face the doctor, and the look he gives him is that of wise men, oracles, statues of saints. Amédée understands it perfectly.

"In any case," the doctor says gently, "there is nothing to be done. When the boy has recovered, he'll leave. It's as simple as that, my friend. He'll be on his way. If parents are waiting for him somewhere, he'll know how to get back to them. And if there aren't, well . . ."

With his frail, scraggly hand, the old man punctuates his words with a period outlined in the air of the evening light. A gesture that flays the heart of Gustave Van Ecke.

BUT JUST AS THE WISE MAN often goes astray, the venerable oracle is badly mistaken, because July comes to an end and the boy remains.

It's true that his health is not completely restored, after-effects subsist—discomfort around his ribs, a pinkie that struggles painfully to bend—but they've taken off his bandages and the splint, and he's been able to get up and move around for several days now. If he were in a rush to leave, all they'd have to do is repair the caravan's axle, and he would be quite capable of doing so. He has not expressed this desire. No one in the house seems in a rush to see him leave either. Who would want that? Emma least of all. One morning the young woman surprised her father by revealing that she had always dreamed of having a brother. "Several, even. A flock of brothers and sisters. Kids everywhere! Running and screeching in every corner, like chicks in a barnyard: Cheep! Cheep! Cheep! Cheep! . . . (She laughs.) A big family, yes, I would have adored that!"

Gustave hadn't known how to respond. At first, treacherously, the doctor's nebulous theory about the rate of reproduction had come to mind—the bacillus of the poor. Nonsense. Quickly swept away, replaced by emotion. He cleared his throat but remained silent, turned around to hide his embarrassment. His daughter's confession moved him. There wasn't a hint of reproach in Emma's voice, but he'd simply never thought of these things. This aspect of things. His tender, his dear, his precious Laure (my life's treasure!) had departed too early to give him other children (my gold, my dawn, why you?). Even if he'd suspected that a mother's presence had been gravely missing from Emma's life, he had never thought of a brother or sister. Should he have? Should he have remarried, if only for this purpose? Should he find, while there's still time, a fresh and new bride—a laying hen, for an abundant brood? Has he been too self-centered?

But that's something that can't be done on command. It's difficult, impossible to force. At least for a man. Surely women, Gustave assumes, are capable of deriving personal benefits from marriages that are imposed on them, but it's an aptitude that the stronger sex does not possess. One does not choose his other half as one acquires a heifer at the fair—take a look at this one: she promises one beautiful little calf each year, and five gallons of milk daily. No, only love, only the will of the heart and soul could compel him, Gustave Van Ecke, to remarry. And that will broke definitively at Laure's passing (my one and only true jewel!).

Excuse me, my daughter, but it was beyond my control.

Nevertheless, since Emma's confession, an idea has insinuated itself. It digs in. Tenaciously. It plots its course. And if one were to follow it, to what, to whom, would it lead?

To the boy, of course.

Is it a sign from above? A belated offering? The unknown boy, who wound up under their wheels, is he the son Gustave never had? The brother that he couldn't give his daughter?

This is madness, Gustave reprimands himself. Put it out of your head.

It's a sweet and pleasant madness, Gustave cajoles himself. Let it be. Don't think about it.

Emma does, though.

Emma acts, moves forward, without the heavy burden of excessive conscience. The young woman has not been wholly transformed since the boy's brutal entrance into their existence, but an undeniable change has occurred. You only have to look at her: yesterday she was glowing, today she shines. She radiates. She attracts light and sends it a hundredfold back out, through all the pores of her skin, from the beams of her eyes, the intense whiteness of her teeth when she smiles, even her laugh illuminates anyone who hears it. That light, but her breath, too. Because if it's not the wind, the sea breeze, that fills her lungs and sends strands of her hair flying around her face, then what is it? Emma, that splendid schooner, had been fully prepared, ready to cast off, but was condemned to remain at the quay because one essential element was missing: her sails. The boy has provided them. Deployed them. Yesterday Emma was floating, today she sails.

She tries all the languages—English, German (*Sprechen Sie Deutsch?*), Italian—of which she knows a few basics. No success. This was at the beginning, three days, four days after the accident. He's bedridden, back propped against a cushion, she's seated side-saddle at the edge of the couch. At each of her linguistic attempts he responds with a big smile, as if it were a few lines of a play she were reciting for him. A comedic role, to entertain him. And his smile brings out her smile. As a result, she continues, repeats: *Come ti chiami, giovane?* emphasizing her tone, exaggerating her facial expression. Until, after a half-hour of this game, she ends with: Very well, since you don't have a tongue, I'll give mine to the cat! and joyously plants a finger between his aching ribs.

The boy jumps, lets out a scream, a stifled groan, while, with a hand over her mouth, she is already babbling excuses, apologies, then reflexively pulls the sheet down and discovers the naked and bruised side of the wounded boy, and leans over to plant a kiss that might relieve his pain, but at the last moment she stops, seized, stupefied by her own gesture, then steps back at once, as if suddenly the bed were ablaze.

There is fire on her forehead—this is rare. Standing there, she looks at him in the spreading silence. His eyes express astonishment. A vague worry. The young woman's reaction was so startling that he fears that it's he who has hurt her. She starts a smile, but it doesn't take. Then she turns around and hurriedly leaves the room in a whistling of fabric and a clicking of heels.

She's gone. The boy places a hand on the still-warm imprint that her body has left on the mattress.

The next day she brings him a pencil and a notebook. Another attempt. She shows him how to make use of these objects by writing her name in the middle of a page: *Emma*. She underlines the word with her index finger before bringing this same index finger to the hollow of her chest, repeating aloud: Emma. He stares at her with round eyes. She sighs. She suspects he won't write, that he doesn't know how, so she also draws a few strokes below her name, a feminine face that could be her own. Here is what she awaits, what she hopes for: a drawing, several perhaps, that might reveal one or two aspects of his mystery. Who he is, where he comes from. She hands him the pencil. Your turn.

It lasts about ten minutes, during which she stands at the window. She turns her back to him. She doesn't want to see before it's over. She hears the light friction of lead on paper. She can't stop herself from imagining things. It softly swells in her chest. A sensation as sensual as it is exasperating. A demand for deliverance. Like the letter from a beloved, awaited for so long, finally arrived, ripped open at last.

When the sound stops, she takes a deep breath and turns around. The boy hands the notebook back. In the movement, the open pages flap heavily, like the wings of a big ocean bird. His heart thumps when she takes it. She glances at it and immediately brings her eyes back to him. (The boy's gaze is a lake. A pure body of water that rises from the depths of the world before this world, the lost world. She can see her reflection in it. But can she drink from it? Can she bathe in it without wrecking it?) Then she manages another breath of air and plunges her eyes into the drawing again.

A six-year-old child could have done it, or a child from the stone age. Primitive figures, crude strokes. She recognizes a house with a square façade, a door, two windows, a triangular roof. Nearby a tree, unless it's a giant plant, disproportionate. In the middle a person, a girl or woman, an indistinct face, but which she convinces herself without hesitating is her own: Emma. Above, the sky gives off a few rays. And then there is another form in the sky, one she cannot identify. Is it an eagle, a star, a comet, a rocket? She'll never know.

That's the entire work. She studies it for a long moment. She hadn't expected this. The mystery remains intact, but she is not disappointed, oh no, certainly not. Her eyes go back to the boy. She doesn't know what to say. She murmurs thank you.

Later, she will carefully rip the sheet from the notebook. She will place the drawing under glass, in a wooden frame, then hang it on the wall in the music room of their apartment on Boulevard du Temple, in Paris, where it will remain until her death.

Between now and then, how many romances will they have lived?

ONE MUST APPRECIATE MENDELSSOHN.

One must appreciate Verlaine.

One must appreciate the blue of the sky, the exceptional clemency of this summer.

One must appreciate the apples.

Raw, cooked, baked, with syrup, in a tart, in a cake, as juice, in marmalade, in compote: the boy eats them in every form. He stuffs himself with them. Behind the house stretches a field of two hectares, planted with eighty-six trees, nothing but apple trees, and each a different type. It's not a lot. There are thousands of types that have been identified and thousands that have yet to be. At one point, Gustave Van Ecke had nearly six hundred and thirty-four varieties in his orchards in the province of Liège. This was during the prosperous years. Gustave had three passions then:

The first was pomology. More precisely the growing of apples. He had dedicated the majority of his life to the study and the cultivation of these fruits. A distinguished specialist, member of several arboriculture and agronomics societies, he is credited with a multitude of articles on the subject as well as a catalog, a treatise, and a famous *History of the Brabant Apple*, which is still an authority today. He is also recognized as the creator of a certain number of cultivars (magnificent hybrids) realized through grafting and budding, patience and dexterity. Gustave's greatest pride has certainly been the creation of original varieties. He patented three new apples that he named after feminine figures who were dear to him. Who knew that it's in fact thanks to him that we find today, in a few market stalls, the *Douce Marie-Anne* (his mother)? We can even try the *Yolande d'automne* (his grandmother), juicy as can be. We can shamelessly crunch into the *Adélaïde parfumée* (his older sister), a variety for which it is advised that the thick, slightly gray, yellow skin be removed beforehand. A delight. For all of these accomplishments, Gustave Van Ecke has, at the very least, earned his place among the crowd of humanity's discreet benefactors that no history textbook ever mentions.

The second of his passions was music. More precisely the oboe. Though he never composed anything, he did transcribe a considerable number of pieces for this instrument, from Bach to Mozart, from Schubert to Schumann, Handel, Haydn, Couperin, Vivaldi, drawing from his favorite repertoire and not hesitating to take, as needed, a few liberties from the original works. He has also written a method of learning, and a very instructive book on the size and carving of reeds—which harkened back to his arboreal preoccupations. For a time he even tried to give private lessons. Although a mediocre musician, he possessed a real pedagogic talent and (most importantly, some would say) didn't make his students pay. Gustave Van Ecke would play, transcribe, teach, and share knowledge of the music solely out of appreciation and pleasure.

His third passion was his wife. More precisely Laure. More precisely the love of his life. Third in chronological order but not in importance or intensity. He had already, and by quite a ways, surpassed the beginning of his thirties, which is when she had thrown herself, through a few winding tributaries, into the course of his existence, and from then on had consumed it. In Gustave's heart, she had supplanted all the trees and all the fruit, all the Mozart and all the Telemann. *Lauro*, *aura*, *aureo*, everything united in one being—and the man on his knees had but one word in his mouth: Laure! Laure! Laure!

But did her beauty really merit the laurels he wove for her? Was her breath, as he whispered to her, as exquisite as the most exquisite of spring breezes? Did the golden sparkle of her irises really make the rays of the sun seem pale?

In reality . . .

In reality, why not?

Isn't it the nature of life to blind and amaze? To render divine what is merely human?

(One must now appreciate Petrarch.)

On the day of her appearance, Laure Koslowski still bore the name of her first, dead husband—a Polish diplomat. She had been a widow for three years. Black complemented her complexion. The prime of her youth had passed. She had lived. She had traveled, crossed borders, seen Europe, visited the world and its many salons. She was weary. She was thinning. She played the piano very well, especially Chopin—a link to her Polish ancestry? Never would Gustave Van Ecke have dared to imagine a woman like her with a man like him.

Six months later she married him.

A before and an after.

During their too few years together, Laure had sincerely, tenderly, peacefully loved Gustave, and she had been, in return, the unique object of his adoration.

What remains of that now?

A daughter. Emma. A pure miracle, according to Gustave. In any case an event that shook his steely atheism, made him lean towards a prudent agnosticism. If there was any chance he had of believing God existed, it was at the birth of this child.

There are memories that resurface out of nowhere, at the sight of a street the two of them used to walk down, a square, a landscape, a church they'd visited, at the sound of a certain timbre of voice, a simple phrase. A perfectly formed image, in absolute clarity, a mortal precision, comes right at him: a terrible and blinding reflection of happier days. He knows, Gustave, he knows. The sudden bedazzlement, the black phosphenes blurring his retina, and the atrocious burning that only tears can appease.

There's vertigo. Opening your eyes to find yourself so close to so deep a chasm. The stupor that follows.

And regrets. Yes, regrets. Of not having been able to compose a symphony or sonata for her. Not even a small, forgotten arietta. Of not having had the time to create a fruit that would bear her name. The perfect apple.

Laure Van Ecke died at thirty-eight and with her all passion intact. Gustave no longer brings his oboe to his lips. He conferred the task of maintaining the field behind his house to a farmer and his son. What does all that matter? What would be the appeal?

Emma and the boy pick apples together. They fill baskets with them. She forbade him from climbing the trees in his state, so she's the one who does so, if necessary, and throws him the fruit, which he catches in flight. Many are already ripe. The Boughs, the Serinkas, the Perkins, the Stettsons, the Pierre le Grands and the Reinette de Wormsleys, the Caroline-Augustes and the Comte Orloffs—whose flesh, the illustrious André Leroy describes for us, is white and tender, and whose juices are "weakly perfumed, possessing a most refreshing acidic flavor."

It's also Emma who prepares them, transforms them into compotes, tatins, other things. She cooks. The rest too. Emma has assumed all management and all household tasks since having decreed, at the age of sixteen, that having servants was nothing but a more hypocritical and more perverse form of slavery, created by the dominant classes in order to give themselves a semblance of good conscience—ultimately one of the greatest examples of what capitalist society can engender—and that it was simply out of the question for such an abomination to persist under her own roof. (She had indeed stopped reading the philosopher Karl Marx—she called him Karl full stop—when she had learned with stupefaction that he had a maid at his service—and she hadn't even heard the rumor that he'd paid her with insatiable ardor . . .)

"But . . . Aren't we ourselves part of these . . . 'dominant classes'?" her father had asked her.

"All the more reason," his daughter had retorted. "It's up to us to set the example."

At that moment Gustave had gotten up, started to pace back and forth, his forehead down, his neck tucked—he looked like a wild boar, an old wild boar backed into a corner.

"Come on, Emma . . . Come on . . . You're not really asking me to fire your fearless Magda? Are you? Magda? Your Magdouchka? . . ."

"I am asking you, Papa, to give her the chance to emancipate herself."

"Emancipate herself? . . . But you adore her! And she adores you too. You'll break her heart!"

"No. I'll break her chains!"

Was the young girl standing on the living room table, fist raised? No. All the same her voice resounded, her eyes shone with the fervor and determination of a passionate leader and the inevitable tears that she later spilled, abundantly, in her bedroom, when, despite her father's plea, she had remained certain of the merits of her convictions and inflexible concerning her decision, and she then saw old Magda, her loyal governess, her devoted Magdouchka, through the window, saw her leave the house forever, a small suitcase in her hand and her eternal black dress on her back, an old-fashioned hat hiding her gray hair.

It was rough, the road to revolution.

What Emma didn't know was that Gustave had continued to send regular emoluments to his former employee, discreetly and for years— until death plucked her, like a flower, from her bed, with a quick and delicate movement of the sickle.

Apart from a few tasks that are too onerous, too specific, Emma has managed everything on her own. This is also changing. During this prodigal summer, she has a helper. But a brother—a brother, yes—is no servant.

One must appreciate the pie crust.

She is the chef and he is the apprentice. They are in the kitchen, the morning is coming to a close, the sun pours diagonally through the window—a cathedral light—shining six white and distinct squares on the burgundy floor tiles. They stand side by side. Before them, on the table, apple slices on a plate, peels and pips on a sheet of newspaper. She's tied an apron around her waist. Her sleeves have been rolled up to reveal her forearms. A long strand of hair has escaped the hairpin and falls over her forehead, from time to time she blows on it by pushing her lip forward in a beautifully simian pout. She shows him how to mix the flour, the butter, the milk. She lets him work the dough. The boy sinks his fingers in, mixes. He likes the texture, it's soft and supple, it's tender, more tender than the balls of mud he used to make in his childhood kingdom. He doesn't want it to end.

One must appreciate the river and the willow.

In the hottest part of the afternoon, when the rest of the planet's inhabitants sleep behind their closed shutters, the two of them go to their deserted island. Eighteen hundred yards across the fields. Beyond a small jungle of alders and poplars. A tiny area carpeted with dark green watercress, almost blue, appears. There looms a gigantic sprawling willow, the tips of its branches dipping lazily in the waves. It's only an island in Emma's head, because the boy, for his part, has never seen an atlas nor a map, has never heard of shipwrecks. (If he had, would he be Robinson? Friday?) The water flows without the least sound. Just a stream, really. That's enough. They're sweating when they get there. Blessed is the coolness that welcomes them. Their shoes fly off. The boy has understood that he should not take off all of his clothes. He rolls up the bottoms of his pants, rolls up the sleeves of his shirt. She wears light dresses that she raises with both hands up to the edge of her thighs, unveiling the alabaster white of her calves, the plump and pink bumps of her knees. He lets her get in first. He adores the cry she lets out, or rather that she sucks in. A shiver runs through her. Skin bristles—hers and his. He meets her in the middle. He waits for her to turn around and for her smile to invite him: her teeth, her eyes. Then they play games in the water. They splash, spray. She lets go of her dress in the current, it flattens against her skin, molded tightly to her, or else spreads in a corolla around her legs, undulating, like the slender, translucent membrane of a giant jellyfish.

When the games are over, they clear away the fallen branches of the willow and slide on all fours into the shadows. They lie down side by side. It's a hut. A cloister. They are antipodes: time and sky are reversed and, for them, for the two of them only, in that part of the world, night has fallen, speckled with a thousand stars, gems, sparkles—a Milky Way in the sunlight. Emma sighs. She's happy. Sometimes the slight buzz of a melody hums at the back of her throat (a piece by Schubert? Perhaps "Auf dem Wasser zu singen"?) then the silence imposes itself. She closes her eyes and abandons herself to sleep, her chest rises and falls, without starts, calmly, and then the boy leans over her, over her face, right up close, so he can feel the warm, subtle breath exhaled through her nostrils, and he observes, he scrutinizes, every wrinkle, every spot, every curve, which keep on amazing him, he knows he can't touch, he knows he can neither lick nor bite, he looks, that's all. But suddenly he withdraws: he thought he saw her eyelashes quiver, her long brown eyelashes, he thought he recognized the trace of a smile on her lips. Is she playing with him? Is she pretending? He no longer dares to move. He is tense, close to a breaking point. There is no sweeter suffering. He wants it to go on forever.

Life.

We must appreciate life.

Peace.

And everything that we barely believe won't be eternal.

We must appreciate bliss.

"FÉLIX," says Emma.

"Félix?" says Gustave.

"It's obvious," says the daughter.

"Not to me," says the father.

"But it is," she says. "Songs. Songs Without Words."

"Emma," he says, "is this a new game? A riddle I have to solve?"

She smiles. She is radiant.

"You know, sometimes I ask myself, my very dear Papa, whether you're going soft in the head."

Everything, alas. Everything goes soft and it didn't start this morning: that's what he thinks, but he doesn't say it. He's mad at himself for having darkened her mood. He settles for a perfunctory grunt.

Although she's his height, she raises herself onto her tiptoes to plant a kiss on his forehead.

"Senile beloved father," she says.

Then come the explanations.

Since the boy has been better, she has started to play piano again—to really play; she's no longer waging war. An hour or two, at night, before dinner. One night she heard a knock at the door: it was him. She sensed that he appreciated the music. She didn't understand to what extent. She had invited him to sit on the only armchair in the room and he had remained there, listening to her—religiously, one might say. She turned around from time to time to glance at him, he had not moved, not a gesture, his eyes hadn't closed, his gaze was fixed: the mask of intense concentration, or even more, a deep trance, something quasi-mystic. She had been impressed. The next night he

175

had come back, and the nights after that. She played, he listened. Without really knowing why, she opted for the Slavs: Mussorgski, Balakirev, Dvořák, the preludes to Scriabine, a bit of Tchaikovsky ("His lullaby," murmurs Gustave, "His lullaby," confirms Emma), with all the usual diversions, Beethoven or Schumann here and there. And then suddenly—through what ineffable inspiration? Through what strange, inexorable charm?—her hands had started unleashing a score that wasn't the one open in the stand. Her hands, with a mind of their own, for her brain had no idea what was happening, it searched in vain for this song that she was in the middle of performing (and with panache!), it didn't know that the notes had been inscribed, etched into the very memory of her bones, carpals, metacarpals, phalanges, like grooves in wax. Her poor cerebellum was pedaling in place, while her fingers ran, flew gracefully, following the fluid movements of her wrists—ah! the muscle memory of the radius and the ulna!

Once her fingers were at rest again, the light had returned to the cave of her conscience and she had finally been able to give a name to what she had just heard: the first of the forty-eight "Songs Without Words" by Mendelssohn. "Lieder ohne Worte" opus 19 n° 1. ("Sweet memories," murmurs Gustave, "Sweet memories," confirms Emma.) An eternity since she had played that. Who, or what, had inspired it that night? From where had this instinct sprung? The final harmony (an E major of great satisfaction, great serenity) is still echoing when she perceived an incongruous noise behind her. She turned around: the boy was on the ground, on his knees.

"Fallen in ecstasy," she says. "In ecstasy, yes! It couldn't be anything else. I was even afraid, at the time. I thought he was in pain. You should have seen him. His expression, his face . . . The Virgin Mary could have appeared and he wouldn't have been any more rapturous. It was . . . it was magnificent!"

Then she tested other pieces from the collection: the effect was essentially the same each time. There was a link, a close connection between the boy's heart and the work of Mendelssohn. These songs in particular: the "Songs . . ."

" . . . Without Words," she says. "Do you understand now?" The boy doesn't speak: that music is his voice. He recognizes it. It fills him, transports him. Liszt saved him, but it's Mendelssohn that fills him with joy!

That's why she decided to name him Félix. The first name of the composer. It's obvious, the young woman seems completely convinced. She's not far from suggesting reincarnation.

"In any event," she says, we can't keep on like this without naming him. It's to deny his very existence—for does something without a name really exist? . . . And 'Félix' suits him marvelously!"

Gustave objects, banters a bit, out of principle, and then gives in. Franz, Robert, Ludwig, Amadeus or Félix: in the end what does it matter?

And it's thus that the boy finds himself equipped with a new identity. A designation, an identifying mark. At least he knows, from now on, which saint to worship.

Gustave Van Ecke stares at his daughter: she smiles, she is radiant. She plants a second kiss on his forehead before slipping out. A subtle caramel scent still in the room, long after she's left.

The old man approaches the window and looks at the immaculate sky without seeing it.

What is she doing there? His daughter, his marvel. His most perfect fruit. His accomplished miracle. Why is she still at his side? . . . And then Gustave is launched into his eternal tirade (silent, all in his head), his refrain, his vain tune, harped on a thousand times . . . Shouldn't she, Emma, at her age, be married by now, warm clothes near the softly purring embers of a good domestic hearth, a nest, a niche, a treasured husband behind her, and two or three flaxen-haired or charcoal-brown-haired children hanging from her skirts? She should, yes. Definitely. However, she is still here, faithful, she has not left her honest little Papa. How far will filial love go? Gustave wonders. Or would it be more fitting to speak of filial "pity." She is certainly not of an easy temperament, but she is not lacking in beauty or intelligence, she has spirit in spades, she is brilliant, generous, "flesh firm, juice agreeably acidic and tasty" in the words of the illustrious André Leroy, and all that for whom? Who profits from that plethora of qualities that nature has gifted her with? It's not for lack of suitors. How many inquiries, timid or frank, has he received on her behalf? Over the years the demoiselle has endured diligent courtships, of which some were nearly assault. But she knows how to look after herself. She knows how to evade. Spar if necessary. He remembers a naval officer, sure of himself, strutting, whom she sank with ironic and acerbic jabs. He remembers a clerk, a pharmacist, a Romanian count, an organist, a professor of rhetoric, the son of a Bonapartist legislator. For all of the men, some more or less handsome, some more or less good, there were just as many rejections. He thought the affair was finally settled when, for an entire winter, she had put up with a renowned actor who recited Lamartine at every opportunity, his eyes half-contorted. But at the return of spring she had sent him back to the stage, calling him a "lotus without a stem." Word had spread rapidly, especially in this realm where sarcasm and jealousy are mere convention, on stage as well as backstage, and a celebrated critic had even used it to demolish a performance by the unfortunate suitor in the role of Don Juan. (Lotus, okay, Gustave said to himself, but what did his daughter mean exactly by "without a stem"?) She had rebuffed all advances. All opportunities. She mocks Saint Catherine and her pious followers, with their ridiculous hats, a bunch of foolish children. But what is she waiting for? What is she hoping for?

Gustave lets out a long sigh. A fine flower of fog forms on the glass in front of his nose. Immediately vanishes.

"Félix . . ." he murmurs.

Shakes his head.

A brother, that's all well and good, but it's no replacement. When will it be time for the fiancé? The husband? The gold ring and the sacred bonds and the solemn nuptials? The subject does not upset Emma, she's rather amused by it. They talk about it sometimes. He's the one who's distressed by it. What he fears and dreads is that under cover of choice hides, in truth, a sacrifice. That she renounces giving herself to another man because she refuses to abandon him. She swears that's not the case, but he knows it's a possibility. He doesn't want that. Not for anything. A father is well and good, but it's no replacement. Nothing, no one can replace that. He hopes that his daughter, one day, will know what he knew with Laure. Will live what he lived. He hopes that his daughter will have a daughter like he had. He could not hope for more for her.

From the room at the end of the hallway come the first notes of the evening. *Andante sostenuto*. Stifled and yet clear, near and distant, like a small music box from another century. Through the walls. Through the seasons.

"'Elegy' . . ." murmurs Gustave Van Ecke.

WITH SEPTEMBER come the Ramsdells, the Blinkbonnys, the Rose de Saint-Florians. The days grow shorter. The sun is obscured. Fruit is gathered or falls, other fruit take its place.

Emma continues to play. The boy to listen. In the vast range of songs, there are sighs, silences, *appoggiatura*, as light, as nimble as a brushing of wings. There are trills that titillate and harmonies full and low that land flat on the heart like an open palm.

The boy is healed.

In the house they no longer speak of departure, no one mentions the notice in the paper, or the eventual search for parents. If one of them happens to think of it, they keep it to themselves.

When she's not playing, Emma reads. She reads to him. She doesn't carry her entire library with her, but she never goes anywhere without her bedside books. Of course she hasn't forgotten the Mendelssohn-Verlaine correspondence (she calls him Paul, full stop). The songs, always. Music above all else. They sit in the living room, or in the grass leaning against a trunk, or else on a low wall, legs dangling. No matter the place, as long as they're together, as long as they are alone. The ritual is that she hands him first the chosen volume. He takes it. He leafs through it, caresses the two covers, above, below, and the spine in the middle that separates and binds them. His gestures possess the sweetness of the first fruit of the season and the solemnity of the sacraments. She doesn't take her eyes off of him. Then he plunges his nose in. More accurately, he brings it to the edge of his nostrils and opens it, delicately fans it and breathes in, inhales deeply, immerses himself in the scents of ink and paper and perhaps, who knows, of the perfume of the words themselves. His eyelids close. He shuts the book and holds it for another moment in his hands, tight. Then he gives it back to her. She takes it.

She clears her throat. She turns the pages. She warms up.

> *See, blossoms, branches, fruit, leaves I have brought,*
> *And then my heart that for you only sighs;*
> *With those white hands of yours, oh, tear it not,*
> *But let the poor gift prosper in your eyes.*

This could go on for hours and he wouldn't bat an eye. He hardly blinks. She doesn't know what he understands, what penetrates him, to what depth, in what proportions. The sounds, certainly, but the meaning? The essence? She has confidence, however. He listens, he hears. That, she's sure of. And it's beautiful, it's rare, this attention, this integrity, no posturing, no artifice, no form of cunning, would she go so far as to say that it's unimaginable? In any case, spending time with him, she realizes that she had stopped waiting, she had stopped maintaining hope, had abandoned it, with no goodbye, with no rupture, had let it slowly die, without even thinking about it: one of those numerous discreet renouncements that life sees to, unbeknownst to us—but without which everything would be unbearable. But now she realizes it. She rediscovers its existence. Everything is there: in the boy's black eyes, in his novel gaze, in his blissful heart, in his innocence, in his absolute sincerity. She loves, she adores reading for him. It could go on for hours, she wouldn't grow weary of it. She hopes to be the first. The only.

> *The dew upon my hair is still undried,—*
> *The morning wind strikes chilly where it fell*
> *Suffer my weariness here at your side*
> *To dream the hour that shall it quite dispel.*

Gradually they desert their island. It's no longer as hot out. They jump in the caravan, which has been brought into the shed. The wheel is not fixed, the hull lists, tips to port. From the outside it resembles, in fact, a lone skiff pitching on frozen waves. From the inside Emma sees it as a dollhouse of Titan scale. She doesn't know that it actually was the den of a giant—here lived an ogre—but how to tell her? She rummages through it. Corners and nooks, niches, she discovers, smiles, a slight wonder when faced with everything in the clever cabinets, she's eager to play tea party on the movable table. She draws the curtains and lies down under the alcove in the position of sleeping beauty. Seeing her like this, tears well in the boy's eyes while, in his head, the inflections of a voice (of those dear ones who have died) remind him of another story, of a hunchback and a gypsy, of a toad and a princess, for whom no common dwelling was permitted, a story, said the voice, that cannot be told.

> *Allow my head, that rings and echoes still*
> *With your last kiss, to lie upon your breast*
> *Till it recover from the stormy thrill,—*
> *And let me sleep a little, since you rest.*

They visit the gelding. It's staying on a neighboring farm. Two mares keep it company. Large stall, good feed. A placid eunuch in his harem. The boy's reunion with the horse was pure and heartwarming. She loved that he started to run at full throttle as soon as he saw the animal. That momentum. That joy lighting up his features. As if ten interminable years had kept them apart. She loved (envied?) their long embrace, his arms around the horse's neck and his cheek against its coat. The boy's eyes were closed, but in those of the gelding she swore she read affection, real and profound. She almost felt like she was in the way.

They give it the usual care. As Brabek had taught him, the boy teaches Emma. As it happened she had never touched animals. She is struck by the force, the power she feels beneath her fingers. It's like embracing the trunk of an ancient tree. Rooted creatures, superb and formidable specimens. She, too, loves the horse.

They take it on a walk. The three of them cross meadows and paths, she and he walking in front, and the horse following like an enormous debonair chaperone, the air playing gently with its blond goatee.

What else? Silly things. Puerile fantasies. The boy shows off what he can do. He slips into chicken coops and steals batches of eggs, and they run away to the yells of farmers and the barking of dogs. They stop, breathless, five hundred yards away. They laugh. The eggs are broken and drip between their fingers. He makes a face as if he wants to wipe himself off on her, and she scurries away, squealing all over again, and he chases her until she falls down and rolls in the grass. They laugh.

One day, despite the doctor's orders, he jumps into a chestnut tree and climbs, agile, nimble, among the branches, higher and higher, while she watches him, head tilted backwards, short of breath, her pulse racing faster the higher he climbs, unable to stop herself from admiring him, from wanting him to keep going, for him to succeed in his ascent and reach the summit, the sky (what other being is she aware of that can escape the control of gravity?) and when the boy's silhouette stands, arms raised, at the top of the tree, when it comes into focus, minuscule and immense, in the ether, something unknots in the young woman's stomach, something explodes and runs free, and she is the one overwhelmed by vertigo.

He makes it rain meteorites. Yellow, green, covered with spikes. He tears them from the branches, he aims and throws them at her from up above, and the projectiles fly, come close to her without touching her, and at the bottom she performs a funny dance: it's the dance of the Bretons. Back rounded, hands on her head, bouncing in place, letting out cries like mice, squee! squee!

They laugh.

They stockpile some horse chestnuts, remove their shells, and carry them like ammunition in their suspicious wanderings. They walk to the churches. The steeples. Station themselves at a strategic location. While she holds the saddlebag like a gunner's assistant, he pulls out the chestnuts and hurls them at the bells. Ding, dong, dong, goes the bronze. The vespers sound at noon, the matins at teatime. Sometimes it happens in the middle of service, a clerk hurries out, he steps outside and scrutinizes the surroundings, circumspect, but they're already hidden or they've already left, so the man raises his nose to the top of the building or perhaps beyond, towards the skies, and he wonders about the ways of the Lord, while inside, on the benches, the anxious parishioners move about, fidget, whisper, pupils dilated and gleaming, always quick to think it might be a sign for them, even if it is the sound of a gong or a bell, why couldn't it be the celestial warning shots, a miracle being foreshadowed?

They laugh. They laugh a lot. Mademoiselle Emma Van Ecke had emerged from adolescence; now she's plunging back in.

Félix, my brother. My soulmate.

One night, before going to sleep, and without laughing this time, she tells herself that life is only worth living for love and art. This idea had never materialized before, had never seemed so obvious to her. A truth that rings out like cymbals and illuminates like lightning. She is happy to have grasped it. She won't let it go again, and its gleam will guide her on the darkest nights and the darkest days to come. Until the end.

Summer fades. They will have to go back to Paris.

On a gloomy afternoon there is one last game with Amédée. A double six finishes it off, which hardly softens the bittersweet taste of this particular victory. His oldest and dearest adversary leaves. The doctor is gloomy. He packs up his bones. He exchanges a long and silent handshake with Gustave. A type of superstition keeps them from saying see you next summer—at their age, is one ever certain of seeing anyone again? Emma kisses him on the cheek. A small sense of satisfaction, despite everything else, when he gives the boy two taps on his shoulder: seeing the strapping lad, there is no doubt about the efficacy of his treatment. The doctor takes one last look at him, his eyes inches from the boy's. Hadn't he always said it? Madeira, nothing like it!

The old man drives off in his sooty buggy.

The next day it's their turn.

Emma has spoken to the boy about Paris. The city, the big city, the city of lights. Have you ever been? No. Do you want to come with us? Yes. What he wants is not to leave her, neither her nor her father. Gustave expresses no objection.

The hardest part was separating him from the gelding. Emma, patiently, explained to him the advantages: the countryside, the space, the lush grass, the quiet, the comfort, no doubt it'll be much better off here. And we'll see it again. It's only for a few months, just a few months. The boy pressed himself against its neck. The animal didn't move. Can a horse cry? she wondered.

They've closed the windows and shutters. Once again, they bring out the infernal machine (De Dion-Bouton, an AW Type, for the connoisseurs). The engine rumbles in the courtyard. They load their luggage. Gustave sits behind the wheel, his daughter at his side. The boy takes his place in the backseat; he is afraid, and he is excited.

On that morning, at the end of September, they take off, leave Seine-et-Oise behind them, and head towards the capital at the staggering speed of twenty-two miles per hour.

1910–1914

FOUR YEARS, OR NEARLY. The next four years of the boy's life, which will be the most beautiful, the most marvelous. The trees were nothing. The elms and the planes and the chestnuts: easy climbs, warm-ups. What he will soon ascend is nothing less than the mountain of civilization. The peak of his existence. The summit of his life on earth. And happiness on top of it all, at his highest point.

After that . . . No, let's not talk about what will come after. Let's enjoy this.

Boulevard du Temple. Here's what it's like: a charming tableau. A beautiful little family. Emma at the piano, Gustave on the oboe, and the young man, there, seated on an easy chair, legs crossed, silk shirt, starched collar, mohair vest, tight pants rolled up in the English style, Derby shoes in kidskin leather (his own clothes, all new, in his size, made to measure) and even, yes, cuff links in the shape of a lyre at his wrists, it's him. It's the boy.

They call him Félix.

Father and daughter play opus 30 n° 6, one of the three "Venetian Gondola Songs" as they were called by Mendelssohn. Gustave transcribed them for his instrument. Emma had to insist that he do so, and in the end he gave in. Exhumed the oboe. Resuscitated it. Gustave carved, scraped, bound the fine strips of wood until the reed was perfect. He pinched it between his lips. He blew. It made him a bit dizzy—it had been such a long time. Fastidious reprise: wrong notes, squeaks, slips, inopportune derailments. In addition to the time off, let's not forget that the oboe is one of the two most difficult instruments to master—the second being the French horn. Gustave's kind eyes implored his daughter. (Please, let this old elephant and his old horn go off to the cemetery . . .) She had not yielded. With practice, and after numerous repetitions, it came back. The sound, the pleasure. When the boy heard the song coming from the salon, he had been transported. Oh! the sluice gates that were opening, the flood, the waves that penetrated his heart, the swell that both submerged and cradled him. Tumult and sweetness. It was the voice of his mother, the rare and precious trickle of words she would suddenly let loose in front of the shack, and which he drank in before the wind carried them towards other realms. They were the crepuscular parabolas that Joseph sometimes unwound at the dinner table, like a blessing. It all came together, harmonized, through a mysterious sonorous alchemy, and it practically made him capsize.

Among the forty-eight songs, it's the three gondola songs that have the most powerful effect on him.

A new year begins. Night falls. It's cold outside. A few snowflakes float here and there but never seem to touch the ground. It's nice inside. The three of them together in the music room. A new kind of trinity—"Father, Daughter, and the Simple Spirit," one of their visiting friends mocked. They celebrate the Magi in their own way. The piano is an Érard, a baby grand piano. The oboe a Buffet-Crampon, not ebony, but grenadilla. The wood shines like black lacquer in the light of the big, four-armed chandeliers. The easy chair is blue velvet.

It develops into a routine. And not limited to Mendelssohn; the repertoire is vast and grows ever larger from week to week. Studies, preludes, nocturnes, fugues, ballads, sonatas, scherzos: everything. Everything is worthy. The important part is in the communion. Osmosis. In those moments the bonds between them tighten, until there's nothing between them but affection and grace.

When they're not playing their instruments, they go to a concert, to the opera. The first time, the boy had been flabbergasted, glued to his seat, clutching onto it. The imprint his fingers left in the fabric of the armrests was visible from afar.

Love and art, as Emma said.

She wanted to teach him. Piano, music. She had a half-dozen students, little girls from six to sixteen years old, to whom she gave weekly lessons. She had asked the boy to attend as well. Then she began to give him private lessons. But it didn't work. Seated at the keyboard, there was a block. The boy understood the advice and instructions, he intellectually absorbed the exercises, but when it came to reproducing them he was incapable. Total paralysis. Just as with words: they simply didn't come out. And it certainly wasn't unwillingness on his part, he enjoyed these lessons and did his best— even if, in truth, it was mostly to please his professor (and, in the truest truth, because a small release shook him every time the young woman touched his hand, his fingers, his back, his chin, in order to correct his posture). Not long after starting, Emma had abandoned the effort.

Likewise for reading and writing. After a few hours spent playing school, she had had to admit the failure of her attempts. And their vanity. For in the end, if she hadn't insisted more, it was because she felt it all risked spoiling the boy, distorting his personality. Inevitably it would have an influence on his spirit, on his way of understanding the world and the things in it—gentle corruption, but corruption all the same—and it was exactly that mode of thinking and that spirit, personal, unique, that fascinated her and that she wanted to preserve at all costs. The teaching she and her peers had received, the education that had been given to them was certainly a window open onto liberty, but wasn't it also a cage? Wasn't it a mold, rigid and functional, from which everything was created, fashioned identically? A single model—designed by whom, destined for what?

Until now, the boy had maneuvered in the margins, outside the precepts and rules. *So, let him continue!* was what, in essence, Emma said. When she observed everything around her, the people who constituted the supposed polite society, what did she see?

Life is elsewhere.

The Van Eckes have introduced the boy to a few select friends. Telling, in minute detail, the circumstances of their encounter, the accident, the convalescence, the mystery of his identity and his origins. The story inevitably engendered all sorts of reactions and comments. The boy's loss of speech, in particular, intrigued them, and, ironically, unleashed their tongues. Every person had their opinion on the subject. When they broached it, Gustave became ashamed, he'd always thought that the crash with the car was the cause of this problem, and consequently deemed himself largely responsible (an intimate conviction that would remain forever stuck in him, like a tiny metal sliver in his flesh). Outside of this limited circle, the introductions were made over many days and at random. Passing some acquaintance, some relation, they took advantage to introduce the boy—Félix—without explaining or expanding. They replied to the questions evasively. With an attitude that made the presence of this stranger seem like the most natural thing in the world, the same as if a distant godson or second cousin had recently arrived from the provinces. But it had the opposite effect, at first. Far from appeasing curiosity, their discretion aroused it. People talked, people gossiped. They embellished, extrapolated. The second cousin became a phenomenon—*I heard that the widowed man has a farmhand . . . A retard . . . Apparently hunters found him in the middle of the forest . . . Would you believe he was raised by a pack of wolves . . . Have you seen the size of his teeth? . . . A missionary, yes, brought him back in his luggage . . . He only eats raw meat . . . Half savage, half . . . I was assured that he eats roots exclusively . . . From a primitive population, over there in who knows what jungle . . . And his eyes, have you seen his eyes? . . . The Arrapaos or the Parrareos, something like that . . . He sees in the dark as well as you or I see in the middle of the day . . . I swear his howls send a shiver down your spine . . . Half monkey, half . . . The Rapparaos, that's it!* And suddenly the curious started to parade through their home, exhausting every far-fetched pretext, every harebrained stratagem, to come get a look for themselves. Never had Gustave and Emma received so many visitors. People went to the Van Eckes' home like they went to the zoo or the natural history museum—or, more cruelly, to the freak show—and they often returned disappointed, because the boy had not perched on the back of an armchair or climbed the curtains, he had not shown his fangs or tried to bite anyone. (Should we demand a refund? At least compensation for lost time?)

Father and daughter had finally understood what was going on. Nothing could have offended them more, especially since they'd taken special care not to exhibit their charge like some vulgar attraction.

"Have you got your tickets?" Emma had said to put an end to it, scowling at the umpteenth curious neighbor who was standing on their landing (a fat lady patroness flanked by two kids dressed as if for the village fair), before slamming the door in her face.

A door that was now only opened sparingly.

Henceforth they were selective. The identification that visitors had to present was the purity of their intentions. Emma and Gustave conferred, evaluated, judged, before granting or denying passage.

Despite that vigilance, they were deceived a few more times. And so on one afternoon, Gustave unleashed a terrible wrath. Their guest that day had seemed above all suspicion. Pierre-Henri Louhans-Mainaut was only a teenager when Gustave had met him, some thirty years earlier. The nephew of a fellow botanist, he often used to accompany his uncle to conventions. Now an honorary member and patron of numerous agronomics societies, to which he'd donated a portion of his inherited fortune. No longer part of that scene, Gustave now only saw him from time to time.

Everything had gone rather well until he was about to leave. Two hours straight they had chatted in the living room, drinking tea and coffee. The boy was present, but their guest had only asked a few questions about him. Rare were the looks he accorded to him and not a single time had he spoken to him. A vase, a lamp had kept more of his attention. On the other hand, the man's features bloomed whenever his eyes landed on Emma, so much so that the young woman had come to the conclusion that the visit's sole purpose was, in reality, to get close to her: the discreet beginnings of a courtship. Which was true.

But as he was about to leave, Pierre-Henri Louhans-Mainaut had gotten up and, still without looking at the boy, addressed him for the first time. And to say what? Simply to tell him to go get his coat. Words all the more humiliating because they seemed so natural in his mouth (that tone, that air). Emma's delicate jaw dropped open. The boy, in his innocent affability, was already carrying out the order when Gustave's voice erupted.

"Félix, don't move!"

That tone, that air . . . The three others, surprised, turned towards him. The old man's eyes had the cold glare of a razor blade. His pale face had rapidly turned purple. One could see the blood fill him, climb, from his neck to his forehead, like a dark wine poured into a glass carafe. When the color had reached the roots of his hair, Gustave exploded.

"What right? . . . How . . . How dare you . . . ? He . . . He . . ." He was stammering, stuttering, spitting. "He's not a servant! Who do you think you are? For God's sake, that boy is not your valet!"

And Gustave the wild boar continued like that, growling, trashing, raving, and advancing towards their visitor, who, frightened, retreated under duress, retreated, retreated, until he stumbled over a low table and tipped backwards, frantically but vainly clutching at the air, and dropping heavily onto his behind, a scene that unleashed in the boy, in his innocent spontaneity, a burst of his thunderous laughter.

Oh how Emma had admired her father in that moment. How proud she had been of her dear, very dear Papa. When she stepped in between him and the odious man, it was mainly because she had been afraid that Gustave would have some kind of apoplectic attack.

Without a word she walked Pierre-Henri Louhans-Mainaut to the exit, handing him, in passing, his infamous coat, which he did not even take the time to put on, fleeing as quickly as possible, clothed only in his shredded vanity.

Adieu, unsavory character.

Finding her father back in the living room, Emma forced him to sit back down, loosened his tie, made him drink a big glass of water, and then, reassured, finally allowed herself to enjoy the hilarity, mixing her own cascade of laughter with the boy's.

This episode closed the book on visitors. In fact, all interest in the phenomenon waned. Novelty doesn't last, we grow bored as we become impassioned: quickly. The affair had hardly lasted three months in their small society. Now they are left in peace. They are free, Gustave, Emma, Félix, to revel in the essential: love, art, and Paris.

WHAT IS PARIS if not the Bar-le-Duc fair, but a hundred times bigger? The bustle, the haggling, the merchandise and merchants and flâneurs and good-for-nothings and thieves and beggars, men of little means and noblemen, bourgeoisies, loose beauties and housewives with heavy shopping baskets and beautiful outfits and rags and, in the air we breathe, all the perfumes, all the odors. And yes, okay, the monuments—temples, arches, obelisks, mausoleums: enormous cherries on top of the cake. When we think of the churches and cathedrals and basilicas, we think of the hundreds of thousands of tons of stones, broken, built, sculpted, transported, lifted, assembled by hundreds of thousands of men, we think of the time and pain devoted, of the sweat and blood spilled solely in order to offer a splendid home, an eternal shelter for a being (a being?) that is no more than a spirit, a pure spirit, perfectly indifferent to bad weather, an immaterial and rot-proof entity, no cold can rattle the flesh it doesn't have, no winter wind can pierce absent bones, we think of the splendor of castles, of the magnificence of palaces that were built by the same hundreds of thousands of men of entire dynasties, Olympuses filled with half-gods, quarter, one-eighth, one-sixteenth, pudgy men whose unique merit was having been born with a certain name, silver spoons in their mouths, and gold crowns on their heads, we think of the hectometers of walls and roofs built around a throne to the glory and honor and interest of lodging their immodest and nevertheless perishable bodies, we think, for a moment, of all of this, and can only ask ourselves, pondering the deepest nature of our species: oh humankind, is it credulity or servility that constitutes the very core of our atoms?

The Eiffel Tower stands tall. Sacré-Coeur starts to pulse.

She wants to show him everything. They walk along the streets and boulevards and on the banks of the river. And as he discovers, she watches his eyes, she watches because in his gaze, the variations of intensity betray surprise, stupefaction, amazement—and the light reflects onto her.

One April morning they find themselves at the foot of Notre Dame. She tells him about the archdeacon Frollo, about the poet Gringoire, about Quasimodo. I'll read you the story, she says. He is transfixed. So, it was true. He goes inside and loses himself. He wanders through the crowd, he searches, in the nave, in the choir, in the chapels, in the shadow of archways and columns, he walks with his nose in the air, he scrutinizes the ceiling, the skies, beneath the vaults, he searches for the creature, the hunchback, he searches for the monster—but there's only him. A long time later he exits, and his eyelids narrow in the brightness of day, and through that crack his gaze sweeps the citizenry in the square, he searches again, among the droves, among the multitudes, he searches for the gypsy, the dancer, he searches for the Egyptian princess in the Cours des Miracles—but there is only her. She sees him. She signals to him, she waves her hand above the heads and hurries over. Her skirt flounces, zigzags between the groups. She had lost him, she finds him again. Everything is restored. Relief throws her into his arms, their foreheads almost collide, their lips, their cheeks brush, he feels her breath in his ear: There you are! she says. And there's nothing else to say.

From the top of the towers the chimeras watch, snicker perhaps.

When Gustave accompanies them, they slow their steps. The man tires. His cane (maple and amber) is no longer only pomp. They go into the gardens together. Montsouris and Buttes-Chaumont, their miniature lakes, their giant trees. Gustave Van Ecke orates: persimmon, beech, Lebanese cedar, American honey locust, gingko biloba—an old family of two hundred seventy million years, he specifies, a hint of emotion in his voice. They go to the Luxembourg Gardens. They stride along the boulevards where the illustrious ones reside (past an ancient, petrified guard house) and there Emma takes the reins, it's her domain, her pantheon. Here is Chopin, she says. And here is Stendhal. And here Flaubert. They attend, in May, the inauguration of the monument to Paul Verlaine. A sign, she says. The bust is unveiled. It's him. Round head, severe gaze, below three women in relief, who seem to want to wrest themselves from their stone prison. They represent, she says, the three souls of the poet: his religious soul, his sensual soul, his child's soul. Pronouncing these words, a distress seizes her, she suddenly asks herself to whom she's speaking. She turns to the boy with a strange look. An abundance of songbirds bursts from the clouds. And here the dancing Fauna (further, later). And here Liberty illuminating the world (but the boy does not make the connection to the one that Brabek had seen born on the other side of the ocean). They go to the Parc Monceau. It's the one he likes best and it's here that, one day, he becomes a hero. How? Like this: just after coming through the gates, they notice a crowd beneath the ample foliage of a tulip tree from Virginia. At the center of this gathering a child is crying. Arms are raised, fingers pointing to indicate the source of his sorrow: a kite stuck between the branches. What to do? It's too high. They need a tall ladder. They need a zeppelin. They throw what they have at the tree to try to dislodge the object, nothing works. And suddenly someone exclaims: "Oh! Look!" They look: it's the boy hoisting himself up the trunk. He's removed his stockings and shoes. He pulls himself up. It seems as easy as climbing the rungs of a stepladder. Such ease! Such flexibility! Even Gustave can't stop himself from thinking, for a brief moment—before chastising himself—of a marmoset, a gibbon, a chimpanzee or some other primate in its natural habitat. In three minutes the boy reaches the branches. He thrusts himself up. He climbs higher. Forty feet below, the crowd murmurs. All those people with their eyes to the sky. Emma smiles. The child is no longer whining, tears and mucus gleam on his chubby face. Now they make out the silhouette moving behind the thick foliage, they follow his movements from branch to branch. The tulip tree shakes. A few flowers fall in big dawn-colored snowflakes. And then it's the kite's turn: unhooked, liberated. It soars through the atmosphere. A bird of paradise with green, red, blue, yellow feathers. Applause rings out. Hurray! Hurray! For once Icarus succeeds. The boy comes back down. He's barely touched the ground when they cheer him, surround him, celebrate him, nearly lifting him up in triumph. What success! What glory! The child's mother plants two noisy kisses on him. And during all this time Emma is hanging ostentatiously from his arm, she squeezes it, she smiles—and the light reflects onto her.

They go to the cemeteries. Montparnasse. Montmartre. They walk among the tombs. At Père-Lachaise they trample the precious compost, the priceless humus—bones, flesh, hair, horn, dust, dust, dust—dust of our dead stars. Here lie the greatest, the most admirable. Here rest the crème de la crème of the passed-away. The void is filled with them. Eternity overflows. Sometimes Emma or Gustave leans over, they point, they read a name, they elaborate. The boy learns. These are little lessons composed on the go, improvised. Brief elegies, portraits, anecdotes, histories from History. All these men, these women, all these dead, they were and remain fragments, microscopic pieces of a unique and gigantic puzzle that no one has the least idea how to solve. For Emma, always, the artists: Molière, Nerval, Musset—dear poets whose own verses devoured them—Bellini, Bizet. For Gustave the men of science, the nearly forgotten scholars. Who remembers Casimir Davaine? And Louis Poinsot? Pierre Flourens? Georges Pouchet? André Thouin? Gaston Planté? Michel Adanson? Gustave points his cane at a headstone: Marie François Xavier Bichat. He is known. Remarkable anatomist. They suspected him of haunting the cemeteries, at night, of desecrating the sepulchers, of stealing the cadavers that he dissected by the hundreds in order to carry out his research. And that man: Philippe Pinel. Another doctor, psychiatric this time. Friend of the mad. The first to attest that they, too, were human beings in their own right, and that we should treat them as such, not with bloodletting or chains or other barbaric medications, but with words. There were numerous people in his time who thought that his patients had rubbed off on him! And then there are those who do not belong to any category. The eccentrics. The special cases. For example, Madame Saqui, famous acrobat and tightrope dancer. Sophie Blanchard, first female balloonist. Marie-Anne Lenormand, necromancer, fortune-teller, pythoness, who acquired such a reputation that all of the most renowned personalities of her time, distinguished revolutionaries, paraded through her office to inquire about their fates. They say that she predicted a clean and concise end for Robespierre. They said she strongly discouraged Marat from indulging in baths. The Empress Joséphine was her most loyal client: they say that this sibyl saw Waterloo in a broken egg, and that the debacle could have been avoided if the emperor had, for once, listened to his better half. They say that through the intervention of a mirror, she prophesied that Alexander I of Russia would die twice, the first time in the robes of the tsar, the second in the rags of a saint.

"As for her own fate," adds Gustave with malice, "Mademoiselle Lenormand had read in the coffee grounds that it would not happen before she had reached one hundred years. But it must have been coffee of mediocre quality, for she died, alas, at only seventy."

"Leaving behind a considerable fortune . . ." concludes Emma.

Father and daughter jeer, accomplices.

It's here again, on a hot spring night, in front of the mausoleum of Héloïse and Abélard (no, it's not by chance), that Emma reveals the story of her scar to the boy.

They are alone. Gustave, sinuses inflamed by a nasty hay fever, had declined the invitation to go for a walk. Emma finishes the story of the exploits and legendary torments of the two lovers. Look, she says, they sleep together now. Lying side by side in their little garden, winter and summer. The grass is soft there. (Sigh.) No matter whether one believes in the heavens or not, it's love that is eternal. Love. Nothing and no one can ever separate them now. Her voice, until now elated, slowly sprawls like a dying wave. Look, she says. She points at the tomb, but it's towards her, towards her face, that the boy turns his eyes. Then frowns. What is it? The heat? A single pearl of sweat, or else . . . Without thinking about it, he extends his arm and gathers, with his fingertips, the clear, transparent fluid that runs over the young woman's cheeks. And when he wants to pull back his hand, she holds it there with a swift gesture, imprisons it, places it back on her skin like a compress, a cool cloth that provides relief. Her eyelids close. (Sigh.) The boy neither stirs nor breathes. His heart beats in his throat. She knows that he feels the scar beneath his palm—the narrow furrow running through the sweet peel. Her eyes are still closed when she says: You want to know?

The silence is her answer. Then a tiny pressure on her cheek, no stronger than the pulse of a infant.

"It's the god of music," she says. "He hit me. He whipped me when I was only a child."

She opens her eyes again. The setting sun bronzes her pupils— coffee, honey, brown sugar. They are opposite each other and in the little space that separates them flutter a few specks of gold, like comets inside a universe under a microscope.

"It was my punishment. My retribution . . . And why did I deserve it? Because of my mother. My mother was a lovely creature, if I can take my father's word for it. And I do. That was precisely my misfortune. For I did not adore her. I adored my father. And I was jealous, I suffered from the adoration that he devoted to her . . . Voilà. The little girl who didn't want to share. Who demanded all the attention and all the time and all the love of her Papa for herself alone. It's so clichéd. My mother was my rival. In my child's mind and heart, she was the one I had to surpass. More than that: I had to, through my intense radiance, tarnish her image, relegate her to the shadows, erase her, permanently remove her from my father's gaze. The role of the princess wasn't enough for me, I wanted to be queen! (Sigh.) A bad fairytale, you see, that's all I have to offer you . . ."

A sad smile blooms on her lips. Her eyes turn towards the big stone bed where the lovers lie: they're said to have been chiseled alive, taken in their sleep by the molten lava—the bubbling lava of their own passion. She squeezes his hand a little tighter. He doesn't move. He is already ready to forgive everything.

"My mother was beautiful, I had to be even more beautiful. My mother was bright, I had to burn even brighter. My mother played the piano admirably . . . Chopin. Chopin above all. She had unraveled his secret—for there always is one. The 'Ballad in F Minor,' the second 'Impromptu': I would have liked for you to hear them played by her fingers. Or rather, no . . . I don't know . . . (Sigh.) It seemed that was what my father loved the most about her. It was the most powerful charm she exerted over him. Through which she controlled him. A spell. You had to see his expression, the happiness, the bliss on his face when he listened to her play. Oh! Lord, for the love of God! She touched the divine. Through Chopin that damned queen reached the status of goddess! . . . So, of course, I had to play even better. I tackled it every day. I devoted hours. Scales and exercises. Dogged labor. The little girl on her stool, clinging with all her claws to the back of the monster. The insidious, the Machiavellian little girl . . . The worst part: she was the one who taught me. The queen. My mother. With gentleness and patience, with rigor, with perseverance she taught me her art. With . . . with love, yes, she prepared me for battle and I set out to annihilate her! My secret, this dark secret that poisoned my soul like venom, she never discovered it. How could she have? How could a mother imagine such abominable designs in the heart of her child? For weeks, months, I stayed glued to my seat. Scales. Exercises.

I toiled on the keys. I seethed. I was incensed. And when she thought she was calming my rage, she did nothing but increase it. But what was I thinking? Stupid little girl . . . (Sigh.) Do you know how much time it takes to master Chopin? I'm not even talking about perfection, just playing without stumbling, without hesitating, simply unleashing it without any kinks. Just that. The smallest prelude. The slightest polonaise. How much time? It can't even be counted in weeks or in months . . . I came to understand that. The queen had too much of a head start. It would have taken me years and years to catch up, and more years still to surpass her, supposing that one day I managed it. I wasn't capable of that much patience. So what could I do? What was left for me? . . . (Sigh.) I wished for her death. Simply. And I wished for it with all my heart and all my poisoned soul. I wished for it so intensely . . . It was granted."

At that moment a finger lowers onto the ivory. She hears it. She was waiting for it. It's the first note, low, deep, terrestrial, of "Nocturne No. 13." In response, a crystalline and high-pitched voice that could only belong to a celestial being. Earth and sky in dialogue. She alone hears it. Her funeral march. The bars go by at that slow cadence and the cortege advances and it's winter.

"Poor Papa. I deprived him of what he held most dear. He doesn't know. I've never told him. I've never told anyone . . ."

She alone sees, from behind, the silhouette seated at the piano. The straight torso, the loose bun and the brown strands that have escaped from it, cascading. Her shoulders barely move. From time to time she stretches her arms, like wings fanning out, deploying. She alone sees her flying. The queen. Her mother. That nocturne, the thirteenth, no one will play it like her ever again.

"I was eighteen when she died. I had won. But I still wasn't satisfied. Because I realized that I couldn't take her place. In my father's heart, we each had our own place, definitively, and it was impossible to change that. The place she had occupied would remain forever empty. A large gaping hole, an immense chasm in my father's heart. And it was my fault . . . (Sigh. Long, long sigh.) One or two weeks later, Papa brought me to visit a piano factory. At the end of the tour, they started to discuss something among themselves. At the other end of the workshop, two workers were busy on the frame of a baby grand piano. They were in the middle of setting the strings. The tension. It's a delicate operation. Do you know how many chords there are in a piano? Two hundred and twenty. You need all of them for Chopin. Two hundred and twenty chords, each one of them exerting a force of around 175 pounds—we had just learned that. Do the math: nearly eighteen tons of tension in total. The nerves of the beast. At that point all you need is one error, no matter how tiny, a faulty grip, a crack in the steel, and anything could happen. Which is to say the worst. Especially if the gods intervene . . . (Sigh.) I approached. The sneaky little girl escaped her Papa's vigilance and sidled over to where the two workers were leaning over the instrument. She stood on her tiptoes to see . . . I saw nothing. I remember only the sound. A whistling. A sort of sharp humming. Vibrating air. The lash of the whip, the arrow that splits the skies at the speed of lightning. It also reminded me of the sound produced by my mother's lungs in the final moments of her death . . ."

She gently brushes her cheek against the boy's palm. But nothing fades, neither the memory nor the remorse.

"Nice lesson, huh? . . . One of the strings snapped. One out of the two hundred and twenty. It lashed me, lacerated me. It flayed my skin down to the bone. And that's how the mean little girl was scarred. By steel. For life."

The nocturne finishes.

"It was, apparently, the F string."

The cortege stops.

"And if . . . And if . . . And if . . ."

How to know what could have been?

She turns her gaze once more towards the mausoleum. A fitting end to the scene would be for the lovers to rouse themselves, sit up, and walk, happily, arm in arm, for everyone to see, away from this spot, cross through the gates and leave the dead behind them.

"We reap what we sow," she says. "But do we sow what we reap?"

He has no response to give her. She removes his hand from her cheek. Before giving it back to him, she kisses his palm. He shivers.

It will soon be night. The boulevards are deserted. It's possible they're the last visitors. The last standing.

The boy scans the surrounding tombs. So, so many tombs. The plaques. The inscriptions. All is summarized there: a name, two dates. A parenthesis. But if there is no name, no dates, who takes us in their arms, who cradles us: oblivion?

"Let's go back," she says.

And the two of them grow distant and walk through the gates, leaving the dead behind them.

THAT YEAR MONTENEGRO and its allies in the Balkan League declare war on the Ottoman Empire.

That year marks the end of the war between the Ottoman Empire and Italy.

That year New Mexico becomes the forty-seventh state of the United States of America.

That year in Fez, Morocco, the treaty is signed that assigns the major part of the Cherifien Empire's territory to the French Protectorate.

That year in Bloemfontein, South Africa, the South African Native National Congress is founded, and will soon become the African National Congress, whose purpose is to defend the rights and interests of the black majority within a country dominated by a white minority. The party will be outlawed in 1960, during apartheid, and will be classified as a terrorist organization by the United States twenty-five years later, under the mandate of president Ronald Reagan.

That year Alfred Lothar Wegener, German astronomer and climatologist, publishes his theory on continental drift.

In Seattle, in the United States, Minoru Yamasaki is born, the son of poor Japanese immigrants and future father of the twin towers of the World Trade Center in New York.

In Paris, France, the Bonnevay law authorizes the creation of the offices of affordable housing.

In Choisy-le-Roi, a crowd made up of dozens of police officers and gendarmes, two companies of the Republican Guard, an artillery regiment, hundreds of individuals armed with rifles and shotguns, and thirty thousand privileged spectators surrounds the pavilion where an anarchist named Jules Bonnot, thirty-five years old, has taken refuge. After hours of siege, amidst the hatred and jubilation of the people, the beast is subdued.

That year in Siberia, Russia, the tsar sends his troops to suppress a protest of workers on strike in the gold mines of Lena. The soldiers fire into the crowd: the total death count is estimated at between 150 and 270, according to various sources.

That year in Saint Petersburg, the Bolshevik journal *Pravda*, which translates to "The Truth," is founded.

At the Olympics in Stockholm, Sweden, in the semi-finals of Greco-Roman wrestling, the Russian Martin Klein defeats the Finnish Alfred Asikainen after eleven hours and forty minutes of competition. Exhausted, he forfeits the finals.

In Montreal, Canada, Louis Cyr, the strongest man in the world, capable, among other exploits, of carrying a platform weighing 4,337 pounds on his back, or even supporting a 530-pound weight on one finger, dies.

That year Arizona becomes the forty-eighth state of the United States of America.

In Los Angeles, California, Carl Laemmle, German immigrant, modest bookkeeper, invests his savings in cinematography and creates Universal Studios.

In Lawrence, Massachusetts, the workers of the textile factories of the American Woolen Company protest, all their demands condensed into a slogan inspired by a James Oppenheim poem: "Bread and Roses."

In Boulogne-Billancourt, France, the workers of the Renault automobile factory go on strike in protest against the timekeeper, another cog in the system of production inspired by a method put in place by the American engineer Frederick Winslow Taylor.

In Division, Pas-de-Calais, a methane explosion in one of the pits of the La Clarence Mining Company causes seventy-nine deaths and twenty-three injuries. Twelve of the victims are younger than fifteen years old, the youngest is thirteen.

In Nogent-sur-Marne, a crowd of dozens of police and gendarmes, a company of the Republican Guard, two battalions of Zouaves, hundreds of individuals armed with rifles and shotguns, and a hundred thousand spectators rush from all the surrounding areas, on foot, on horse, on bike, in taxis, to surround the pavilion where the anarchists René Valet, twenty-one, and Octave Garnier, twenty-two, have taken refuge. After ten hours of siege, amidst the hatred and jubilation of the people, the beasts are subdued. The forces of order cannot contain the human mob that rushes in: they stomp on the still-warm cadavers, they plunder the house, they collect the casings and the bullets and the tiniest debris, to keep as a souvenir or sell to the highest bidder. The elegant dip their handkerchiefs in the blood. In Octave Garnier's pocket they find these words:

Let's reflect. Our women and our children pile up in hovels while thousands of villas remain empty. We build palaces and we live in shacks. Worker, develop your life, your intelligence and your strength. You are a sheep: the sergeants are dogs and the bourgeois are shepherds. Our blood pays for the luxury of the rich. Our enemy is our master. Long live anarchy.

That year in Munich, Germany, Eva Braun comes into the world.

In Berlin, the Social Democrats of the SPD win the Reichstag elections with 34.8% of the vote. The liberals, frightened by this socialist push, refuse any alliance. The radical conservatives talk of "Jewish elections."

That year the Nobel Prize for medicine is awarded to Alexis Carrel, a brilliant French doctor capable, among other feats, of maintaining the beating heart of a chicken in vitro for between twenty-eight and thirty-seven years, according to sources. Later, in a celebrated attempt, Alexis Carrel will introduce and develop a model of society founded on eugenics, advocating selection through genetics, re-education by the whip, and the pure and simple elimination of the handicapped, murderers, and other individuals afflicted with any physical, intellectual, or social defect, those capable of delaying the accession of the perfect human race.

That year in Pyongyang, Korea, Kim Il-sung, founder, director, Great Leader and eternal President of North Korea, is born.

In Lyon, France, Henri Grouès, whom society's collective mind will remember as Abbé Pierre, is born.

That year Maurice Barrès, writer, deputy Boulangist, nationalist, president of the League of Patriots, anti-Dreyfusard, anti-Semite, and member of the Académie Française, refuses to vote for the loans that the government wants to allocate to the celebration of the bicentennial of the birth of Jean-Jacques Rousseau, claiming that one cannot honor a man that he considers to be the spiritual father of a certain Jules Bonnot and his band.

That year Pierre Rousseau, forty-eight years old, head chef; Auguste Coutin, twenty-eight years old, entrée chef; Claude Janin, twenty-nine years old, potager; Pierre Villarlange, nineteen years old, assistant potager; Alphonse Vicat, nineteen years old, poissonier; Louis Dornier, twenty years old, assistant poissonier; Adrien Chaboisson, twenty-five years old, rotisseur; Marcel Cornaire, nineteen years old, assistant rotisseur ; Georges Jouannault, twenty-four years old, assistant saucier; Henri Jaillet, twenty-eight years old, pastry chef; Louis Desvernine, twenty years old, assistant pastry chef; Jean Pachéra, nineteen years old, assistant entremetier; Maurice Debreucq, eighteen years old, assistant server; and Jean Baptise Blumet, twenty-six years old, dishwasher, perish off the coast of Newfoundland, at 41° 46' N latitude and 50° 14' W longitude, in the shipwreck of the unsinkable transatlantic liner baptized *Titanic*.

GENESIS DOES NOT SPECIFY what it is. The battle rages on among the scriptural experts. The pomologists, serious and reasonable men, don't get involved (none of them would dare call a fruit "forbidden"). The date, the grape, the fig, the pomegranate, sometimes even the cherry are proffered. Curiously, never the pêche, peach, as a symbol of *peché*, sin. The most commonly accepted idea is the apple. If it is an apple, all they'd have to do is reach up. Their garden is nothing but a vast orchard. The temptation is great.

The century is twelve years old, the boy eighteen. Hand to the fire. This hand, in fact, the same one that the young woman placed against her cheek one evening among the tombs. Now life is carrying him along.

Since then there has been another summer and a fall and a winter. Seasons without hell. As ephemeral as petals. Full and crescent moons. There were other books and other readings, face-to-face or shoulder-to-shoulder, their heads bent, their hair mingling, mixing, suddenly standing on end due to brief electrical discharge. There were other bursts of laughter. Other urges. Other treks. In the city, in the fields. Bridges crossed, picnics and siestas in the oases of greenery. Baths in the river. There were other tarts. Other recipes. Other whispers. Other concerts, in public, in halls, on balconies, beneath the gilding, beneath the high and large cupolas with luxurious clusters of hanging lights and their thousand shining crystal beads, and there was their own little chamber music, exclusive, intimate, exclusive, distilled by the monastic but warm glow of candles in the dedicated room, the quasi-altar, of their apartment on Boulevard du Temple.

You can count on the fingers of one hand (this hand, the same one) the hours they didn't spend together.

And the night doesn't interrupt any of this. The nights. One and many. Having crossed the threshold of darkness, they find each other again. Reunite. Each one asleep in their room, in their bed, alone, they don't leave each other. Their dreams are porous. They close their eyes and it's worse. As soon as the prayers are over, the shadows come. The shadows? But how bright they are, how luminous, and how lifelike, so lifelike, the succubus or the incubus, it depends, that visited each of them. Tender are the male's scratches, traversing the entire territory of the young woman, her hills, her valleys. Tender and abundant is the female's fleece of hair, in which the boy is enveloped, indulged, the heady odor intoxicating him. All that and more. Behind the covers of their eyelids, in the enclave of their dreams, under veil of secrecy, she tells him what she cannot not tell him, he does to her what he cannot not do to her. Is it really an illusion? A chimera? For the effects are certainly real. Their nerves, their muscles taut in sleep. And the abrupt contractions in the stomach. And the stabbing pain in the small of the back. The convulsions. And the torpor that follows.

In the morning they're exhausted, bodies worn out and clammy, minds in a daze, while their rumpled sheets show the proof of a feverish tussle, a suave calvary.

Brother Éros, sister Oniris: infernal couple. Souls divinely damned.

We can count the nights they don't spend together on the devil's cloven hooves.

What to do about it? Remember the petrified lovers: the molten lava the arteries transport can't be stopped. No more than the booming clouds. We can't tame the volcano.

They fought, they lost.

There's nothing left for them to do but savor their defeat.

It happens for the first time in the kitchen of their Parisian apartment. A Sunday. Early afternoon. Spring blossoms. From day to day the sun spreads, and the heat. Good old Gustave is in the living room, in his armchair, dozing after his meal. His spectacles balance at the end of his nose, a folded newspaper rests on his stomach. He snores softly.

Standing in front of the sink, Emma and the boy do the dishes. A tub of frothy water, another of clear water. She washes and scrubs, he rinses and dries. They're used to it. The routine is well established, their hearts and gestures light. Nothing weighs on those who share the load. As usual, she's humming. It's Verdi, Giuseppe. An Italian tune. Between the splashing and the clanging of the glassware and the rubbing of the sponge, we recognize snippets of *Rigoletto*. The young woman wears a white silk chiffon tunic adorned with a corsage of honeycomb lace. Over it a short cotton apron cinches her waist, also white. A virginal white. That's all she wears. She looks like a maid and also like a wife. Like a child taking first communion, a novice touched by grace. At this moment she could be one or the other, whichever she chooses. *La donna è mobile.* The flowing fabric veils and unveils her body, transparently. Is this why the boy has been wall-eyed recently? Sweat beads on his forehead, which he wipes regularly with his forearm. Minutes pass like this. Verdi. The aria. A spring Sunday in the peninsula, in Calabria or Campania, in Mantua, Venice, Verona, in Naples in the sulfurous shadow of Vesuvius. The aquatic minuetto of silverware and dishes. The bubbles. She washes, he rinses. And it could have wrapped up nicely like that, but no. Things topple suddenly, and life spins out of control.

All it takes is a little nothing. The boy is a little restless, distracted. The muslin dish rag lends itself to clumsiness. After the last plate, the rag slips from his grasp and falls into the tub. Immediately he pulls it back out, disgusted, holds it in the air between his thumb and index finger, as if he had just fished some filth out of the river, some nasty insect, a dead rat, and he turns towards her with an expression at once nauseated and contrite. She stops humming and bursts out laughing. Then smiles at him. Big oaf. She lightly lifts a portion of her apron and presents it to him, so that he can wipe himself on it. The boy leaves the rag soaking in a corner of the sink. He moves his hands towards her and grabs the cotton and it's in this movement that everything happens. Here. Now. It's just a fleeting touch, but the fabric is so fine that he feels it: beneath the apron the tunic, and beneath the tunic the secret little hill, the mound, soft and fertile, and beneath his fingers the moss that grows there. She feels it too, evidenced by that jolt and the sort of hiccup that she can't hold back. And of course in the seconds that follow they freeze, petrified (remember the lava, the veins, the volcano) and more long seconds go by and stretch in the silence, heavy now, charged, fully formed, while they both remain absolutely immobile, like two dogs in a standoff, breathless, throats dry, looking into each other's eyes, confounded by the same stupor, the same exquisite panic, seized by the same urge and the same fear and the same desire to succumb to it, and their ears start to ring, and the temperature rises, and the heat burns their cheeks and surrounds their foreheads and temples.

One date, two names. Written in the sky with fiery letters.

And it's Emma who makes the first move. *Bella figlia dell'amore.* And it's Emma who sets herself in motion. Who commands her pelvis to move forward with a sudden momentum (oh! slowly, very slowly at first). Who approaches him. Who reaches him. The boy is still holding the apron tightly in a ball in his left fist. His other hand (this hand, the same one) is free. Slips under the cotton. He only has to open it, he only has to unfurl his fingers to receive what she has to offer him. Which he does. And his skin brushes the material, once again. But already she is withdrawing. She retreats, once more. Then she comes back. She leaves again. She comes back. Like one testing bathwater before sliding in. Too hot, too cold. Come back, leave again. A swing in the garden, beneath the branches of an acacia tree. Sorcerer's pendulum. Ticking in double time, two beats per measure, two pulses. Largo. It's the cycle of moons and tides. Push and pull. An ocean to drink up, but honey, syrup, nectar. And this slow, this very slow to-and-fro, lasts and lasts.

Standing in front of the sink.

Is it still a dream?

The boy doesn't move. Their eyes stay riveted to each other. Their lips are squeezed tight. A hoarse sound emerges from Emma's throat. A sort of growl. She breathes loudly. The air chirps, whistles through her nostrils like an excess of steam. Her chest rises and with it the lid of the sky. Closed, open. Shadows, light. Go, come back. Go . . . And then suddenly a blunt thrust of her hips. Her pubis juts out. She plasters herself, crushes herself against him. He holds her. That's it. In his palm. He envelops her. So tight is the silk that it counts for nothing. He feels her beneath his fingers, beneath the flesh of his fingertips, everything, the mount and the moss, the spring, the furrow, the other furrow, the other scar, far deeper and softer. He feels it spread open, split like a ripe fig, or a date, a pomegranate, an apricot, a fruit, whatever it is, whose juice flows abundantly, and all that juice that bathes, soaks, permeates the fabric and her skin within it, streams in a trickle along Emma's legs, descends, licks, caresses the inside of her thighs, then her calves, then her ankles. He doesn't move. It's her. She's the one who moves, who rubs, low to high, high to low, her movements becoming more and more rapid, crescendo, allegro, movement that is no longer a swing but a file, an emery board, a saw, the cadence of a lumberjack at work—but who is the blade and who is the trunk? He watches her. She is beautiful. He's never seen anything more beautiful. Emma the brunette. Lovely Emma. Her mouth, her forehead, her eyes. Her eyes are fixed, a veil, something thinner and more translucent than the muslin makes them gleam, her irises, her retinas shine like diamonds. She rubs. *Più mosso. Più moto.* At the back of her throat the rumbling intensifies. At her feet the little puddle spreads. She rubs, she files, she saws, *prestissimo. Con fuoco.* And then suddenly the blade pierces through the trunk, pierces the bark, the pulp, the flesh, everything, from her stomach to her shoulders, a wave shakes her, overwhelms her, her eyelids close, her teeth bite her lower lip until it bleeds, her neck tenses, her body buckles, reflexively she grabs onto the edge of the sink so as not to collapse, while at the same moment the lava rises from the depths of the boy's loins and spurts in a series of burning jets. *A piacere*. It's the awakening. It's the eruption.

A spring Sunday in Italy.

But they have hardly any time to regain their footing. When their blood ebbs, when their eardrums come unblocked, right away they hear the scraping of soles, steps dragging, approaching. Gustave. He appears in the corridor, hair disheveled, white cowlicks on his head. He walks to the threshold and stops. His eyelids are heavy, still sleepy, his complexion rubicund. In the doorframe he looks at them for a few seconds while fanning himself with his newspaper. Then he says, his speech slurred:

"Is it just me, or is it stifling in here?"

THUS BEGINS A PERIOD that can only be described, without a doubt, as frenetic. They can't control themselves anymore. Everywhere, all the time. She gives and he takes and vice versa.

They love each other.

It is indeed love.

In the waning hours of that Sunday, among all that is blessed, they lose their virginities. In the middle of the night. The city is asleep. The boy walks down the corridor that separates them on his tiptoes. Ethereal, silent. (Here's the *Fauna Dansant*! And here *Liberté*!) He scratches at her door. She doesn't ask who it is. She opens the door for him. She has been waiting for him. Enter, my prince. A candle is lit on the bedside table. On the ground, a two-hundred-year-old rug that formerly covered the floor of the bedroom of a distant Flemish ancestor. Heavy, thick, deep like the humus of forests, a motif of roses and acanthus leaves, colors faded. It's there, for they are fearful of making the box springs squeak, that the hymn of the hymen plays out. Rests and *fermate*. No, they're not dreaming anymore. It's real. Angels and demons are incarnated, and their shadows move, crawl, and commingle on the floor in all their splendid nudity. In the morning a new flower, bloomed, spreads its scarlet petals amid her ancestor's ancient roses.

It's only the beginning.

What happens next is an explosion.

Opportunity makes the thief, and these two make their own opportunities. Each room of the apartment is thus baptized. And each corner of the house in Toussus-le-Noble. And in their intimate geography there is not a square inch of skin, not a section of flesh, not a molecule or an atom that is not transformed into an incandescent erogenous zone. Pores, hair, flesh all fan the flames. The spirit is aroused, blood boils and passions flow, are expressed, let loose at will. The décor varies; their bodies are the true theater of their concupiscence.

So many performances! So many acts!

There is no censorship, there are no shackles to restrict them except Gustave's gaze. They take care to avoid it. Gustave doesn't know. He doesn't suspect a thing, and his daughter and his adoptive son make sure it stays that way. It's fair to ask: is the charade driven by real moral concern, something atavistic? Or is it simply a pinch of spice that enhances the secret? The nature of one's motivation in posing such a question reveals a certain corruption within the person who's posed it. (And incidentally, in the infamous story, from which all others allegedly stem, who is more perverse: the one who grows the fruit and risks its consumption by a non-believer, asking him to not taste it at all—a cruel edict—or the one who ends up sinking his teeth into it? Who is more vicious: the tempter or the tempted?) Let it be known that they are pure! Their desire is pure, their hearts are pure, their souls are pure. Without this profound and veritable innocence, they would be incapable of offering themselves with such fervor, with such liberty, incapable of embodying this nearly total absence of restraint. They inhabit a wholly terrestrial paradise, and they stay there. Protected. The time has not yet come for them be expelled from it. The curse has not yet been pronounced, the terrible and unjust anathema. No supreme entity blames them, no angels pass over their heads. Or do they simply not see them? Blind to the eyes of their judges. They don't look for excuses, no justification for their behavior—does the bird have to explain why it flies? The lion why it roars? Remorse and repentance are foreign to them. They don't atone. They have nothing to declare besides a phenomenal cargo of hormones at the bottom of the hold. A different kind of confession.

Neither god nor master when all is said and done. Anarchy of the senses. A joyous mess. As soon as their father has his back turned, they get to it. They ruse, invent, improvise or organize in order to draw out the best of all the possibilities that present themselves. All the moments, all the precious minutes stolen, snatched, and all those hours royally decreed, all their existence's free time henceforth dedicated to this single goal, devoted to this sole project: pleasure.

Give rise to it. Nurture it. Then relish it.

Their appetite is ferocious. And the hunger, they both understand, justifies the means. Thus "do the dishes" becomes, in Emma's mouth, a sort of password, a key opening a chamber of delicacies. As soon as she has pronounced these words, they become aroused. Never has the world seen such haste, such enthusiasm for this chore as displayed by the two of them. It's only one example of many.

Another: piano lessons. As if by accident, they begin again. Regular and constant—that at least, yes! It's obvious that the music is nothing but a pretext. It's no longer about acquiring skill in this domain. The boy will not be a virtuoso nor even a humble player. But at least during those hours they have the leisure of being alone, cloistered between four walls. A godsend. They take advantage of it. The boy takes his seat on the bench, Emma at his side. And while, clumsy, awkward, he begins to abuse the keys with his ten fingers, a skilled and slender hand works its way in, below. It's no longer the student's posture or the positioning of his wrists that she corrects, but another part of his anatomy. And it works this time! His form is impeccable. His stature perfect. And when she increases the exercise's intensity and leans over him and comes into contact with his instrument? Music lovers, protect your ears! Because the boy, elbows rounded, lifted high, in the uncouth posture of a playful bear, persists in crushing his paws on the ivory, creating clusters of agglomerated notes at random, torrents of repetitive and discordant harmonies that display no grace, except perhaps many years later to the ears of a handful of serialism enthusiasts.

Meanwhile, they assassinate Mozart! They deafen Beethoven! But amidst all of this, in stark contrast, an entirely different melody plays, a recorder, a clarinet, a cornet, a slide trombone, as harmonious as the other is dissonant, as exquisite as the other is execrable. Scales and arpeggios at will. Broad range. Such dexterity! Such smoothness! Such audacity in the execution!

So is this the famous Méthode Rose? In the hands of beginners, it seems. Devilishly efficient. Almost every afternoon, Emma and the boy perform it diligently. Never has anyone seen a more studious student, nor a more meticulous professor.

But it's still in the summer, in their island, beneath their willow, that their sensuality really takes flight.

The place is ideal, everything they need. Here they are children beneath the maternal skirts of the tree. Here they are princes reigning beneath a majestic canopy. A sultan and his favorite concubine beneath the palm leaves of an oasis. Lovers in the darkness of an enclosed bedroom, blinds lowered, sheltered from the eyes of snoops and the tongues of vipers (only the quiet quacking of rails and mallards).

In this chosen place they surrender.

The sweetness of the air, the murmur of the waves, the playful light brings exquisite pleasure. And, with all due respect to Verlaine, their languor is not monotonous.

Love, the big everything.

ALTHOUGH MUCH OLDER, Emma does not possess any more experience than the boy. They discover and explore together. Empirical learning at first: touching and tasting and smelling—the boy now understands the ogre's advice—and listening and observing and practicing often, three or four or five times in a row and more than a hundred, more than a thousand repetitions over time. No reticence. No restrictions. Together they learn, and they learn quickly. Determined seekers, willing guinea pigs. Master and disciple in turns. Companions in fortune. They mutually instruct, and what joy they have in filling their shortcomings and gaps. It's good and noble raw material that they mine and fashion, a supple and malleable clay, as elastic as can be. They make, unmake, do, redo. Strengthened by a curiosity without limits and the hunger of wolves, which is also greed, which is also gluttony, and which seems insatiable. This is why there are those, always the same hypocrites and wet blankets, who cannot stop themselves from wondering, in bitter tones, if this quest isn't endless, condemned to an eternal dissatisfaction, a failure for centuries and centuries, like Sisyphus and his consorts, it's undeniable, isn't it? A damned shame that they don't have anything more exalting to propose than this frenzied search for bliss to fill the bottomless pit of their miserable existence. And if they do, why not share it with everyone else? For if it's only about preparing oneself to die, it cannot really be taken seriously.

The lovers are off, nothing can restrain them. Even the sky itself is not up to the task of reversing the trend. As proof, a shower is sent to them in the middle of the month of August and in the middle of their transport. Like a bucket of water over dogs in heat. They couldn't care less. They revel in it.

They are naked beneath the willow. Standing. Her leaning, chest forward, bottom thrust back, offering the most beautiful view there is of her roundness, and him behind, anchored to her hips, those sublime curves, womanly gifts, angelic bays, those beaches, those coves where one drops anchor, pirate and buccaneer, corsair, smuggler, fisher of pearls or thief of amphora, to accost and find refuge inside those lands.

The boy has plunged deep.

From a distance, through the curtain of frayed branches, they resemble a strange Minotaur. She holds on to the tree, she embraces the trunk while he embraces her neck, she bites the bark while he bites her neck. And it's in this moment, a sudden roll of thunder. The clouds are tallow-gray, a daytime night that surprises them. They didn't see it coming. The first drop, heavy, pierces their perforated roof and runs down Emma's back. A long shiver runs through her, from her shoulders down to the tops of her thighs, adding a novel nuance, an unprecedented sensation to her sweetness. Then another drop follows, and another, heavy, like tears of resin falling from the willow (Is it crying, their dear tree? With joy? With elation?) and hitting her spine with a little suction sound, from the edges that gradually come unglued, and then with a sinister crack the skies split open and it's a shower. Torrents, waterfalls pelt down onto them. But far from curbing their ardor it seems, to the contrary, to heighten it. She pushes on his arms to stretch herself even more. He tightens his grip and penetrates deeper, harder. The elements unleash and so do they. They are the squall. They are the storm. Rolling waves of thunder shake the earth to its foundations. The tree quivers at its roots. The ground vibrates beneath their feet. The phosphorescent flashes illuminate the dark bedroom where they play, captured, immortalized for a brief moment in their bestial postures, in their scowls and their grimaces, like flashes of magnesium in a tabloid photo. He grunts, she pants, she moans, he gasps, and all these sounds melt into the din that surrounds them. The rain streams over their bodies, it drips down their faces and over their eyes and blinds them. The water cascades between Emma's shoulder blades, hurtles down her spine before collecting in the curve of her lower back, forming a tiny pool, a miniature lagoon, the boy leans over and wets his lips, and licks and laps and drinks. His thirst is immense. She begs. He gives. He accelerates. She scratches the trunk. He scratches her flesh. The storm intensifies. The flashes blaze. She demands. He pounds. He crushes. They are torrential waterfalls. They are torment. She shines. He radiates. The clouds unload. The sky empties itself. Still they want more. They are the deluge. They are nature. And it's in an ultimate crash of thunder, immaculate, that their cry explodes and disappears.

Oh, creator of all species, multiply your bounty.

Day after night, stone after stone, they construct an ark of exquisite pleasure, a palace, they erect a kingdom. It's a world of passion. Their world. A universe in the heart of which, of their own free will, they withdraw and imprison themselves.

Félix, my love. My lover.

She says Félix again and again, in every tone. The boy finds himself there. In the end he doesn't really care, she could call him Primrose or Vinegar or Pimple as long as it's her calling to him, as long as it's him she's talking about.

She says things like Take me. Spread me. Split me. Penetrate me. Eat me. Drench me. And he takes and splits and eats, and he adds to it as he likes without her asking.

Their universe is expanding. And they grow with it. They evolve. They change. In the immense boiling pot, in the mysterious recipe, in the nebulous potion that brings them to ecstasy, they throw in new ingredients. Over time their innocence evaporates. Sublimates. Their taste sharpens. Imagination decants. From the sugary sweetness of the beginning succeeds the fire of spices. They sprinkle. They vary.

Alternating good old popular and rustic dishes (those that stuff, those that fill) with the refinements of gourmet cuisine. Tradition and gastronomy. The menu expands, and to end this culinary metaphor let's say that they are capable after a few months of offering up a complete menu to the sturdiest stomachs and the most demanding taste buds: from aperitif to digestif, without skipping over the entremet or *trou normand*—ah! the trou normand!

It contains a certain amount of sport and malice. They are brats, insolent, cheeky, but so endearing, adorable rascals for whom love-making and merrymaking go together. Gavroches in their sexual revolution. Their flag flies in the winds of joy. Lust is a celebration, it's a merry-go-round, a Ferris wheel, a roller coaster, it's a flare blinding the night. They never stop laughing. They enjoy themselves. Precocious libertines who abide by no rules, no limits other than those set in the moment.

She loves his semen. She likes its taste, its texture. She likes to make it show itself, to extract it, collect it, feel it on her skin, impetuous milky bursts, spread it on her palm like a cream, a rich ointment, lubricate her stomach, polish the domes of her breasts with it, the tips of her nipples. She likes to take it in her mouth and keep it on her tongue, under her pallet, sample it like a rare liqueur, unctuous, an exceptional spirit. She likes to swallow it and feel it slide down her throat.

And he's not left out, he adores lying down, presenting himself at a perfect bisecting angle to the one she forms with the compass points of her legs wide open, pointing his nose towards the top and taking advantage of the stunning view offered by this position. He examines. He revels. He gently spreads the fine hair, those threads of black silk, tangled, shielding access to the temple of the goddess. He excavates and uncovers with the delicateness of an archeologist on a site that's sacred—or sacrilegious. This is where the world is born. The cradle of humanity. A treasure whose riches he never tires of searching for and rediscovering. His approach is slow and precise (she did not hesitate, the first few times, to guide him with her voice and gestures). He spreads her lips with his lips. Pink through and through. And below, in a hue barely more vibrant, the last frieze on the perimeter, here the nymphs, graceful, serrated, chiseled, like the wings of an emerging butterfly lightly traced—a half-peacock sphinx—in flight indefinitely, cast off. He caresses them, teases them with small strokes of the tongue, supple and sharp: a cat lapping its milk. The nymphs quiver. He blows, a trickle of taut and fresh air that wrests a sigh from the goddess and covers the walls of her thighs with a deliciously fleshy plaster. The angle of the compass grows. The branches spread. The corolla opens, coral red, wet, all shiny with a dew that he collects on his tongue, flat and smooth. Going back to the spring he finds the precious clitoris, the one and only, the rose bud concealed in the calyx and already engorged, saturated, gleaming, he forms a hood over it with his lips, pinches it softly, presses it, sucks it, breathes on it, he bevels it with his mouth, he polishes it with his saliva while his thumb simultaneously slips into the sanctuary and floods it, probes it, from the narthex to the apse, the vault to the crypt, and what is that voice they suddenly hear? It's her. It's the goddess herself, she cantillates, she extols, she implores, she begs and beseeches her servant to continue, these primitive incantations born in her stomach, the eternal prayer arises from her throat.

And the ceremony continues.

There is another game that they thoroughly enjoy. Emma baptized it the sexicon (derived from "sex" and "lexicon"). A dictionary in sum. Maybe it's her taste for words? Maybe it's her vocation as a teacher surfacing again, making its way through diverted paths and side roads? Her invented exercise consists quite simply of naming things. The maximum number of synonyms must be found for their quotidian names. But not for just anything: exclusively for parts of the human body. And among those only the ones that mark the difference between masculine and feminine—anatomically speaking.

Thus the game takes shape and grows complicated.

Dear mistress . . .

They play facing each other. They stand very close, like a full-length mirror of each other, with their skin as their only clothing. A half-minute of concentration, then:

"You may begin," she says.

A small look of defiance levels his face. The game begins. After a glance at the model opposite him and the variety of her landscape, the boy chooses. He places a hand (this same one or its twin, it depends), for example, on the young woman's breast. So be it. Very well. She lifts her chin, takes a breath and begins—it is agreed that she speaks on his behalf:

"My chest," she says. "My throat . . . My breasts . . . My nipples . . . My mammary glands . . . (Counting each added term on her fingers.) My teats . . . My hills . . . My shells—not of very big caliber, it's true! . . . My globes . . ."

And the boy trying to perturb her, distract her, make her lose her train of thought (she cannot repeat herself) through cheap tricks, through sly means like surreptitiously titillating her nipple, like insidiously rubbing her mauve and grainy areola.

" . . . My spheres . . . My buoys . . . My balloons . . . My hot-air balloons!"

And she stops there. Rather proud and breathless as though she'd been holding her breath for a long time.

"Twelve," she says. "Twelve to zero . . . My turn!"

No hesitation on her part: the masculine features are not as numerous and there is already one pointed beneath her nose. She quickly gets in position and grabs hold of it. Then begins again, playing for herself this time.

"Your rod," she says. "Your penis . . . Your phallus . . . Your nightingale—sing, nightingale, sing! . . . Your flute . . . Your candy cane . . . Your shaft . . . Your hummingbird—no, I take it back: a hummingbird is too small! . . . Your scepter . . . Your fishing pole . . . Your bludgeon . . . Your ax handle . . ."

But isn't she cheating a bit, nonchalantly accompanying each of these terms with a subtle milking motion, teat in hand? The boy appears completely discombobulated.

" . . . Your member . . . Your pine . . . Your branch . . . Your épée—what am I saying, your épée? Your saber! . . . Your gladiator sword . . . Your javelin . . . Your spear . . . Your fire hose . . . Your trunk . . . Your boa constrictor . . ."

Nouns so brazen, so evocative that sometimes the thing itself turns red and puffs up with importance.

" . . . Your tower . . . Your knob . . . Your broomstick—that witches straddle!" (Commentary is a bonus.) "Your spindle . . . Your corkscrew . . . Your maypole!"

When she stops abruptly, the object in question, as if swollen by the tributaries of all those denominations, has doubled, tripled in size. Emma's hand is full. Its eye sparkles. In a victorious, but nevertheless distracted tone, she announces:

"Thirty! Minus the hummingbird that flew away, that makes twenty-nine. I'm in the lead, and by far!"

Does he understand? Eyelids half-closed, vision blurred, lips hanging open, the boy wears an expression usually reserved for idiots and drunks. As though drool might soon flow over his chin. Without even realizing it he has taken over the movement she had started and that she had suspended at the end of her list. Now it's he who slides himself between his adversary's fingers: a sort of manual fellatio that plunges him into a euphoric stupor.

But she suddenly lets go, leaving him orphaned, lost, teetering at the edge of a precipice. The game isn't over.

"Your turn," she says. "You still have a chance to catch up to me."

With a brief swoon she points to the boy's palm, which he cups between her thighs. Then she catches her breath and starts up again:

"My vulva," she says. "My vagina . . . My cunt . . . My mound . . . My hole . . . My piggybank—slide a coin into the slot, little piggy! . . . My hold . . . My muff . . . My burning bush . . ."

She gradually weakens, her chest leaning slowly but surely towards him, and, following a parallel slope, her voice diminishes, becomes muted, hoarse, rasping, until it's just a gravelly murmur in the boy's ear.

" . . . My fissure . . . My vermilion rift . . . My pussy . . . My candy—oh, you like it, my candy, huh? You like to suck on it, don't you? . . . My doorway . . . My gap . . . My golden lyre—for you to play . . . My well . . . My cavern . . . My center—enter, that's right! Yes, go on! Enter my center, you scoundrel! . . ."

That's usually the last round. It's rare that they finish. The points get lost in the shuffle and in the end everyone wins. The lesson is complete: biology, anatomy, language. Their knowledge is increased. Their vocabulary is enriched. Undeniably they are improved. Learning in bliss: a highly pedagogic method that a number of learned bores, the old warts, would do well to take inspiration from.

There are constantly new entries in the dictionary of lovers. Selected terms, add-ons unknown to the outmoded provosts and other doddery old academic men. They're composing an original collection, flourishing, vibrant. But where do they fish for these words? Where they are: in the stream. And in books.

THROUGHOUT HISTORY, authors, and more than a few of them, out of
derision, out of fantasy, out of defiance, out of appetite, have dipped
their quills in the fountain of man—and of woman above all.

An excerpt:

> *Greetings, fat Whore, whose noisy gurgles*
> *Have engendered three generations of ejaculation,*
> *And whose old hands have fondled more balls*
> *Than there are golden stars in the constellations!*

Who wrote that?

Monsieur Guy de Maupassant. In a poem soberly titled: "69."
The next stanza, to save the best for last:

> *I love your fat breasts, your fat ass, your fat gut,*
> *Your belly button in the middle, black and hollow as a rut*
> *Where it accumulates the dust of time,*
> *Your damp and swollen skin, so like a pig's,*
> *And which so many pricks have pumped with jizz*
> *The sticky stuff oozes down your thighs!*

Incredible realism! As though you're there with them.

And then this one:

> *Her cunt no secret nor no mystery has,*
> *So on that night, I quickly took her ass.*

She was asleep, so I had to do it silently,
She never knew a thing, it was over in a flash.

And who is this?

The inescapable, indispensable, incomparable father of *Les Misérables*, the master of Parnassus himself: Victor Hugo. We recognize the temperament and the implacable meter, chanting his pelvic thrusts in this first quatrain of a parodic sonnet: "Le Sonnet d'Arvers . . . à revers."

No, this is not just second-rate cacography scribbled in a notebook. Rimbaud. Rimbaud, yes. The young King Arthur, enlightened prince, cursed archangel, he too turned his irreverence towards poetry into verses in which obscenity and mockery are spelled out with decadence and good-natured farce. See his "Stupra." See that black pearl—if one dares—inserted into the *Album zutique* that he created with his partner in crime Paul Verlaine and that they named "Sonnet of an Asshole" (*Dark and pleated like a violet carnation . . .*) and that Emma cannot recite to the boy without a ravishing turning up of the nostrils expressing both her disgust and her excitement (*Filaments like tears of milk . . .*) nor without biting her lips to suppress a budding laugh (*Cried, beneath the cruel wind that spurns them . . .*). We can envision them, the two genius schoolchildren, composing, laughing, a glass of absinthe or cheap wine in hand, playing around and throwing in each other's faces their Alexandrines, their enjambments, their caesuras, fashioning half-lines of empty measures that house their subjects (*Feminine Canaan in the enclosed moistness!*).

They just have to procure them. Literature overflows with these licentious pages. When the young lovers find themselves in Paris again—and free of Gustave's chaperoning—the first destination of their promenades changes: rather than gardens or cemeteries, henceforth they prefer the quays of the Seine. Romantic walks along the water? Absolutely not. The hunt for sorcerers and bookish monsters, fishing for the exiled and excommunicated: that's what draws them. They skim the book stalls on the banks, rummage through the boxes, search in this sheaf of old paper for a volume that morality has cast out and the law censured. For those works whose success is often guaranteed by an official condemnation. Clandestine publication, circulation—and reading—under the table, under the coat, under the skirt. Emma's fingers are dirty from letting them run over the dusty covers and spines, on the sepia sheets, sometimes completely stiff and covered with an ink that looks powdered. By the end of the day traces of anthracite smudge her skin as if she had rubbed the venomous petals of some flower of evil. She searches. The boy can only barely help her in this task but he is there, near her, if only to see her expression, the gleam of her face when she finds it, when she discovers the nugget, extracts it from the clutter, the gleam of her eyes when she looks towards him, book in hand—the printed promise of a deliciously delinquent moment—the look she gives him in that instant lights a flame in the most intimate regions of his being. For nothing in the world would he want to miss that.

When the quest remains fruitless it is sometimes necessary to specify the object to the bookseller, to ask him, to let him in on the secret in veiled terms ("You understand?" "Yes, young lady, I understand perfectly well . . .") for it's the kind of item that is not displayed carelessly, that is often hidden behind boxes in backrooms, under piles, in secret false bottoms, and then with a bit of luck the gentleman speedily unearths the hidden treasure and just as speedily pockets his payment and they return, Emma and the boy, on the alert and hearts racing, towards the discreet corner where they can at leisure lean over their latest acquisition.

One morning they set out, carrying in their pocket—or rather in a basket, hidden beneath a voluminous bundle of leeks—a very beautiful octavo entitled *Le Portier des Chartreux*, whose dark cover in onager-skin gives away nothing of the bacchanals that unfurl within, imagined by a certain Gervaise de Latouche. ("Latouche . . . Latouche . . . Just his name makes your mouth water," she says, the cheeky girl. "And when I say mouth . . .") Another day, they carry, beneath a bed of asparagus, a numbered edition (14 of 110) from an 1845 publication (CHEZ UN BOURGEOIS DE PARIS—Rue du Coq Hardi) of *Gamiani ou Deux nuits d'excès*, a novel long published anonymously, finally attributed to Alfred de Musset, and phenomenally successful ("The most reprinted book of the last century!" said the buxom bookseller on quay Saint-Michel with an emphatic wink), whose reading and rereading and re-rereading struck the boy with a painful priapism and kept them coming back to it for a good fortnight straight.

Disappointments are not very frequent. They found Ovid rather boring; there was nothing in *Ars amatoria* that they didn't already know. As soon as she read it Emma resold the volume, at a loss—not a big loss, she estimated. The antiques, the classics, Latin and Greek primarily, and everything more than three centuries old, seemed to them outmoded, if not in content at least in form. The eroticism too allusive. What they want, what they hope for is flesh and muscle. Raw. Crude terms, phrases without embellishment and without diversion, expositions in full light, detailed scenes, illustrations that illustrate. Nothing allegorical, nothing clinical—or as little as possible.

Left bank, right bank, the booksellers spread the word. They now recognize the young lady and her . . . (her what? valet? gigolo? porter? stallion?) ambling along the quays. Regarding her, there is rife speculation. Countess, some bet. Or duchess or baroness or some other titled noble who wants to remain anonymous. Others imagine she's the wife of a representative of the Chamber. ("And quite the chamber. Ha! Ha! Ha!") The mistress perhaps. A courtesan. A socialite, or socialist. A Cléo, a Liane, an Otéro. A rich heiress. A defrocked nun. A neurotic.

A pervert. A nymphomaniac. An erotomaniac. A priestess of black masses. But in any event, business is business, and she is above all a valued customer. She pays cash and doesn't haggle. They set aside the books that might interest her. They grab her in passing to show her their latest finds. ("One of a kind, take a look! Unobtainable!") They adopt mischievous or conspiratorial tones. They try—once, not twice—to pull the wool over her eyes. The young lady is not a fool. She also knows how to say no.

And then one day Emma gets wind of an address. A knowledgeable collector mentioned it to her (whispered it to her, on the sly, like a password between insiders). It's a bookstore, Rue Chadenat. Rare books. She and the boy go immediately. They walk in circles for a half hour before finding it. No sign, only a metallic plaque the size of a business card under an awning, its oxidized copper letters illegible. They have to pass through the doorway. They have to cross an interior courtyard where the crabgrass dislodges the cobblestones. They have to climb the front steps made of three large slabs of cracked stone. They have to push a tall glazed door coated in a layer of dust thicker than the glass itself and which doesn't let in, nor let escape, the least bit of light. No doorbell, no chime announcing the entrance of a client, nothing other than the sinister meowing of the door on its hinges. Then the silence of the interior, and the darkness.

No one.

What happens then is a mystery.

For you remain there, in place, frozen. Incapable of taking another step. Incapable of retracing your steps though the desire suddenly takes over you. Too late. You know it. The die is cast. The magic spell. You feel your free will annihilated. Incapable of opening your mouth, of hailing or coughing to signal your presence—sacrilege, any noise that you produce. Your very presence seems supernumerary and of a total incongruity. You barely breathe. You wish you could suspend the flow of blood through your veins, the drum of your heart resounding so loudly. You scrutinize the shadows and you are at the mercy of what you hope and dread to see emerge.

Then the shadows open. They fade. Or is it that you recover your sight? Little by little a dull, dusty halo, dawn of a gray day rises or falls—we don't know, we don't understand where this gleam comes from. Night dilutes and beneath your eyes the décor takes shape and relief. You think first of a chapel. But the dark perimeter continues to enlarge, to recede, the borders of the shadows are pushed further back, and you think of a cathedral. The Lord. Such are the dimensions of the place. Such are the proportions. A room, a hall, unique and monumental. And pillars, columns of books. Benches, racks of books. Stalls, corridors, passageways, mazes of books. You think of a pigsty. You think of a gigantic cabinet of literary curiosities. And it's this, it's all of this. You raise your head, following, scaling the shelves with your eyes, the stacks, the successive strata of books, and you reach the arcade, the gallery bordering the three walls, and from there rises a new floor, a new cliff, a new steep incline of books that lose themselves up above in the realms that vertigo forbids you from measuring. Prudently you go back down the corniche and move along it carefully and circumspectly, but despite all your precautions you tremble and nearly drop when there in the middle you pass two charcoal orbs—eyes!—black and yet ardent, observing you.

You think of the barn owl in the forest.

You think of the devil on his throne.

Your heart beats, you blink a few times, and the dark embers disappear.

The man—for it's certainly a man, it has to be, it could not be otherwise—moves. In the twists and turns of paper you don't see him. You don't hear him. It's by his odor that you are able to track him. Bitter, unpleasantly sweet aromas that you associate with a kind of poisonous mushroom or some decomposing organic tissue. But it's too late. He

233

is there. He is already there, facing you. Though you were on the alert, you jump again. You shiver. The Lord. Horror and disgust steel your heart. Fascination transfixes you.

What is it?

You think (Emma thinks) of a satyr, a gnome. He has the look of the first, the stature of the second. You think (the boy thinks) of a bat, a vampire. And instinctually he closes his fist as if around a bludgeon.

The man—for he is one, no matter what you might think—is dressed in black from head to toe. A loose, shapeless article of clothing covers him, a coat or frock or canvas sack. Black boots and black gloves hide his extremities. Only his face emerges: brown.

He's of mixed blood. Diverse heritages. But not one of those magnificent specimens most often obtained through the harmonious mixing of races and pigments. Alas no. You think of a mongrel. You think of a cruel joke of nature. Of a ruined experiment. Of a residue. Of the dregs. Of an ugly duckling.

The man—yes, the man, get that through your skull—is small in fact. He is ugly. He is skinny, bony, stooped, disfigured, and he stinks.

But that's not all.

If you look closer. If you manage not to turn your eyes away. If you make an effort. If you suppress your nausea and dare to stare at him, you will notice how his poor face is ravaged. Wounds sully it. Rosacea or ash-colored blemishes devastate it. Crevices deform it. Here and there dead skin flakes off like old scales. Hideous and reptilian sloughed skin.

You think (the boy thinks) of a burn victim.

You think (Emma thinks) of a leper.

Backing away, you think again of the gloves, the shadow, the silence of the place. The solitude. You think you understand, but you are mistaken. And you will probably always be mistaken, not ever knowing the whole story, namely: lupus.

The Big Bad Wolf.

But that's not all.

Look again. More, further. Swallow once more this spurt of bile that rises in your throat and plumb those eyes that plumb you. Behind the charcoal, behind the embers, behind the ashes, do you see?

There is something—a tiny gleam, an ultimate flash—expressing both derision and misery. Is this what they call the irony of despair? It's a morose and silent sarcasm. The manifestation of the consciousness of a condition that is excessively and inexorably painful. The poignant smile of the dying clown. It's something profoundly human. Something that determines humanity. Something that is, yes—much more than the laugh—unique to man. His very essence.

Now you can no longer have any doubts.

The man—for the third time, the man—clearly knows the effects caused by his odor and his appearance. He stands six feet away. He stares at Emma, ignoring the boy. His gaze and what it contains does not allow for pity. He says nothing. He waits.

Slowly Emma comes back to herself. The strong impression settles down, her free will fortifies. It's no longer so much the evil charm, the gnawing, irrational terror, that keeps her in a state of muteness and inertia, but a type of embarrassment, of shame, the feelings surrounding a request that's inappropriate for this particular interlocutor. Is she going to bring up in front of him the texts in praise of pleasure, is she going to speak of odes to ecstasy and delight to this being who is eaten away by cankers?

Suddenly the boy grabs her elbow: he wants to leave. This contact makes her shudder for a third time. But rattles her, makes up her mind, too. She clears her throat and begins, all at once she exposes, explains, describes the type of books she's searching for. The words are precise, the flow taut. It takes her less than a minute.

The man listens to her, impassive. After she's done, another minute goes by. The boy doesn't let go of her elbow. Then the man says:

"The divine Marquis."

His voice is not the least of the surprises. They had been expecting it to be meek, nasal; it's full and deep, almost smooth. Perhaps he is possessed. Perhaps there is a second creature deep inside him.

The fine line of Emma's brow breaks.

"Pardon?"

The man then—and for this they were even less prepared—cracks an imperceptible smile. Just a hint. Just the edge that rises on the horizon—behind the ruins of his face.

"Sade," he says. "Donatien Alphonse François de Sade. Based on what you said, he's the author that I think will best correspond to your yearnings."

"Yes," says Emma. "I'm familiar with him."

Lie. Pride. She has never heard the name.

"Sade," she repeats.

"*Justine, or The Misfortunes of Virtue*," says the man.

"Perfect."

"The edition I'm thinking of," says the man, "is an exceptional piece. Anonymous publication. From La Haye, the workshop of Laurent Demuink, bookseller. Fake name, fake address, naturally. Small folio illustrated with a frontispiece and eighteen engravings in intaglio. Cover in light calfskin. Spine in five loops decorated with geometric shapes and golden jewels. Frontispieces covered in triple golden threads and woven flowers. Endpapers of pink Tabis, geometric wheels framing the inside covers. All the pages gilded. A bookplate of ink on flyleaf: 'By Comte Charles Caissot de Chiusi.' And the most remarkable part: a personal autograph signed by the author."

Emma acquiesces. Approves of the proprietor as a connoisseur. She will not tell him that she is not a bibliophile, that the vial doesn't excite her much, only the perfume, the elixir, only the intoxication.

"Can we see it?" she asks.

"No," says the man.

"No? Why not?"

"Because it is not in my possession."

"You don't have it?"

"I will have it," says the man, "have no fear. On the condition that you are certain of wanting to acquire it."

"I would like it," says Emma.

"It comes at a price," says the man.

"I'll pay it."

"A price in accordance with its exceptional character," says the man.

"Don't worry about that," says Emma. "I have the necessary means."

Once again the smile—a trickle, a blade. After which for the first time the man's little black eyes quit Emma's and begin on a very slow and sinuous descent along the young woman's body. His gaze slides, creeps over its prey, like a boa constrictor; indeed he seems to possess a similar indolence and viscosity. Emma cannot stop herself from clenching her enchanting backside, and the boy squeezes her elbow tighter and squeezes the imaginary bludgeon with his other.

"Come back in a week," says the man, arriving at her feet.

HE DIDN'T LIE. He knows his trade. And she did not recoil despite her aversion. It costs her a small fortune but eight days later they set off again (of course the boy accompanies her) with the precious volume in their grasp. To which a second was added on the spot. "Allow me to suggest to you . . ." The man was already holding the book wide open in front of her. Where on earth did he pull it out from? Sure enough the praiseworthy and very explicit paintings reproduced on the spread he showed her had the double effect of heating the blood of the young woman and relieving her of a more substantial part of her savings. "There are forty of them. Forty tableaux of the same quality . . ." Make her blush and make her pay: that's what he wanted. Both goals were achieved. She bought the second book without hesitating. The man could have watched them leave, rubbing his hands together—which the black gloves were still protecting—but he didn't do it, either out of respect, or more likely out of the fear of anyone seeing his atrocious peeling skin, revealed through this simple gesture.

Walking away from the bookstore, Emma swears out loud that she'll never step foot in there again. She knows that, in his way, the man had possessed her. Her pride is wounded and the wound festers with anger. Walking, she spits out "Midget!" between her teeth. "Runt!" "Little maggot!" "Earthworm!" "Fleabag!" "Walking boil!" "Pig's wart!" "Stinking rat fart!" So much so that halfway home a laugh erupts at her side. It's the boy. She stops and looks at him—he's holding his sides, the poor simpleton—surprised at first, then vexed, outraged, furious, then suddenly won over by this contagious hilarity, vanquished, she cedes in her own turn and her laughter bursts out to join his. It's fine.

All this bile evacuated, they turn to basking in the exciting prospect of warming themselves up by the firebrand they're carrying. They anticipate, they fantasize (two pyromaniacs with matches in their pockets). However it's not until deep into the night that their project materializes. In Emma's bedroom, cross-legged on the rug, by candlelight, they turn the pages.

Sade first.

It's important to remember that she's the one who reads. In a low voice in order not to wake up her father. Whispered, murmured, whispered words. You have to imagine the panache of the Marquis between the lips of the young woman. The thread of the narrative sometimes broken, breath cut short by the crudeness of a phrase, by the enormity of a situation. The look that they then exchange. These are extremes they have not yet explored. The unknown opens before them—to where? to where?—the abysses and the heavens, and they stop short for a moment on the edge, on the border, frightened but curious, eager, reckless. They have to keep going. Emma swallows her saliva and begins again.

Sade is too much.

Beyond the salacious, beyond the bawdy, beyond the erotic and even the pornographic. Within his writing is another dimension that they perceive only with unease. The cruelty overwhelms them. For them the pleasure stops on the threshold of pain, inflicted or endured. They don't adhere to the particular perversion to which the Marquis lends his name.

And yet they read until the end. After three nights and three successive candles the adventures of Justine are no longer a mystery to them—nor that unfortunate virtue undoubtedly abused. And it was worth it. To know. To understand. To expand their horizons. Also, in a certain way, to pay homage to the courage of the author. For one must not forget that this liberty of thought and tone, this liberty of spirit, the Marquis paid for with his physical liberty: twenty-seven years of imprisonment—jail, asylum, prison. Twenty-seven years of his life.

The writings remain, fortunately.

They won't regret Sade, but they won't return to him either.

The second book is very different. What does it recount? They have no idea—and they'll never know. Emma is not even capable of deciphering the title. In this moment she finds herself as bereft as the boy. There are signs, symbols, a very beautiful graphic system, very elegant, certainly, but incomprehensible. A foreign and exotic language. Chinese, she says. As she might have said Hebrew, Yiddish, hieroglyphs.

In reality it's Sanskrit. If she hadn't been in such a hurry to leave the bookstore, if she hadn't so abruptly cut off the walking boil's long-winded speech, she would have known that. As he was going to explain to her, it's a book entitled *Kama Sutra*, this edition dating from nearly a century ago, published in Rajasthan and in the manner of works that were formerly produced by the most celebrated art school of the Mughal Empire—the school of Bikaner. Hence the extreme care accorded to the illustrations. Hence the splendor of the paintings. And that's the essential part. No need for words this time, the images suffice. In the warm colors of illuminators, each of them represents a position of coupling. The bookseller had promised forty. Forty tableaux: as many variations. Exquisite pleasure in (almost) every way.

This book suits them more. Their attentive consultation of the collection quickly inspires passionate romps. You have to remember that the reading is done naked, and that it's difficult in these conditions, notably for the boy, to hide his excitement—hoho! observes Emma, teasing. Contrary to the work of the Marquis, they return to it, a hundred times rather than once. Certain positions they know already. A good number surprise and delight them—the Hindu art in all its refinement. And soon, as we might have suspected, the book becomes the basis for a new game: one of them flips through the pages until the other, eyes blindfolded, stops them. The challenge is to then reproduce the position chosen by chance. It's thus that, without knowing it, they execute *The Cavalier*, *The Reverse Cavalier*, *The Embrace of the Panda*, *The Propeller*, or *The Dance of Enticement*. They try them out for the first time. They improve. There are some that are more of an acrobatic performance, even circus-like, than an act of love. Setting aside gravity, only attraction remains! Flexibility, balance, strength, and endurance are required. And perfect coordination—to fit the pieces together. It's the oil in the engine. In order to imitate *The Doe in Heat*, the boy's muscles, all of his muscles, are harshly called upon. As for *Teetering Tripod*, he teeters so much that he ends up truly tumbling onto the Flemish rug (unleashing in the effort an umpteenth fit of hysterical laughter that rattles them and exhausts them more thoroughly than any coitus).

But in this range of positions, the one that gives them the most difficulty is without contest *The Noose*. A supreme challenge. The Annapurna, the Everest of the amorous pantomime. They will finally succeed in summiting it, but after how many tries? After how much effort? More falls, slips, aches, cramps, and in the end Emma will come out of it with a nasty crick in her spine (she explained to Gustave that she put out her back out while doing the laundry . . .) which will condemn her to two days and two nights of immobility during which she will be able to do nothing other than rest stretched on her back and submit, passively, to the boy's whims.

Books, books, books. Over the months they accumulate and pile up. Emma organizes them in an armoire in her bedroom, thus constituting, over time, their little forbidden library, their den of iniquity. Not a day goes by without them borrowing from it. Sometimes at random, often according to their desires. It's not that their inspiration is lacking, it's just another joy. An added pleasure.

And how to resist this:

Let's Love, let's Fuck, these are pleasures
That one must never separate;
Enjoyment and lust are rare treasures
For the soul to cultivate.
A Prick, a Cunt, and two fond hearts
Create sweet songs in many parts,
Which the holy wrongly blame.
Amaryllis, ponder this:
Love without sex is a paltry flame,
Sex without love is empty bliss.

"La Fontaine," she says in a sigh, "I will forever drink from your spring."

"YOU SEE, I wore my most beautiful dress tonight. Do you like it? Marvelous, isn't it? But I would say simply: a jewelry box befitting the jewel it contains. Yes! For you must know, my sweetheart, that before cloaking it in this piece of high-priced fabric, I soaked my body for nearly an hour straight in water delicately sprinkled with jasmine salt and lily of the valley essences. Then I dried my body, and I oiled it, in order to make it soft, with a chamomile and white lily cream, known for its emollient virtues. Nevertheless, after much reflection, I feared that it was becoming a bit too soft and relaxed, even dangly, like that appendage that acts as a chin, a double chin, on Madame Loue—you know, the baker. Gobble, gobble! Would you enjoy kissing a turkey neck? . . . No. I didn't think so. So, to prevent the risk of flaccidity, I chose to oil myself once more with another cream, one with extracts of flax seed and sea buckthorn, recommended for re-firming skin . . . What? You want to see for yourself? You want to feel the firmness? Tsk tsk! Hands off, you sly dog! You'll have plenty of time to do so once I'm done. Patience. Know that I achieved this magnificent composition by adding a few drops of the very last creation of Monsieur Coty. What a fragrance! Smell it . . . Hey! My hand only, little rascal! So? . . . I agree: a divine fragrance. *Iris*: that's its name. A new flower essence. No longer a jewel—a bouquet! A garden! I am a garden unto myself! And that's quite fitting, as it turns out. Do you know why? . . . Go on, think. Think a little . . . No, it's not that I'm suddenly interested in horticulture. What day is it? You don't know. I'll whisper it to you: it's April 25. Saint Mark's Day, if that helps. And why is it special, this date? Why is it, in theory, so memorable? What happened on April

25, let's say, last year for example? . . . You still don't know? You know, birdbrain, others would be rather upset by this! Come closer, I prefer to say it in your ear . . . In your ear, I said! . . . So, it was exactly a year ago today, I . . . you . . . we . . . Well, I gave you my flower, in fact! Don't tell me you don't remember. It was the night of April 25 in the year 1912 of our era. My flower, my one and only, I offered it to you. And it's to you that now I want to offer an entire garden. Which is to say what has grown since! It's true, my poor simpleton, that you have planted a lot, a lot. Brazen strikes of the pickaxe! Brazen strikes of the spade! And the sap hasn't disappointed. In the end, maybe you're the horticulturist, emphasis on the first syllable, of course . . . In short, it's our anniversary, today. Happy anniversary, my love! I gave you my flower. I gave you my name. I gave you my heart . . . Like a refrain in a song by . . . who is it again? Muguette? Mistinguett! 'I gave you my flower, I gave you my name, I gave you my heart, ba-bum-ba-bum doo-ta-doo . . .' I give you my soul, my love. It belongs to you, too. Everything. Everything that I have, I give to you. And what I am. Everything belongs to you. Does that not merit a little ceremony? Look: I bow. I kneel down before you . . . No, scoundrel, not for that! Patience, for heaven's sake! . . . I get down on my knees now to take an oath. Promises, as we know, aren't made standing up. And what am I going to swear to you? This. Listen. I, Emma Van Ecke, on this April 25 of the year 1913 after Jesus Christ, solemnly swear to not let anyone other than you cultivate my garden. My secret garden. My garden of love. I swear that no one other than you will ever enter the gate, which I hope you will not let rust. I swear that no one other than you will ever come to trample my flower beds—which are not so flat, you must admit. No other will come to water them. No other will sow as they please. Never! Never! Never! It's my vow, it's my wish, it's my promise. And now, I beg you, knight me . . . Jesus, not like that! Put that away! Knight, I said! Have you never heard of knights? It's called a rite—and a rhyme comes to my lips, which I nonetheless have the wisdom to save for our next sexicon. But if I tell you that it's practiced ordinarily with an épée, what are you going to take out this time? Keep yours for a better use, patience, patience, its sheath awaits. Since we don't have a real épée at our disposal, you will use ... Hmm ... Let's see ... There! The feather duster! That will do. You will place it first on my left shoulder, then on my right, then on the top of my head, not to remember that we are dust and will return to dust—we'll have plenty of time to think about that—but to make me a chevalière ... Can we say 'chevalière' for a female knight? Why not? We say 'écuyère' for a horsewoman. We say 'épicière' for a female grocer and 'poisson-nière' for a female fishmonger. A bit of noblesse won't harm our sex. Especially since we're using the feather duster: etiquette has been redeemed. So you will make me, by the grace of earthly and celestial powers, chevalière of ... of ... of the Garden of Delights! That's good. Chevalière of Eden! That's even better. Don't be at all afraid of blas-phemy. The Eternal is love, we affirm it. Eve and Emma: the same fight. Go on, proceed, my king. One shoulder, then the other ... Ooh! That tickles! ... Through this sacrament I renew my promise to you of loyalty and happiness for this entire life and for all those that might one day follow and carry on its essence ... I'm shaking, look! In a good way. My heart is filled with emotion. My soul is full and overflows. These tears in my eyes ... No, no, leave them! They're from happiness. It's the nurturing rain that irrigates and fertilizes my garden. I've never been so happy, my love. And it's you, it's you who is responsible. You have the gift of making me drip from everywhere ... Your turn, now! On your knees! Give me that feather duster and take a knee. I'll make you a chevalier. By the order of the Divine Horticulturists, since we are on this terrain. Do you swear to be and to remain my ardent Adam? Do you swear to maintain to the best of your ability, and exclusively, this garden that you gave rise to and that is entirely dedicated to you? Do you swear, I insist, to never labor elsewhere? To never pluck, nor even sniff, flowers other than those that grow in this patch that belongs to you? You swear? . . . No, don't spit, this poor rug has already endured enough affronts as it is. But allow me all the same to open a parenthesis here: Do you know what would happen if, by chance, by accident, by misfortune, you were to break your word? If, by my own eyes or by the intervention of some perfidious and viperous tongue, I were to learn that you betrayed my confidence? If you should prove to be disloyal and unfaithful. If you were to lie, cheat, scorn. If through such an ignominious action you were to crush my heart, dishonor my name, devastate my soul and pulverize my being. Oh my vile love, do you know what would happen then? . . . Well, you see, it's simple: I would behave like the chevalière that I now am. It seems to me a rather basic precept: accepting a title, we are bound to apply its principles. In this case that means that I would arm myself not with a harmless feather duster like this, but with a real épée, honed, sharp, with which I would first have a grand time cutting off, one by one, the limbs of the squalid sow with whom you had shared a bed and sty—brrr! I'm shivering at the thought—ending with her snout, so that she'll have ample time to appreciate her agony, then her horrible swine head, with a proper decapitation. Whack! That's it for her. Yes, I said 'sow' and I maintain and pledge: whether she be blue-blooded or lowborn, whether she be a virgin or a harlot, whether she be young or old, tall or a dwarf, beautiful or deformed, she will never be to my eyes anything but the most abominable specimen of swine that the earth has ever seen, though that's more of an insult to the animal that's otherwise endearing. But the work of justice would not be finished just because her fate has been sealed. It's then on to you, oh renegade gardener, oh naughty piggy, it's to you, yes, that I would be forced to turn. Whose fault is that? Tears in my eyes, heart in tatters, soul in shreds, but still armed, I would be content, for your expiation, to slice the instrument of your crime clean off. Yes, that very one. The one I love so much. That I cherish. That I venerate. Whack, once again!—Oh, my God, I beg of you, make it so that we never arrive at such extremes! The instrument of my happiness turned to that of my affliction, and me condemned to subject it to my épée. Condemned, yes! For in punishing you, I would be punishing myself at the same time. You castigated and castrated, me murderer and maimed. Red with your blood, pale with horror. What else could I do but turn the blade back on myself? Pierce my abandoned body. Ravage my broken heart. Free my tortured soul. Die, in a word. Die with the hope of rejoining you, my love, of finding you again in the realms of the very first garden, original and pure: Félix, Emma, my Adam, your Eve, reconciled and reunited, and for eternity this time, in that mythical Eden where nothing, nothing, no nasty sow will ever come to stick her nasty snout! . . . That's it. I close the parenthesis. And I finish consecrating you a chevalier, with this . . . Come on, don't be afraid! It's only a feather duster. You're supposed to be a valiant knight! The man who is afraid of being dusted! You are indeed very funny, my love. But tell me, and be frank: does all of this seem, in your eyes, like grotesque and childish affectations? Nonsense? Poppycock? This ceremony, do you find it ridiculous?—This word inspires me, I confess, to make a pun, one that a certain Marquis would not renounce . . . No, you don't think so? Really? Oof! I'm delighted. Wait, please. Don't get up just yet. I have another surprise for you. Yes. It's an auspicious day, take advantage of it. This dress, you see, this marvelous and rather pricey dress, well, I'm going to take it off. I'm going to lift it and throw it away like a vulgar rag. All so your gaze—your gaze, first—can revel in my garden in all its splendor. The full extent of it. Complete panorama. I know that you have already seen it and seen it again, but not . . . No, I shouldn't say it. My tongue, my tongue, I have to restrain it another few moments. Ready? . . . Okay, I'm taking it off. I'm uncovering myself. Unveiling myself . . . Haha! You didn't expect that, huh? . . . So? . . . I see it has a funny effect on you. I myself am not yet used to it. But, actually, it's not such a big deal: to continue the metaphor, let's say that I simply trimmed the field. Pffft! Cleared, cut, razed. Clean sweep. Is it such a big change?

It's different, it's true. And I admit that it wasn't without a bit of pain and apprehension. I had to be a contortionist. I had to use a mirror. I had to stop my hand from trembling the whole time. Can you imagine the damage that could have caused? My motivation had to be as great as the risks! But what wouldn't I do for you, my love! For you! I really wanted to offer you this treat. I wanted to mark this day and render it unforgettable. Are you happy? Do you like it, at least? . . . Allow me, all the same, to verify . . . Dear god! Beyond a doubt! Thank you. Thank you for being so appreciative of it. And now, would you like to assess the sweetness, this new novel sweetness? Do you want, since you find yourself in a position that lends itself to it, to have a taste? Yes, you may now. Your patience—and mine!—will finally be rewarded. I am virgin once again, my love. I present myself to you in the appearance of my younger years in order to celebrate the joy begun on this day, and all those, countless, that will follow. Touch, yes! Taste! Take it, you have the right! Treat yourself! Treat me! Happy anniv . . . Ooh! You savage!"

CAN THE WORDS of a woman in love—and a chevalière on top of it—be doubted?

Two weeks after this consecration, while the brown moss on the mound gently grows back, Emma is given the opportunity to demonstrate that she does not take her oath lightly.

You flirt with danger, you can't avoid an accident.

The one who bears the consequences is a young girl of seventeen years old. One of her students. Emma had been teaching the girl piano and music theory for a half-dozen years. She had not yet noticed how much her appearance had changed during that time. Her charm, her bearing, her body have changed. The roundness of her cheeks has shifted towards her bosom. While her face was thinning, while her height was soaring, elsewhere shapes were budding and blossoming. To her advantage, indisputably. Today Emma takes notice. One might even say that this observation strikes her full force. The little Isabelle—the name of the demoiselle—is no longer a child. She's a sow.

The dreaded sow.

The perfect sow.

On the day of the lesson it's the boy, as usual, who goes to open the apartment door and escorts the student to the music room. Emma is busy preparing the sheet music. She turns around just as the two of them cross the threshold, and the welcoming smile that she had on her lips instantly wilts, shrivels, and dissolves like raw flesh in acid.

She detects admiration, desire, and even lechery in the look that the boy is giving the demoiselle. And, worst of all, she is reciprocating. They understand each other. Accomplices in concupiscence. Why is she fishing for this? We don't know. The heart has its reasons. And it's precisely in the heart that the sharp point of jealousy plants itself at that moment.

A poison arrow.

The young girl sits at the piano. The boy takes his place in the fireside chair. He seems to have decided to sit in on the lesson: which is nothing exceptional—the opposite would have been—but which causes extra ripples of doubt in the now-troubled pool reflecting Emma's spirit. The whole hour that follows she spends worried, agitated, going in circles around her student, sometimes scrutinizing her appearance (which reveals itself, from minute to minute, to be even more charming, more appetizing, more swinish to her), sometimes surveying the effects on the boy. And trying to uncover the slightest sign of connivance between these two, a word, a gesture, an attitude that might betray them. Alas, looking at it, it seems to her that there are a quite a few! The way the boy keeps time by tapping his finger on the velvet: why this rhythm? Why this finger? This manner the girl has of tilting her head at the rise of an arpeggio: what purpose does that serve if not to show off her neck, its fineness? Unless . . . Can they glimpse each other in the glossy varnish of the piano? Better to stand between them, just in case. But from what side: here or there? And why is she clearing her throat nonstop? Is the mademoiselle hoarse? Does she have a cold, the poor thing? Or has the cat got your tongue? A pussy, no doubt! Meowing. Calling. A pussy in heat!

Emma sees nothing, but she sees everything. Thinks she sees. Thinks she intercepts. She interprets. Each sound, each movement, insignificant not so long ago, is suddenly susceptible to transforming into proof of their foul duplicity. All wood can catch fire. Emma knows it. Emma feels it. If her eyes are not certain, her heart—her pierced heart filling with venom—is convinced of it. The young lass bats her eyelashes: the coquettish doe. The boy coughs: he's the roaring stag. Ruses and subterfuges. Until that sharp note, that one sharp note that the pianist in training desperately tries to execute, ten times, twenty times, and which does not exist in this particular key (in this one it's a natural, silly girl!). What does this wrong note mean? What code is there in their invented language?

The lesson comes to a close, but Emma goes back over it again and again, well into the night. She dissects, analyzes the minor events with a magnifying glass, the tiniest details. Her judgment claims—imagines—itself as objective, but the poison has already taken effect. From her heart it's spread to her brain. It flows through her veins. The damage is done. It is everywhere.

Tortured by suspicion, Emma suffers.

When the boy joins her that night in the bedroom, she doesn't fall into his arms or any other part of him. She is neither nude nor half-nude. Neither Musset nor *Kama Sutra* in sight: no book. He finds her seated on the edge of the bed. She signals for him to sit at her side. He sits down. She takes his hand, fingers interlaced, and looks at him for a long moment without saying anything. She sighs. She smiles—a weak smile. Tell me, she says, am I old? The boy raises his eyebrows. Tell me, she says. He shakes his head no. However, I am ten or twelve years older than that . . . that Isabelle. Isabelle, you see? He nods his head yes. Yes, she says, you see. She sighs again. I'm maybe a good ten years older than you, too. In sum . . . Her voice derails. She clears it. In sum, she says, in terms of age you are much closer to her than to me. He does nothing this time. He watches her with his big black eyes. You would make a lovely couple, she says. In fact, what do you think of that? I mean to say: What do you think of her, that . . . Isabelle? The boy shrugs his shoulders. Well, I for one find her charming. No? The boy pouts. (What's a pout? It's not much. It's not no.) Certainly, she says, intelligence is not her strong suit. Nature did not spoil her on that front, we can agree. A real idiot! And not in her musical talent either. No ear, no hands: difficult to do less. With such limited ability, Bach himself would have given up! But is it her

251

fault, that . . . that little girl? Heaven is not generous in all things. The gifts are not always equally distributed. She has received others. Beauty, for example. Because she is beautiful, no? The boy pouts. (A pout, a pout is not a frank and solid no.) Yes, she says, she is beautiful. We cannot take that from her—what would she have left? More precisely, she is pretty. She is gracious. She is precious. An idiot, yes, but made of porcelain! She seems so fragile. If I were a man, I think I would die of desire to take her in my arms to protect her. Dear little idiot, come here, come to me, I am so afraid that you might break . . . I am certain that that's what you feel, too. Are you dying of desire to squeeze her in your arms? Finally there it is, the no. Clear and frank. Too frank. Too clear. Too rushed to be honest. It's the no of a man backed into a corner. The no of a guilty man caught in the act who denies the evidence. She lets go of his hand and stands up, uncoils like a spring. She walks. She turns in circles. We think we can hear her growl. Dignified daughter of a warthog. She urges herself to be calm. Calm, calm. Breathe. She stands opposite him. She smiles—a menacing smile. Come on, she says, a sin confessed is . . . She breaks off. She can't say that. Cliché. Pure convention. If she demands the truth she cannot lie. She is not sure, she is not at all sure of being able to forgive him, neither halfway nor a quarter nor a hundredth. You maintain, she says, that you are not attracted to her? He nods his head yes. You maintain that you feel no desire for that . . . that tramp? He nods his head yes. She shakes her head no. I'm not stupid, she says. I'm not blind. I saw. I saw everything! He doesn't know what to do. He watches her with his big black eyes that are now tinted with worry and incomprehension. Come on, she says, admit that you like her. He shakes his head no. Admit it, she says. He shakes no. Admit it! He shakes no. Admit it! No. Admit it! No. She remains open-mouthed, silent. Her lips start to tremble. All at once tears fill her eyes. He stands up and throws himself on her and squeezes her in his arms. Squeezes her, squeezes her.

The scene replays the whole week. Variations on the same theme. She tries sweetness, threats. She hassles, badgers, takes a roundabout approach, or else she charges head-on. He won't admit it. She goes through various phases, various states, from dejection to fulmination, from exhaustion to ire, to fury, to rage. He won't admit it. She is miserable. He is too.

Poison.

Then comes the day of the next lesson. Countless times she's thought of cancelling it. She didn't do so. She asked the boy not to be there for it. She asked him (ordered him) not even to show himself, to remain cloistered in his bedroom. He consented—mercifully hoping to help heal her, to chase this sickness that she has contracted and of which he does not know how to relieve her.

It's Emma who goes to open the door. Oh, the pretty little face. It gets worse and worse. Comely, truly. A delicate carnivorous plant. To think that within this ravishing box a snake is sleeping. The snake watches. Emma grinds her teeth. Emma withdraws her claws. Manages a smile. Teacher Emma Van Ecke accompanies her student to the piano room. Enter. Sit down. What is she looking for? Right profile, left profile. No, you see, the male is not here. We are alone. Student, teacher. Serpent, panther. There's just you and me. Emma closes the door behind them.

Notes arise one after another. The usual exercises. Emma doesn't listen. Doesn't intervene. She who ordinarily corrects errors with tact, who kindly points out faults, who always has a word of encouragement, she doesn't loosen her lips. What difference would that make? In any event you didn't come for that. You didn't come for the music. Likely story! I know perfectly well why you're here, traitor. Just like during the last lesson, she remains silent. Her steps trace an arc that skirts around the young girl from behind, from one end of the keyboard to the other, from high to low, back, forth. She doesn't listen but she watches her, yes. She observes her. Scrutinizes her. Examines her.

Everything is subject to her gaze, outfit included, from her shoes to her dress. That neckline, my God. That chasm. That abyss. Deeper than the Sargasso Sea. How can a mother allow her daughter to go out dressed like that? Undressed like that, rather. Who is it for, is it for Czerny? For Brahms? Is it father Handel that you're trying to seduce with that? Of course. If you think that I don't see right through you. I am not your mother. No matter what you think, slut, I am not old enough to be your mother. What's going on? You're simpering less this time. Why don't I see it pricking up, your little tongue? And her eyelashes: they are certainly prudent, calm, have they been glued? What's going on, sweetheart? Is it, by chance, the absence of the male that saddens you? That's such a shame. No nose to shove your little tits under. It's all for nothing. What? Yes, play. Play again, if you like. Start over. You can begin again a thousand times; never will you be capable of playing it correctly. You are not here for that. You know it, I know it, we know it. There is only you and me here. The only thing you are capable of playing is farce. Play, if you like. But it won't work on me.

Emma doesn't hear the "Canon". Pachelbel. The canonical. It could be anything, she isn't listening. Emma paces. Emma comes and goes while fiddling with her fingers. Emma is hot. Her eyes linger on the young girl's neck. Today it is exposed. Blond hair collected in a voluminous bun. We see her neck. Her slender neck. Her swan's neck. Her snake's neck. Her sow's neck. Stop! Emma suddenly raises her eyes, she turns her head from left to right: she searches for an épée. For a few seconds, very seriously, she searches for an épée in the room. Or an ax, why not. An ax would do the job. It's obvious that she isn't fully in her right mind. The poison is violent. It is everywhere, in each cell, in each atom. She doesn't find an ax, or an épée. What she finds is the boy's drawing, under glass, hung on the wall. Her eyes fall on it. She is hot. She is very hot. The drawing of the child, so naïve and innocent. We see the house, the tree, the sun: a peaceful place. And the woman in the center of the sheet. The unknown woman. The woman or the girl. The girl? She stares at the drawing and remembers the day when he gave it to her. She remembers everything. My love, she thinks. So, so hot. As if she were suffocating. Whack! The ax of Pachelbel. There it is. Brusquely she sets herself in motion, she takes two steps towards the piano, plunges into what she will later call a big black hole. The sow is playing. The girl? Teacher Emma Van Ecke pivots on her heels to face her student—oh, the pretty little face—and in the same movement inadvertently slams the keyboard lid on the girl's fingers with all her strength. Whack!

The "Canon" stops.

It will not begin again. The young Isabelle, we quickly learn, has a broken pinky (precisely the same finger, twist of fate, as the boy). The trapezium and scaphoid of her right hand are crushed. But above all she is deeply traumatized, emotionally and psychologically: The demoiselle is convinced that her teacher did it on purpose. Intimate and profound conviction that she keeps to herself—who would understand that? She would come off as crazy at the mere suggestion of it. She keeps quiet, but the fear is there, crouching low, anchored. The after-effects persist. Long after her bones are reconstituted, she will continue to be terrorized by the idea of returning there and will find every pretext to avoid it. At the end of the day the young girl will get her wish: the music lessons are finished. Boulevard du Temple will never see her pretty little face again.

It takes a lot less time for Emma to forget. A dash of remorse, not an ounce of regret. It wasn't me, she will say to the boy (and to no one else), evoking then this famous black hole by way of explanation. A journey outside of herself, outside of time, outside of everything. An absence. A non-event. She wouldn't know how to describe it any better. The proof is that her memory is void of those moments. She barely remembers the screams that tore her from the void where she found herself. Like . . . like, yes, a sow being slaughtered. Since she was absent from her own consciousness, what could she have done?

From her point of view, it could have been worse. I could have killed her, she will say (without being overly emotional about it). Let's be happy about that.

The fact is that she is. Purged of a dose of poison that was eating away at her. Heart and mind freed. Fresh blood. Her other students are too young or too ugly: she treats them with all the benevolence they merit, and which incidentally she had always demonstrated. Emma Van Ecke is an excellent teacher.

And the boy is happy, too. So happy to see her cured, to find her as she used to be again, and perhaps even more spirited, more zealous. With no restraint she presents him with a case that manages to sweep away the last specks of doubt. No more ax, no more épée: a broom!

She retrieves the books from the armoire. She opens the gates to her sumptuous garden once more (the lawn has grown back, soft and wild grass). And it's thus that after a bit of time, the good life and the great love regain their course.

BUT IT GOES BY SO QUICKLY. It's already almost passed. The happy times and the sad times are not of equal measure or equal value. (Does that add up, sonny?) One contracts when the other stretches and expands. One races while the other drags on. A simple comma and it's four years of existence. Is it possible? This includes love, joy, tenderness, laughter, music, poetry, desire, pleasure, peace, grace, harmony, serenity, plenitude, in a word, happiness, as they say. And we don't realize it. We are lifted, lifted, unbeknownst to us. We are carried. We reach the summit. The high-altitude air intoxicates us, makes our heads spin. Heads full of ether. See how beautiful it is. There is nothing higher.

Once we're here, we cannot go back down. Teetering on the other slope. North. In one step we lose our laurels and our necklaces. The ground is damned low, the boy will be forced to remember.

One last thing, however, before the apocalypse: Emma has started to write. Restarted, in fact. She had tried during puberty. She had aspirations at that age, lofty and noble aims (Hugo, or nothing!), the dreams and illusions that go along with it. The limits of her talent, surrounded by an implacable lucidity, had driven her to renounce them. She comes back to them, but this time without the manifest ambition of leaving her imprint on literature. Her plans are much more modest. No enduring masterpieces in sight. No intention other than having a good time. A game, one more game, and nothing else. A game for the two infatuated lovers.

Strongly influenced by the readings of these last months, she writes in a bawdy, risqué style, sometimes crude, that charms and excites them, her and the boy. To start with, she imitates. Parodies ("The Social Cuntract," to give just one example), and parodies of parodies: odes, sonnets, epigrams with colorful rhymes that she takes shamelessly from her sexicon. Then the production is enriched with a few tales in which debauched animals or ithyphallic divinities frolic. An orgy in the barnyard, orgy on Olympus or in Arcadia: always an orgy. The fables that she invents are of dubious morals, when they have any. She also creates short plays, scenes that she has a great deal of fun directing, at night, on the ancestral rug that is the setting for both the stage and the wings. She plays all the female roles and the boy puts on the costumes (often rather skimpy) of the masculine characters. We are far, very far, from his lamentable performance as an actor in the nativity scene. He doesn't play the Exalted One; he is exalted. He will perform as often as she wants. There will be as many acts as she wants.

Emma is inspired. Each day she sets to work with her quill and makes the most of it for the boy. The best of her writing is brief poems for him alone, intelligible to him alone, for these texts possess secret drawers that conceal their true meaning, their key entrusted to him alone. Here is an example:

> Come, pretty chickadee, come. Emerge fearlessly from the brush,
> Unleash your melodious song. Spread your joy for everyone.
> Your trills soar far and wide among the lush
> Wood and fly and sparkle like a thousand radiant suns.
> O little angel, beautiful blue bird, your arpeggios
> Melt on the tongue of the gods: it's spring.
> My soul is reborn, pure and virgin like the snow
> As we listen to it fall when we are twenty-something.

Bucolic and charming in appearance. But should we read only the first word of each line, in a kind of acrostic poem, then the tone changes and this innocent story of a chickadee takes a turn in another direction for an entirely different meaning.

The young woman produces messages like this in abundance. Though he knows the various codes, it's not always an easy task for the boy to decipher them. He doesn't read them, so he has to retain everything before extracting and then reassembling in the proper order. Brainteasers that require an infallible memory and a nimble recall. Sometimes he gets lost, most of the time he finds the thread again and enjoys the challenge.

Emma is so happy with this little game that she wants to pursue it more widely. The idea is to unite a few strangers in order to allow to them share in the splendor of her creations. A fantasy that's a bit perverse, there's no denying it, because she does indeed intend to deliver her crude messages right under the noses of her ignorant audience. Salt, voilà! Spice.

When the seed of this project is planted, they are once again on holiday in Toussus-le-Noble. Consequently the number of potential insiders is necessarily limited. But no matter, the quality will make up for the quantity. And so it happens that, in the beginning of the month of July, she opens the first literary salon that the village has ever known. Besides Emma and the boy, only two other people have the honor of taking part: Gustave and the loyal Doctor Théoux. The physician's last contact with poetry was when he was courting his future spouse: a few gallant stanzas of a courtly poet that he had memorized and recited down on one knee, as he had thought was fitting to do. Today still he remains convinced that it's this master stroke that allowed him to win her over and lead the beauty to the altar—when in reality the betrothed was much more receptive to his recent medical degree than to this gobbledygook in archaic French of which she hadn't been able to understand a single word.

It's time. The meal is over. The dessert consumed, Emma stands and clinks her glass (we will remember this small crystalline noise, joyous, pleasant, when the alarm bells sound). Standing in front of the attentive audience, she opens her notebook and begins to read. They are prosaic texts, without anything questionable, written for the occasion. They are admired and applauded. Gustave is proud of his daughter. Amédée savors the readings as he savors a pear: a gourmand's expression, tiny bites. Emma smiles modestly. Then she unleashes her secret weapon. With a complicit wink the boy is forewarned: the next one is for him. For the two of them. It's a poem, she tells the audience, that she has titled "Oblivion." Her tone is serious, her gaze sparkles. She begins:

> I would like in this moment
> To abolish the past.
> For you to raise your sword,
> O benevolent oblivion,
> And sink your blade
> Into my tortured soul.
> Through the slant of my lips
> I pray to forget.
> May you open me and cleave me,
> O merciful one,
> Right here. Strip
> My eyes of memory
> And wrest from me all at once
> All regret, all remorse,
> —Those cursed items of clothing
> That dress my wrongs—
> And take me right now
> That atrocious memory.
> Oh! yes, come, I beg of you!
> Have pity on my old bones!
> Quickly, unload

My soul of the burden that resides
So very deep inside of me!
O benevolent oblivion,
In this moment I would like
To be reborn in sweetness.
To feel the spurt of your stream
To appease my heart
Burning like lightning.

Be aware that the she-devil has upped the difficulty of both the composition and the decoding. The key has changed: it's no longer the first words of each line that constitute the message, but every other line.

Naturally, those who are not in the know see nothing but smoke. But even for the initiated the task is arduous. Imagine for a moment the mental gymnastics necessary to comprehend a cryptogram when one does not have it beneath one's eyes. A challenge. Gustave's applause, Amédée's praise have already died down and the boy is still racking his brain on the other end of the table. Concentrating, eyebrows gathered, the intensity of the effort can be read on his face (where is the caesura? where is the enjambment?). This lasts a good two or three minutes. And then suddenly his features relax, his face illuminates. He stands up with a jump and starts in his own turn to clap his hands, a blissful smile on his lips.

Emma laughs. But not the doctor, who is surprised by the delayed reaction. He stares at the boy with an alarmed and then worried expression. He thinks of the accident again. Of the cranial trauma. Of the irreversible after-effects . . . Turning around he meets the gaze of his friend Gustave, who displays an expression like a brave compassionate priest while at the same time giving the hint of a vaguely embarrassed, vaguely guilty pout. And as Emma closes her notebook again, the old man wonders whether the treatment prescribed to the boy—Madeira: a half-glass morning and night—was in the end the most appropriate.

Ah, happy days.

The experiment will happen again, they will hold salons several more times, enlarging the circle of participants to seven (adding the sharecropper and his son as well as a cousin of Amédée, a demoiselle of seventy years old who showed up at his house unannounced and well versed in spiritualism—they will be subjected to the totality of a madrigal by Madame de Coligny, Countess of La Suze, recited monotonously from the beyond and letter by letter by the very spirit of the author).

The rest of the time the lovers love each other.

But this passes, it passes so quickly.

No matter what anyone says, it's the last summer. Even worse, it's truncated by half because it ends on August 1 at precisely four in the afternoon.

Terrible heat that day. They, she and he, are lying on their blue watercress bed, on the banks of the river. The willow spread above, its branches tracing Mashrabiya shadows on their nude skin. Lazy, they sleep side by side, emptied and sated, full of each other. Empty of sweat and sap. That's where they are when they hear, in the distance, as if in a dream, the ringing of the bells.

1914–1915

SO THAT EVERYTHING IS CLEAR: George Frederick Ernest Albert, called George V, King of the United Kingdom, of Canada, of Australia, of New Zealand, of South Africa, of Ireland, and Emperor of India, is the German cousin of Nikolai Aleksandrovitch Romanov, called Nicholas II, called Nicky for short by those close to him, Emperor of Russia, King of Poland and Great Prince of Finland, himself son of Alexander III and Marie Sophie Frederikke Dagmar of Schleswig-Holstein-Sonderburg-Glücksburg, called Dagmar of Denmark, Empress of Russia under the name of Maria Fedorovna, who is the sister of Frederick VIII, King of Denmark, and of George I, King of Greece, and of Alexandra Caroline Marie Charlotte Louise Julie of Schleswig-Holstein-Sonderburg-Glücksburg, wife of Edward VII, who is consequently son-in-law of Princess Louise of Hesse-Cassel, who is included then among the grandchildren of Christian X of Denmark, as well as the aforementioned George V and Nicholas II, whose uncle, Nicholas Nikolaievitch of Russia, is the brother-in-law of the King of Italy, Victor Emmanuel III, called Vicky by those close to him, called the dwarf by the insolent—because, unlike his paternal second cousin, Amedeo II of Savoia-Aosta, a giant at nearly six and a half feet, Victor-Emmanuel barely exceeds four feet nine inches— himself son of Umberto I and of Margherita of Savoie and grandson of Marie Adelaide of Habsburg-Lorraine, as well as Constantine of Schleswig-Holstein-Sonderburg-Glücksburg, called Constantine I of Greece, older son of the Grand Duchess Olga Constantinovna of Russia and great-grandson of Tsar Nicholas I and husband of Princess Sophie of Prussia, herself daughter of Emperor Frederick III of Germany and mother of Irene of Greece, herself wife of Aimone of Savoia-Aosta, King of Croatia under the name of Tomislav II, as well as Haakon VII of Norway, husband of his German cousin Maud Charlotte Mary Victoria of Saxe-Coburg-Gotha, called Maud of Wales, Princess of Great Britain and of Ireland and daughter of Edward VII and the Queen Alexandra—which explains all the more the rather striking resemblance between Tsar Nicholas II and King George V—and son of Louise of Sweden, herself daughter of Charles XV and Princess Louise of the Netherlands, herself granddaughter of the King of Prussia, Frederic III, and niece of Augusta Victoria of Schleswig-Holstein-Sonderburg-Augustenburg and of her husband Friedrich Wilhelm Viktor Albert of Hohenzollern, called Wilhelm II, called Willy by those close to him, Emperor of Germany, who, it's worth noting, was never invited, as a child, to enjoy the sumptuous snacks that his brave grandmother, Louise of Hesse-Cassel, organized each summer for all the other cousins and nephews, poor little Willy, such frustration, he who already had a terrible complex because of his atrophied arm, a birth defect that one was never able to console his mother over, the Kaiserin Victoria, Empress of Austria, who was none other than the daughter of Queen Victoria and of Prince Consort Albert of Saxe-Coburg-Gotha, himself cousin of King Léopold II of Belgium, himself brother of Empress Charlotte of Mexico, herself wife of Ferdinand Maximilin Joseph of Habsburg-Lorraine, called Maximilian I, Archduke of Austria, Royal Prince of Hungary and of Bohemia, Vice-King of Lombardy-Venetia, and sister-in-law of Marie of Hohenzollern-Sigmaringen, herself sister of Stephanie, Queen of Portugal, and of Charles, King of Romania, and granddaughter of Grand Duke Charles II of Baden and of the Grand Duchess born Stéphanie de Beauharnais, while on her side Ferdinand I, Prince of the house of Saxe-Coburg-Gotha, Tsar of the Bulgarians, is the fifth and last child of Prince Auguste of Saxe-Coburg-Kohary, himself son of Ferdinand of Saxe-Coburg-Saafeld and of the Hungarian Princess

Antoinette of Kohary, and brother of King Consort Ferdinand II of Portugal and of the Duchess of Nemours, and nephew of Léopold I of Belgium, and German cousin of Prince Consort Albert and of his wife Queen Victoria, and dignified husband of Clémentine of Orléans, herself daughter of Louis-Philippe and of Maria Amalia of Bourbon, Princess of the Two Sicilies, who is mother of numerous progeny including another August of Saxe-Coburg-Kohary, husband of Leopoldina of Braganza, Princess of Brazil and daughter of Emperor Pedro II, as well as Philipp of Saxe-Coburg-Kohary, husband of Princess Louise of Belgium, eldest daughter of King Léopold II, himself uncle of Albert I, Prince of Saxe-Coburg-Gotha, son of Prince Philippe and of Princess Marie of Hohenzollern-Sigmaringen, as well as Clothilde of Saxe-Coburg-Kohary, wife of Archduke Joseph of Habsburg-Hungary, as well as Amalie of Saxe-Coburg-Kohary, wife of Maximilian-Emanuel of Wittelsbach, Duke of Bavaria and brother of Empress Elizabeth of Austria, called Sissi, naturally, and it goes without saying that the aforementioned Ferdinand I of Bulgaria, sometimes called Oui-Oui, is no longer but a shadow of himself, it seems, when he marries Princess Marie-Louise of Bourbon-Parma, daughter of Robert I, Duke of Parma, of Piacenza and of Guastalla, who, conversely, valiant and vigorous, marries in a first marriage Princess Pia of the Two Sicilies, then in a second marriage Antonia of Braganza, daughter of Miguel I of Portugal, and engenders over the course of these two unions no fewer than twenty-four children, of which a good quarter, alas, turn out to be mentally retarded, but of whom the remaining three quarters are quasi-sane, among which include, in addition to Marie-Louise, previously cited, Zita, Empress of Austria and Queen of Hungary, wife of Charles I, as well as René, husband of Margaret of Denmark and father of Queen Anne of Romania, as well as Elias, husband of the Archduchess Maria-Anna of Austria, who is none other than the daughter of the Archduke Frederick of Teschen and his wife Princess Isabella of Croy, who has as a female companion a certain Sophie Chotek, who is herself a Countess and descendant of Rudolph I of the Holy Roman Empire, who marries out of love and morganatically, Franz-Ferdinand of Habsburg-Este, Archduke heir to Austria-Hungary, who, it must be said, is an unparalleled shooter, a passionate and efficient hunter as proven in his hunting notebooks, preciously preserved, from which it is revealed that the Archduke killed over the course of his life two hundred seventy-four thousand eight hundred eighty-nine animals of all species, of which a good number were exotic, like tigers, lions, and elephants, many of which can be physically admired, dead and mounted, among the hundreds of thousand trophies displayed in his chateau in Konopiště, in Bohemia, in the middle of his superb collection of antiques, another great passion of Franz-Ferdinand's, who, incidentally, is himself shot like a rabbit, by Princip, first name Gavrilo, a poor unfortunate Yugoslav nationalist, on June 28, 1914, in Sarajevo.

In sum, it's a family affair.

Airing dirty laundry: nineteen million dead.

And we're still asking ourselves why Poincaré had to get involved!

"BELGIUM," says Gustave.

"Belgium?" says Emma.

"They've crossed the border," says the father.

"How?" says the daughter. "What about the principle of neutrality?"

"Flouted," he says. "Trampled."

"But they have no right!" she says.

"The right? . . ."

Gustave Van Ecke stops, looks at his daughter. She is sitting at the kitchen table, a bowl of warm milk in front of her. He looks at the boy, sitting at the same table, a bowl of hot chocolate in front of him. He turns back to his daughter.

"It's written in black and white," he says. "See for yourself."

He puts a newspaper beneath her eyes. Emma doesn't move. She doesn't touch it. She sees the big headlines, the bold letters, it's enough. Gustave sets himself in motion again.

"A 'scrap of paper,'" he says. "See how the German chancellor described the treaty ratifying Belgian neutrality. That's what he dared reply to the British ambassador."

"Germany signed that treaty!" says Emma.

"Yes," says Gustave. "And yesterday, at the crack of dawn, his troops entered the country by force!"

He stops again. Deals a blow to the table. The wood gives a muted sound at the contact with his fist.

"At this very moment," he says, "the soldiers of the Reich are quickly heading to the town of Liège."

Emma tenses.

"Liège?"

Father and daughter stare at each other. There is, under Gustave's heavy, drooping eyelids, anguish, indignation, anger, revolt. Emma sees it. She sees all of this.

Liège. Grâce-Hollogne. She was only a child. Her memories are sporadic and hazy. Mirages? An impression of immensity. Of plantations. Of infinite orchards. Apple trees. The sound of rain on the leaves, a crackling that could be heard from inside the house with the windows closed. The deceitful spring snow. The white flakes in the breeze. The thousands of aligned tree trunks. An army in the countryside. An army of flowering trees.

"Who will stop them?" asks Gustave.

He starts pacing again.

His mother, his sisters, his uncles and aunts, they are dead or else they left the country a long time ago. There must be, spread out, a few distant cousins still there, a few second and third nieces and nephews. Some drops of his blood. Strangers. Is it them he's thinking of? Is it the trees?

"They're wolves," he says. "A hoard of famished wolves. They care nothing for rights, except for those of the strongest."

Emma gently shakes her head.

"No, Papa," she says. "They are men. Nothing more."

Her tone is suddenly calm, poised.

Gustave shakes his head in his turn, but it seems more painful.

"In that case," he says, "it's worse."

Emma turns towards the boy. He's standing behind her chair. Hair tousled. A white shirt on his back. He is barefoot. She finds him handsome. She shaved him the day before. Mustache and beard. That's how she prefers him: smooth-faced. Just his skin. Often, she's the one who shaves him.

"They will never be satisfied," says Gustave. "If we sit by, they will devour everyone and everything."

Emma lets out a sigh, restrained, discreet, then turns around to her beloved.

"I don't believe," she says, "that we have any intention of sitting by. I remind you that France is mobilized. And if I've understood, England will also get involved. Not to mention Russia and I don't know what other country. That seems to me to be a lot already."

"You don't know the Germans," says Gustave.

"I know a few," says Emma. "They're named Bach, Schumann, Beethoven, Wagner, Goethe, Schiller. They're named Mendelssohn..."

"Alas, they are not the ones in power," says Gustave. "They don't preside over the destiny of their people."

"That's true," says Emma. "They speak to all of humanity."

"Good God!" says Gustave. "I know what these artists are worth, and I appreciate them as much as you. But we are not talking about music or literature. We are not talking about creation. We are talking about the exact opposite. We're talking about war, Emma!"

Red. Redder than ever.

It's a strange word. War. In the mouth of her father. As if she's hearing it for the first time. What rhymes? *Guerre, père, mère, frère* ... Look for the odd one out. Weak rhymes. *Atterre, cratère, enterre, cimitère, enfer, vers, vers qui, vers quoi, Werther, souffrances ... Je vais quitter cette chaumière et rentrer dans ma prison.* No, that doesn't rhyme anymore. Neither weak nor strong.

Emma lowers her eyes. Her bowl on the table. The milk grows cold. Not a wrinkle on the surface. The truth is at the bottom. She had planned to make crepes this afternoon. For the afternoon snack. The boy loves crepes. He can gobble down a dozen in a row. She loves to watch him devour them.

"They are masters of this domain, too," says Gustave. "This isn't their first time. You hadn't been born yet in the seventies, but I was there!"

Bismarck. The mastiff. The spiked helmets. He remembers, yes. Back then they were called the Prussians. The young Gustave was of fighting age. But Gustave Van Ecke was a Belgian citizen and Belgium was neutral. In those times treaties were respected, even by a dog. Gustave had not taken up arms. He had not batted an eyelid. He had endeavored to grow apples.

"History doesn't repeat itself," he says, "it only gets worse. They will always want more. Always more! Always more!"

More what?

Crepes with orange blossom. Crepes with honey. Crepes with cane syrup. With blueberry jam. How can he swallow all that? How can he digest it? When they're alone again, after, she covers his stomach with a thousand little kisses. She pecks at it. His tummy, she calls it. Very taut, very full. It's like bread dough. She puts her cheek on it. Her ear. She listens. Things are happening below. Funny sounds. Gurgles, rumblings. Who knows how to imitate the cry of the greedy enzyme better than her? It's a sight to see her grimace when she does it: like a badly congested frog. They laugh.

I know not whether it is day or night; the whole world is nothing to me.

"Let's hope you're wrong," she says. "Let's hope the men who govern Germany will quickly come back to reason."

"Reason? . . ."

"And if that doesn't happen, our only hope will be that our army will know how to rebuff them."

"And us?" says Gustave.

Emma raises her head.

"Us?"

Her father looks at her. Looks at the boy. Back to his daughter.

"Me," he says. "What do I do? . . . The barbarians are at the gates. Belgium, my home country, is being attacked. France, my adopted country, is in danger. What am I supposed to do? Wait? Hope, as you say? Perhaps get down on my knees and pray, too? In case God, for once, might take pity on good men!"

War.

It is already here.

It is in the good eyes of Gustave, in his crimson face, in the veins of his inflamed neck. Emma sees it. She wants him to loosen his collar. Loosen your collar, Papa.

"No," says Gustave. "I am not going to stay here with my arms crossed waiting for it to happen. I will not let other men act alone, on my behalf, to defend my liberty, my life. I am not going to give myself over to divine grace nor to the German military!"

It is in his voice.

It is in his words, in all the words that spew from his mouth.

"Since all of France is mobilized," says Gustave, "there is no reason that I shouldn't be too. I've thought about it: I will volunteer. I will enlist."

A sound comes out of Emma's throat. The beginning of a laugh, nervous, that she cannot hold back, that recalls her imitation of the boy's gurgles.

"Enlist?" she says.

Father and daughter stare hard at each other.

"Come on, Papa . . ."

"I know that age is not working in my favor," says Gustave. "But that doesn't . . ."

"Not only age," says Emma. "Everything. Your health. Your inexperience. Your . . . your incompetence! Excuse me, but have you ever held a rifle in your hands?"

"That can be learned," says Gustave. "Plus, there are other ways of serving. I presume they won't send me to fight on the front lines, unless the end is near. However, they will also need people in the back. For maintenance, for distribution, for taking care of the wounded, who knows? I can help. No matter the task they choose to entrust me with, I am confident that I will be capable of accomplishing it. And no matter what, I will be more useful than if I stay here."

"This is foolish," says Emma. "It's impossible. You can't do that."

"My daughter," says Gustave, "I am not asking your permission. My decision has been made. I am informing you, that's all."

It is here.

It is even in the silence itself.

"I feel that it is my duty," says Gustave. "And to be frank, I feel that it's not just mine . . ."

He looks at the boy. The boy looks at him. Emma looks at them, one, then the other. Quick movements of the eyes. Her eyelids flicker, once, twice. And she stands abruptly, jostling the table. The bowl pitches and spills, the drink spreads. By reflex the boy unglues his thighs from the chair to try to stop the flow, but immediately something stops him. He freezes. He looks at Emma. He looks at Gustave.

Father and daughter stare at each other.

"What do you mean to say?" says Emma.

Gustave inhales. His chest inflates beneath his shirt.

"I mean to say that Félix . . ."

"No," says Emma. "Don't mix Félix up in this."

She turns towards the boy.

"Sit down," she says.

He looks at her. He slowly sits back down on his chair. The milk continues to spread in a rivulet, towards the edge of the table.

Gustave sighs.

"Whether we like it or not," he says, "we are all mixed up in this, Emma."

"Not him," she says.

"Him just like everyone else," says Gustave.

"No," says Emma. "As far as I know, he is not a soldier."

"Neither are the majority of the troops," says Gustave. "None of those young people are soldiers by profession."

"Félix has nothing to do with them," says Emma. "He has nothing to do with any of it."

"He's a man," says Gustave. "Of enlisting age."

"Precisely," says Emma. "You, you are perhaps too old for them to send to fight, but him? Him, they won't hesitate. Him and all those young people you speak of, they'll send them into the fire. Without any qualms. And it's them who will find themselves facing the enemy. It's them who will be on the front lines."

"It's war, Emma. You don't seem to understand . . ."

"It's you who doesn't seem to understand. Do you realize that he could be hurt? That he could even . . . That he could even . . ."

She can't say it. The word doesn't come. She brings her hand to her throat. She shakes her head forcefully. No, she says.

A fly lands in the puddle of milk. Black on white. It drinks, it breathes. For the insect it's a godsend. A fortuitous spring.

"Do we really have a choice?" says Gustave.

"Yes, we have one," says Emma. "We always have a choice. It's just a matter of saying no. If all the soldiers, from both sides, if all of them said no, what would your chancellor do? Your military, what would they do?"

"Those are fine words, Emma. But futile. Wishful thinking. Unfortunately that's not how it works."

"Sheep," says Emma. "Sheep being led to slaughter. It's just a matter of leaving the herd."

"It's just a matter of this . . . It's just a matter of that . . . No," says Gustave, "it's not that simple. Like it or not: it's the law."

"The law is wrong," says Emma.

"It's the law," says Gustave. "Be realistic. If Félix doesn't show up on his own, one day or another they'll end up coming to search for him. It's called desertion, and it's subject to capital punishment."

"Who knows about him?" says Emma. "Who knows where he is? No one. No one even knows his identity. How could they come to search for him? Are you . . . Are you going to inform on him?"

Gustave goes pale. His hands are on the back of a chair. His fingers squeeze the wooden crosstie.

"Do you really think I'm capable of that?" he says.

Emma doesn't respond.

War only rhymes with war.

"People other than me will take it upon themselves," says Gustave. "Neighbors, here or in town. People who will not understand why their father, their brother, their husband had to leave, and not him. Families who will consider it an injustice, and deservedly so."

"And if he's German?" says Emma.

"What do you . . ."

"We don't know where he's from, in the end who's to say he wasn't born in Berlin? Or in Munich? That would be great, wouldn't it? The enemy seed sown right in the middle of the French army."

"Emma . . ." says Gustave.

She shakes her head.

"No," she says.

Gustave starts pacing again. Does a hundred steps around the table. Wild boar. Sentinel. Emma doesn't move. The boy watches them, him, her.

"You're the one who was talking about sheep," says Gustave. "What else will we be when Germany invades us? When we have to live under their yoke. Under their boots. Bleating and submissive."

"All things considered," says Emma, "I prefer a living sheep to a dead hero."

She said it. The word. She pronounced it.

"You don't believe that," says Gustave. "Not you."

"One more or one less soldier won't change anything," says Emma.

"And as for his conscience?" says Gustave.

"His conscience?"

"Can we endure watching others leave? Compatriots. Comrades. Knowing that they're fighting for us, that they're giving their strength and their blood for us, and all the while remaining tranquilly sheltered in our cocoons? What decent man can endure that?"

"Isn't that what all the leaders do?" says Emma. "Those who command. The generals, the leaders. Those who bark the loudest against
the enemy. Who extol courage and sacrifice for the love of the country.
Will they fight, those men? Certainly not. The courage of others, the
sacrifice of others: that's enough for them. I don't get the impression
that their consciences suffer for it."

"They're not all like that," says Gustave.

"Is that right?" says Emma. "Would you like for us to add it up
when it's all over?"

The fly has drunk. It is sated. It is full and heavy. Too heavy. When
it wants to take off, it no longer can.

"And your conscience?" says Emma.

"Mine?" says Gustave.

"I thought you considered Félix your son," says Emma. "How can
a father send his own child into such great peril? How can he accept
that his life will be at stake?"

"Don't be unfair," says Gustave. "I didn't want for this to happen.
If it were only up to . . ."

"That's exactly what everyone will say," says Emma. "That they
didn't want it. That it wasn't their fault. That they were obliged and
forced. Of course. No one wants war, and yet we wage it. And what's
the difference in the end? The dead will be dead, and they won't come
back. I assure you, it's just a matter of saying no."

She said it again. Two times.

"Félix's life, yours, mine," says Gustave, "what are they worth? Can
you tell me, Emma . . . Can you tell me, in all honesty, in all sincerity,
what meaning our lives will have if we are stripped of liberty? What
value will they have in the clutches of a tyrant?"

Father and daughter stare at each other.

"My dear Papa," says Emma, "if that is your conviction, if this is
how you think you can ease your conscience, if it's not possible make
you come back to reason . . . well, then do it. Go. Enlist. Try, at least. I

can tell you, in all honesty, in all sincerity, that my heart will be broken to see you leave. But I cannot go against your wishes. It's your right, fine . . . That said, it doesn't give you the right to drag Félix in your wake. That, no. You cannot force him."

"I have no intention of doing so," says Gustave.

"You cannot decide for him," says Emma.

"You are right," says Gustave. "That decision is his alone. So why not ask him the question?"

He turns towards the boy.

"Félix?" he says.

The boy looks at him.

The fly is drowning in the milk. Its legs are stuck. Its wings flap, vibrate in vain.

"Félix?" says Emma.

The boy looks at her.

It is here.

It is in his eyes.

Emma sees it. She turns pale.

The boy gets up. Slowly he gets up.

Emma shakes her head.

He is standing.

Pale and pallid and breathless she shakes her head.

"No," she says.

Tomorrow the traveler shall come, he shall come, who beheld me in beauty: his eye shall seek me in the field around, but he shall not find me.

The fly is dead.

Look: a dead fly in a puddle of milk. Black and white.

OF THE TWO OF THEM, she will be the first to fight. She who looked for gold and found lead. With all her strength and with all her weapons, she fought. She argued, begged, cried, she hit (her fists beating on the boy's chest). He responded to her with passivity, a sad and contrite look that exasperated her all the more, that drove her crazy. She wasn't far from strangling him with her bare hands to keep him from going to get himself killed.

She doesn't understand. But the boy, even if he had been endowed with speech, would not have been able to explain it to her. Men wage war: there is no other explanation.

They returned to Paris. Here, as in Toussus, she wanders. She goes back into each room where they laughed, where they read, where they compulsively or tenderly made love, she contemplates these places with the eyes of an old woman: like fragments of another life, so long ago, perhaps before this one, perhaps just dreamed, imaginary.

She is mad at her father. She is mad at the boy. At the entire universe.

And during this time period Gustave lobbies the committees. Persistent and flushed he continues his soliciting. He has found, in his memory and in his notebooks, the names of people that he used to spend time with, acquaintances, relations, who might be able to help him now. Men who work in the administration, cabinets and ministries or close to it.

But it's not necessary: with the sudden demand the army very quickly opens recruitment centers to foreign volunteers. They go, the boy and him. They are not alone. There are thousands of immigrants of all nationalities, ready to give their lives for the country that took them in. They march in the streets crying "Vive la France!" The crowd cheers them. They are here.

Gustave left his cane at the house. He straightens his chest and sucks in his stomach, struggles not to give in to the pain in his hip. His gait is so stiff that it looks martial. When he presents himself they don't laugh in his face. They appreciate his intention. They admire his sense of duty. They refuse him nevertheless. Gustave insists. They finally tell him, with all due respect, that his presence among a regiment would be more of a burden than a relief. It's a no.

Emma was right: they don't want him. The war has little use for an old arborist.

However, if it's any consolation, they accept the boy. They are not concerned about his origins nor his identity. He is young, virile, those are the important criteria, the only ones that matter. They won't ask him to read or write, they won't ask him to speak. They will ask him for obedience and devotion. For the rest they will teach him everything he needs to know. The enemy has already crossed the Marne, time is of the essence, sign here.

The boy takes the quill they hand him. The nonsensical scribbles that he executes at the bottom of the document mean something to him: Mazeppa. The name of a survivor. Emma insisted—he gives her this, at least.

Leaving, Gustave stumbles. The boy has to support him. "My son . . ." moans the old man. He is one hundred years old. He is one thousand years old. "My son . . ." A tortured tone, a frightened look. What have I done? he seems to say. He grips the boy's arm. His eyelids are lined with red, his eyes mist over. He looks away suddenly.

That night he sits slumped in the living room armchair, his false collar askew, his tie hanging, his shirt rumpled. The boy is seated on the floor at his feet, his cheek placed on his thighs. Gustave caresses his head. He's let himself drink too much mediocre wine from Xérès that had been prescribed to him by his doctor and friend Amédée. Night falls. He cannot hold back. There have already been so many others. There have already been too many for him. He speaks. His voice is heavy and monotonous, his words muddled. He speaks of former times. He speaks of Laure. Laure's beauty. Laure's generosity. That distant and marvelous time. He cannot hold back. Laure's hands. Ivory on ivory. Sometimes a large tear overflows, rolls down the limp skin of his cheek and gets lost in the white of his beard. Laure's smile. The boy is tempted to turn around because he can't believe that these words are meant for him. But yes, but yes. That miraculous time. She lived and walked and laughed and slept and all at his side. He could look at her. Contemplate her. He could, oh! Heavens above, he could touch her. Laure's hair. Nothing intoxicated him more than burying his face in it. He closes his eyes and breathes; his nostrils grow wider. He opens his eyes again. Another tear. It glistens in the orb of his eyelid. It slides in silence. There have been so many days and so many nights since then. No one thought to draw the curtains. The moon is full, it's not visible but they sense it through the panes, the room bathes in its milky powder. Laure found. Laure vanished. Gustave talks and cries. The boy listens. His eyes are open. On his temple the fingers of the old man, his breath, his drunken breath. Men are weak. Men are crazy. They can't be restrained. She had given birth to her child. Their child. As true as the stars in the sky. As true as the fact that they are born and shine in order to guide us in the night. And when they go out where do we go? Where is the path? He thought about offering her a concerto, a symphony that would bear her name. Laure. But too late, too late. Laure of his life. Can we believe that the stars die? After a long while, Gustave's voice runs dry. His tears dry. He nods off. And the boy stays there, head on his knees, until dawn.

The date is fixed. A chalky September day.

Emma is in the bedroom. She will not accompany him. It's beyond her strength. Gustave signals to the boy: Go say goodbye to her. He waits. The boy crosses the corridor and knocks twice on the door. No response. He knocks a little louder. Then he turns the handle and softly pushes. He pokes his head in and sees her. She is standing facing the window. She's wearing a mauve silk dressing gown whose belt, untied, hangs on each side. Underneath, an eggshell nightshirt. Her hair falls over her shoulders. She is pale, her features haggard. For how long has she not been able to sleep? The boy enters and closes the door behind him. On the threshold he hesitates for a moment, then advances. She brusquely extends her hand, palm forward.

"Don't come any closer," she says.

He stops.

Between them the length of the rug. That rug where so many times, so many times. They look at each other. She breathes quickly, as after a race. He can see beneath the silk, beneath the shell, her chest rises and falls, her breasts swell. The silence continues. Then:

"Will you come back?" she says.

He nods yes. He seems convinced, determined.

"You see this window?" she says. "Look at it. Look at it hard. If you don't come back, I'll throw myself from it. And I won't fly away!"

She clenches her jaw. Her scar seems to pulse beneath her contracting cheek muscles.

He knows that she is capable of it.

Yes, he says.

He wants to feel her against him. To throw himself at her knees and wrap her in his arms. He takes a step but once again she stops him with a gesture and with her voice.

"No," she says. "Go away!"

He remains immobile, fists clenched. Two turtledoves fly through the sky behind the glass. Her eyes sting him. He pivots suddenly and leaves the bedroom rapidly, without turning around.

As soon as he has left Emma buckles—the sound of the door closing: like a punch to the stomach. She bites her lips to keep from crying.

Then she suddenly curls them and her entire face tenses, creases, a hideous grimace disfigures her. Her legs give way, she sinks, she falls to her knees, she falls on all fours on the rug—that rug where so many times—and her arms give out in their turn, she falls on her side and she remains there, curled up, shriveled, breathing in big gulps of that air that is missing him, and exhaling it in a sort of moan, a deep whine, continuous, harrowing, that has nothing human about it except its essence, she stays like that for a long time, a long time.

The streets are full of people. Cars, horses, pedestrians. Surrounding the train station it's worse. The driver complains. The boy helps Gustave get out of the taxi. He no longer has an age, Gustave. On the platform they're jostled. The trains whistle and spit, white steam, black soot beneath the framework, the cars swallow men and animals. Here and there couples embrace as though for a final waltz, silent, in suspense, the dancers deaf to all sound other than that of their hearts, deaf to cries, to songs, to interjections, to bravado, to barked orders, to wailing, and the hands advance on the big clock above their heads. Then Gustave throws all his weight against the boy. He embraces him, he squeezes him and nearly suffocates him. His rough wild boar skin scrapes his neck. Forgive me, he whispers. Forgive me! . . . (Listen, listen to his voice because it's the last time you'll hear it.) His words are drowned in the racket. Another whistle, another hissing of the smoke escaping from the machine's nostrils, and then the grinding of the wheels on the rails, the train starts going, the train grows distant and disappears, carrying the boy with it. And others are arriving already, other trains and other men, but Gustave is still there, standing on the platform, leaning on his cane, in the same spot, and he seems set on staying there for all eternity.

Of the two of them, he will be the first to die.

EMMA WRITES:

My love,

　　My love, my love, my love, my love, my love, my love, my love, my love, my love, my love, this is not ink, this is my blood. I give it in place of yours. I give it so that you won't have to spill a single drop of your own.

E.

THE COMMANDER-IN-CHIEF DECREES:

"A troop that cannot advance must, at any price, keep the conquered land and be killed on the spot rather than retreat. In the current circumstances, no weakness can be tolerated."

JOFFRE

LET'S GO CHILDREN. Charge! . . . The torso emerges. He sees it. He sees the open mouth, the large hole beneath the mustache, a pale pink tongue, almost white. The arm traces a circular arc, the thin line of a rifle pointing towards the sky like a lance, so thin, so frail beneath the immense gray sky. The scream is lost in the roar of the shells. The earth is sprinkled. A baptism. A geyser. Flashes of steel. A shadow passes, barely a brush, and the face of a man is cleanly sliced in two, neatly lopped like the top of a boiled egg. Everything above the nose is carried away, and, flabbergasted, he sees something fall back behind, on the other slope of the trench, something that rolls to the bottom. The man's skull. A man without a skull. Truncated. Just the stump of the neck and a sprout above, an unknown plant, carnivorous, a cropped mustache, black and red, more and more red, and in the gaping jaws, a tongue that still moves, he sees it. Then everything teeters, all of it together, the arm and the torso and the stump and the plant, all of it plunges forward, and the large gaping hole of the mouth moves to eat the mud. The glorious day. The glorious day has arrived. Charge! Everyone with me! Another person takes over. And if it's not him it's another. The same. All the same. Aligned. Uniform. He screams from less than a yard away, but the enormous noise eats all the sounds, devours them. The cotton in their eardrums like feverish nights. It whistles and buzzes, he hears his own breath inside, it echoes in his skull. Move your hide, my boy! He melts into the wall, but the beast has stirred, moves, the long body of the earthworm undulates in the tunnel, each ring counts, he is part of it, he must follow. Cut off its head, it grows back. Cut off its tail, it grows back. He is among the last men to exit. He hoists himself above the embankment and he sees it: no man's land. It is full of men. They run. He runs. Machine gun to the right! Stooped, back rounded. Arms encumbered by a rifle, one hand over the breech, one hand on the butt. He doesn't shoot, he runs. In place or almost. Like feverish nights. Each step costs so much effort. The greasy earth that wants to hold him back, that grips, that clings, that sucks his boots. He has to wrest himself. Two pounds beneath his foot, four pounds. Each stride is worth its weight in clay. He slides. He falls. He gets back up. He runs. He doesn't know towards what. A hundred yards further is nothing but smoke, and rings of fire and an abundance of that dirty glebe that spurts and rises and rains lumps onto their backs. And through that screen they penetrate and disappear, he sees them, creatures roaring or silent, that look clumsy, grotesque, terrifying, like a horde of phantoms, a legion of slimy specters emerged from their sepulchers, from the deepest shadows, from the last putrid cellblock of hell, only to return there after nabbing everything they can, flesh and souls, on the way. My leg! My leg! In front, behind, around. The living dead. He is one of them. He follows the surge. He breathes. The air burns. Sweat drips into his eyes. He runs. And always the sound, the sound so massive and harsh that you can touch it, bang into it, a wall of sound, a rock, an avalanche of sound that keeps rolling, rolling, and that makes the air vibrate and the ground tremble and that knocks him out, crushes him, buries him. Son of a bitch! I've been hit! He sees them fall. He runs avoiding the holes, the craters, the burial mounds that arise and are flattened in the same handful of seconds like wheels, waves, a brown swell come from the open sea and its Isles of the Dead. He rushes in front of the corpses, he brakes and skids, all those bodies, he sees them, more and more, those sprawled bodies, those bodies in the way, those heaps of bodies, those pieces of bodies, he doesn't dare step over them. He sees a man dancing to his right. He sees him spinning around, arms outspread, on one leg, the other one absent, vanished, in its place hang fringes, shreds, he turns around on his only foot like a weather vane in the wind, like a frantic scarecrow, a sad simulacrum, no one laughs, the birds left a long time ago. It's the men that fly. He sees them. Three at once projected into the sky, one, two, three suns that don't shine, scattered, nude, dislocated. Empty pants unfurl and float for a moment, fold back like an accordion and drop. The bloody flags. He sees each detail. Fragments as if they were magnified a thousand times that permeate his retinas with an incredible precision. He sees the open eyes of the dead. The veins on white eyeballs. He sees the stitched stripes. He sees the grenades on the leather buttons. He sees the medals. He sees the belt buckles. He sees the bubble of blood beneath the nostrils. He can count the beads on the rosaries around their wrists. He can count each bullet that passes with its hornet whistling. Listen. And yet he doesn't see the whole. That escapes him. It's blurry and fluctuating, it's elusive. Do you hear the howls? Don't leave me! His foot suddenly blocked, he almost falls again. He lowers his head. He sees the fingers squeezing his ankle. The hand. The arm. The encrusted face. The big blue eyes raised towards him. He sees the punctured stomach, split open, and the rosy guts, the violet intestines spilling out, the other hand rummaging in this magma. Don't leave me! It's only a wheeze, it's only a murmur between the lips through a bubbling pink froth, but he hears it. He stays there staring at the man. Perhaps a second. Perhaps a minute. He's seeing Death in the flesh. Then a spluttering, a burst, the hornets sting the ground in front of him, splash his greatcoat. He jumps. Those ferocious soldiers. He tries to take back his leg, but Death holds on. Groveling Death. He pulls harder and the man weakens, he sees the entrails move, viscous, a nest of tangled serpents. Death's talons cling to his gaiters, hold him back. Don't leave . . . He pulls sharply and liberates himself. Onward to battle. One step. One step. March. He leans over and vomits bile as he keeps marching. March. March. Then he starts to run. But the odor follows him. No wind. The air reeks. It smells like sulfur and gunpowder and shit and blood and the bottoms of wells and charred flesh. Henri! Death stinks. He runs and everywhere he goes he brings the odor, which weighs on his lungs and on his heart. Henri! Suddenly the earth opens, his heels falls into the void, he teeters and tumbles and rolls. On his back, feet in the air like a woodlouse. The sky opposite: his entire field of vision. He feels a burning gust above his head, on the edge of the crater, a dragon's ferruginous breath. He closes his eyes. He opens them again. Always the gray sky. Henri, where are you? He no longer has his rifle. He looks for it, and he sees it two yards away planted by the bayonet. He's back on his knees, on all fours, he tries to get up but a shadow surges, like an immense bat, it jumps into the hole and lands at his side. Keep down! A weight on the top of his skull sinks his face into the ground. Mouth full of dirt. Nuptial embrace. My love, my love made of mud. Slug lips. The taste of silt on his tongue. It squeaks between his teeth. It plugs up his nostrils. He suffocates. He struggles. He gets free. Henri! He spits and coughs and spurts clots of blackish mucus from his nose. With a wipe of his sleeve he dries his eyes and discovers the bat. It has a red beard and is missing an ear. Auricle, lobe, cartilage, nothing left, nothing more than a wound in which pus and blood gleam. The bat crouched, cape folded, seems so calm, not hurt, not afraid, chewing tobacco or something else, staring at a line right above the rim, the horizon or something else, it seems to count the strikes, does it hear them through the bleeding hole? Doesn't look at him. He sees the copper jaw chew, he sees the drips on the neck, on the collar. Impure blood. And then it jumps again, the bat the size of an albatross, it deploys, the wingspan, the sails, it embraces the sky and takes flight. Henri, I can't see you anymore! He doesn't want to be alone. He gets up. He grabs the Lebel. He climbs the slope and gets out of there. He runs. He sees the bodies, other bodies, more and more, roses and bedstraw grow in the shadow of burial mounds. Grow, grow, bloom, as far as the eye can see. Bouquets. Clusters. Entire fields. Fertile humus. Fetid compost. And the great sowing of steel continues. Scattered limbs and entrails. A vast plow, the blade sinks and returns and splits. Quenches. He doesn't hesitate, he steps over or he crushes. He sees the screaming man. Henri! Henri! He sees him move aside the curtain of smoke with vague gestures of his arms, like a slow wave, a weightless breaststroke. The solitary man. The blind man. Quenches. Quenches. The man wanders at random, disarmed, disoriented, lost, because it is the darkest of all abysses, a place darker than the blackness where the damned themselves are sent to wander for eternity, there is always a deeper circle of hell. Henri! The man staggers, stumbles, yells the name of his friend or brother, his twin, or perhaps his son that he will no longer see, or perhaps his father who preceded him to the other side, to the other shore, who calls to him, too, who waits for him, or perhaps it's his own name that he repeats, perhaps it's himself that he's searching for, what he was, what he had been, what he no longer is. Go! Charge! Whatever the cost. Cut off the head. Cut off the tail. He runs. And still the odor and worse. And still the racket. Hornets, wasps, bees, swarms, enraged, tenacious. Whistles and claps. Thunder. *Ultima ratio regis.* The strikes repeated infinitely, the echo of the echo of the echo never fades. Over there the haze has a thousand pairs of eyes that blink. Yellow eyes, orange, the color of fire. And their tears burn. And their looks kill. All these dead, the living dead. He sees them. No phantom comes back from behind the screen. The fog is stronger than them. As many as there are it swallows them, regiment, battalion, company, it breathes them, it gulps them down and grinds them and sucks the marrow from their bones and probably their souls with it and what it regurgitates is a soft and inconsistent pile of who knows what. And that's where he runs to. Mazeppa. His name is Mazeppa, but they call him something else. They call him soldier. They call him infantryman. They call him a number. But who calls him? Captain down! Someone help me! He sees the man leaning over a shapeless pile and straightening back up and signaling, waving his hand as if to say goodbye, farewell. It's a small creature made of mud, brown and blue. A homunculus. An imp. Farewell. Farewell. A projectile slashes his neck. He sees the line break. He sees the spring spurt, the scarlet stream. He sees the kepi go askew. It's a farce. He sees him gesticulate. He sees him collapse with his uniform like the ones the djinns wore in the desert at the opera house. In the distance a tree catches fire. The only tree. It blazes. A burning bush. Living torch. He sees it. He saw the fires of Saint John burn in the plains. It was beautiful. From the top of his boulder. He was an eagle. What is he now? One of them. Legion and cohort. Soldier, phantom, bat, woodlouse, specter, scarecrow. Same. All the same. Ectoplasm. Living-dead. Living. Dead. Living. Dead. Chance or something else. He runs between graves. And suddenly a mute throbbing, that then sharpens, rips through the cloud. That one among them all, why? When he notices it he knows that it's for him. He knows it. His ears plug. And he receives the blow, the whip, the dragon's breath, the enormous flatulence. He loses his footing. He takes off. Floats. Falls back down. The avalanche covers him. The glebe on his back, in piles, in heaps. The sky disappears. The mouth closes. He doesn't see anything anymore. Black. Black and silence. Farewell. Farewell. A shroud of clay. He is underground. He is in his cave. Dead. Living. Dead. What is he? The loud noise now deafening, light years away. All he hears is his heart. His cannon heart, his mortar heart. Ultima ratio. So fast and so strong that it's going to implode. He panics. He wants to get out. He wants air and smoke, the blaze, the thunder, the bees. He wants to move but his body is draped, it's weighed down, squeezed, he squirms in his pod like a larva, a caterpillar in its cocoon. He was an eagle and now? A fetus. An embryo. He wants to be born. He needs air. He spreads his jaw but it's earth that enters, that fills his mouth, that obstructs his throat. My love another kiss my love. Tongue and palate, gums. He swallows earth. The earth swallows him. He asphyxiates. Dead. And then a tremor, another one. The ground vibrates. The earth shaken. His body rears, a limp rag, a meager dance, a bucking. In a flash he sees the sky. He winds up flat on his stomach. He vomits. He breathes with his mouth wide open. The air. The air and the smoke and the gray sky. He reaps. His shoulder hurts him, ants in his bones. Living. He doesn't have a rifle anymore. He doesn't have a shoe or a sock on his left foot. He sees his bare foot. He sees his toes. Henri! It's a hole. The bottom of a funnel. He sees the sky above. So vast. The birdless sky. Henri, where are you? His ears unplug and his eardrums whistle and it's that noise once again, intense, horrendous, the cataclysms, the big metallic organs, forged iron, broken pipes, white hot. The odor again. The gunpowder and the blood and the shit and the tissue and the charred flesh. He breathes. In his nostrils, in his lungs the rank exhalation, the deleterious miasma. It stinks. The punctured guts. The carrion. Death stinks. Life stinks. But this odor is his own. This stench is him. What is he? What is he not anymore? His name is Mazeppa. He has shit himself.

My love,

    A cloud, just one. A tiny little cloud of white cotton in a great blue sky. I thought of a chick. The most brazen of the brood. The most mischievous. The one that makes his mama sweat. The one that makes her laugh too (but she hides it in front of the brothers and sisters). The adorable rascal. He must have escaped from her surveillance. A runaway. A gust of wind and off he goes! He's free. A field of azure all for him. A boundless plot. He plays. You know how those silly little clouds are: always wanting to show off. Ready to do anything to amuse their audience. He launches into a series of tricks that would make any illusionist green with envy. The celebrated Houdini and that Chinese magician the whole world talks about, Mister What's-His-Name, are charlatans by comparison. Imposters. Slackers. He, the little cloud, transforms in plain sight. No need for a wand or an abracadabra-type spell. No snags. Transformations at will and without cheating. What an act! He gathered himself, lay down, tousled, split in two, stuck himself back together again. From a bowler hat he turned into a fish. A trout. A salmon going upstream. Then a croissant. Then an almond. Feather. Sprig of lily of the valley. He was a shellfish, a cauliflower, a coxcomb. From the head of a tawny owl he turned into an island, an archipelago in the middle of the ocean. And all seamlessly. Without forcing it. Very slow stretches, almost voluptuous. From a viol to a violin, from a violin to the bow. No ruse.

It was precisely ten o'clock when he appeared. I know, I count the hours. There isn't a single one that escapes me. I raised my eyes and I saw him. I was looking out the window. I was watching for the postman. Cursed postman. I have no news from you. I don't wait for any. I don't want any. I know that you won't write: if there is a postman, he could only be a gruesome messenger. With his bicycle, his bags. It's only a disguise. Grotesque. Who is he fooling? Each piece of mail is a threat. That's where the danger comes from. Every day shells, thousands of shells delivered through the mail. Stamped. Proper. Bullets headed home. At point-blank range. How many victims fallen in silence in front of their mailbox or in their kitchen, in their living room? I am not a dupe. The disguised archangel and Death crouching in the sealed envelopes. White paper. A rubber stamp and it's the announcement and the defeat, the ultimate defeat. I don't want it. In the same way I watch for the official vulture. Military, gendarme, what do I know? I imagine him in a uniform. A uniform for him, too, to conceal his black, lugubrious wings. Stiff expression. Condolences. Salute. He has already turned on his heels. He has already left, and I am here, I am still here. I tremble. I crumple on the landing. No, I don't want it. To the devil with them. I cross my fingers, I make the sign of the horns to chase them away, all of them, the messenger boys, the ones doing the dirty work. I have invented spells that I hurl at them.

I write to you every day. I speak to you. I recount for you. I have the right. I simply hope that you receive these letters. That you keep them with you. On you. That they accompany you. You will open them perhaps. You will bring them to your nose to sniff them, like the pages of Paul, of Musset. You will smell my perfume. You will smell my sweat, my saliva, my thoughts, my tears, you will smell the spring that flows through my secret garden, through your garden (no matter what I do it flows, it streams when I think of you), you will feel my love. I know that you know what is inside.

One tiny little cloud between the sun and me. At half past it transformed a final time. It spread, spread. It filled the sky. Its shadow over the roofs, over the entire earth. I thought it was starting to rain. But no, it was just my eyes.

E.

AND NOW THEY MARCH.

It's a country of plows. A country of farms, of villages, of wheat, of vineyards, of cows, of churches. It's a country of udders and saints. It used to be. The magic of war. It transforms everything, men and maps. Put a helmet on the skull of a baker and he becomes a soldier. Put an eagle on his helmet and he becomes the enemy. Sow, plant seeds of steel in a field of beets and it becomes a mass grave. Grander than W. C. Harding. More expansive. The great circus, the caravan. The monster parade.

They march.

The French infantry includes one hundred seventy-three regiments of three or four battalions made of four companies, nineteen battalions of foot soldiers, twelve battalions of mountain infantrymen, four regiments of Zouaves, nine regiments of indigenous infantrymen, two regiments of the Foreign Legion including four regiments of foot soldiers, five battalions of light infantry from Africa, three Saharan companies, a regiment of firefighters from Paris, nine special operations units. A regiment includes between three thousand and four thousand men.

They march.

The role of the infantry is to conquer and keep the terrain. The official regulations stipulate that it is the infantry to whom this most formidable but also most glorious task is entrusted. Its two methods of fighting are shooting and moving forward.

They march.

It's summer then it's autumn. It's dawn. It's noon or midnight. No matter the weather.

They don't know to what end, towards what destination. They're not told to where or until when. They're not told anything. They don't know. "Strategy, my ass!" says the Wise Man. They advance. They come and go, then retrace their steps. They climb up. They come back down. They circumvent. They drift. The paths become blurred. Mazes and twists and turns. Mysteries. "Tactics, my ass!" says the Wise Man. "The real truth is that the men with the stripes are just as lost as the rest of us. Not one of them would be able to tell you the how or the why. They fart in the bath and it bubbles, and those bubbles are us!" In columns, in lines, in clusters. The boots pummel and scrape, the mess kits jingle. Cling-cling, clop-clop, cling-cling. It's almost funny. A troop of comics. Fifty pounds of supplies on their shoulders. Peddlers. Hawkers. What do men do when they don't walk with their houses on their backs? Him like the rest of them. Would he understand now if he were told that there are nearly two billion of them, and that three fourths of them will pay the price, in one way or another, will inevitably suffer? Because this is black magic, my boy. And would he laugh if there weren't so many dead—more cadavers on the plains than starlings in the sky—would he let loose his thundering laugh?

They have nothing to sell but their skin.

They march.

"The colonel shits. The corporal barks. And who takes the fall?" Champagne. Ardennes. Argonne. Victory is near. The distances grow longer. The fatigue is immeasurable. Sleep. No matter when and no matter where. Woods, forest, thickets, embankments. Cave, hay loft, stable. Often a barn. Among the animals. All kinds of animals. Straw is a luxury. They are numerous. They pack together. They stick together. In the shadows they hear wet coughs and wheezing coughs, they hear the groans and the snores and the gas. Prayers whistle between their lips. Sacred Virgin. Holy Mary Mother of God. Muffled crying: it's exhaustion. It's fear and bitterness. It's dregs of the soul—worn out like the rest. Happy are those who don't dream. A few hours, barely.

They are awoken. They are shaken. They take off again. They sleep standing up. Cling-cling, clop-clop, cling-cling, clop-clop. Who are they pursuing? Who is pursuing them? They are told everything and its opposite. "Step-by-step, my ass! Joffre the capable, yes! A small happiness for some, a great unhappiness for others." They sweat. They shiver. They have fevers. They have diarrhea. They are hungry. They are thirsty.

They march.

Beneath the President of the Republic there is the Minister of War, beneath the Minister there is the Marshal of France, beneath the Marshal there is the General of the Army, beneath the General of the Army there is the General of the Army Corps, beneath the General of the Army Corps there is the Major General, beneath the Major General there is the Brigadier General, beneath the Brigadier General there is the Colonel, beneath the Colonel there is the Lieutenant-Colonel, beneath the Lieutenant-Colonel there is the Commander, beneath the Commander there is the Captain, beneath the Captain there is the Lieutenant, beneath the Lieutenant there is the Sublieutenant, beneath the Sublieutenant there is the Major, beneath the Major there is the Chief Warrant Officer, beneath the Chief Warrant Officer there is the Warrant Officer, beneath the Warrant Officer there is the Sergeant, beneath the Sergeant there is the Master Corporal, beneath the Master Corporal there is the Corporal, beneath the Corporal there is the Private, beneath the Private there is the void. A space of a few inches, ten, twelve, between his soles and the floorboards. A knocked-over milking stool. A small brown puddle, dry. The wood is soaked through. It's a legionnaire. 2nd Light Infantry Regiment of the 1st Foreign Brigade. They find him hanging from the beam of a hay loft. He has departed. Perhaps for the Black Sea, perhaps another sea. He came from Odessa, that's all they know about him.

They march.

Two days later there are six men of the same company, six all lined up and shot. They say executed by firing squad. Insubordination. They didn't want to march. Apostates. "Hijos de putas," says Guso. He's talking about the shooters, the executioners. He clears his throat and spits at the officer's feet. The officer pretends not to have seen. Six graves are dug in the clay earth. Six crosses are planted. Someone sings a sad song in his mother tongue. Three hours later a violent shower whips the graves and the crosses.

They march.

Victory is certain. They say General Dubail beat the German left flank, Field Marshal French the right flank. They say that in Berlin the people are revolting. The empress escaped by pretending to be her chambermaid.

They march.

They pass fugitives. Vagrants. Forced migrants. Gaunt and haggard. Leaving the smoking embers of their existence behind them. The cottage, the business, the shack, the patches of kohlrabi. The entire village. All of it razed. There are mothers of families and gangs of kids and the elderly. No fathers. It could be their own mothers or their own wives, their brothers and sisters, their grandparents. Swaying and lurching, in heaps in a cart along with the mattress, the clock, the table, the straw chairs and the pans and sometimes the dresser. Pulling the carts. Pushing the wheelbarrows. Something like rag pickers. Mirror images of the infantrymen. Cling-cling, clop-clop. Skinny dogs as escorts.

They march.

On the roadsides there are dead horses. There are dead donkeys and dead mules. Dead oxen. A disemboweled duck pecked at by crows. What is this country where garlands of viscera hang from the branches? Where tatters of pelts decorate the bushes and hedges? The stench lingers in their mucus.

They march.

Here, there. Here an old man is led by the hand by a man even older than him. He wears a woman's coat on his back and a woman's hat on his head. There two young girls with white hair, twins, albinos, unless there are elves in this strange country. They are six or seven years old, the age of maturity. The girls watch them go by without a word and without a gesture. Absolutely alone. Absolutely identical except that one of them is holding a black cat in her arms. Some cross themselves in passing, because of the cat or because of the children's white hair.

They march.

Victory is imminent. They say one hundred and twenty thousand Japanese have landed in Toulon. Hungary separates from Austria. Lille is surrounded by Hindus.

They march.

They pass a convoy of prisoners. They appear no more exhausted than them. No more lamentable. No more defeated. The officers have big cigars in their mouths. "Hijos de putas," says Guso. He clears his throat and spits. "Good for nothing but curling their mustaches!" says the Wise Man. That very night they are privy to a spectacle: in a train yard, a stockpile of merchandise burns all night. A long snake of fire. The bright red scales. Chinese dragon. Then the mills catch fire in the middle of the countryside. Three, four, five, six fires. They count. They calculate the loss of income, all that good hay lost. They stretch their necks and inhale the smoke, eyes half-closed, they dream of hearths and stoves, of ovens, of warm bread. At the hour when the matins should be ringing they meet a procession of nuns along the road. There are thirty of them. Sisters of Providence, white as geese. Four among them carry a large Christ on the cross on their shoulders: it's all they were able to salvage from the rubble of their chapel. An entire wing of the convent collapsed under shelling. But it would take more to knock them down. Keep the faith, soldiers, the Lord accompanies you. The nuns bless them. The nuns distribute bars of chocolate that they appear to extract, as if by miracle, from the folds of their scapulars. "And the little bread loaves, where are those?" laughs Fuller. Krestorsky shoves an elbow into his ribs: "Shut up!" The sisters take off again with a song of hope and mercy on their lips, they grow distant, their silhouettes grow thin and disappear, the Christ with them, but the song remains, it's all that remains to them, and more than the traces of cacao on their fingers it's those pure and crystalline voices that they will hold on to as the proof of their appearance, as the precious receipt of their passage.

They march.

Victory is won. They say that the Kronprinz has been assassinated by one of his officers. They say that his body has been transported to England. The Germans have offered forty thousand prisoners in exchange, the English refused.

They march.

They bivouac for a day in a half-devastated village. They cook apples. An old woman drags her chair and sets it up in the sun at the foot of her door. Her house doesn't exist anymore, it's a ruin, an enormous rotten tooth, decayed. Sitting in front of the vestiges she takes out her needles and her pin cushion and knits. Just like she always has. That afternoon they improvise an auction where objects confiscated from the enemy are put up for sale. Spoils of war, relics, trophies. Personal and derisory things. Souvenirs from the Krauts. The auctioneer is a scrawny guy with the traces of a mustache. Backwards kepi. To make himself look taller he stands on a crate and hits a cooking pot three times. His assessors present, jeering. A Mauser cartridge. A tobacco pouch. Ten cents over here. Twenty. Who can top that? A blank postcard representing the main square of a large town in Bavaria. A watch. A purse. A bayonet. Two cents. Sold. It's all in good humor. The officers let it happen. The tone changes at nightfall when they find the mayor in his cellar, calling a German number. Spy. Vile traitor. He is shot on the spot. Executed. Guso falls to the ground. They clear the camp and leave the village as if the plague now ruled there.

They march.

Cold and ice mix. Early morning a lace-like pattern of frost cracks beneath their boots. Sometimes it lasts until noon. Cling-cling, crack-crack, cling-cling. They swaddle themselves. The icy air rushes into their lungs, leaves them breathless. They advance, heads lowered. They swear. They breathe between their fingers. Lips chapped, lips cracked and split. They try hard to smoke. Through the nose, the mouth, the skin, the men and the animals, steam-men, steam-horses, one single breath rises, like the dust beneath the troops' footsteps. Cling-cling, clop-clop.

They march.

The first snow arrives. It was almost beautiful. All that white. An immense bandage on the wounds. Carcasses, brambles, barbed wire, everything blends together, everything sparkles. Christmas is coming. They have high hopes. The snowflakes fall. Is it possible that something besides shrapnel can fall on their faces? The sisters said it: The Lord is with them. They still await His grace from above. Pure. Unsoiled. The flakes hook into their beards and eyelashes. They stick out their tongues to receive this cold Host. Eternal choir boys. Aren't they innocent? Him like them. They are enthralled for an hour or two, until the snow penetrates their greatcoats. Then their flesh. Then their bones. Until it changes into a filthy sludge beneath their soles.

They march.

On a cloudless night a small group forms, separates, out in the field. There are eight of them. They raise their heads and point their fingers: above, just beneath Ursa Major. A pair of binoculars circles, and each person points in his turn towards the stars. A young lieutenant is among them. He is a member of the Flammarion Astronomical Society. He explains. It's the Delavan comet honoring us with a visit. Very beautiful. See its brilliant plume, see its long tail, tousled. Take advantage, messieurs. "According to our calculations," says the lieutenant, "it won't pass again for another eighty million years." Distant times. And us? And us? They want to know. The future. What will become of us? "My lieutenant, will the Earth still exist then?" The question is crucial. They look at the young officer like an oracle, like the prophet on the mountain. He smiles with all his immaculate teeth. "Not only will it exist," he says, "but thanks be to God we will be rid of the German vermin!" A happy portent, duly acclaimed. They congratulate each other. They make vows. They pass the binoculars around again to better admire this sibyl that the sky has sent to them. Their celestial godmother. The word "tail" enchants them. There are eight of them and none among them will see next season's wheat harvested.

They march.

They march.

Cling-cling, clop-clop, cling-cling, clop-clop, cling-cling.

They march.

The light fades. Darkness falls for a long time.

They march.

Victory is always for tomorrow.

❦

My love,

Do you know that there was a secret meeting yesterday in Aix-la-Chapelle? The pope was present and demanded peace. France and Germany were ready to accept, but Russia and England were opposed.

Do you know that the children of Maubeuge saw the Virgin and that she revealed to them that the conflict would end next April 4 at two fifteen in the afternoon?

Do you know that in Laon the Boches have typhus? Which explains the silence of the cannon: the French soldiers retreated for fear of contagion.

Do you know that Germany is on the verge of declaring war on Sweden?

Do you know that in this very moment there are no fewer than six million Russians advancing on Berlin, sowing terror everywhere?

And best of all—I hope that you are up to date—that's it, it's done, Lorraine and Alsace have been recaptured!

Voilà.

That's what we hear in the streets, at the market, in the shops. Everywhere. And this is just a small compendium. Make your choice. It's fresh, all my news is fresh! Of the highest quality. And guaranteed from reliable sources, of course. Listen: Madame Loue knows someone who knows someone whose sister is the wife of a gendarme who works in Aisne, and this gendarme was charged with escorting prisoners, and he told his wife that these prisoners were all Bavarians of at least fifty years old, old farts who were wearing uniforms and boots dating from the 1870 campaign! And the funniest part, imagine, is that their leaders confirmed to these poor old soldiers that they weren't charging directly on Paris not because the French army was blocking their path, but because of the cholera spreading there. And those stupid imbeciles believed it!

I heard it. I swear to you that I heard it with my own ears, Madame Loue delivers this kind of nonsense to her customers. It wouldn't be so bad if she were the only one, but it's a real pandemic. It gushes from all sides, it runs, it propagates like gangrene. Noise, rumors. Everyone has their own. People talk. They know. The gods don't keep any secrets from them. You have to see the importance they give themselves. War, they know it, believe me. War, they wage it over two loaves of white bread, over a pound of green beans and a cup of lard. By the pound. So, how much of my news should I put you down for?

I'm ashamed. I'm ashamed of all of us.

And the newspapers are hardly any better, they basically lend credibility to this gossip. The newspapers speak of victories, of conquered territory, of courageous and hard-nosed combatants, heroic tasks. In fact, I have one in front of me now. You want to know what it says? "The battle was settled, an incontestable success for the Allies . . . 138 cannons seized, 55 machine guns, 20,000 prisoners of enemy ranks, 200,000 men knocked out of action . . . A French plane destroyed an ammunitions train . . . The Germans are retreating from Namur and Waterloo . . . We await the impending reunion of the Belgians and the Allies in Tournai . . ." That's what's written. Who to trust? We would so like to believe it. That these lies are truths. I promised myself that I wouldn't read anymore but I can't stop myself. I buy them for Papa. I think it's the only thing left keeping his heart beating. Reading these few lines. The rest of the time he remains closed in on himself, in a kind of morbid prostration. He doesn't go out anymore. We hardly speak. It's a very old man that I see opposite me.

Our father isn't doing well. He feels guilty. He wages his own fight against his own enemy: remorse. Formidable adversary. Apparently Papa's progress doesn't go hand in hand with that of our army. I fear that he will not come out a winner. I am not even sure that he hasn't already surrendered. What can I do? He's sinking, he's falling, and I don't have a pole to hold out to him. I wouldn't be sincere if I said that I wasn't mad at him. That I have totally forgiven him. Should I also lie, out of compassion? Should I cheat? The truth is that I am also suffering for him.

My love, never have I felt so alone! I now realize that I didn't know what solitude was. And it's a terrible thing. It's a slippery and black and hard stone. Harder than granite. Harder than marble. A compact stone, without the slightest crack. It's a monolith that nothing seems to be able to break. And it weighs, weighs, crushes you.

I thought of enlisting, too. Offering my services as a nurse or something similar. My only motivation was to be with you again, to find you again somewhere. However, I realized that there wasn't one chance in a million that it would happen. That we would be reunited. So what good would that be? I don't want to see any soldiers other than you. I don't want to care for the wounded, the mutilated. I don't want to serve them soup, empty their bed pans. All that disgusts me. The war disgusts me. Even the idea of it. I don't have the calling of a saint. I don't have the spirit of sacrifice. Does that mean I don't have a heart? Oh! yes, I have one. But it's completely filled with you. It is entirely and exclusively devoted to you. Is it my fault if there no place for anything or anyone else?

What sort of person am I if I can coldly envisage the death of all those men, but not yours? May they all die, may the Earth burn, I don't give a damn, as long as you are returned to me!

E.

AND NOW THEY BURY EACH OTHER.

They dig. They dig. A vast labyrinthine grid of tunnels and galleries. Shovels and pickaxes in hand. Halfway between the mole and the worm, on the border between the termite and the rat. Man supposedly at the end of the chain, anchored at the beginning of time, going back link after link, era by era, since the time of the infinitesimal, fermented in the primordial soup, Pasteur leaning over his microscope, the trilobite, the mammal, the primate, and then Socrates, Diogenes, Aristotle, and then Dante and Leonardo, Copernicus, Michelangelo, Montaigne, Cervantes and Shakespeare, and then Galileo, Descartes, Racine, Pascal, and then Mozart, and then Darwin, and all that to end up here?

Shadows in the light . . .

They delouse. They eat like monkeys. They sprawl in the mud. They wash themselves in cesspits. They defecate in public. Their hair grows. They growl. They tremble. They are afraid of the dark and the invisible. They are afraid of silence. They are afraid of noise. They wait.

Winter approaches.

The boy starts to get to know them. Those in the company, in his section. Those who remain. Little by little, one by one, they detach themselves from the mass. Their silhouettes materialize. Their features clarify. Beyond the registration numbers, each has his gaze, his voice, his experience. The boy listens. They say that they are his brothers. However, one must not be too touched, one cannot go so far as loving them, because, soon, soon they will no longer be.

This is the story of those who will die.

The Wise Man is one of them. A surname. An ironic monicker due to the pertinence of the reflections he offers as they wander, a philosophical range as long as a musket. He's named Agassagian. Twenty-three years old. Private First Class. A metalworker in civilian society. He'll lose his cheekiness under fire in the battle of Carency. And Stein. The serious, the anxious, the meticulous Stein. Gray hair at twenty-six years old. The kind of guy to recount his ammunition three times before going to sleep. Ten times before the assault. Clockmaker by profession. For him the large hand will remain eternally stuck beneath the leaden sky of Sainte-Marie-aux-Mines. And Guso, the Spaniard, or the Mexican, or the Colombian, who knows? The size of a toreador, the stare of a furious young bull, like coal, eyes of storm and lightning, and raw nerves, always smoking, nostrils and saliva on the edges of his lips. Olé! The crowd gets up and it's over. Already. For Rafael Guso Álvarez the great corrida will take place in the Souchez arena, in Artois, far from the sun of Seville. And Campana. Thirty-three years old. Almost an old man. Baritone in the opera. A voice like gold. Campana whose reason will desert him over time. A mania that will cause him to scale the railing to unload his rifle on an enemy that he alone will see, imitating the noise of a Hotchkiss with his mouth. Campana the nut job. And then the day will come when he will get confused and pull the pin on a grenade before trying to launch it with a mortar: the device will explode in his face, carrying away his splendid mustache and his nose and a good portion of his jaw. Sing, beautiful blackbird. Sing, now, to see. And Fuller. And Wachfeld. And Thill. Sixty years to the three of them. Submerged together in a collapsed trench, buried together in the shelter beneath which they were sleeping. And Gardot. Tawer. Skin riddled with holes from French artillery, his own camp, yes, who will take him for a target on the summit of Vimy one spring night. Sorry, friend, those are the risks. And Cormuz, the Swiss. And Krestorsky, the Pole. A coal miner. He knows how to find mines, too. Good Christian. He prays, he kisses his crucifix before charging. Notre-Dame-de-Lorette will get the better of him. A methane explosion like he never could have imagined. He'll rise to the sky like vapor. Sublimated. Go, Polack, go. God will glue the pieces back together. Here on earth, in the shadows of slag heaps, Johanna will grow old without you. And Madsen. And Demetrenko. And Hadida. And Biele, Ace of Spades. A stateless man from Montmartre. Player, cheater, stealer. Pickpocket artist of great talent. In the blink of an eye he is capable of confiscating the medals from a commandant without him noticing. A funny man. If a pipe, a lighter, a kepi, a pocket knife goes missing, everyone turns towards him. He taunts you with his funny expressions, eyebrows raised, simpering. It's a joke. Gone, the Ace. Totally eviscerated on the field of honor. The smoke dissipates, and he is no longer there. They won't find any trace of him, not a single ring, not an ounce of his jaundiced skin. Certain people will say that he stole himself, on his own and entirely, just like that, a final scam, certain people will say that he's now on the other side picking the pockets of the Boches—if they start missing cartridges we will know for sure. And Cavendish. And Field. And Dulac. A predestined name. Luxembourger of nineteen years old. Has never seen the sea but dreams of setting sail. He speaks of the merchant marines. He speaks of oceans. He speaks of crossings. He will drown in six feet of water, in a sinkhole the size of a cooking pot, the fifty pounds of his gear inexorably dragging him down. You dreamed of a ship, sailor. You won't dream anymore. And Feoroff, the Russian. Marksman. A giant who will become a dwarf after the brutal and fortuitous eradication of both of his entire legs in Verdun. Feoroff who will manage, despite this, to drag himself, in his soapbox racer, six months after the armistice, beneath the wheels of a streetcar. And Merthens, the Belgian. Virgin and obsessed. A 77mm shell will take his virginity in the vicinity of Suippes. And Novak, the Czech. And Babik, the gypsy. And Cauditi, the Sardinian. Bugler. That will play Schumann for them, at night, at the back of the barn. "In der Fremde."

Far from home. To soothe your soul. All those tender soldiers who discreetly sniff while listening, eyes wet. What he can do with a heart and three valves. Cauditi the bugler who will spend two days and two nights moaning, stomach open, attached to a stretcher between the two camps, before one of his companions finds the courage to turn his Lebel on him to put an end to his suffering. A taste of copper between the teeth. And Pereira, the Portuguese. And Ross, the Canadian. And Wayne, the cowboy from Arizona. And Vandelahert, the Dutch, flying in the ether filled with cordite and falling back down torn to shreds on the lands of Givenchy. And Blumenfeld. Dead. And Fernandez. Dead. And Karadjian. Dead. And Hosberg. Dead. And Panossian. Dead. And Racovitch. And Simonian. And Sijas. And Berecki. Dead, dead, dead, dead. Killed by the enemy they say.

And him.

No one will be spared. No one will get out unscathed.

But for now, they don't know that. They are busy. They are asked to dig, they dig. They drill. They support. They caulk. Bags of sand and timber. Sheet metal. Planks. The trenches have women's names. The bayonets too. Clarisse, Rosalie. The momentum is broken. The bellicose intoxication from the beginning. The kisses sent, the flowers on their departure. The cheers. And the polished gun, the uniform, the pack. The adventure. All that, far away. The fervor is dampened. They saw what they saw. Their eyes have been opened. They've been taught about battle, the Kaiser and the Germans.

But for now, they are alive. It's flowing inside. The red blood, the blue veins. The gray breath. The smoke bombs disperse. The night has come. One more. It's an immense screed above their heads. The veiled moon. Feet in the mire they look at the sky. They scan. The comet has left. Venus remains, faithful. There are other planets, but of them all, which is the most beautiful? Ours? Someone coughs and it echoes like in a cavern, a grotto, high and deep. The cannons have died off. A great calm reigns. A glacial silence cracked by the tiniest noise.

310

"I don't like this," someone says.

He pricks up his ears. They are worried.

"And over there?" someone asks.

They lean and observe through the fissures. They scrutinize. Nothing moves. They get up, their necks, despite everything, sunk into their shoulders. Shrunken by reflex. The weight of silence and night. The celestial vault is much too vast for them. They sigh. They wait.

For the right time.

Winter approaches and they are hiding themselves.

EMMA WRITES:

My love,

Whose fault is it? I ask myself. All of this, who do we blame? All this distress and this suffering, all this waste: Who? Truthfully I would like to know. I'm seething. There are nights like this. Long, so long. I don't even try anymore to sleep, to close my eyes, to wait for a slumber that won't come. I walk. Our old rug, I must have paced across it a hundred thousand times. Enough to burn the soles of my feet. If you were to see me, I look like a crazy person! Though who knows, maybe I'm in the process of becoming one? Who's to say that I am not already one? In a straitjacket night shirt. I talk to myself. I talk to my shadow. I question it, but it doesn't respond to me. Nor does anyone else. But I need answers! This horror, who dreamed it up? Who rendered it? Who orchestrates it from a distance? I need to hold people responsible, do you understand? I need them to be shown to me. For them to be pointed out to me, objectively. Him, and him, and him. Them. I want names. I want faces. Take off the masks! I want to know into whose vile faces I must sink my claws if I were to cross their paths!

They are out there, I'm sure of it. Below. Behind. I want people to stop boring me with the "context," with the "situation," with the "alliances," with the "national interests," words, words to confuse the issue. Anonymous and uncertain responsibility, impalpable. Perfectly in the spirit of the times, is that it? Is that what they would have me believe? Responsibility without responsible parties! No. I refuse. We must never forget that those who make the decisions are beings of flesh and bone. Sheep, sheep, okay, but there must be, somewhere, a repugnant shepherd that guided you, that threw you into the mouth of the wolf. Where is he, that man? Where are they? Interests, yes. I refuse to accept this. Certainly not national. Certainly not for the good of us all. So whose interests, exactly?

The Kaiser? Of course that's who comes to mind first. (Ptui!) Easy target. Obvious. A bit too obvious, it seems to me. What, by himself alone that old porker unleashed the fires of hell over the entire continent? That's giving a lot of credit to a one-armed man. Are we not confusing Willy with Lucifer, by chance? I'm not saying he's had nothing to do with it. He has his part, certainly, but . . . But so be it, since we're already talking about this mob, let's get into it!

Kings. Emperors. How can that still exist in our time? The "Lords," the "Majesties," the "Royal Highnesses." How can we still accept that? How can we still swallow this enormous tall tale? The crown and all that goes with it. Kings! And in the name of what, can you tell me? In the name of blood. Noble, aristocratic blood. And the divine right, moreover. You understand that? It's not any old fairy that will be leaning over their coffins, no, it's God Himself. Sacred monarchs! Incubated, pampered, blessed by the Eternal God Himself. Straight from the loins of Jupiter. Gosh! And for centuries and centuries. Because the deception persists. It's congenital. From lord to lord, then from father to son, from son to father, from generation to gener-ation, long, long, long, unending litany of first names and numbers. Hereditary power. Hereditary fortune. Hereditary privileges. And it's crucial that they never leave their precious bosom! And us, mere subjects, we swallow this? We don't get tired of it? Better, worse, we ask for more. We yield, we kneel down, we revere, we kiss the luxurious boots that stomp on us. When I think of all those peasants who hurry and jostle to see their carriages pass! They applaud. They throw petals. They cheer and admire. How is it possible? Haven't we talked about revolution? At least an emancipation? Haven't we proclaimed the advent of a sovereign people, masters of our own destiny? This new era that should have begun, where is it? Someone explain to me what changed. We cut off a few heads but there are so many branches, so many roots. Hydra cannot die! Look: those nine-tenths of the world are still under its thumb. Kings, tsars. Despots and good-for-nothings. A lot of one and little of the others, no matter what they say. Even the weakest weigh something. Their influence is considerable. And France? You tell me. Our beautiful country. Our exemplary republic. Oh yes? What difference? Because we elect our leaders? False. Not me. Not women. Not wives. Not fiancées. Not sisters. Not mothers. None of us. None of those who give life. Not children. Three-fourths of the population are excluded from this right. What remains? Give us a ballot and then we'll see! . . . And even then. Vote for whom? Deputies, senators, ministers: a wretched clique of profiteers only concerned with their little wheels and deals. Humanists? Democrats? Come on! Here, listen to this:

"I would however like to see him grow, the true democrat, he who would live with six thousand francs, who would dress like a civil servant, and who would take the bus. Who would walk in his tattered jacket from the Post Office to Commerce, from Public Education to Finances, bearing his integrity. I see him giving fifty thousand francs of his ministerial salary to the poor, ignoring the cars, the actresses, and the little suppers; dreaded by his colleagues; celebrated and loved everywhere. Later president, dressed like you and me, and receiving kings without ceremony. That's a plan that would please a truly ambitious person. Wealth would be returned to its rank; and that would already be nearly all of justice served."

Those aren't my words, they're Alain's, the philosopher. I transcribe it word for word. Isn't it an admirable portrait? That of a man to whom we would happily give his suffrage. A true representative. A person of reason and heart. But how many are there, on the benches of the Assembly, who can claim to resemble him? How many seats of the Counsel? Those pipsqueaks! Gargoyles. Grimaces, grimaces. Grocers who make money hand over fist and count their till. Politics: business assets. Their shop: the Nation. Careerists and sellers. Not ideal. Not in the long run. And no scruples, naturally. Everything is bought, and everything sells—with a profit margin!

I seethe, yes. I am enraged. And would we be here if we had not been governed by that handful of hawkish and ravenous people? If the wealth had been equitably shared. If there had been the slightest concern for justice in this world. If, if, if. If we put more resources into instruction and education than into weaponry. More books and less cannons! Those aren't my words, they're Hugo's this time. We never listen to poets! No, it's not utopia. It's common sense. It's the voice of intelligence and soul. It's potential harmony and peace. Happiness as a focal point. It's making the well-being of humanity the principle aspiration, the goal to reach, essential and primary.

But there are those who don't want to hear talk of it, this ambition. There are those for whom this would not suit their business. Who? We always come back to the same question, you see. Who? Who pulls the strings? Who holds the reins and the chains? Who profits from the crime? Names! Should we look at the great industrialists? The scrap metal merchants. Those who melt metal and steel to make bullets, shells, cruisers, trains. Or else the big money-lenders? Those who play with the lifeblood of war. The financiers, the bankers, who invest, who lend, who give credit. Those who bet on the course of life and death. But aren't they in cahoots with each other? It's possible. United for the occasion. Associates in the juicy affair. Investments, production, benefits. Boards of directors: Who sits around the table? Isn't this it, the headquarters of Almighty Capital that Karl described? But who, in reality? Names! Faces! Show yourselves, cowards!

They're powerful, you know. They are cunning. They are Machiavellian. They are capable of anything. Even my father, even my sweet and gentle Papa succeeded in poisoning his spirit with their adulterated patriotism. For all the means are good. All the resources. All the vices and diversions. They don't hesitate to wave the flag to make the beast charge. Suspicion. Suspicion when we suddenly start seeing the flags fly again. The blue the white the red. They are beautiful, these colors. And I love them, too, but as a backdrop, to remind us of the values that we have chosen to defend, remember, the inscription in gold letters, the profession of faith, the promise, the vow: Liberty—Equality—Fraternity. Otherwise, no. I reject them. I loathe those three colors when they aim to cover up all the others, abolish them. A trichromatic world? Not for me, thank you. The nuances are infinite, and I want all of them. I want the entire palette of the rainbow! I want all of Rimbaud's vowels!

Oh, forgive me, my love. Forgive me. I digress. It's lamentable. I'm mad at myself for inflicting my meager harebrained thoughts on you when these letters should be a balm; they should be your joy and your consolation. Sometimes I tell myself that it's for the best that you can't read them. How petty my agonies are compared to the sufferings that you must be enduring. Forgive me, I beg of you.

It's that the night is so long. The night never ends. I meant it when I said I felt I was going crazy. I wait. I spin in circles. The bedroom. The rug. I walk. I have to hold on. Hold on. I take the quill to keep my hands from trembling. I'm afraid. I'm cold. When the anger fades, my blood freezes. I am so cold, if only you knew. Walk, write, what other choice do I have? I count my steps, I blacken the pages to hold on until dawn, until I fall, until I collapse onto my bed. I have to get through the night. This one and the one after. And the one after. And the one after. How many more? My love, how many more nights?

E.

AND NOW THEY CRAWL.

Between the white earth and the white sky. Dressed all in white. It's a trick. A makeshift camouflage made on short notice from large pieces of sheets. It's not Guirand of Scévola but a simple reservist from the 230th who had had to pervert his modest talents for the occasion. For each soldier, he cut a sort of roomy blouse to be worn over the greatcoat, as well as a pair of trousers to put on over the uniform pants. Far from bespoke. They didn't ask him to make them beautiful but to make them discreet. Invisibility. A false seasonal molting. "Think of ermine," the captain had said. "Think of the Siberian jackrabbit." But it's another kind of beast that the troop thinks of when he discovers one last accoutrement. Apart from the blouse and the immaculate pants, they wrap their heads in a kind of headscarf made from the same fabric. The boys struggle to keep themselves from erupting in laughter. Wayne was not embarrassed. "Pretty snowmen!" His laugh resembled a whinny, perhaps because the cowboy has horse teeth. The captain, however, was satisfied with the result. "What did I tell you? Mother Nature still has lessons to give!"

Thus decked out, they are supposed to melt into the landscape. Neither seen nor heard. And here they are sliding flat on their stomachs on a crust of hard snow. Like seals on an ice floe.

There are six of them.

It might look like clowning around but it's not. The operation was conceived of by the captain. An idea pulled from his kepi under pressure from his superiors. They wanted information. They wanted to know what was afoot on the opposite side, what dirty trick was germinating in the dirty noggins of the Boches. And who better than the Germans themselves could help them to learn it? Prisoners: that's what they needed. "Bring me one of those pigs," the colonel had said, "and I guarantee you we'll be able to cook it!" If it wasn't an order it sounded like one. The captain had searched for a way to execute it. He'd found this one.

They advance in single file. In a single crawling movement. Each man with his nose on the soles of the man before him. Lieutenant Barlier in the front. He regularly stops and consults his compass. He calculates. His eyes squint as he surveys the haze, tries to pierce its mystery. They can't see more than twenty feet in front of them. More than five. The sun is risen but doesn't show itself. The day is bathed in a milky gray. In front of their eyes blankets glide, drift, ripple, smoke rings cross and rip. Phantoms of phantoms, neutral, indifferent. Perhaps wandering spirits. If limbo exists this is what it looks like. Hell must not be far off.

The captain was rather proud of his plan. Audacious, it had been deemed by the higher-ups. Suicidal, Lieutenant Barlier had translated to himself. "A fucking stupid plan," Fuller had simply stated, thus summarizing the general opinion. No matter. The colonel had given his approval and the honor of leading the mission fell to the lieutenant, seconded by Sergeant Olivetti. They had estimated that an additional four men were required.

"Any volunteers?" the sergeant had asked.

Guso was the first to leave the ranks. Without hesitating. Little bull. Bad-tempered and impatient. His foot was already scraping the dirt. He had spit on the ground.

"What's in it for us?" Wachfeld had asked.

Sergeant Olivetti was a veteran, it would take more for him to fly off the handle.

"Glory, soldier."

"Fuck all," Wachfeld had said.

He had spit also. More half-heartedly.

The boys looked around at each other, from left to right, surreptitious glances.

"So? Are you going to force me to draw straws?"

"That wouldn't be fair, Sergeant. Pereira is sure to lose: everyone knows that he's the shortest!"

The Wise Man (who else?). His witticism came at just the right time: laughing relieved them. And laugh they did. Pereira too, in good spirits without knowing why, his comprehension of French limited to one word out of ten. The sergeant had waited for it to die down, then repeated:

"So?"

Thill had volunteered, closely followed by Panossian. For the final place there had been two people to come forward, both at exactly the same time: Merthens and the boy. It was one too many.

"You," the sergeant had decided.

More than an hour already since they had left. Every inch counts. Every second. They can't go any faster. Admittedly, their camouflage is working. It is nearly impossible to spot them in the snow. Their packs and everything else covered in white cloth. Inside, grenades. A cautionary measure. In principle they shouldn't have to use them. In principle they shouldn't even have to exchange a single shot. They didn't bring their rifles. They only have their sidearms and blades on them. Revolvers, daggers. The success of the operation depends on the element of surprise and persuasion. In principle. How may among them would bank on that?

The lieutenant stops again. He glances at his compass, then he unfolds the map that he drew himself. He verifies. He lifts his eyes and compares. Nothing. Nothing in common between what's on the paper and what's in front of him. White, gray. Wisps of smoke. His own breath mixing with it. Chimeras. The boys were right: a fucking stupid plan. Populist wisdom. A furious desire to give up everything overwhelms him. He would just have to make one gesture and. No. He cannot. He too has his pride. He has responsibilities. He feels the presence of the men at his back. The weight of their expectations, of their silence, of their fears, of their confidence. The lieutenant Barlier folds his map back up. It's only a question of time and distance. Every second, every inch counts. Not far from here the target will be in sight. Not far from here they will have Boches in front of them. And Boches behind them.

"Bring me one of those fucking pigs," the captain had said, "and I assure you I'll be able to cook it!"

The phrase pleased him. He had made it his own, and he delivered it with a grave and resolute tone at the moment of departure. After which he had watched the small group charge into the haze while bringing a long and fat cigar with a musky aroma to his nostrils. It was one of the Havanas he had received the day before among an assortment of sweets and presents, including a small box of pastries and a twelve-year-old cognac. Exquisite care. He recognized the distinct taste of his mother and the tenderness she devoted to him. The dear woman had not been stingy for her son's Christmas.

The least of the consolations would be to know that captain Armand de Villiers would die of esophageal cancer a month after the end of hostilities.

The plan born of his brain consisted in attacking the advanced post of the Germans located five hundred feet from the French lines. The clever part ("Do you understand the trick, Lieutenant?") was to approach not from the front, as they had already tried in vain, but from the back. A space of a hundred and twenty feet separated this bastion from the first enemy trench. So they needed to skirt the post by its western flank, tracing a circle around the Ronsard forest, before going back to the east, towards the center, in order to breach the open field between the lines, then make one last turn, forty-five degrees north, in order to come full circle and take the target from the rear.

"And that's it! That's the trick. My trick. Haha! Who would expect that?"

No one, thought the lieutenant.

"Pure logic, when you think about it. What do the lookouts look out for? The adversary. And where does their gaze naturally point? Forwards. Towards the trenches opposite. They won't think to survey behind them, where their own troops are stationed. Thus the genius of such a strategy! An assault from behind. And gently . . . For the goal of the maneuver, let's not forget, is above all to bring back one of those swine in our nets. And alive!"

The element of surprise. Persuasion. The words smacked around in the captain's mouth. Unstoppable tactic. In all probability (what probability?) the number of sentinels occupying the post could not be more than two. Three, at the absolute maximum. All we have to do is discreetly sneak up on them and neutralize them before they're able to alert anyone.

The noble strategist puffs on his porcelain pipe. He had not yet received the package from Madame de Villiers.

"Like clockwork," he had concluded. "You see, Lieutenant, the only question is this: Why didn't we think of it earlier?"

They had had four days to prepare. The mission was planned for the morning of December 25. They were counting on two aligning circumstances: schnapps and fog. The Teutons would certainly have celebrated the birthday of the divine child. They would be sleeping off their hooch. Attention and reflexes dulled, heads softened, as groggy as the weather. Factors to take into consideration.

It might look like clowning around but it's not.

They crawl. They drag themselves. Behind the lieutenant comes Private Guso, then Thill, Panossian, the boy, Sergeant Olivetti at the tail of the squad. They're hot and cold at the same time, as if caught between a feverish dream and stark icy reality, moving, wandering between the two—if limbo exists. Are they really there? Are they really doing what they're doing? There's still the possibility that reality is nothing but a waking nightmare.

Suddenly the lieutenant raises a hand. The men freeze. They heard it too. Or they think they heard it. A sound. Abrupt, muffled. They keep from breathing. They listen. Time, the dream, reality hang on by a thread. They wait.

The sound repeats. Once, twice. Regular. It's something between yowling and hissing. An animal? Guso forms a silent word with his lips: *pala*. And then a section of haze half-opens before the rest of them and they have their answer. Stark and icy reality.

They are there.

The post is on their left, thirty steps away. Much closer than Lieutenant Barlier imagined. As this revelation crushes him, he feels flattened by an invisible, powerful, merciless hand, a hand that can only be that of destiny. For a few seconds he's breathless. As is each member of the group. All seized. All overwhelmed. Hearts, pulses in suspense. May those who know prayers say them, it's now or never.

There's a slight bulge in the terrain, a kind of hillock with the German bastion on the summit. Their eyes scrutinize the diaphanous veil. They make out the edge of the shelter, heaped up sandbags, a dim bluish gleam that might well be the reflection of a machine gun. No human silhouettes. They can't see the lookouts. But they're there. That noise, it's a shovel digging into the snow—pala.

Little by little fear dilutes in their veins, excitement takes over. A burst of adrenaline. Senses and consciousness honed to the extreme. The lieutenant's hand is still raised above his head. He extends his index and middle fingers: it's not the V of victory but the number two. Okay. They practiced. They know what they have to do.

The patrol splits. The lieutenant takes off, Guso and Thill in his wake. They follow on the same axis, parallel to the trenches. After a few yards the fog swallows them. So the others take off too, heading north, straight towards the summit of the hill, and not in single file but side by side, climbing the incline slowly, slowly, every second, every breath, every movement, every inch counts, moving over the white land, all dressed in white, like legless larvae, like enormous pale leeches.

The first group quickly reaches the perpendicular tunnel that joins the advance post of the first German line. The three men slide in. It's a narrow, enclosed path. On each side the walls are higher than two yards. They stand still for a good minute crouched, ears pricked. The screeching of the shovel seems to have stopped. They take out their revolvers. They start back on the route. A canopy of fog undulates above their heads. The more they approach, the more the temperature rises: a hot tide that swells in them, invades them, nearly numbs them. Saliva accumulates in Private Guso's mouth. He restrains himself from spitting. The element of surprise, repeats Lieutenant Barlier. The element of surprise. Fucking stupid plan.

The second group is immobilized. Sergeant Olivetti and Panossian and the boy. Lying low, flat on their stomachs, sticking to the ground with all their limbs, with all the surface of their bodies, and their souls too probably (neither remorse nor contrition in this moment, rather, an attitude of allegiance, of total submission to the forces that preside, no matter what they are, good or evil). Weapons drawn. They are six feet from the target. Now they can see everything above the trenches: the bags and the logs of the parapet, the slabs of sheet metal, the roof of the bunker made of entire tree trunks, two machine gun nests, a periscope. The post spreads about fifteen yards long and around three yards wide. The sentinels are in the hollows. They still can't see them, but they hear them: feet in the snow, voices, a few words in that idiom that they associate henceforth with the language of barbarism (they haven't read Schiller, they haven't read Hölderlin), from time to time a brief burst of laughter that cuts them to the quick. Enjoy yourselves, you bastards. Have a good laugh. Panossian cries. It's the fear and the tension. Private Anton Panossian, twenty-two years old.

Tears run down the length of his nose. Perhaps he isn't even aware of it. Perhaps he chalks it up to the air, the cold, the needles of frost on his eyelids. Lying at his side the boy appears dead he's so motionless. The old hunting reflexes: make yourself forgotten until you forget yourself, be a rock among the rocks, a stone among the stones, grass in the prairie, blend in. Not so long ago, as a child, he would chase the lizard and the vole, would hunt the hare, for fun or for food. For hours he would keep watch in front of the burrow. His body remembers. Only his nostrils palpitate. He smells the odor of tobacco. Enjoy yourselves, you bastards. Laugh, smoke, you . . .

Suddenly the cry of the nighthawk. In the middle of the day? Here? The nighthawk is the only bird that Guso knows how to imitate and Guso is the only one who knows how to imitate any animal at all: they didn't have a choice.

The signal.

Panossian and the boy turn towards the sergeant. The sergeant crouches. They imitate him. Then they start to run. In a few strides they're at the top. The trench opens beneath their eyes. The first thing they see is a snowman. Hastily and clumsily formed, wearing a kepi from the French army. One of the sentinels was getting ready to pelt it with a snowball—that's what the laughter was—but the soldier is petrified, arm in the air and snowball in his hand. With an expression of stupefied terror, he stares at the three white phantoms that have just emerged from the haze. A second sentinel is seated on a log bench. He has his back to them. All at once he stands up and pivots and turns his head towards them, his cigarette in the corner of his mouth, an eye half closed. The man makes as if to shoulder his gun, but Sergeant Olivetti points his revolver at him and he puts an index finger over his mouth and the man obeys this mute injunction and gives up his plan. At that moment the second group arrives. Barlier, Guso, Thill. They arrive at a light trot behind the shelter. They have with them a third German soldier, arms raised, that the lieutenant has in his aim

THE BOY

and pushes in front of him. Three sentinels: three prisoners. Flawless. The lieutenant doesn't want to cry victory too early, but he starts to believe it and something like euphoria spreads over him, inflates his chest, makes his heart beat to the rhythm of a triumphant march. He gestures to the guns: to add to the spoils. Guso hurries towards one to dismantle it, Thill towards the other. Sergeant Olivetti descends with his hundred and fifty pounds into the trench. The boy puts his weapon in its holster and nimbly jumps in to join them. Panossian wants to do the same but his foot slips on the edge and he hurtles down the incline on his back and ends up below groaning and swearing. The lieutenant shoots him a death stare. The sergeant cannot suppress a smile, and this smile is still floating in the middle of his large round face when a fourth Teuton devil bursts from the bunker yelling: "Gott mit uns!" He's a very young soldier, no helmet, with shaved blond hair that shines on his head like the wheat of his native Westphalia. He holds his Mauser like a pitchfork and fires without aiming and if there had been a single nighthawk in the vicinity it would have taken off at the sound of the detonation, and Panossian brings his hands to his stomach as if he wanted to keep the bird in that cage, and he falls suddenly on his butt, mouth open and eyes wide and he topples slowly backwards and even before his back hits the ground he is dead and the cage deserted. Sergeant Olivetti reacts first, responding with his revolver but he misses his target, the bullet lands in the wood six inches from the young soldier's skull, and already the young soldier has reloaded, he points his rifle at the sergeant and fires at him in return and the sergeant is hit in the shoulder, under the impact he makes a rapid and curious rotating movement, similar to a toreador's pass, then he loses balance and collapses with all his weight against the wall. "Hijo de puta!" spits Guso. Knee on the ground, he aims his weapon at the blond devil, but he doesn't have time to squeeze the trigger before the bastard collapses, a bullet straight to his forehead. Guso turns around and he sees Thill in shooting position

325

and he sees the wisp of smoke that escapes from the cannon of his revolver. Lieutenant Barlier extends his arms, he waves his hands, he cries "Stop! Stop! Don't shoot . . ." but a projectile pierces him before he can finish his sentence, the burning steel perforates his heart and then his chest deflates and the lieutenant slumps and stops his triumphant march. The shot came from the second sentinel, who took advantage of the confusion to pick up his gun again, and now he pivots and points his gun at Thill. The boy is two yards away. He drops down and grabs a shovel on the ground and he leaps forward and he raises the shovel and he strikes with all his strength, using the sharp edge of the tool. The steel diagonally penetrates the soldier's jaw and splits his face in two. He collapses on his back, his helmet flies off and his finger tightens over the trigger of the Mauser and the shot flies and gets lost in the heights. The boy leans over and looks at the man, he sees the split mouth and lips, the wound, the hole, the broken teeth, the atrocious grin, and the man looks at him, looks at the boy and who knows what he sees but he laughs, with that big bloody and silent smile. The boy raises the shovel, and he hits again. He hits. And in that moment the snowflakes begin to fall. They fall slowly, and they are sparse, each looks lonely, solitary in its descent, as finely chiseled as lace, as light as foam, and in the very second when they land they dissolve and disappear. The boy hits. He hits again. The shovel splits the air and every strike hits its target, and the more he hits the more the man's smile enlarges, mouth, lips, chin, cheeks, the metal works the flesh and chops and grinds and shreds of skin come loose and splinters of bone and pulp of gums and fragments of enamel of teeth and droplets of blood splatter the surrounding snow and stud the boy's white outfit and he receives a splash in the eye that forces him to close his eyelid and in front of his other eye the haze becomes red and he hits, he hits, he hits, and the snowflakes fall, they fall softly, sprinkling the face of the man, or rather what was the face of what was a man and who is now at present nothing but pulp, magma, minced meat, and who the boy would continue to attack if Sergeant Olivetti hadn't gotten up, if he hadn't grabbed him around the waist from behind, with his one working and powerful arm, if he wasn't now squeezing him against himself to keep him from hitting, from moving, from trembling. "It's okay, it's okay, it's okay . . ." the sergeant murmurs in the boy's ear. And while this is happening Guso rummages in his satchel, he takes out a grenade and pulls the pin and throws it inside the shelter. "Salud!" He throws himself flat on his stomach. The explosion shakes the trunks of the frame and a gray smoke climbs from the entrails of the earth, escapes from the black mouth of the hut. There's movement in the German lines. The haze hides them from Boche eyes but they perceive muffled noises, bursts of voices. "Fall back!" yells Sergeant Olivetti. He's still holding the boy in the vise of his arm, his other arm hangs like a broken branch at his side and a star of blood spreads over the sheet around his shoulder. "Fall back!" repeats the sergeant. It's then that the first lookout chooses to try to escape. He gains momentum and clings onto the edge of the trench and he starts to bring his legs under him when Thill fires and hits him in the calf. The man takes the hit but still manages to stand up straight, he advances towards his camp dragging his leg and screaming "Franzosen! Franzosen!" and immediately a burst of machine gun answers him in echo, sweeping the snow in front of him and opening a path for him and in the end shutting him up by hitting his legs and stomach, and the man falls and he dies with a hand stretched towards his compatriots, his brothers, perhaps to signal to them to cease fire or perhaps only to bid them farewell. And the machine gun continues to spray blindly. The chunks of earth and snow fly over the crest. Sergeant Olivetti turns back towards what remains of the troop. He lifts up the boy, he nearly carries him. The last German sentinel still has his hands in the air. Beneath his helmet the soldier has a pale face. He seems on the point of bursting into tears. He seeks the gaze of one and then the other and he says: "Kamerad . . . Kamerad . . ." he says it and he repeats it like a mantra, like a supplication, as if he were saying "Mercy . . . Mercy . . ." reaching a final stage of begging, not to save his soul but simply his skin, he loves them, yes, his French friends, he would be ready to kiss their hands, to kiss their feet, and they understand, and anyone in his place would do the same, but the good Kamerad Thill approaches him and charitably shoots him in the back of the neck at point blank range. Private Thill, eighteen years old. "Fall back!" orders Sergeant Olivetti for the third time. He drags the boy towards the other side, Thill follows on their heels, and while they start to climb Guso covers their retreat with grenade strikes. The small bull settled on his back legs and emptying his bag, launching explosives hand over fist towards the German lines yelling "Hijos de putas!" then throwing the empty bag before making an about-turn and joining the others, following in the direction of a sign made out of a piece of beet crate nailed to a beam and on which they'd traced, in charcoal, the inscription: *Nach Paris*. The four men pass the parapet. They clumsily cross the interlaced barbed wire deployed in front of the post. Then they run, bent over, hunched in half, caught between enemy fire and their own artillery firing back, between the Boche machine guns and the French cannons, between the feverish dream and the icy reality, they run and they pray that none of the whistling bullets, that none of the shells wailing above their heads, knock them down, they run and they sink into the fog and little by little they dissolve and disappear, between the white earth and the white sky, all dressed in white and red.

EMMA WRITES:

My love,
  Listen to this:

"Stunned and bewildered, she stands upon a precipice. All is
darkness around her. No prospect, no hope, no consolation—
forsaken by him in whom her existence was centered! She sees
nothing of the wide world before her, thinks nothing of the
many individuals who might supply the void in her heart; she
feels herself deserted, forsaken by the world."

*Goethe. Werther. I regret not reading it to you before. But how could
I have guessed?*
  *Today, this is the hundredth letter that I write to you. That means
it's been a hundred days since you left. No sadder anniversary. It's
raining on the city. The poet only had to open my heart to soak his
quill. I couldn't have said it better myself: the universe without my
lover is an atrocious wasteland.*

                                                                    E.

THE FIRST LETTERS reach him in January, the day of the Epiphany. After following a postal route that no one would be able to retrace. The boy had never received a letter in his life. He receives twenty-eight all at once. "Jackpot!" says Wayne. A bouquet of missives that the postman takes a sly pleasure in distributing to him one by one, under the astonished eyes (then the dumbstruck eyes, the sardonic eyes, the envious eyes) of the company. "Get a load of this sly little fox! The King of Morocco! He doesn't just have a woman, but a whole harem!"

The boy carries the bundle and goes to sit on a crate, off to the side. He remains there without moving. The letters between his hands, his hands on his thighs. His face is like marble. Then he goes over each of the envelopes, slowly, one after the other. Some are thick, they must contain several sheets. He doesn't open them. He doesn't smell them. He looks at the words written on the back. The black ink. He looks at the stamps and the postmarks. After which he undoes the buttons of his greatcoat and slips the letters inside, against his chest. He closes his greatcoat.

It's man, sonny. Man alone who holds the clay in the palm of his hand: What will he do with it?

As he contemplates the envelopes, he contemplates his hands. It's become a habit. He holds them flat in front of him, fingers slightly spread. He observes them, and he waits for them to turn red. For the blood to spring through his skin and envelop them. He's astonished when it doesn't happen. His hands are dirty and tanned but not red. They are short and strong. Sometimes they tremble. A barely

330

perceptible movement, something like the rippling of water in the breath of the breeze, or like the first signs of boiling. When it happens, he rests them on his thighs and it passes. After a moment it passes.

It's man, sonny.

So be it.

But is he still a man?

"Despite what some of you might think," affirmed the medical officer, "war represents the highest degree of civilization!"

The practitioner addressed everyone and no one. Witty and lively, he went from one wounded man to another, from one wound to another, followed like a shadow by a giant, horse-like nurse, who probably owed the stiffness of her bearing to the presence of a stick, perhaps a broom handle, in her posterior, introduced long ago in the early years of her Victorian and Anglican education. She was carrying a tray on which lay bandages and compresses, utensils and instruments. A precious assistant, certainly, but the sight of this woman reminded him, foremost, of a severe nanny (she is the horse-nanny) studying, from very close up, the acts and gestures of an overgrown child, capricious and turbulent.

"Who created it?" said the doctor. "It's man. Who practices it? Man. And him alone. War, messieurs, is the prerogative of our species—Homo sapiens."

His powerful tenor voice dominated the chorus of wheezes and groans constituting the background noise of the room. Sorrow and distress. Feeble laments, punctuated by hoarse coughs. From a distant straw mattress stream the litanies of an artilleryman invoking in the same ethereal delirium both his mother and a certain Iphigenia. The unfortunate man now has only holes in place of eyes. The boy was standing in a corner, his arms slack. When they returned from the mission they had driven him here with Sergeant Olivetti. Blood smearing his camouflage uniform, and his face, his neck, his hands. After a rapid cleaning it turned out that he had no wound. Not even a tiny gash. The blood wasn't his own. There was nothing wrong with the boy.

"There exists no other creature on earth," said the doctor, "who can boast of putting so much intelligence, so much imagination, so much talent into the manner of slaying his fellow being. None that devotes so many members and means to the destruction of his own peers."

Now he was leaning over the sergeant's bare chest and tinkering with his insides with long steel pliers.

"None!" he said. "War is indeed specific to man. And I would go even further: it is the principal component of the definition of humanity! . . . Who, among you, would dare complain about taking part in it?"

"That'th a load of bullthit, that ith!" yelped an anonymous voice, in all likelihood from a dislocated jaw.

"Haha! We can agree on that, soldier. If it's not that exactly, it's at least a load of bullshit erected in the name of art! . . . Look at this," the doctor had said, brandishing at the end of his pliers the 7.92mm bullet just extracted from the shoulder of Sergeant Olivetti. "This is the tangible proof—and it is indeed tangible, isn't it, Sergeant?—of the superiority of our species over all the others. Would the most cunning fox have been able to invent the Mauser? No. Would the cow, the rat, the lion, the tiger have been able to conceive of a hand grenade? A 155 cannon? Not that either. They wouldn't even dream of it! And no more would those who are supposedly our distant cousins: chimpanzees, gorillas, orangutans. None of these primitive primates would be capable of creating the work of art that is a fragmentation grenade!"

The nurse held out the tray to him. The doctor dropped the projectile onto it—a small metallic sound like a coin in a beggar's metal cup.

"The more our instruments of destruction become ingenious, efficient, and numerous, the more we will see our level of civilization increase. And the more our supremacy will be confirmed! . . . Compress, please, Miss Hiddink."

A little later the expert passed in front of the boy again.

"You're still here?" he said. "What are you waiting for? . . . Go on, to your post, soldier! You're fit for a second tour."

Authoritarian and paternal.

And prove yourself worthy of mankind, he might have added.

Just behind him, Horse-Nanny looked him up and down. Hieratic, a red cross over her forehead.

They know.

Sergeant Olivetti had stayed in the ambulance. The boy had gone back to his company, alone and on foot.

It's man, sonny.

So be it.

Man, more than ever. He has not yet asked himself whether it's a good thing in the end. Whether it's a desirable thing. He has not yet told himself that it's meaningless.

He places his hands flat on his thighs. He lifts his eyes.

After a moment it passes.

My love,

I came.

I came in my dream and I came in reality.

It was four in the afternoon. Exhausted by an umpteenth night without sleep, I nodded off on my bed. I dreamed. In my dream we were in your caravan, the one that you were driving when our paths first crossed. The wheel was not broken, and the caravan was carrying us along. I don't know who was holding the reins for we were both inside. We heard the clicking of the horse hooves and we saw the trees go by through the windows. The shadow of trees. It was beautiful and hot. We were naked in the alcove and our bodies were sweating. I recognized the texture of your skin. I recognized its taste. You were lying on your back and your penis was upright, it was rigid and swollen, and you offered it to me, you were waiting for me to take it. Your penis, your shaft, your arrow. For me. It was a gift and it was a command. Take it! I read it in your gaze. In your gaze I saw pride, impatience, feverishness, and that harsher flash that shines in the eyes of someone who requires and who orders. Take it! . . . Yes, master. Yes, my prince. Yes, my love. I obeyed. I leaned over, and I took it. In my mouth. Your stake, your sword. I slid it into the sheath of my lips. I polished it and smoothed it. I licked it. I enveloped it and sucked it. I sharpened it. For all I was doing, in truth, was preparing it to slay me. Who commands, do you think? Who requires? I forged your blade in the fire of my mouth, and I impaled myself on it. Take it!

I swear to you that I thought I was dying. A marvelous, ecstatic death. The sublime burning. You pierced me. You filled me. Never had you ever penetrated so deep in me. The wheels continued to turn, the caravan bounced softly on the path and the countryside went by. The shadow. The sun. The shadow. Who was driving? No one. The two of us. I straddled you and you transported me, and it was a voyage that we could take together, you and me, lover and lover, master and mistress, slaves to each other, united, chained by intrinsic and indestructible links, like clouds and water, like sun and shadow, and the voyage neared its end, I felt it coming, the dazzling, the formidable devastation of matter and spirit, the miraculous chaos, I felt it rise, rise . . .

I don't know how long it lasted. I woke up. I opened my eyes. Beyond the windows night was falling. But I still had the taste of you in my mouth. I really had it, do you understand? There, in the room, on my bed, I still had your eyes fixed on me. And your skin. And your sweat. And your penis deep inside my stomach.

I did nothing other than prolong the dream, my love. Continue the voyage. Ours. Finish it.

My thighs were already open, my hand already in place. Who commands? Who orders? My vulva was burning and swollen. My juice was running—it was running so much, if only you knew! And my fingers were already moving. But they weren't my fingers, they were yours. My fingers were your fingers. My fingers were your tongue. My fingers were your powerful stake that nailed me and lifted me and carried me towards the highest realms. Outside of me. Outside of everything, soul, flesh, spirit and matter. Trance. Searing. Incandescent. I had to bite myself to keep from screaming.

You made me come, my love.

It was the first time since you left. For a long time I struggled. I resisted. I told you: I think of you and there is fear, there is anguish that chokes me and keeps me from breathing, but there is also desire. How can I help it? I think of you and I drip. Desire is there. It's terrible.

For a long time I rebuffed its assaults because morality forbade me from succumbing to it. You know me well enough to know that I'm not talking about common, general morality (decorum, sin, that kind of hard-to-swallow broth that they serve to us by the ladleful—this soup of nonsense never made anyone grow), it's not about that but a personal morality. A sort of pact that I made alone, based on a mixture of modesty, fidelity, respect, decency, duty. Duty, yes. A duty of abstinence that I imposed on myself, out of respect for you. Your absence, your situation, all those horrors that you must be seeing and enduring: that's what was holding me back. But in the end, is it so far off from the absurd common broth? I don't think so. I don't think so.

For a long time I was mistaken.

What I think now is that there is no better homage that I can offer you. There is no greater proof of love that I can give to you. In this way I honor you. You make me wet. You make me come. As far away as you are, you hold me. You command my hand, you command my fingers, and I obey. I am yours. From now on I won't resist anymore. I won't refuse the fight. It will be my desire and my ecstasy against all those atrocities. They will be my arms. You see, at present night has fallen and I'm a bit less afraid. I'm a bit less cold. And thinking again of my dream and of what followed, in describing it to you, I feel the wave rising again already. It comes back. Look. Touch . . . You see? I'm already soaked! And my legs spread again. My thighs. I keep one hand for the quill and the other, yours, I move beneath my dress. I slide it into my slit. You're going to make me come again, my love. And I would like . . . Oh! yes, I would like for you to come too. With me. Together. Nothing would satisfy me more. Make yourself come, my love. Make yourself come! Now, right away, wherever you are. I beg of you. Let yourself. Let me. It's my hand, you see, it's mine. It's mine that grabs your member and makes it swell beneath my fingers. Make yourself come! I want it. I need it. Obey. It's my hand and it's yours. Take it! Take care of my cunt. Rub it. Stuff it. Like that, yes.

Like that. Keep going. I can feel your sap rising. I want your cock to tense and grow and get even harder and then explode. The two of us, together. Make yourself come. Make me come. Make me come, my love. And spurt your cum at the mouths of the cannons!

E.

THEY SPEND THE REST of the winter and a part of spring in Somme. Battles and fights, offense and defense. First line, second, third, rest—organizing the chain, planning the tasks, optimization, industrial cadence: slaughter and its business. Added to that the boy is on all the patrols, all the small missions. Voluntarily. Reconnaissance. Ambushes. Blitzes. Sneak attacks. Sabotage and cleaning and harassment. Dirty work. The boy takes on more than his share. He observes, and he imitates, and soon he surpasses, by his audacity and his temerity, by his efficiency. The old rediscovered reflexes mix with the new sciences he acquires. Intuition and intelligence add to each other and complete each other. Instinct and experience. His natural dispositions, his chameleon-like gift for camouflage, his dexterity, his agility, his mastery of movement and silence: it all serves him. Because this is a return to the time of predation. The time of hunting.

In a few weeks it's not a name he makes for himself but several. Among the section they call him the Shadow. They call him the Sioux. Ross the Canadian calls him the Lynx. Wayne the cowboy calls him the Wolf. No matter the name they give him, it's pronounced with a certain amount of respect. Even admiration. These are the times, and these are the standards wherein a man's value is often measured by the number of scalps he brings back. They've seen the boy in action, they know his worth.

He kills.

This wouldn't have been so extraordinary if he hadn't almost exclusively used blades. There was a period, in the beginning, when he had sharpened the edge of his shovel so well that he could have used it as a razor. A single strike precisely measured and applied was enough to bring down any adversary. Then he tried the sickle. Then he tried the ax. Later he converted to the machete: a sword picked up from the corpse of a Senegalese infantryman, which he now wears on a belt in a leather sheath. In addition to this weapon, he shares with these colonial troops the principle of taking, despite orders, neither mercy nor prisoners.

The boy intrigues. Sometimes he becomes frightened. His muteness contributes to the mystery. His various nicknames regularly come up in the mealtime conversations. There are first-hand witnesses of his actions, those who have seen with their own eyes and who recount, who exaggerate, a bit, a lot, who one-up in bravura or in horror, who embellish in exploit or in carnage, who glorify, with the feeling or hope that a parcel of that glory will reflect onto them by the simple fact of having been there, present, at his side. There are those who hear talk and pass it on, and in their mouths, too, the story can transform into an epic as they adopt, without even realizing it, the tones of their ancestors gathered around the fire narrating the adventures of a legendary character, of a mythic being. Thus, word circulates. And thus, the stories become legend. Listening to them, the boy does not really have the traits of a hero, he is also not a demon nor the devil himself, he is instead something like the Angel of Death. Angelic and deathly: Isn't that the most dangerous creature, the one with such paradoxical characteristics? A celestial warrior descended to raise hell.

This ambiguous prestige, this macabre sort of aura that surrounds him and the sentiments that he inspires, the boy does not seek them out. In reality his companions are far from knowing everything. Most of the time he acts alone and without witnesses. And when his section is in the first line, he takes great liberties with the rules. He slips away. Without asking permission or even informing anyone. Nocturnal sorties usually. He leaves in the dead of night and comes back at the break of dawn. Between those two poles, what has he done? Where has he gone? He explores. No man's land and beyond. He snakes through the lines, grazes them, skirts them, crosses them. From one camp to another. No barrier confines him. He plays with the barbed wire like a toy. He tames the Frisian horses. He opens breaches. He thrusts himself through, when he feels like it, as far as enemy territory. He makes himself lighter than air and darker than night—a breath in the wind, a shadow in the darkness: How to distinguish them? Sometimes he wanders for a long while inside of a German camp. Furtive, silent. The Angel passes . . . At dawn the Boches find one or two of their own with their throats cut. It's not rare. But sometimes he also just simply, patiently observes, posted, for example, astride a branch, ten, twelve, fifty yards above the ground. He once sat like this for several hours straight, directly above a squadron of Uhlans. Their camp was set up in a clearing. Rather quickly the horses had sensed his presence, manifesting their concern through whinnying and nervous stamping and rolling of their big porcelain eyes—the whites of their eyeballs shining in the crescent moon. Signals that the cavaliers didn't know how to interpret. Once, only once, the boy was caught during his peregrinations: identified by the nose of a guard dog. It was one of those formidable giants from Rottweil, Germany. Luckily, the animal had at first just bared its teeth, a hoarse growl vibrated in its throat. The boy had not allowed him to bark. He used the ax: with one strike he split the dog's skull. But the blade had been so deeply anchored in the bone that he could not withdraw it before its master was already on him. A man as ferocious as the beast and with a similar growl, but weighing three or four times as much. A giant. Then followed hand-to-hand combat, during which the boy had had to tear the nose of his adversary off with his teeth in order to get himself away. Then there had been a second swing of the ax to the man's neck. Taking off that night he had wanted to scream at the stars. The blood the blood the blood the night the blood the moon the air the blood the blood. No password required, he weaves in and out under the noses of the sentinels whether they be enemies or allies. Without a trace.

Some among the company are skeptical. They are careful not to ask questions. They can imagine. Only the corporal of the squad is formally up to date, for the simple reason that they ran into each other, the boy and him, by chance during one of these expeditions. Both out of bounds, seeing to their nocturnal lives, they had come upon each other and very nearly killed each other. They returned to camp together. The corporal doesn't know everything either, but he knows that. He understands. He too has secrets.

"Why do we take such risks, Mazeppa?" he says to the boy one day. "We're working overtime. We're not obliged. We want someone to pump us full of lead so we don't have to do it ourselves, is that it?"

He nods his head. Thin smile and cigarette in his mouth, an ironic gleam in his eyes.

Swiss. A legionnaire, due to the circumstances. The regiment had seen so many losses during the first months that the battalions had been reorganized, regroupings had occurred during winter, that's how they had found each other.

The corporal has a gray-green look, intense, penetrating. One that cuts straight to the soul. The men like him. Everyone in the group. But over time he has forged a particular bond with the boy. Closer. Perhaps because they have something in common: being there, totally and fully there, and at the same time somewhere else.

"You remind me of someone, Mazeppa," he says to him one day. "Someone that doesn't exist. He hasn't been born yet. For now he is here."—placing his finger on his own forehead: "He's growing. He's getting taller. He's fed by all this, all this disgusting crap. He soaks it all in . . . But I'll have to give birth to him one of these days. The thing is, I'm afraid he'll be a terrible guy. A goddamned asshole! The worst little rugrat . . . What can I do about it? Dogs don't make cats."

The corporal is also the only one to call him by the name on his ID card: Mazeppa. He had immediately recognized the inspiration. He cited Hugo. He cited Liszt. As if he were evoking two friends currently trudging through the trenches with them all. Friends, nothing more nor less. And then the keen smile again, the piercing gaze. "Well-chosen," he had said. A funny guy.

One thing is certain: as far as his escapades are concerned, the corporal covers for him. The Angel of Death can continue to spread his wings. Is it him? Is it his noxious flight that we sense above the devastated fields? Possible. The blood the night the moon the blood. Harvest.

The scarlet season has begun. It is far from over.

IN MAY THEY PUSH to Artois, Pas-de-Calais. It's the home of the Ouvrages Blancs, Hill 140, the Carency cemetery, in Souchez. Over there people will speak of their bravery for a long time. They will speak of their sacrifice. Then they will be forgotten.

A month later they are in Alsace. Sainte-Marie-aux-Mines: the center of everything. The same sound of bells tolling. The fights are epic, the combatants heroic. They are valiant, they are pugnacious, they are intrepid, they are courageous, they are gallant, they are killed. Mausoleums will be erected for them. Their names will be inscribed. They will be commemorated. Then they will be forgotten.

The men pass through. Villages that were unknown yesterday enter into history. And history continues.

It's on the way back from Vosges that a tragic episode unfolds for the boy. If there is one thing that can still make the heart of the Angel bleed, it's this:

The route they've been following since dawn is an open wound in the large body of the moribund country. Devastation, devastation. An iron storm had recently preceded them, a hail of fire and steel that flattened the trees and buildings, the roofs, the walls, the bells, it hacked, it disemboweled, it burned and blackened. Everywhere ruins and rubble, carbonized heaps that give rise, here and there, to flimsy columns of anthracite smoke that sting the nose. Some natives rummage through the wreckage in search of a buried relative or a paltry lost treasure. They are rare, those who remain and are still alive. It's nearly midday and it's hot. The sky is a cruelly pure blue. Dead beasts lie on the ground. The fat bloated bellies of cows, their limp and wilted udders, useless. The flies are already there, in great numbers, in clouds. Crows and ravens gather in preparation for the feast. The promised meal. Carrion and vultures and those who march, who pass through, are not out of place in the middle of this desolation. A handful of scruffy soldiers in rags. They move slowly, heads lowered beneath the harsh rays of the sun, like convicts going back to their cells after a day of penal servitude. You can almost hear the clinking of invisible chains shackling their ankles.

A bit further on they fall on the remains of a company no less wretched than their own. The deluge struck them full force. The damages are considerable. The losses. Half the troop. The wounded, the killed. Overturned vehicles blocking the path: field kitchen, ambulance, supply trucks. A pasture stretches on one side of the road, sprinkled with poppies. Between the stains of brilliant red one can see, like enormous molehills, a series of graves, freshly dug and filled. Troops in sweaters dig them. They hurried to bury the men, and now it's time for the horses. A dozen animals. One grave for all of them. They cut them up to save room. They cut off their legs. And it's then that the boy suddenly detaches from the troop. He rushes through the ranks and jumps over the embankment and hurries to two soldiers leaning, saw in hand, over the corpse of a horse. He pushes them away with such violence that the men fall to the ground. They get back up, surprised, furious. When one of them charges back, the boy draws his machete. The man rears back. "Leave him!" says a voice. It's the corporal who arrives, running. He is soon joined by the men of the squad. They don't know what's happening, but they follow, in solidarity. A crowd forms. Things get heated. The men are exhausted, on edge, they wouldn't be far from knocking each other around if not for the intelligence and authority of the corporal. Tempers eventually calm down. The gravediggers take off mumbling, set off to tackle another nasty job a bit further on.

During the entire altercation the boy has not flinched. He is still standing with his machete, in front of the dead horse, as if detached from everything that's happening around him. Now his companions are quiet and they observe him, they wait. After a moment the boy gently lets himself fall to his knees in front of the animal's corpse. Then he extends a hand and places it flat against its ears. Blessing or sacrament or simple caress. He looks at it. He looks at the large chest, the vast flanks, like a ship's hull, the depleted but still robust carcass, the legs that death has turned rigid, the enormous pasterns. It's the gelding. Beneath the dust, beneath the mud and the dried blood the boy had recognized the bay-colored coat that he has currycombed, corked, brushed so many times. It's the gelding. Requisitioned, wrested from its peaceful retirement like all who are mounted or who carry, who load, who pull, men and beasts, all living strength, all flesh that can contribute to nourishing the most famished monster, the greediest there is. It's the gelding. Like no other. The horse has one eye open, glassy, its eyelid hemmed by black flies—the insects leaning over the pale surface of this lake as if to suck it down to the last tear's salt. Its pupil is fixed on the blue of the sky. Its bared lips reveal long teeth, a yellow frozen smile. A thin trickle of blood oozes from its nostrils. And the formerly blond goatee is now an ashy gray. It's the gelding. Among the red poppies.

The boy watches. Chest raised by a slow and deep breath. He remembers. It was another time. Perhaps another world. Here and now the horse is lying on the ground and he is on his knees and standing around them, as a rampart, is the clustered guard formed by the corporal and all the men of the squad. And the men are still there, later, beside the boy, when the flames take hold of the gelding's cadaver, and no one can truly know what part of them soars in the smoke along with the dead horse.

❦

My love,

I hear that they are watching the mail. They open the letters. They censor if need be. Certain things, it seems, are forbidden. Which things? Supposedly the information related to the military, strategic domain. Information concerning your positions, your displacements, the attacks you plan, perhaps the weapons you use, what do I know? They fear spies. My love, if you wrote to me, you wouldn't be able to reveal to me how many bullets remain in your rifle nor what sumptuous massacre the formidable Marshal Joffre is preparing for you. You will note that I wrote "sumptuous" and "formidable." And look, I'll add "admirable"! Thus I am more than abiding by the rules, no? They can reproach me for nothing. This in the event that those messieurs decide to also throw an inquisitive glance over the innocent little letters that I send you. Does it work in both directions? It wouldn't surprise me at all, in the end. For I believe, for my part, that this control of the mail has other motivations and other aims than those that I have just listed. Less honorable ends. I believe that they simply do not want us to know the truth. What you live and what you really think, you, over there. What we live and what we think, us, over here. It cannot be known. The dead, the wounded, the mutilated, the wait, the fear, the anguish, the madness, the despair: no no no, that doesn't exist. News from the front is good. According to the newspaper we read, it's even excellent. On that subject, as I already told you, the official press is unanimous: our soldiers are valiant and the hour is near when the German eagle,

346

that rapacious villain, will be driven out, plucked clean, from our beautiful country. That's what we need to know. It's rare that some grouchy journalist dares to venture a doubt or an objection in his article. A discordant note in the middle of the harmonious concert. The bastard! He didn't do his job properly! Fortunately the conductor is there in the pit, keeping watch. Bang! A rap of the stick on the fingers of the offender, and the marvelous symphony is back in unison. That's how it works. They will not allow us the tiniest false note. What needs to be said is that here, too, in the rear, all is going well. Thanks to you. Thanks to you our assets and our lives are preserved. Thanks to you we still have hope. We are wholeheartedly with you. We are proud of you. We count on you. We admire your courage and we encourage you to continue the fight. Yes, yes, continue! Continue! Rest assured that your sacrifice is necessary and fully justified!

You see, I think that these messieurs the censors worry about our qualms. Not out of empathy or a sudden burst of compassion, but out of necessity. Nothing that might sap the morale of our troops can show through in our letters. We must maintain the flame, the fire, the immense devastating blaze. And to do that all suspicion of defeatism must be banned. Any potential drop of water on the fire. No doubt will be permitted. No questioning. Imagine if we could share our true sentiments, our real sincere thoughts, imagine if we could finally be aware, all of us, you over there, us over here, and even the Germans in their country, if we could collectively become aware of the uselessness, of the absurdity, of the inanity of this war, of the pain and suffering that it engenders on all sides, of the evil they inflict on us by obliging us to act in this atrocious play. Can you imagine that? You can bet that after an exposé like this, all the world would fall into agreement and immediately cease this magnificent, this sublime carnage ("magnificent," messieurs, "sublime," I insist). Act IV, Scene 3: "And the fight ceased for lack of combatants" . . . What a catastrophe that would be!

No, better to prevent it by avoiding the spread of the tiniest drop of that poison in our mail. Prudence and vigilance. Also, if we want to write usefully, they place at our disposal superb postcards. There are several designs. On each we find represented one of our young and beautiful soldiers. Such allure! Chest bulging, proud gaze, starched uniform, shoes and rifle perfectly polished. And each card has a caption. Which would you like to receive, my love? The one that says:

"Glory to the 75! Everywhere it goes
a laurel tree grows."

Or would you prefer:

"By the flag of the Republic
He who seeks trouble will find it!"

I admit to being totally swayed by these Alexandrines:

"So close to the enemy my heart fills with rage
If he comes, I'll know how to fight him with courage."

Proof, if there is any, that wartime patriotism is not exempt from poetry.
But I can offer you another rousing one:

"We will take them!"

Sober, classic, efficient.
As you see, I have an embarrassment of choices with which to express my tender thoughts to you. While we're at it, they also strongly urge us to participate in the war effort: "Sign up for the National Defense bonds," they say to us. I waver, I waver, as you can imagine . . .

A smile comes to my lips when I think of what these messieurs might find shoving their dirty snouts into my letters. They would learn some things. Certain lines would really boil those pigs' blood, and why not send their corkscrew tails wriggling!

Nevertheless I would like, and in advance, to excuse myself for the possible spelling errors that they might notice. And since I know that this will not be the case for you, my love, here is one last message that I am very tempted to deliver. The caption says simply:

"To Hell with the person reading this!"

E.

GUSTAVE IS A RAT. The first time the boy heard this name pronounced he swiftly turned his head, searching for the father figure that he knew so well. He saw nothing but one of the thousands of rodents, dead, a soldier was holding it by its tail. His morning trophy. Dirty creature. The third plague after the Boches and the mud. Gustave, that was its name. Which goes to show how the universe has been transformed. Which goes to show the proportions to which it has been reduced, the new face that has been given to it.

July. They are stationed in Somme again. It was never officially decreed, but their squad is now considered a kind of unattached unit. It is composed of about fifteen men, the corporal at the head. They've all proven themselves. Hard nuts to crack. Mercenaries without salaries whose conception of discipline is closer to anarchy than that of any hierarchical system. The corporal is just about the only one they listen to. If he gives orders, they execute them. They are entrusted with the most perilous missions. Atypical. In exchange for which they have relatively great liberty. Without chores, tasks, exercises. They organize themselves as they see fit. Blind eyes are turned to their little affairs. In a word, they are left alone.

From the boy's original unit eight men remain: Wayne, Hosberg, Babik, Racovitch, Cormuz, Hadida, Blumenfeld and him. Some of the Russians, Italians, and Belgians have joined their respective armies. The Wise Man is dead. Guso is dead. Ross, Stein, Wachfeld, Gardot, Thill, Krestorsky, Pereira and all the others, dead. They've been replaced. Their dead replacements have been replaced in their turn, as well as the replacements of the replacements. The boy has seen a lot of P.F.M., as the old timers say. Provisions of Fresh Meat. Some smartasses painted the three letters on the freight cars carrying the reserve soldiers—requisitioned civilian vehicles on which the destinations *Galeries Lafayette* or *Madeleine-Bastille* were still displayed. "Change of destination, boys. Over there is L'enfert-Bochereau. End of the line, everyone get off! Welcome to Hell! Haha!" (The men are mischievous.) He has seen some of these new recruits fail to even get past their own baptism. Mowed down on the spot during the first attack, annihilated after four minutes. Blues forevermore.

Here are those who remain—can we call them the lucky ones? Strong heads. They have made their own little tranquil hamlet. Their shack is outfitted with objects gathered here and there from the ruins and abandoned houses. Furniture and trinkets. Babik has a penchant for paintings. There are more on the walls of his shanty than there ever were in his gypsy caravan. He brings back every painting he finds, gouaches and watercolors, landscapes and portraits—like those austere faces of illustrious ancestors of illustrious but unknown origins—and even two empty frames in gilded wood. "The museum of scabs," Cormuz says ironically. Cormuz sleeps folded on a child's bed made of wrought iron. A cormorant in a canary cage. He says it reminds him of when he was a kid. He says it's nostalgic. Hadida says that what he's lapping up now isn't mother's milk. Hadida acts like a bourgeois. He unearthed a pair of Louis XV armchairs that were nearly intact, he who had never planted his butt on anything other than straw or wood. And the best of all: a crystal chandelier that he hung from the ceiling. At night when he's alone he sits in his living room and he crosses his legs and puffs on a cigar, not lit because he doesn't know how to smoke, and he leafs through an old copy of *Gaulois* that he holds upside down half the time because he doesn't know how to read. No more than Wayne knows how to play music, but the American moved heaven and earth for people to help him carry an antique Pape upright piano made in 1834 into his room. From time to time he presses down on a key at random and it's as if he were setting the tune before launching into one of those songs from the Old West that talks about a poor cowherd and his sweetheart and the deserted plains beneath the moonlight. One day the corporal surprises his men by sitting in front of this very piano to extract all the juice of a Bach cantata from its carcass: "Jesus bleibet meine Freude." Further proof that German genius produced more than the Big Bertha. Although the instrument had been nearly destroyed and was very poorly tuned, it played surprisingly well and sent a shiver down all of their spines. The corporal had drunk more than his share, his eyes were closed, and his fingers seemed to be walking on the keyboard by themselves and they seemed to sparkle like the reflections of the sun in a torrent in the middle of summer. If he was sleepwalking no one would have wished for his awakening. If he was possessed it could only have been by a celestial and luminous power and may it remain thus, may his joy linger and ours too. It was the one and only time that the corporal touched the Pape. Normally, instead, he could be found visiting with Blumenfeld, who was a chemistry professor in his former life. The two men chat. The décor is less luxurious but the words fly a little higher. Along the lines of:

"Besides a proven existence what's the difference between God and Wilhelm II?" asks Blumenfeld. "Between God and Napoléon? Between God and Attila? For one as for the others, there is always, on top of everything, thousands, millions of victims, all done with the sole aim of spreading their glory, of establishing their almighty power and affirming their hegemony."

"Not God, old boy," replies the corporal. "It's not about Him but only about those who claim to be His representatives. Usurpers. Those who speak in His name and in reality do nothing but distort His word. You confuse the enemy with the messenger, Blum."

"It doesn't matter. Without an enemy, the messenger wouldn't be there. You must admit that in terms of number of dead, religion, no matter which one, is the worst scourge of humanity. And I have an inkling that it's far from over."

This kind of speech.

Outside of time spent taking it easy, what do they do? They hunt. Their favorite prey is hooch. Any liquid containing a certain proof: they're not picky. The quantity first. The ordinary quart does not suffice for them, nor the half-pint. Always in search of a bottle or a supplementary cask. They ferret about in the depots and the trailers, they help themselves to the reserves of the company, of all the companies, they don't hesitate to bribe, to pilfer, to extort. (What a memorable celebration they had for the boy when he brought them back a case of champagne reclaimed from a small German fort during one of his outings: the most beautiful of his spoils of war.) Sometimes they go off gallivanting for miles on foot to wind up in some watering hole in the rear. Hosberg is the son of a well-to-do family, his wallet is stocked, it's he who treats. They drink, they taunt the table of wretched sub-officers who have already drunk their wretched salaries. They provoke them and end up getting into fights with them, or else with a flock of gendarmes they pass on their return, at dawn. They invite themselves into black barracks, hanging about with the immigrants, Turco, Babakoute troops, share their soup, dance the African dances during the impromptu concerts, dancing to the sharp sounds of flutes, to the rhythm of tin cans, dance, dance, get drunk and dance and turn and spin around like tops before going to puke their guts out beneath the stars at the gate of the casbahs.

They hunt other prey too: rabbits, hedgehogs, cats. To change up the mundane meals. Racovitch prepares them in a ragout, in a stew. Poultry sometimes, ducks and gallinules. They haunt the marshes on an old patched-up barge. Strange gondoliers roaming the twists and turns of the Somme river at dusk or in early morning, silently splitting the curtain of fog, of bulrush, of reeds, spectral apparition that brings to mind the legendary phantom crew of the *Mary Celeste*.

But it's not just them. Freshwater pirates. In a vast bog they found an eel breeding ground, they hunt there regularly. Racovitch prepares them with cheap wine. Racovitch did his training in palace canteens, he can cook anything.

Marauders, certainly, but let's not relegate them to the ranks of those organized pillagers, shameless, who follow the armies step by step and emerge as soon as the battle is over to methodically pilfer the gutted houses and rob the still-warm cadavers. They profit ignobly from misfortune, feed like parasites on the vile beast, cynically displaying a Red Cross armband that serves as their passport to go between the lines. Despicable mob. Above all, don't lump them together!

Waiting for the next Gehenna, they take a nap. They play *manille*. They think of women. They speak of women. The ones they knew and the ones they brag about knowing and the ones they invent and that they'll never know and who are certainly the most beautiful of all, who have the prettiest eyes and the reddest and softest lips and the cheekiest smiles and the most delicious breasts to pinch, and who aren't prudish about it, not the least bit shy, to the contrary, the passion, goddamn, the passion, the ardor, the eagerness, gourmands for God's sake you have to see it, and when the boy finds himself witness to these conversations he lowers his head and looks at his hands and he places them flat on his thighs and it passes, after a moment it passes.

"Madelon, she's nothing but a whore when you think about it!"

From the case of champagne bottles Hadida constructed a beehive. It holds a nest of bees transported on the end of a pole. He is really hopeful of getting honey from it. He also hopes to extract a bit of wax to fabricate an altar candle, as he saw a brigadier do in Meuse. When they burned, his candles smelled good.

Wayne adopted a ferret. He's domesticating it. He gave it the nickname Bill and he speaks to it in the language of Shakespeare. Or at least in the language of Shakespeare's horse. His idea is to train the animal to hunt rats. He wants to turn it into a veritable rat killer, the most famous rat killer in the country. And when this fucking war is over he'll bring his champion with him back to Arizona and he'll make himself a load of money organizing fights and pocketing the bets. He's fully convinced of it.

The corporal fashioned himself a hammock. He suspends it between two beech trees and he sleeps under the stars. When the alcohol doesn't manage to knock him out, he contemplates the fireworks raging in the distance during the night. He counts the rockets. Tries to distinguish the French from the Germans—the good from the bad.

These are the first days of summer. So goes their life and it will last as long as it lasts.

THE BOY CONTINUES his solitary excursions. He scours the country-side. Barefoot, always with his sword on his hip and his bag over his shoulder, the unread letters crammed inside. He sees all sorts of things and all sorts of people. He reigns for a few hours over the abandoned, deserted villages. Not a living soul. Old rocks and lizards boil there. He goes into the manors and the chateaus that are now open to all visitors. Where are the former lords? Perhaps these cold ashes in the hearths of giant chimneys are all that remains of them. The gaping doors. The high ceilings. The drafts of air. What was not plundered has been destroyed or soiled. Leprosy runs through the rooms. In the kingdom of the mentally ill, who are the kings?

His steps carry him further and further, for more and more time. He has unexpected encounters. One day a cavalry soldier in the under-growth. The skeleton of a soldier resting on the moss, in the shadows. The uniform that seems barely wrinkled, the brown underpants, the sky-blue tunic, barely faded—but what blue? of what sky? He doesn't spit fire or flames anymore. Where are the hussars of former times? A ray of light filters between the branches, illuminating the hollowed face. The perfectly eroded, polished, blanched bones. From a hollow eye socket runs a column of ants, like a gloomy lachrymal stream, endless. Does he cry over his own fate, or over that of the one staring at him? Disarmed does not mean in peace. A tuft of hair, rough like horsehair, gray like lichen, emerges from beneath his helmet. His hair must have continued to grow. There's a nursery rhyme that goes like this: "Cavalryman, cavalryman—what does the echo promise? Cavalryman, cavalryman—if not the wine of youth and the gallop's bliss." No trace of the mount in the area. A bird made his nest on the cavalryman's cadaver, between the shoulder and the neck. On the rug of twigs lie three little beige eggs speckled with brown. The boy leans over and grabs them and continues on his way.

On another day in Flanders, he happens upon a painter. Since the morning he's been walking along the Deûle. Another hot day. He had stopped for a moment to urinate in the water when a call rings out behind him: "Fuchs! . . . Fuchs!" The accent is German. The boy turns around. Ten feet away stands a little white fox-terrier, staring up at him. The dog neither growls nor barks. Muzzle slightly tilted, he seems more curious than frightened. Without taking his eyes off him the boy slowly pulls the machete from its sheath. The animal does not shy away. Another call: "Fuchs!" followed by a whistle. This time the dog's ear moves. For a few seconds he seems to hesitate, then a quick movement of the head, as if to express a regret or an invitation. He turns around and takes off scampering away, his nose along the ground. The boy follows him. Fifty yards away the animal disappears into a thicket. He can hear the voice of the master who greets him. A tone of false anger. A laugh. The boy glances through the bushes. He discovers a clearing, a small strip of land surrounded by yews and poplars. Behind the trees a stretch of river, in the center a bicycle lying in the grass, a standing easel, a man, in front, with his back to him. The Angel flies. The dog is seated at the foot of the easel and watches him approach. The master has gone back to his work. He is in a knit sweater. On the frame of the bicycle is a jacket from the uniform of a Bavarian regiment. Next to it an open bag, a big sketch book inside. The only weapon the man has is his paintbrush. He caresses the paper with slow, applied gestures. He dips the tip in a box of colors, in a metal cup filled with water. The boy stops three steps behind him, he looks over the painter's shoulder. A watercolor. He recognizes the slender silhouettes of poplars, the sky, the sun, in the diluted azure and gold. It's prettier than the paintings displayed in Babik's shack.

And suddenly the painter becomes aware of the boy's presence. He pivots, his paintbrush in his hand, then becomes petrified. His face is extremely pale, his complexion as though diluted, which makes his short waxed mustache of black and coarse hair stand out even more. The boy faces him. The machete hangs at the end of his arm. The blade shines, sends a flash of silver over the green grass. Only the murmur of the Deûle disturbs the silence, like the slight rustling of leaves in the wind. Then the man's lips move. It's not that they're trying to form words, it's that they're trembling. And very quickly the trembling intensifies and spreads, reaching the other limbs, from head to toe, contaminating the flesh, the muscles, the nerves and down to the bones, and suddenly the entire man is shaking with terrible, uncontrollable spasms. It's too strong: his legs buckle, he falls to his knees. In the same movement he lets go of the paintbrush and brings together his trembling palms in a sign of prayer and presents himself in the pose of a penitent in front of the boy, imploring, mutely asking for mercy, begging with his eyes, from the very depths of his terrified being. Tears run down his cheeks. In that moment the fox-terrier approaches, stands on his hind legs and places his front legs on the chest of his master and he runs a pink tongue along his face, he licks his cheeks, his mustache, he wipes away his tears. The boy looks at the man and the dog. He looks at the watercolor on the easel. An ocher color gently spreads towards the bottom of the canvas. Then his gaze returns to the man on his knees. He lifts his machete towards the sky, and for a brief moment the steel seems to burst into flame in the sunshine. The man sinks even more, his neck sunk between his shoulder blades while a kind of sharp whining escapes from between his lips. His face tenses. He closes his eyes, squeezes them with all his might, as if the light were hurting him or as if he wanted to forever preserve this final vision—and perhaps he will. When he opens them again, the Angel has gone.

He's gone for nearly a week. His longest absence. He brings back two hares and a wild boar weighing fifty pounds that he drags at the end of a rope: feed for the squad. The lads celebrate him accordingly.

"I thought you'd ditched us for good," says the corporal. "It would have surprised me, but you never know . . . Here, I kept this for you."

It's a packet of letters. Five of them. They've continued to arrive since January. The boy opens his bag to shove them in with the others. A handful of envelopes overflow and fall to the ground. All of them sealed. The corporal helps the boy to gather them. He keeps the last one in his hand.

"I read Hadida's mail to him," he said. "I read it to Krestorsky, too, and to another boy that you didn't know—Hot-piss, we called him. A pimp from Pigalle. I even replied for him. That guy kept up correspondence with a dozen high-earning hookers. He got more mail than a minister."

The boy looks at him. He waits for what's next. The corporal takes a drag of his cigarette, discards the butt. He exhales the smoke.

"I know how to be discreet when I need to be," he said. "Silent as the grave . . ."

A crooked grin. With a nod of the chin he indicates the bag.

"If you need . . ." he said. "Up to you, Mazeppa."

He gives the envelope back to the boy.

The next day the boy comes to find him and hands him the bag, and it's much more than a packet of letters that he entrusts to him with this gesture. His gray-green eyes say that it's the right decision, a decision that honors both of them.

From this day on the ritual is established. They isolate themselves, the boy pulls an envelope from the pile, the corporal opens it and reads it to him. He respects his promise of discretion. He keeps a neutral tone and doesn't make any commentary. If he were reading the official mail to the chief of police he wouldn't conduct himself any differently. Over the course of a few weeks there is only one occasion when he permits himself to express a personal sentiment: after having put the pages back in the envelope, he remains silent for a long moment, staring into the void. Then he says:

"This woman . . ." He taps the letter with his fingertips. "You know, not everyone is like this . . ."

He breaks off. His voice is more hoarse than usual. He straightens his chest, takes a deep breath. Then lets out a sigh.

"Yeah . . ." he says. "I think you'd better make it out alive, Mazeppa."

My love,
    You alone will understand:

> Hell is, after all these winters, for there to
> Be only one summer. So many dark nights before
> Mist clears for a single dawn. The lantern has burned down.
> Are we to be granted a dreamless rest forevermore?

> Pop of stars dying, the sky now empty,
> A universe lacking in light completely.
> Is there an eternity? No longer a possibility.
> No gold that melts to the bottom for the greedy.

> More darkness, more night. The skies have opened.
> Gone is the music, only a glacial silence.
> For now only worms in apples hum.
> Ever since this horrific turn, we have wished for an end.

                                                         E.

THE COMMANDER-IN-CHIEF DECREES:

"Soldiers of the Republic! After months of waiting, which allowed us to build our strength and our resources, while the adversary used up his own, the hour has come to attack, to vanquish, to add new stories of glory to those of Marne and Flanders, of Vosges and Arras. Behind the iron storm and the raging fire, thanks to the labor of France's factories, where your brothers have worked night and day for you, you will go to battle together, on all fronts, in close union with the armies of the Allies. Your momentum will be unstoppable. It will carry you from your first steps all the way to the batteries of the adversary, beyond the fortified lines that stand in our way. You will grant them neither truce nor rest until victory is won. Go wholeheartedly for the deliverance of the soil of the motherland, for the triumph of law and liberty."

JOFFRE

CHAMPAGNE!

Champagne again!

Champagne all around!

The generalissimo buys this round. He seems to have a weakness for the land of Champagne. After the failure in Artois he wants to concentrate his forces on this sector. These men are his forces.

They move. They bid adieu to their quarters. Adieu chandelier and piano and paintings and beehive, adieu hunting and marauding. Adieu cage with no bars. Wayne brings the ferret hidden in his gear. He rejoins the ranks. They are gathered. The Legion. 2nd Light Infantry Regiment of the 1st Foreign Brigade.

Summer is drawing to an end.

HQ shows its cards. It prepares the offensive. The second one. The big one. The proper one. The one that will allow them to penetrate the enemy front. A feeling of déjà-vu? Let there be no mistake: this will be worse. It's always worse.

Here's how it happens for them:

On September 1, 1915, they head out for Plancher-les-Mines. A pack of firefighters has joined them. They move the earth. They dig tunnels.

On September 8, General Urbal signs 10th Army order number 102, recognizing the capture of Ouvrages Blancs, and the regiment earns its first citation in an official army commendation: "On May 9, following orders issued by Lieutenant Colonel Cot to seize, by bayonet if necessary, a German position that was very strongly entrenched, the unit launched an assault led by the officers, possessing superb strength of will, gaining several square miles of terrain all at once,

363

despite a very active resistance by the enemy and the violent fire of machine guns." End of citation.

Superb strength of will.

On September 13 there's a big spectacle in the presence of the President of the French Republic, Raymond Poincaré, for the presentation of the flag. The president affixes the Cross of War, with distinction, to it. And then the president returns to his home.

On September 17 they board the train at Champagne and the next day they set up in the woods on Hill 160, northeast of Suippes. They dig tunnels. They move the earth.

The day and the hour approach.

The weather is beautiful and clear.

The future combat zone is not a circle of seven yards in diameter—we don't give a damn about the noble art—but a vast stretch forty miles wide: a chalky landscape, gray and gloomy plains, nearly bare, only pockmarked by a few depressions and bristled here and there with small wooded areas that they call the Carré woods, the Losange woods, the Trapèze woods, etc. Other rare landmarks are designated with origins that are even more obscure and that vaguely evoke names of insignificant and ridiculous constellations lost in the far corners of the universe: Vedegrange's Thorn, Bricot's Hole, Navarin's Farm, Massiges' Hand, The Two Mamelles, Toothbrush . . . Who would be willing to die for these stars?

General Castelnau is in charge of organizing the offensive. He utilizes the 2nd Army under General Pétain and the 4th Army under General Langle de Cary, making in total twenty-nine divisions and two cavalry corps.

Opposite them stands the 3rd German Army under General von Einem, augmented by three infantry divisions commanded by the Kronprinz himself, making seven and a half divisions. A lesser number, certainly, but perfectly entrenched and organized in advantageous positions.

The French infantrymen are provided with new uniforms, hori-zon-blue in color (since when is the horizon blue?). They have swapped their kepis for helmets. Many are wearing new boots.

Private Cormuz suffers from acute diarrhea. A charitable soul procures a paregoric elixir for him.

Everything is nearly calm. Nearly immobile and silent.

When suddenly . . .

Stupor and tremors.

On September 22 they begin firing the artillery. For seventy-five uninterrupted hours the thunder of cannons and mortars of 75mm, 90, 105, 120, 155, 220, 270, 370—with their 700-pound shells—can be heard, and then there's also the manna from heaven released by the planes endlessly crossing above the German lines. Afterwards, they will calculate that over a surface area one hundred yards wide and eight hundred long, approximately three thousand six hundred projectiles fell per hour. One hundred years later they will still unearth them in the fields, like curious mushrooms.

This intensive bombardment is meant to destroy the adversary's defenses, crush the trenches, the shelters, the tunnels, the wires, and the defenders themselves.

From September 24 to 25, while the cannonade continues, the troops spend the night on the parade grounds. Sleep if you can. A soldier announces that for those wanting to confess their sins, a chaplain is at their disposal in one of the shacks. There are a few who relieve their consciences.

But it was too good to last.

At midnight the sky becomes overcast. Enormous clouds accumu-late, then open. Torrents of water rain down and the blanched earth softens, the chalk dilutes, becomes mud, stream, swamp.

At one in the morning, the A Battalion of the 2nd Regiment of the 1st Foreign Brigade takes its combat positions. They station themselves in the Japan tunnel, between the Navarre and Nivernais tunnels.

At two in the morning, the B Battalion takes its place in the Japan tunnel, between the Navarre tunnel and the Souain road.

At four in the morning, everyone is in position.

Day appears, bleak.

At nine fifteen in the morning, the attack is launched.

A bugler rises over the embankment and sounds the charge. A command rings out: "Forward! Vive la France!"

The infantrymen burst from the parallel starting positions. Over the forty miles of the front an immense wave unfurls. Horizon-blue.

A barrage welcomes them. From the parapets constructed on the edge of their territory, the German machine guns spit, blowing away anyone who presents themselves. And the heavy artillery is not long in following. The air fills with suffocating tear gas.

At eleven the regiment receives orders to go to the top of the Place de l'Opéra. Then the order is given to continue to the trenches while clearing the Presbourg foxholes still equipped with machine guns. The movement is executed under redoubled fire.

Racovitch falls.

The tunnels are packed with German cadavers.

The monstrous wave progresses. At many points the first line of the adversary is reached. Beyond the crests, however, the enemy soldiers shelter themselves in trenches dug running in the opposite direction, invisible to French artillery. Small forts and barbed wire are intact. Information that HQ was not aware of. Their barrage is insurmountable. The momentum is stopped in front of this second line.

A critical moment. The defensive bombardment continues, and the forces of the Legion suffer heavy losses. Until four in the afternoon they maintain their positions, then they withdraw into the surrounding woods.

On September 26, the deluge continues, water, fire, rockets, grenades, shells, wreaking devastation in the legionary ranks.

On September 27, the men camp in a wood neighboring the Archduchess tunnel, where they spend the day building shelters to try to protect themselves from the enemy's relentless shots. The losses pile up. The balance sheet gets heavy, like their clothes, like their hearts. The beautiful uniform weighs on their shoulders, soaked, soiled, the blue is maroon, the horizon is mud. They need water, they're dying of thirst. Cormuz clutches his elixir, the opium tightening his guts and emptying his mind. Wayne shares his cans of sardines with his ferret. The body lice eat away their skin.

The troops have only gained a few yards.

General Pétain suspends the attack.

On September 28, General Joffre and General de Castelnau talk over the telephone. From HQ the generalissimo promises a reinforcement of fresh divisions. More! More!

At four o'clock, General de Castelnau relaunches the offensive.

This time the objective given to these two regiments from the Legion is one of those sad constellations called Navarin's Farm.

The farm is a heap of ruins and no one knows who this Navarin is nor if he ever even existed. Beyond the curtain of rain, the men can make out something outlined against a background of carbonized sky. The stars no longer shine. A formidable lattice of trenches and barbed wire stretches in front of them. On the other side is a fearsome reserve of automatic weapons and combatants.

Given their starting position, it is useless to try an attack from the sides: they have to go through the front.

The men charge.

Superb strength of will.

It's better to keep the mind separate and let the body act, the body alone. Muscles and limbs. Legs carry, arms shoot, launch, the heart pumps. Reflexes. Instinct. But sometimes a thought that is hardly a thought sneaks insidiously to the level of consciousness, something bordering on pride. A thought that says: I am immortal. The others fall, but not me. My comrades, my brothers, but not me. I am stronger. I am more cunning, or I am luckier. I am the chosen one. I will be the last. I may be the only one, but this bullet, that shell, this fatal blow cannot be destined for me. The cadaver that the rats will feed on cannot be mine. A horrid dislocated puppet, disfigured, no. An unspeakable heap of viscera, an inanimate thing, no, no. Not here. Not like that. Not me. And when suddenly this belief is extinguished, blown out like the flame of a candle, when the illusion breaks and smashes to smithereens, what replaces it is the exact opposite: the certitude that we will not get out, that we will not come out alive. I will die. That's it. Blind faith collides head on with a wall of that gruesome revelation. Oh well, too bad! The nausea, the disgust consumes us. We accept it. We resign ourselves to it. Enough, enough, enough! Lassitude. Renouncement. And then anger, suddenly. Die, bastard! The final burst of rage. Die, because it has to be that way! Finally we don't think anymore. We charge. The body, the body alone carries us to meet our destiny. We run, we run. We've never run with so much fervor, towards death. Die, swine! Die, pig! Die!

Hosberg falls.

Blumenfeld falls.

The ferret escapes from the bag where Wayne had been keeping it. The animal leaps and takes off. Wayne slows his pace, slides on the ground, gets up. For a few seconds we see him scurry into the middle of the battlefield, frenzied, his eyes riveted to the ground, yelling above the racket: "Bill! Bill! Come on, Bill! . . ." Until a bullet blows off his mouth.

The cowboy falls.

The adversary's lines of defense are barely dented. Firefighters armed with shears hurry to the rows of barbed wire. They are mowed down one after another. Wave after wave under the machine gun, decimated by the intense fire. The legionaries can't advance more than a few dozen yards. They persist.

Hadida falls.

Babik falls.

The rain falls.

The shells fall.

Cormuz marches, face smeared with blood, a dumb smile on his lips. The top of his helmet is pierced with two holes that look like empty eye sockets. Absent gaze. He marches. He moves through a patch of gas and smoke and for a moment he is crowned with a bluish halo. Then a grenade propels him into the air. He smiles at the angels.

Cormuz falls back down.

Somewhere a bugle continuously sounds the hymn of Boudin. The salvos continuously respond. The enemy seems to have concentrated all their artillery on this bit of land. The massacre continues.

The breeches of their guns burn their fingers. Their arms are tired from launching grenades. The companies in front are nearly annihilated. Hundreds of bodies are clinging to the wires.

They persist.

Out of the corner of his eye the boy suddenly perceives the corporal, who drops onto his behind. He goes over to him. The corporal's face is streaming. His gray-green gaze is veiled. His right arm doesn't exist anymore. In its place a stump has grown, an excrescence of tissue and flesh in tatters, pouring blood. The torn limb lies two yards behind, the hand turned towards the sky and seeming to surge from the muck like a strange orchid, a mandrake, a spray rose with crimson sepals. The boy slides beneath the corporal's left armpit and helps him up. They walk, their backs to the farm. It takes them more than a quarter of an hour to reach a foxhole, where the boy leaves the wounded man in the care of two stretcher bearers. Just as he turns to leave, the corporal grabs him by the collar, forces him to lean over. With a clenched jaw he whispers: "My arm . . ."

The boy straightens. Their gazes lock on each other. Then the boy does an about-turn and takes off at a run.

He searches. He searches the area. He searches for the corporal's hand. The red-blossomed flower in a bed of chalk. He sweeps a decent parcel of land down on all fours, feverish, head lowered like a dog tracking a scent, here, there, he searches, he scrapes the soft earth with his nails while the waves continue to unfurl around him, bodies rush past him, jostle him, boots trudge and splash him, bursts of machine gun fire makes the mud in front of his nose erupt.

He doesn't find it.

He stands up and stays there for a moment, immobile, stupefied.

And suddenly a shock to his hip. The round spares his skin but perforates his rucksack, tearing it open. Like the feathers of a pillow the letters escape and scatter. And already the rain plasters them to the ground, the white paper wilts, the ink dilutes, already the mud covers them and absorbs them. One soldier crushes them beneath the soles of his boots. Then a second.

The boy stares at the pile of sullied envelopes, trampled, stuck together, reduced to a pulp.

My love, she said. *My love*.

Look, here comes the cavalry, here comes the cavalry.

The bugle sounds.

Then the boy, throat tilted back, lets out a big silent cry towards the sky. Then he turns towards the German fortress—cursed star—and takes out his machete. Die, swine! Die, pig! Die! Die! Die!

Sword straight in the air, he charges forward.

Champagne!

My love,

Today marks a year. Day after day after day after day after night . . .

If one were to paint the hours, what would they look like?

Time passes, it's true. This time from which we have been dispossessed. This time that they have robbed us of through threat and force. O motherland. O kingdom. For you, this sacrifice. We bow down.

If you told me it had been ten years, I would believe it. If you told me one hundred years. And yet Beauty doesn't sleep.

I truly suffer, you know. I'm not proud to admit it. My arms are too weak. They can't kill. The beast barely feels the sting. It snorts and laughs with its hyena laugh.

And yet I persist.

This is what I decided to do today:

I am going to play. For you. For us. I am going to play Mendelssohn. All the songs without words. Yours. "The Departure," "Unrest," "Regrets," "Lost Happiness," "Sadness of Soul," "Sighing Wind," "Consolation," "Confidence," "Hope," "The Return" . . . All of them. I'm going to play Schubert. I'm going to play Schumann. Of course I'm going to play Liszt as well. "Mazeppa." As best I can I will accompany his ride, I will carry it as far as I can, to relieve his sadness. So that he doesn't die. I am going to play Chopin so that my mother's soul will forgive me and support me. I am going to play "Ballad in F Minor" and the second "Impromptu." For her. For me. For us. And all the Preludes and all the

371

Nocturnes. I am going to play the entire day and perhaps the night to follow, and a year, ten years, one hundred more years if necessary. That's what I'll do.

Because I love you.

Because love is my motherland and art my sole kingdom.

Because I still want to believe that we will emerge triumphant.

E.

ACHEN MICHEL AUGUSTIN, born June 12, 1885 in Troisvierges, Luxembourg, killed September 26, 1915 in Souain. Achoud Georges Auguste, born February 7, 1889 in Beirut, Lebanon, killed by the enemy September 28, 1915 in Souain. Alvarez Julien, born August 19, 1891 in Madrid, Spain, died September 28, 1915 in Souain. Ananiantz Achot, born October 20, 1893 in Tauris, Iran, killed by the enemy September 28, 1915 in Souain. André Claude Emile Joseph, born January 3, 1886 in Freycenet-la-Tour in the Loire Valley, killed September 28, 1915 in Souain. Aradas Clemente Bandelio Laurenzo, called Aradou, born September 3, 1890 in Banyoles, Spain, killed September 28, 1915 in Souain. Arambouro Eulage, born October 13, 1982 in Miogno, Spain, died September 28, 1915 in Souain. Assa Rafaël, born May 27, 1891 in Constantinople, Turkey, killed September 28, 1915 in Souain. Azzi Joseph, born February 14, 1875 in Dosolo, Italy, died September 28, 1915 in Souain. Babik, killed September 28, 1915 in Souain. Bainier Marcel, born July 1, 1896 in Courfaivre, Switzerland, killed September 28, 1915 in Souain. Bak Joéli, born August 21, 1889 in Bucharest, Romania, killed September 28, 1915 in Souain. Bauler Henri, born July 15, 1894 in Scheidgen, Luxembourg, killed by the enemy September 28, 1915 in Souain. Beller Jean Aimé, born July 17, 1878 in Arbus in the Basses-Pyrénées, died September 28, 1915 in Souain. Belmessieri Joseph Jean Dante, born February 20, 1874 in Pellegrino, Italy, killed September 28, 1915 in Souain. Berla David, born October 8 1886 in Panein, Romania, killed by the enemy September 27, 1915 in Souain. Bernard, killed September 28, 1915 in Souain. Bertin André Grat Joseph, born September 14, 1885 in Etroubles, Italy, killed by the enemy

September 27, 1915 in Souain. Beullens Henri, born February 2, 1868 in Marcinelle, Belgium, killed September 28, 1915 in Souain. Bianchi Léopold Louis Justin, born November 22, 1892 in Vernix, Switzerland, killed September 25, 1915 in Souain. Blanes Jose Huesca, born June 1, 1888 in San-Vicente, in Spain, killed September 28, 1915 in Souain. Blaser Hans, born September 12, 1891 in Lauperswil, Switzerland, killed September 29, 1915 in Souain. Blumenfeld Isadore, born May 29, 1883 in Buchus, Romania, killed September 28, 1915 in Souain. Bochinsky Martin, born December 15, 1877 in Krotoszyn, Poland, died September 28, 1915 in Souain. Boers Hermann, born June 11, 1886 in Amsterdam in the Netherlands, killed by the enemy September 28, 1915 in Souain. Bouffoni Armand, born October 31, 1893 in Albertacce, Haute-Corse, killed September 28, 1915 in Souain. Boutonnet Louis Jacques Marie, born December 28, 1886 in Dreux, Eure-et-Loir, killed by the enemy September 27, 1915 in the north of Souain. Breithoff Michel, born September 24, 1895 in Paris, killed by the enemy September 28, 1915 in Souain. Brodler Adolphe, born March 5, 1878 in Basel in Switzerland, died September 28, 1915 in Souain. Brun Joseph, born October 3, 1881 in Schaffhausen, Switzerland, killed September 28, 1915 Souain. Burel Eugène Fortuné, born March 29, 1859 in Alfortville, killed September 28, 1915 in Souain. Cabau François or Cabaud, born February 19, 1885 in Génos in the Hautes-Pyrénées, killed September 28, 1915 in Souain. Cabraz Louis Joseph, born August 17, 1888 in Valpelline, Italy, died September 28, 1915 in Souain. Canavaros Georges, born May 1893 in Laconia, Greece, killed September 25, 1915 in Souain. Carachian Léon, born 1888 in Constantinople, Turkey, killed by the enemy September 28, 1915 in Souain. Cerda Honoré Gomila, born February 8, 1883 in the Balearic Islands in Spain, died September 28, 1915 in Souain. Cerutti Séraphin Jean, born October 30, 1889 in Yvonand, Switzerland, killed September 28, 1915 in Souain. Chanut Jean Marie, born February 20, 1880 in Le Falgoux, Cantal, killed September 29, 1915 in Souain. Chappuis

Claudius, born October 28, 1887 in La Motte-en-Bauges, Savoie, killed September 28, 1915 in Souain. Chautems Samuel Adrien, born November 23, 1885 in Geneva, Switzerland, killed by the enemy September 29, 1915 in Souain. Cipriani Alexandre, called Simonetti, born July 9, 1888 in Castellare-di-Mercurio, Haute-Corse, killed September 28, 1915 in Souain. Clerici Charles, born September 30, 1876 in Lurate-Abate, Italy, killed by the enemy September 27, 1915 in Souain. Cohenoff Simon, born April 24, 1878 in Vidin, Bulgaria, died September 28, 1915 in Souain. Collet Émile, born August 21, 1881 in Geneva, Switzerland, died September 28, 1915 in Souain. Cormuz Germain, born August 23, 1893 in Riaz, Switzerland, died September 28, 1915 in Souain. Coudrachow Georges, born July 6, 1884 in Kurmarsk, Russia, died September 25, 1915 in Saint-Hilaire-le-Grand. Couri Georges, born October 24, 1887 in Baïme, Syria, died September 17, 1915 in Souain. Coutoupis Dimitrios, born October 24, 1893 in Thasos, Greece, died September 25, 1915 in the Sabot woods. Cuello Auguste, born August 28, 1896 in Escalona, Spain, died September 28, 1915 in Souain. Da Costa Valentin, born September 1, 1883 in Lisbon, Portugal, killed by the enemy September 26, 1915 in Souain. Dalla Costa Michel Antoine, born May 10, 1890 in Cevins, Savoie, killed September 28, 1915 in Souain. De Carvalho Raphaël Xavier, born April 22, 1896 in Porto, Portugal, killed September 29, 1915 in Souain. De Cellery d'Allens Jean Marie Georges Joseph, born March 15, 1865 in Arnave, Ariège, killed September 28, 1915 in Souain. Declève Eugène Jules, born February 5, 1865 in Bordeaux, Gironde, killed September 28, 1915 in Souain. De Souza Manoel, born December 8, 1878 in Amieira, Portugal, died September 28, 1915 in Souain. Delpech Louis Raymond, born January 22, 1890 in Chambon-sur-Voueize, Creuse, killed September 28, 1915 in Souain. Delrue Alfred, called Delruc, born February 24, 1888 in Lannoy, Nord, killed September 29, 1915 in Souain. Dimech Paul, called Dimeck, born April 22, 1887 in Bône, Constantine, killed September 28, 1915 in Souain. Dimitresco Thomas born February

9, 1886 in Bucharest, Romania, killed September 28, 1915 in Souain. Disdero Joseph, born July 17, 1891 in Sampeyre, Italy, killed September 29, 1915 in Souain. Doroszynski Thadane Vincent, born April 5, 1878 in Poson, Poland, killed September 28, 1915 in Souain. Drtad Kotchian, born October 11, 1884 in Trabzon, Turkey, killed September 29, 1915 in Souain. Dubois Émile Paul Auguste, born December 12, 1876 in Laval, Mayenne, died September 28, 1915 in Souain. Duborgel Louis Paul, born August 1, 1889 in Paris, killed September 28, 1915 in Souain. Dunesme Léon, born April 15, 1884 in Schaerbeek, Belgium, died September 28, 1915 in Souain. Egli Heinrich, born May 24, 1888 in Zurich, Switzerland, killed by the enemy September 26, 1915 in Souain. Eminian Hampart, born in August 1896 in Constantinople, Turkey, killed September 28, 1915 in Souain. Enard Alfred Gustave, born August 14, 1892 in Munich, Germany, killed by the enemy September 28, 1915 in the north of Souain. Eskenazi Haïm or Eskissazi Heisse, born 1889 in Constantinople, Turkey, killed September 18, 1915 in Souain. Espartero Bartholome, born July 24, 1980 in Barcelona, Spain, killed September 28, 1915 in Souain. Esposito Daniel, born January 12, 1890 in Spain, killed by the enemy September 28, 1915 in Souain. Farre Augustin, born August 20, 1887 in Jou, Spain, killed September 28, 1915 in Souain. Feldmay Jacob, born December 22, 1891 in Iași, Romania, died September 28, 1915 in Souain. Fillietroz Léon, born July 28, 1889 in Quart, Italy, died September 28, 1915 in Souain. Forcella Louis François, born April 2, 1886 in Montpellier in the Hérault, killed September 28, 1915 in Souain. Freiburghaus Alfred, born July 15, 1881 in Villars-sous-Yens, Switzerland, killed by the enemy September 29, 1915 in Souain. Gache Samuel, born December 12, 1888 in Buenos Aires, Argentina, killed by the enemy September 1915 in Souain. Gaibrois Louis Henri, born January 8, 1894 in Colombes in Seine, died September 28, 1915 in Souain. Gasi Pierre, born April 3, 1893 in Geneva, Switzerland, killed by the enemy September 28, 1915 in the north of Souain. Gaultier Louis Georges Marie, born May 2, 1889 in

Saint-Sulpice-sur-Risle, Orne, killed by the enemy September 28, 1915 in Souain. Gerber Antonin Rémy Charles, born July 22, 1887 in Lyon, Rhône, killed by the enemy September 28, 1915 in Souain. Gertsch Hermann Henri, born June 2, 1895 in Neuchâtel, Switzerland, killed by the enemy September 28, 1915 in Souain. Ghinsberg Jacob, born April 7, 1893 in Bucharest, Romania, killed September 28, 1915 in Souain. Gilabert Joseph, born July 6, 1895 in Sidi Bel Abbès, Oran, died September 28, 1915 in Souain. Gisello, killed September 28, 1915 in Souain. Golda Marcel, born August 9, 1892 in Vevey, Switzerland, died September 28, 1915 in Souain. Golderon Bernard, born May 22, 1890 in Varlin, Romania, died September 27, 1915 in Souain. Goldstein Moïse, born May 5, 1888 in Toulelia, Romania, killed September 18, 1915 in Souain. Gouaux Noël Henri Joseph, born December 25, 1832 in Bordères in the Hautes-Pyrénées, killed September 28, 1915 in Souain. Grad Bernard, born November 1, 1884 in Caïffa, Syria, killed September 28, 1915 in Souain. Graziani Dominique, born December 18, 1883 in Puerto Rico, killed by the enemy September 28, 1915 in Souain. Gruber Alfred, called Maillard, born December 21, 1883 in Eschau in Bas-Rhin, killed September 28, 1915 in Souain. Hadida Samuel, born February 7, 1889 in Sousse, Tunisia, killed by the enemy September 28, 1915 in Souain. Hamed Emile, born August 21, 1892 in Pressenn, Albania, died September 28, 1915 in Souain. Herdler Charles Jules, born January 29, 1887 in Schmölln in Germany, killed by the enemy September 28, 1915 in Souain. Hosberg David, born November 4, 1894 in Bucharest, Romania, killed by the enemy September 28, 1915 in Souain. Itzig Henry, born June 16, 1890 in Mexico City, Mexico, killed September 29, 1915 in Souain. Izquierdo Justo, born March 27, 1889 in Hunel-del-Mercado, Spain, killed September 28, 1915 in Souain. Jentgen Mathias, born March 25, 1884 in Schifflange, Luxembourg, killed by the enemy September 28, 1915 in Souain. Jimenez Élie Louis Désiré, born March 31, 1894 in Curzay-sur-Vonne in Vienna, died September 28, 1915 in Souain. Jiranch François, born

July 27, 1892 in Mladá Boleslav, Bohemia-Moravia, killed by the enemy September 26, 1915 in Souain. Junod Jacob Édouard, born February 3, 1875 in Plainpalais, Switzerland, killed September 29, 1915 in Souain. Karels Dominique Pierre, born December 9, 1882 in Winscler, Luxembourg, killed by the enemy September 27, 1915 in Souain. Kauf Charles Alfred, born December 12, 1897 in Paris, killed September 28, 1915 in Souain. Kellaris Charalambos, born August 10, 1892 in Lemnos, Greece, killed by the enemy September 28, 1915 in Souain. Kiener Charles, born March 28, 1878 in Muri, Switzerland, killed September 28, 1915 in Souain. Kummer Jean, born March 9, 1875 in Berne, Switzerland, killed September 28, 1915 in Souain. Lacoudrée Armand Jules Albert, born May 10, 1888 in Combray, Calvados, killed September 28, 1915 in Souain. Lacroix-Andrevet Marcel Pierre, born July 5, 1877 in Paris, killed by the enemy September 25, 1915 in Souain. Lambert Louis, born January 1, 1895 in Neuchâtel, Switzerland, died September 28, 1915 in Souain. Lammens Fernand Louis Maximilien, born January 24, 1891 in Anderlecht, Belgium, died September 28, 1915 in Souain. Larcher Charles François, born June 17, 1893 in Italy, killed by the enemy September 27, 1915 in Souain. Lauvray Ernest Adrien, born May 27, 1891 in Lesse, Moselle, killed by the enemy September 27, 1915 in Wez-Prunay, near Mourmelon. Lecoultre Arnold, born December 29, 1894 in Le Bouveret, Switzerland, killed September 28, 1915 in Souain. Leibovici Israël, born August 10, 1893 in Bucharest, Romania, died September 28, 1915 in Souain. Leone Benedetto, born January 14, 1895 in Vallebona, Italy, killed September 1915 in Souain. Lestrade François Eugène, born March 27, 1886 in Paris, killed September 26, 1915 in Souain. Longchamp Irénée, born December 21, 1883 in Ponthaux, Switzerland, killed September 28, 1915 in Souain. Looss Georges Théodore Jacques Léon, born April 11, 1883 in Poitiers in Vienne, killed September 29, 1915 in Souain. Lucas Pierre Marie, born September 21, 1877 in Loyat, Morbihan, killed September 28, 1915 in Souain. Manfredini Umberto Edmondo Santo, born March 27, 1880 in Ferrara, Italy, killed September 28, 1915 in Souain. Marchand Auguste, born August 24, 1891 in Paris, killed September 29, 1915 in Souain. Marco Jean, born January 6, 1887 in Algiers, Algeria, killed September 28, 1915 in Souain. Marengo Giuseppe Giovanni, born November 20, 1894 in Turin, Italy, died September 28, 1915 in the north of Souain. Masson Paul Edmond, born June 8, 1897 in Saint-Maurice, Switzerland, died September 28, 1915 in the north of Souain. Mathurin-Lecocq Juan, born February 20, 1885 in Montevideo, Uruguay, killed by the enemy September 28, 1915 in Souain. Melik-Sarkissiantz Arsène, called Melick, born May 20, 1889 in Taurus, Turkey, killed September 28, 1915 in Souain. Moretti Jean, born August 12, 1885 in Locatella, Italy, killed September 28, 1915 in Souain. Nincewich Antonio, born January 14, 1892 in Taraš, Serbia, died September 28, 1915 in Souain. Olivier Henri Louis, born January 20, 1890 in Geneva, Switzerland, killed September 29, 1915 in Suippes. Omet Jean, born June 14, 1897 in Olsenitza, Romania, killed September 28, 1915 in Souain. Pache Gustave Louis, born February 12, 1885 in Épalinges, Switzerland, killed September 28, 1915 in Souain. Pages Louis Léon, born August 3, 1892 in Saint-Victor-la-Coste in the Gard, killed September 28, 1915 in Souain. Paris Francisco, born 1885 in Tourris, Spain, killed September 28, 1915 in Souain. Pedrini Basilio, born October 30, 1894 in Milan, Italy, killed October 1, 1915 in the north of Souain. Pernau y Sans Juan, born March 14, 1886 in Arba, Spain, killed by the enemy September 27, 1915 in Souain. Pesciotti Jean, born May 4, 1895 in Pessano, Italy, killed September 28, 1915 in Souain. Pichon Eugène Ernest, born February 11, 1886 in Brest, Finistère, killed September 28, 1915 in Souain. Pieracci Nazzarano, born August 28, 1887 in Città di Castello, Italy, died September 28, 1915 in Souain. Pilger Pierre, born December 19, 1884 in Willerscheidgen, Luxembourg, killed September 28, 1915 in Souain. Pini Jean Hector, born June 8, 1894 in Barrettali, Haute-Corse, killed September 28, 1915 in Souain. Pisantin Gaspard, killed September 28, 1915 in Souain.

Pivaro Jean Baptiste, born August 21, 1876 in Pontecchio, Italy, killed September 28, 1915 in Souain. Poch Jaime, called Rock, born June 30, 1893 in Barcelona, Spain, killed September 27, 1915 in Souain. Racovitch Mirko, born November 26, 1890 in Belgrade, Serbia, killed September 25, 1915 in Souain. Ramus Charles, born July 13, 1875 in Basel, Switzerland, killed September 28, 1915 in Souain. Reichert Camille, born June 5, 1891 in L'Île-Saint-Denis, Seine, killed September 28, 1915 in Souain. Repik Laurent, born January 5, 1884 in Wracour, Czechoslovakia killed by the enemy September 28, 1915 in Souain. Riessen Théophile, born February 10, 1890 in Lenwarden in the Netherlands, killed September 28, 1915 in Souain. Riondel Antoine, born May 21, 1882 in Versoy, Switzerland, died September 28, 1915 in Souain. Rios Nicolas Gonzales, born March 15, 1874 in Beria, Spain, killed by the enemy September 28, 1915 in Souain. Rivera Pablo, born April 28, 1888 in Pardial, Spain, killed September 22, 1915 in Souain. Rober Gustave Alvin, born January 29, 1896 in Heiden, Switzerland, killed September 28, 1915 in Souain. Rosenspain Don, born August 18, 1888 in Brăila, Romania, died September 28, 1915 in Souain. Rosenspier Isaac, born September 10, 1881 in Routchouch, Bulgaria, died September 28, 1915 in Souain. Rubio Eduardo, called Roubic, born October 13, 1880 in Madrid, Spain, killed September 27, 1915 in Souain. Sarfati Albert Abraham, born July 16, 1884 in Constantinople, Turkey, killed September 28, 1915 in Souain. Sastre de Castroverde Manuel, born March 31, 1888 in Lorca, Spain, died September 28, 1915 in Souain. Saugy Georges Émile, born May 8, 1883 in Lode, Switzerland, killed September 26, 1915 in Souain. Schaer Paul Jean Élie, born August 14, 1894 in Paris, killed September 28, 1915 in Souain. Schaller Léopold Lucien, born May 8, 1887 in Méziré, Territoire de Belfort, killed September 28, 1915 in Souain. Schlegel Jean, born September 25, 1882 in Saint-Gall, Switzerland, died September 25, 1915 in Souain. Seguin de la Salle Louis Georges, born February 10, 1872 in Paris, killed October 7, 1915 in Souain. Sekler Léon, born July

17, 1893 in Wiesen, Switzerland, killed September 27, 1915 in Souain. Senmarti Jean Tomas Mariano, born August 30, 1878 in Mallén, Spain, killed September 29, 1915 in Souain. Serrano Mariano Vicente, born September 8, 1888 in Zaragoza, Spain, killed by the enemy September 27, 1915 in Souain. Seyrig Jean Roger, born March 6, 1897 in Hérimoncourt, Doubs, killed October 2, 1915 in Souain. Soreff Jacques, born August 15, 1894 in Andrinople, Turkey, died September 28, 1915 in the north of Souain. Sourdan Joseph, killed September 30, 1915 in Souain. Speck Alfred, born September 25, 1880 in Fribourg, Switzerland, died September 28, 1915 in the north of Souain. Sprauck Jean, born January 13, 1893 in Alzingen, Luxembourg, killed by the enemy September 25, 1915 in the vicinity of Souain. Stretti Giuseppe Mariano Gaetano, born July 13, 1890 in Livorno, Italy, killed September 28, 1915 in Souain. Sush Aloïs, born June 3, 1886 in Parine, Czechoslovakia, died September 28, 1915 in Souain. Szafraniec called Franice Joseph, born March 6, 1879 in Dambréa, Poland annexed by the Russians, killed September 28, 1915 in Souain. Talone da Costa e Silva Valentin, born September 1, 1883 in Lisbon, Portugal, killed by the enemy September 28, 1915 in the north of Souain. Tarice Joseph, called Taricco, born December 11, 1881 in Turin, Italy, killed September 28, 1915 in Souain. Teran Marian, born September 22, 1891 in Burgos, Spain, killed by the enemy September 28, 1915 in the north of Souain. Toresani Charles Louis Frédéric, born May 11, 1889 in Milan, Italy, killed September 28, 1915 in Souain. Torres Joseph Marie, born January 22, 1882 in San Pedro del Valle, Spain, killed by the enemy September 29, 1915 in Souain. Tortel Édouard, born May 26, 1878 in Montélimar, Drôme, killed by the enemy September 28, 1915 in the region of Souain. Touron Victor, born December 18, 1887 in Brussels, Belgium, died September 28, 1915 in Souain. Treboul Jean, killed September 28, 1915 in Souain. Tronick Wolf, born in 1891 in Alavenic, Russia, killed September 26, 1915 in Souain. Urcun Jean Jacques, born February 28, 1875 in Charleroi in Belgium, died September 28, 1915 in Souain.

Valente Raymond, born April 22, 1884 in Gaeta, Italy, killed September 28, 1915 in Souain. Vek Aloïs, born July 25, 1883 in Brandyse-sur-Elle, Austria, killed by the enemy September 27, 1915 in Souain. Vernet Gustave Léon, born May 31, 1879 in Meysse, Ardèche, died September 29, 1915 in Souain. Verney Edmond, born June 14, 1880 in Besançon, Doubs, killed June 26, 1915 in Souain. Vernez Henri, born February 27, 1868 in Villarzel, Switzerland, killed September 28, 1915 in Souain. Volanthen François, born February 2, 1893 in Guin, Switzerland, killed September 29, 1915 in Souain. Vuille Auguste, born March 18, 1896 in Saint-Imier, Switzerland, killed September 28, 1915 in Souain. Vullierme François Marie, called Perrier, born December 23, 1876 in Annecy-le-Vieux, Savoie, killed September 28, 1915 in Souain. Wanty Émile, born February 2, 1885 in Beaumont, Belgium, killed September 28, 1915 in Souain. Wayne John Douglas, born May 20, 1892 in Tucson in the United States, killed September 28, 1915 in Souain. Weingartner Paul Louis Lucien, born January 8, 1894 in Algiers, Algeria, killed by the enemy September 28, 1915 in Souain. Zimocki Alphonse Lucien Etienne, born July 18, 1883 in Longwy, Meurthe-et-Moselle, killed by the enemy September 30, 1915 in Souain. Zolotareff Nicolas, born May 8, 1877 in Rybinsk, Russia, killed September 25, 1915 in Vienne-le-Château in Marne.

These men are only from among the ranks of the legionaries of the 2nd Light Infantry Regiment of the 1st Foreign Brigade.

In total, the second battle of Champagne incurred nearly twenty-eight thousand deaths, ninety-eight thousand wounded, fifty-four thousand missing and imprisoned from the French side. The German army suffered far fewer losses.

The front advanced two and a half miles.

On January 30, 1916, General Gouraud will sign 4th Army order number 478 recognizing the battle at Navarin's Farm, earning the regiment its second citation in an official army commendation: "During the operations of September 20 to October 21, 1915, under the command of Lieutenant Colonel Cot, the brilliant qualities of courage, determination, and endurance were on full display. On September 28, with an admirable spirit of sacrifice, the attack was launched on a position that had to be taken at all costs, and despite the violent fire of the enemy machine guns, they reached the German trenches." End of citation.

1916–1938

A PALE GLEAM SPREADS behind his closed eyelids. Little by little it intensifies, burns brighter, denser. From the pink of dawn to the phosphorescence of noon. He feels the heat caress his face, bathe it, envelop it—emollient gauze.

As a child he used to lie naked on the ground at the hottest time of the day and let the sun transport him. His body would dissolve. He was vapor. Particles. He would rise. Lighter than air. He would remain like that for as long as possible. When he got up again his skin had been branded. His head would be spinning. He would stagger a bit. Fireflies would appear, disappear, darting before his eyes. Will o' the wisps. Sparks. He liked that.

Then a shadow passes. A stroke. As would happen long ago when a large bird crossed overhead, positioning itself between him and the solar star—a sparrow hawk on the hunt, a gull.

The shadow passes again, provoking a sort of tic, a nervous palpitation of his eyelids.

Suddenly he opens his eyes.

He sees, in the background, an out-of-focus face. He sees, a few inches from his own face—and perfectly distinct—the sharp edge of a steel blade. A knife. A straight razor. The blade moves towards his throat. He doesn't have time to see anything else. His whole body contracts, then explodes. His left arm reaches out and pushes the blade aside in a quick movement while his right arm simultaneously throws a punch. Struck right in the face, the adversary falls back. The boy wants to take advantage of this to finish the deed, but the pain that he feels in that moment devastates him, wrests an animal groan from his chest. His arms falls back down. He is incapable of moving. His muscles no longer obey him. He realizes that he is lying down. Nailed to the ground. Totally at the enemy's mercy.

The enemy gets back up. The handle of the razor still squeezed in a fist. A bloody nose wiped softly with the back of a hand, while staring intently down at the boy. The hand moves away, leaving a purplish smear beneath the nostrils. Then their lips stretch into a broad smile, tears flood their eyes at the same time, giving the irises a brilliant mahogany gloss. Then they open their mouth and say:

"Hello, my love . . ."

And in the silence that follows a tear swells and trembles and slides along her cheek, following the course of her scar.

And this vision hurts the boy so much that he hastens to close his eyes again.

IT WILL TAKE TIME. More time. It will take patience. It will take perseverance and gentleness and humility. It will take an ocean of love and an unwavering faith in that love.

And that will not be enough.

Never will things go back to how they were.

For days the boy avoids her gaze. He can't do it. Images assail him and weigh on him, atrocious visual residues that appear superimposed over the young woman's face. They form a screen between her and him. He is afraid of sullying her, of ruining her. Out of fear of this contagion, he prefers to turn his eyes away or keep them closed. He secretly observes her sometimes, managing to foil the vigilance of his own mind for a few seconds, to keep his own infected memory at bay. What he sees at first glance delights him, then ravages him. So great is the beauty of the world and he is so small. Emma. Emma's eyes. Emma's smile. And what they call the heart and what they call the soul. If he had been worthy of her one day, he no longer is. Shame, shame, shame on him. Emma's beauty reminds him of his own ugliness. The luminous purity of Emma contrasts with the blackness of his disgrace. Emma's love floating atop the muck among the rats and the tortured bodies, a love that she exhales and offers to him and which reminds him of the fear, the terror, the pain that he doled out along with death.

She is the sublime mirror and he the repugnant reflection.

He cannot do it.

But how to tell her? How to explain all of this to her?

The fact that he avoids her is what causes her the most suffering. She wasn't expecting this. She couldn't have imagined it. She struggles not to react. From early morning to late at night she remains at the boy's bedside. No doctor, no nurse could stop her. They didn't try. They quickly grow accustomed to her presence. Especially as she relieves them of a good part of their daily care for the wounded soldier. She takes it on herself. She has already done it. She has already wrested him from the shadows once, you remember. She bandaged him and cared for him and healed him and she will do it again. If sometimes her confidence wavers, it doesn't disappear. All along the dreary corridor there is always at least the little flame from this woman keeping vigil.

They will remain in the military hospital, number 44 in Falaise, in Calvados, for nearly five months. It's where the boy wound up when his condition allowed for him to be transported. It's where she had found him again.

The boy was hit with four bullets. One struck him in the groin. One perforated his abdomen down to the peritoneum. One passed right through his left collar bone. One penetrated his thorax and his right lung before lodging in his right shoulder. He did not die. He underwent seven surgeries. He stewed in the cauldrons of fever and chattered his teeth in the fortresses of ice and wandered in the mysteries of delirium. A chaplain with a blond beard gave him his last rites, placed the cold metal of a crucifix on his lips. He escaped tetanus and septicemia and gangrene. He lost twenty-four pounds of flesh and muscle. He did not die.

The doctors spoke of rare exceptions. They spoke of robustness, of solid constitution, of luck—damned good luck, too! The sisters in their white smocks speak of a miracle. Emma hears Liszt in these affirmations. "Mazeppa." The transcendent étude. The forty-eight ballads of Mendelssohn. What's the difference?

She took up residence in a neighborhood that they call Val d'Ante. A small river snakes between the old stones. She rents a room in the house of a widow named Majon. The woman had lost her husband in 1870, during the campaign against the Prussians. He was twenty-three years old, like her. They had recited their vows in front of the priest a month before he enlisted in the regiment. She had not remade her life. "One does not remake one's life," she says. "It's life that remakes us." Emma avoids her as much as possible, she does not want to hear this, especially not with her accent that Emma has a hard time understanding and which makes it so that she has to repeat every sentence three times.

The room is very modest. The walls are thick. It's cold. At night she sleeps fully dressed beneath a triple layer of duvet and covers. She thinks of her love. She can't wait to sleep at his side, to warm herself with his skin.

In the morning, when she opens the blinds, she can see William the Conqueror towering over the enormous mass of fortified castle, situated on a rocky overhang, having protected the city for nine centuries. Another William. Another conqueror. And dead men, and widowed women, always at their feet. Time changes nothing. In the enclosure of the castle they've constructed a temporary hospital reserved for Muslim soldiers. Colonial subjects. Brave children of Africa who came to defend the motherland and who certainly never expected to find themselves so close to their roots, to their ancestors, to their brothers, those Gallic blonds from Normandy.

The hospital where the boy is cared for is on the property of the École Supérieure for young girls. Starting at eight a.m., Emma is there. She enters with a gust of air, a fresh and pure halo that for a brief moment overpowers the odors of antiseptics, cleanses the confined atmosphere of the room. Each time her heartbeat accelerates, along with her stride, when she sees the boy's silhouette sprawled on the sheets. She has to keep herself from running. She stops at the foot of the bed and she leans on the steel support with both hands and she looks at him. She never gets tired of looking at him. She can hardly believe that he is really there. She smiles. She could cry, let this emotion that fills her and subsumes her overflow. She holds herself back.

Her overcoat gently steams. She would like to lie down on top of him. She would like to caress his face, cover it with kisses, bury herself in the hollow of his neck, breathe him in, she would like to squeeze him against her and taste his skin, she would like to eat him. She keeps herself from doing all of it.

The newcomers think she's an actual nurse. She quickly sets them straight: the boy is her only patient. Beyond the time spent giving him the necessary care, she speaks to him. Seated on a chair, leaning over his ear. She doesn't know whether he received her letters. What she said to him in writing she says to him again out loud, everything and more. In a long and calm and clear murmur her life flows through her lips, her lived experiences, her horrible existence far from his love. The absence of his love that took up all the space of her life. The hours, the days, the nights, the weeks, the months, the years. The void. The wait. The dizzying anguish. The endless struggle to repel the terrible omens. The perpetual oppression. The suffocation. The powerless rage. And everything else that in simpler terms means I love you, I love you, I love you, he has to know, it must be said and repeated.

It's not, however, until the end of the second week that she speaks of Gustave.

"We have lost our father," she says.

(Certainly she has not yet fully understood the extent of everything they've truly lost.)

She says that she told him in a letter, in the form of an encrypted poem because it was impossible for her to express it otherwise. She says that she couldn't manage to associate the word "father" with the word "death." Her mind couldn't comprehend it. Her hand couldn't write the words. They are so hard sometimes. They possess such cruelty. If we try to expose them as is, stark and crude and in their most brutal truth, then their shockwaves are so powerful that reason builds walls to protect us, it shuts down and rejects words because it is incapable of assimilating them.

"His light went out in his armchair," she says. "I say 'went out' because that's exactly what it felt like. I don't think there was much left: a little bit of wick on a tiny smudge of wax. Our father had come to the end. All it took was one breath, a light breeze . . . An afternoon that seemed like any other afternoon, he read the newspaper, then he folded it back up and placed it on his knees, then he closed his eyes, and he never opened them again. That's all. Just like that. I remained perhaps two hours, perhaps three, in the same room as him before realizing. I thought he was sleeping. I was trying not to make any noise. I was walking on the tips of my toes so as not to wake him, because sleep was precious. For him and for me, sleep, at that time, it was a rare commodity. It came only with difficulty. It was a break, a parcel of oblivion oh so beneficent and we couldn't waste it when by chance it was bestowed upon us. I wanted . . . I wanted him to rest in peace, yes. How could I have imagined that he would leave without saying goodbye to me? Not a word, not a gesture of farewell. My father! Our father! Not even a tiny sign. Nothing. He read the newspaper, and he closed his eyes, and it was over. Pfft! Hardly a breath . . . No, it wasn't supposed to happen like that."

She raises her head and observes the boy. He is lying with his arms along his body, absolutely immobile. He stares at the ceiling. He doesn't blink. His gaze is impenetrable. She sighs. She leans towards his ear once again, as if it were only to this part of him that she was speaking, as if it were the only breach through which to reach him.

"I wish I could assure you that he didn't suffer," she says. "But that would be a lie. His pain wasn't visible. No wounds or marks on his body, no scars. An interior pain. That gnaws, that devours, that spreads, that destroys. Like a worm in fruit, the pomologist would have said. I talked about it in my letters. You can call it an infection of conscience. You can call it gangrene of the soul. An insidious and fatal pain. There is a species of termite that can devastate the most solid framework without anyone noticing. The wood is hollowed, emptied. In appearance the surface is intact but inside everything is rotten. And one day, suddenly, the roof collapses. All it takes is one breath . . .

"Our father," she says, "died from having made a mistake. An error so heavy for him that it turned into a transgression, his transgression, his rather large transgression, crushing, invasive, unbearable. You have to give him credit for that. He knew how to recognize his wrongs. He judged himself and he didn't need anyone to condemn him. Proof of his immense sense of morality, his integrity. How many, in his place, would have striven to acquit themselves? How many would have washed their hands of it? How many would have gone so far as to glorify themselves?

"Look," she says, "look around you: these wounded men, dying. This room is filled with the transgressions of a handful of men, and there are hundreds of rooms like this one, and there are thousands of graveyards, and this handful of men will never be judged by themselves nor by a third party. These are cowardly or cynical or greedy or amoral beings, maybe all at once, but they will never be found guilty. I wouldn't have wanted our father to resemble them. His own transgression was far smaller and the pain that he inflicted on himself as elevated as his soul."

She says that it's regrettable but that she wasn't able to help him.

A feeble ray of sunlight pierces through one of the windows of the façade and lands on the sheet. Emma slowly moves her hand forward and covers the boy's. The boy closes his eyes. Perhaps to avoid having to see the blood as it reddens his fingers, his knuckles, his nails. His hand trembles but he fights. It's a terrible effort for him but he doesn't pull his hand away.

HE GETS UP. He walks. In mid-April he takes his first steps outside, in the school's gardens. Emma accompanies him. Always, no matter where he goes, she is at his side. She supports him. The wounds in his thorax and collar bone prevent the boy from using crutches. His muscles have atrophied. His sense of balance is fragile. He reminds her of a fledgling that's just hatched. Every time the weather allows, they go out. Slow walks interrupted with breaks on a bench, beneath the trees. While the boy rests Emma gathers little wild flowers for him, makes tiny bouquets. She then places them in a glass on his bedside table. They are blue, yellow, mauve.

The boy regains his strength. The head doctor calls his progress remarkable, surprising, undreamed of, even dazzling. The sisters call it miraculous. Emma smiles proudly. The flame shines, tall and bright, during this time. In the young woman's mind there is no doubt that the future will be an exact copy of the past. The cursed parenthesis has been closed, life and love will regain their course. Tomorrow like yesterday. Like before. The golden age.

She can now touch the boy. She can shave him, attend to his hair (his hair grows back, his mane), she can caress his face and hold his hand without him pulling away, without provoking any painful tensing, a cold sweat that used to instantly cover his forehead during the first weeks. And best of all she can look deeply into his eyes without him fleeing or cloistering himself.

A hundred times per day she murmurs to him my love, my love . . .

In June the boy is given permission to leave the hospital. Emma fills out the paperwork for him. She signs the name Mazeppa and spontaneously invents an address (rue des Martyrs, in Liège) where she is sure that they will never find them. She hands the form to the administrator with a big smile.

They don't leave town right away. She doesn't want to take any risks. They're not in a hurry. Here or anywhere else. She extends her room rental by a month. The widow raises her eyebrows a bit when she sees the boy. Emma introduces him as her husband. The widow grumbles a tirade from which Emma is able to make out something like: "He come back, yours . . . Not 'n the same boat . . . Have to b'lieve that the good Lord plays fav'rites!" She doubles the price of the room. Emma does not argue.

It's their first night. Their first night together in nearly two years.

Emma has lit a pair of candles. While the boy is sleeping beneath the sheets, the young woman undresses. Standing in front of him. Slowly. Suavely. Without taking her eyes off of him. She wants him to look at her. She wants to look at him while he looks at her. One by one she takes off her articles of clothing and lets them fall to the ground, and soon she is standing naked at the foot of the bed. She no longer feels the cold. The light of the flames licks her body. The shadows play on her skin, like clouds passing over a rolling landscape, they veil, they unveil: the mounds, the hills, the bulges, the acres of woods, the dark thicket nestled in the hollows of pale expanses, chalk-colored . . . Yes, voilà, there it is, battlefields no more, now fields of peace, no longer a land of desolation but of fertility, of sowing, life, voilà, a haven, no longer a tomb, vault, sarcophagus, but a cradle, and everywhere sublime constellations to conquer, stars finally worthy of the name, Champagne, voilà, that's it, Champagne my love, Champagne. And the boy contemplates her, and what he sees is still and will remain the most beautiful thing he's seen in his entire existence, he is breathless and he is in pain again because to a certain extent the spectacle of beauty can cause suffering.

Emma joins him. Nude, side by side. She has dreamed of this for so long. She turns onto her side and presses herself against him, gently, careful not to put too much pressure on his wounds. The burning she feels at contact with his skin is exquisite, radiating down to the bottom of her stomach. The boy doesn't move. She leans on an elbow and roams over his body with her fingertips, grazes it, brushes it, in slow arabesques she seems to be charming it, bewitching it, a shaman's gestures, it lasts for a long time, after which she gets on her knees and starts over, with her mouth this time, with her lips she follows the same circuit, reproduces the same caresses. Then she delicately places her cheek on each of the boy's wounds. Scar against scars. A sealed pact. My love, my love . . . Drunk on these words that she whispers on a loop, drunk off the odor of the boy, the pigments, the opium of his skin that she breathes in, that she inhales, numbed by the voluptuous heat that spreads into her stomach, Emma floats. A state of half-consciousness. So much so that she is perhaps not as astonished as she might have been when she reaches for the boy's penis and finds it completely shriveled and flaccid, curled up. She is reminded again of the fledgling that has just been born, so small, so fragile in its cozy nest. Will she need to add the hummingbird to her sexicon after all? She smiles to herself. She is happy. It's not a big deal. It's nothing. It's too early, certainly. She will wait. He is there with her and that's the important thing.

Later she sleeps holding the bird in her hand.

She is awoken in the middle of the night by a sort of groan. One of the candles has gone out, the flame of the other trembles. The shadows dance in the room, walls and ceiling seem to be moving. Emma sits up and turns towards the boy. The noise is coming from him. His face is pale and shining, strands of hair are glued to his temples. And his eyes roll beneath his eyelids. And the muscles of his jaws jut out. And from the bottom of his throat a sort of moaning continues to rise, a wheeze that filters, in spasms, through his clenched jaw. Emma touches his forehead as if checking for a fever.

"My love . . ." she whispers.

The reaction is abrupt, immediate. In a heartbeat the boy bolts upright, opens his eyes. His dilated pupils take up all the space of the irises: black on black, a sky without stars, without a single light. He doesn't see the room. He doesn't see Emma. He doesn't see the beauty anymore. The total eclipse of his gaze conceals utter horror. Blinding, staggering horror. Horror in all its magnificence.

The boy pants. Convulsions rattle him again. Through caresses and sweet murmurs, Emma manages to bring him back to the present time and place. The tension loosens, little by little. The boy calms down. Emma takes him in her arms. She cradles him against her chest. The demons have evolved: that's when she understands. His own demons. And her own will have to submit to them. While the last candle burns out, while its flame vanishes in a brief crackle, suddenly lowering a dark curtain over the room, the young woman glimpses, in a flash of lucidity, the new form that their love will take. And she is already fully prepared to accept it.

"SUCH A PITY! . . . Such a pity! . . ."

It's said in an exhale. Always in the same tone. The old man shakes his head. His bright eyes are more tearful than ever.

"Such misfortune, my children! . . ."

How to respond?

Emma acquiesces in silence. Yes, a pity. A pity, yes.

In the beginning, Amédée's lament, of a sinister concision, concerned only the death of Gustave. It was obvious that the doctor was not only grieving the loss of his dominoes partner—in fact his oldest, his most faithful adversary, the only, the last. Even if he saw himself henceforth condemned to play dominoes alone, it was first and foremost the friend that he was crying for.

And then, over the course of many visits, the pity has spread to more and more events. Today it has latched on to everything.

"Bernard, you remember Bernard, the sharecropper's son? Well, he died on the battlefield too! In Douamont, in the Meuse . . . Barely seventeen years old . . . A kid. He wanted to grow up too fast. His father didn't want him to, but of course the simpleton didn't listen. And there you have it . . . His parents received the notice just last month. Their only son, imagine! 'Lost in combat.' That's what was written. Lost! What does that mean? Killed, I can understand, but how does one get lost?"

The old man turns towards the boy. Distraught, his lipless mouth is half-gaping. It's a real question.

The boy could tell him, he could explain to him how it's possible for a man to disappear. Totally. To evaporate. By some magic. In absolute terms, he can, yes.

"Such misfortune! . . ." sighs Amédée.

Emma does in fact remember the young man. Bernard. His short pants, his chubby face, his pink cheeks. She had seen him grow up over the summers, always in the shadow of his father. His timid, overwhelmed look each time he entered her house. She remembers having managed to lure the two of them, father and son, into her literary salon experiment. The poor things! The stupefied faces they made listening to her recite poetry! And as if that weren't enough, on that day, as a bonus, they had had to bear witness to a séance by the doctor's elderly cousin!

A furtive smile passes over the young woman's lips. It was great. It was nice. It seems so long ago now.

Did he, Bernard, remember this before getting lost? Can the remains of a man communicate from the beyond?

"There are twelve," says the doctor. "Like the apostles. Twelve from the village that have been mobilized since the beginning of this war. We already know that three will not return. And we know of two more who are close to leaving us: if this lasts, they will soon be of the age . . . Good Lord! A veritable hemorrhage! And what is the remedy? . . . Tell me: what is the remedy for this?"

It's towards Emma, this time, that he turns his parchment face, his limpid eyes, misted over. Another real question.

Emma could also respond to him. Emma has already responded. She has said it and repeated it. But she knows that men don't listen. She won't say it again. She doesn't even want to think about it anymore.

"These days," sighs Amédée, "I thank the heavens for giving me only daughters . . ."

His head, covered with fine strands of white hair, nods.

During his first visit he had insisted on examining the boy. Perhaps he'd been preparing to offer some sort of critique of the work done by the doctors who had fixed him up. Perhaps it was his intention to add his two cents. His own method, completely personal—the good old recipes of Doctor Théoux. His confidence in modern medicine is rather tepid. But upon seeing the boy's wounds, he remained silent. No commentary except "Such misfortune!", which soon became a refrain. He hadn't even thought to prescribe one of his famous treatments, Madeira or something else, whose virtues and efficiency he normally extols. No. "Such misfortune!" Nothing more to add.

The old man doesn't come every day, and it's just as well. They like him well enough, but they prefer to be alone. Sometimes they pretend not to hear when he knocks on their door, they remain hidden inside until the sound of the wheels on the ancient buggy, pulled by an emaciated cow, disappears.

Emma and the boy arrived here at the beginning of July. The village. The house. In each room, each corner, on each landing they encounter Gustave's ghost. They don't dare hold hands. But it passes. They tame it. The shadow of the shadow of the old wild boar fades. Who is there to hide from now?

No one has picked the apples in the orchard. They rotted on the tree or fell, withered, overripe, riddled with holes, shriveled, they finish decomposing on the ground. They gather the least ruined. Not for tarts since flour is increasingly rare. Emma makes compotes. Which contain vitamins. It's good for you, she says.

Each day their walks grow longer. They gain more distance. The boy's stride has changed—a consequence of the wound in his groin. He hobbles a bit. This slight limp will fade, then cease completely, but he will have a particular gait until the end of his life, his left leg remaining straight and the right opening towards the outside at an angle of about twenty-five degrees. A sort of half-duck. Emma wonders whether he'll ever again, one day, be capable of climbing to those great heights.

At the end of the month he reaches the willow. It's an important accomplishment. They bathe naked in the stream. A long and deep scar diagonally crosses the boy's torso, and two smaller ones cross this long one. (The sign. The mark. The glyphs of a barbaric civilization, inscribed in the flesh. All a symbol—for those who know how to read it.) They lie naked on the watercress. One near the other beneath the canopy of greenery. It doesn't go any further than that. It's already a lot: that's what Emma tells herself. Sometimes, however, she grabs the boy's hand and places it between her thighs. And the boy doesn't withdraw. They both close their eyes and let the heat rise and let the hours go by.

The willow.

(Will it weep, their dear tree? From nostalgia? From tenderness?)

Emma hasn't brought her books to the village. She had left Paris as quickly as possible, as soon as she knew, with a minimum of bags. A dozen books lie around the house, mostly on the subject of apples and pears and general botany. Gustave's legacy. Some passages may turn out to be delicious, but only a few. She doesn't want to read any of that to the boy. Even less the newspapers. (Out of the question! May Verdun die and Nivelle with it!) She manages to recall poems she'd learned by heart. Her favorites. Wonders. The most wondrous wonders of the universe. Verses to damn you. Verses to make you believe in God. She recites them for him. She is happy to see that he enjoys it. Still. At least there's that. She recites them for him. She draws on her reserves. And then she invents. Stories. She imagines them and tells them to him piece by piece. She doesn't write, she doesn't write anymore (too many letters have separated them), she recounts.

She had planned for them to leave again at the beginning of September, but in the end, why not stay?

They extend their trip.

When autumn arrives, they start planning their travels.

THE FIRST TIME it happens by accident. A rainy afternoon. They'd gone out to the shed. In the gray light the caravan appeared before them. She didn't move. She studied it. The wheel had never been repaired. Dust covered the gold—the inscriptions on the sides. You would have had to know beforehand that *Brabek, the Ogre of the Carpathians* hides beneath. Vestiges. They have to tear at the spider webs to enter. The boy's heart races, palpitates beneath the swollen scar. Inside nothing has changed. Just the musty odor. Emma opens the windows. Glancing at the bed, suddenly, she remembers her dream. The images shoot back by surprise: the boy lying, his penis rigid, swollen, his gladiator sword standing for her—take it!—and her impaling herself on it, the blade that lashes her, a divine lash, beyond compare, that kills her. In the space of a moment a wave moves through her, her legs tremble, then she gets a hold of herself again. She chases away the nightmares. There are other dreams to have. They lie down in the alcove.

"Later," she says, "we will travel. When this is over. (They both know what that means.) What's stopping us? We will be free. We have this caravan, and that's enough. It's perfect. It will be our home. We will take off. We will take the roads and paths, you and me, together, in our mobile home. We will travel the world. Do you know the world, my love? I don't even know what you've seen. What countries you've visited. What continents. No matter, if you've already seen the world, you will see it again. With me. You will show it to me. I want to see everything. Everything! . . . We'll have the time. We'll take it. We'll stop in the towns and villages, in the squares. To make money we'll do what entertainers do. 'Come closer, mesdames and messieurs, come closer!

Come see the internationally renowned artists, Emma & Félix, Félix & Emma, come see their sensational numbers!' I can do that, you know. I'll recite poetry. I'll sing. I'll dance barefoot while hitting a tambourine. I can do that. I'm capable. But I'd better warn you: while dancing I'll lift my skirts rather high so that the gentlemen can get an eyeful, so that they clamor for me and aren't stingy with their wallets! Oh yes, whatever it takes, my love! And for the ladies, I'll play piano . . . Do you think we can get the piano into this caravan? Why not? We'll squeeze it in. We'll make some room for Wolfgang Amadeus. And for Franz, Robert, Frédéric, Ludwig, Vincenzo, Joseph. You see, they'll be like our children. Oh! A charming litter! We'll bring them everywhere with us. All those mouths to feed: they'll have to participate, too. Get to work, kids! Music! The ladies will adore it . . . And then I'll read their fortunes. Good, good, always good. Marvelous. With me, the future will be radiant. Nothing but tomorrows that sing and zing. They will entrust their hands to me and I will read between the lines and they won't be disappointed. It's easy: all I'll have to do is tell them what they want to hear. I know how to do that. Where's the sorcery in that? I will be the new demoiselle Lenormand! (But when she says this, he thinks of another fortune-teller, another sibyl with onyx eyes.) I will be the oracle of happy days! 'The good word, mesdames and messieurs! Come discover the fabulous destiny that awaits you!'"

Emma smiles. She is enjoying herself. That's already a lot.

"And what about you?" she says. "What will you do, my love, to earn our daily bread? Don't forget that the family has gotten bigger. Now we have a heap of little prodigies that sleep in the piano. They're hungry. They're crying. What do you propose? . . . I know! All you'll have to do is stand in front of the crowd and lift your shirt. Ooh! Lord, get a load of those stitches! 'Félix the Scarred Man.' Imagine the faces they'll make? . . . 'Oh my! Don't touch, little lady! It's a penny if you want to feel! Five cents for you to take a photo with the specimen! Sorry, but whatever it takes, my love . . . ' Have I already told you about Doctor

Frankenstein? (But when she says this, it's another creature, another monster, that he thinks of.) What do you say? Isn't it a good idea? . . . Or else, you could be a juggler. Or a fire-eater. Or better yet: a bear tamer. Would you be able to train one of those enormous beasts and teach it a few tricks? Leaps, pirouettes . . . But will we have room to house a bear between the piano and all of our little brats? Hmm . . . Perhaps it would be better if you were a flea trainer instead!"

Her eyes shine in the alcove, in the dull gleam of the late afternoon. The light has dimmed. They can hear the rain softly pattering on the roof of the shed. The boy's eyes shine too. He is nestled against her, his cheek on her shoulder.

"Where shall we begin? What will be our first destination? I want to see everything, I told you that, but I want to see Italy first. Do you know Italy? Have you already been there? I haven't. I want to see Rome! The Seven Hills. The thousand churches. We'll share the bounty. I'll leave you the pope and I'll take Michelangelo. The Sistine Chapel. The golden ratio. The frescos. The celestial bodies on the ceiling. The hand of God. The spark. The chubby-cheeked angels. Apparently, if you stare at the plump thighs of the cherubs it looks like they're moving. Apparently, you'll die of desire to bite into them! . . . I'll take Caravaggio too, and the great Leonardo—veni, vidi, vici. I'll take the Temple of Venus. You can take the House of the Vestals: the chaste priestesses, the sacred virgins, I'll leave those to you—generous, huh? We'll share the Colosseum! The ancestral arena. The immense ring. It'll make our heads spin. We won't be the only ones: it can contain up to seventy-five thousand spectators, they say. There, all around us, on the benches . . . Are you listening? They say that if you really concentrate you can still make out the clamor of the crowd when the gladiators enter. It's the plebs. It's us. It's Rome! . . . And then Venice. Oh! yes, I want to see Venice. Is there anything more romantic? More romantic than ancient Rome! I want to see the palaces. The Doges. I want to swim in the canal. I want to dive from the Bridge. I want to lose myself in the labyrinth of those liquid lanes. Have you ever seen anything as beautiful as the sunrise over the canals? . . . And from there, since we'll be there, we'll be just a little jump away from Verona. Why Verona, you ask? . . . For the lovers, of course! For him, for her. For Juliet and Romeo. How could we forget them? How could we not pay them homage? We will go, you and me, my love, engrave our names on the walls of the house of the Capulets. Don't listen to the people who tell you it doesn't exist. That's nonsense. That's the drivel of jealousy. How could it not exist when Mister Shakespeare himself invented it? Mister William Shakespeare, of all people! And apparently you can visit the house. We will go. 'Pull on the string, and the cap will fall': that's the password to enter. I know it, believe me. Look, the doors are opening. Let's go inside. The kitchen, the living room, the bedrooms, the antechambers, the boudoirs, the long dark corridors, and there finally the majestic ballroom where their gazes met. The spark. The hand of God—or of the devil! Call it love at first sight, if you like. This is where everything began. Apparently, we can even kiss on the balcony where they declared their passion. Do you know that the sweetheart was only fourteen years old? Precocious, the Veronese! As for her suitor, he was about your age. But passion isn't determined by the number of years, is it? . . . Of course we will continue our journey to the monastery of San Francesco where they put an end to their days. This is where everything culminates. Did you know that in the end they only had one night of love? How sad! And yet, you see, centuries have passed and still we talk about them. They are still there. We honor them. We celebrate them. We envy them. No, in truth the story is far from over. Didn't I tell you that love was eternal, my love? Don't listen to those who tell you the contrary. Liars! Jealous! Don't pay them any mind . . . Let's continue, let's continue, bella Italia calls to us! The boots of seven hundred leagues. We will cross it from end to end, from north to south, you and me—and our astonishing brood—in our caravan. We will go along the Po Valley in the footsteps of Fabrice . . .

Fabrice! But of course! You remember: Fabrice del Dongo. Parma, my love. Parma! Other than ham and cheese, which is excellent of course, there is Chartreuse. There is the citadel, the fortress, the tall Farnese Tower from which our young hero escaped—it exists just as much as the Capulet house. Another story of cursed lovers. Indeed! Is this fate reserved for everyone? Is love a curse, my love? . . . I will tell you what I really think: it's not little Clélia whom he should have chosen, but Gina. The Duchess Sanseverina. She is his aunt, but she could have been his sister, his lover, his mother. She could have been his everything. She is his true beloved! If it had been me who had written the story . . . But anyway. It's ours we need to write. We will leave Parma and after an obligatory detour to see our reflections in Lake Como, we will head for Florence. Then from Florence to Bologna. Then from Bologna to Ravenna. None of that sounds familiar? . . . It's the itinerary of Dante. I want for us to retrace his path. I want for us to lie on his deathbed—Signor Alighieri, per favore! . . . Did you know that it's precisely there, a few steps from Ravenna—the entrance to Paradise. Admit that it's worth it to go investigate. Paradise! We will stop at the poet's old tombstone, warmed by the sun, and I will read you his verses, and you will see, you will see what Paradise is! . . . Ah, the *Divine Comedy*! Ah, those terrible and poignant verses! Ah, those admirable hendecasyllables! . . . That means eleven, my love. Eleven feet: one less than those of Alexander. One might imagine, to put it another way, that we will carry on, limping, all wobbly, and we might think that we'll miss a step at each landing. But no. That's exactly the gait required, the perfect cadence to climb the slope: from hell to the heavens. Bravo, maestro! . . . In our language, in my humble opinion, there's no equal except for Paul. Only he was able to successfully adopt this singular pace. *Il faut, voyez-vous, nous pardonner les choses* . . . Do you hear that? A splendid blunder. The horse with three legs, but with wings to compensate . . . *Ô que nous mêlions, âmes soeurs que nous sommes / À nos voeux confus la douceur puérile! / De cheminer loin des femmes et des hommes / Dans le frais oubli de ce qui nous exile!* A Dantean gait! My love, it is possible to be both wobbly and sublime—if you see what I mean . . . And at the same time, we will reignite our romance! The songs without words. The silent songs. Yours, mine, ours. A connection made through the grace of poets—whether we limp or not! . . . Is it really our story? The cursed lovers. The soulmates. The long and perilous journey between Hell and Paradise . . . We will take a break, there, sitting on the old tombstone, warm and worn out, we will let ourselves be overtaken by the sweet heat, I will read you those verses. Will we be, my love, at the halfway point of our lives? Will we be at a crossroads? At the edge of a dark forest whose narrow path is lost? . . . No! No! Not yet. Not just yet. We still have so much to discover. Italy is vast. Up! We will get up and continue on the route. South, still further south. Abruzzo. Apulia. Yes, I want to see Apulia! I adore that name. It makes me think of . . . No, nothing. Yes! Of wine! Apparently, their wine is utterly divine. The blood of the Madonna! Vino rosso. Vino negro. Vino puro. I want to see what it looks like, Apulia. Their vineyards. And their olive trees. And their palm trees. And their orange trees. And all those white cities on the Adriatic. The south, further south forever. The tip of the boot. The heel! . . . I would so like to see Syracuse. Messina and Catania and Palermo, and all the volcanoes of Sicily and all the islands of the archipelago that are, they say, like gemstones, like precious jewels set in the blue of the Mediterranean. The sea, my love! Have you ever seen it? Sea! Sea! We will dive into it. We will bathe in it. Apparently on the coast of Lampedusa you can swim with the dolphins. Apparently even the sirens wash up on the shore, lured, dazzled by its sand so white, so fine. Lampedusa, my love! The beach! The sirens! Do you see them?"

He sees them.

He sees, through the window, the sun and the shadow, the pale light of Tuscany, of Campania, the azure. He sees. The landscape goes by. The rain falls softly on the roof.

Thus, they took their first trip.

Others follow. They go back there often. They invade the caravan and take off for journeys so long and so distant that sometimes it lasts all afternoon.

They do a tour of the world.

Who can say whether they believe it or whether they're pretending? Knowing the conditions required for their trips to take place one day. Knowing that the cannons would have to go quiet. That the old wagon would have to be refurbished. The wheel and the axle repaired. Knowing that they would above all need the gelding to be there, between the shafts, to bring them still further on the roads and the paths.

THEN THEY GO BACK TO PARIS. Boulevard du Temple. Here, too, weeks pass before the specter of their father stops haunting the apartment. His absence is even more obvious when Emma sits at the piano. They don't speak but the two of them remember their former concerts, their chamber music. The trio has lost a member. The oboe player has gone quiet. The instrument remains in its case, closed. A flag at half-mast. They miss his voice, the singing that the boy loved so much. Emma plays alone. She plays for him. For them.

The boy's nightmares have not stopped. They will never stop (even in the jungle, two thousand leagues from here, from everything, they will follow him). One night out of two, two out of three, he battles his ghosts. And the ghosts have nasty faces. And the fights are bloody. And he's not the one who wins—not this time. The dead avenge themselves. They eat him, they devour him cold. They have time. They have eternity. The pity he didn't display, they don't either. How many silent screams will he have to unleash? The boy wakes up soaked in sweat, he emerges, gasping at the air, mouth open, eyes wide, blind—remembering the glassy eyeballs, the opaque jelly where the crows jabbed with their beaks, remembering the hollow and darkened sockets of the cadavers. Sweat coats his forehead. Emma wipes it with a corner of the sheet. Her gestures are slow. She caresses his hair, his temples. "It's okay, it's okay, it's okay . . ." she murmurs quietly to him. What else can she do? The boy's pain is beyond her grasp, she doesn't know its face. She would like to wrest it from him and make it her own. At least take on her part, share it, but it's impossible. Her compassion is immense. She has to fight against her own pain, which chokes her, which suffocates her, against her tightened throat and her rising tears. "It's okay, it's okay . . ." She takes the boy in her arms. She cradles him gently against her breast.

Félix, my child. My little one.

He is afraid of the dark. The candle that she leaves lit on the bedside table changes nothing. The darkness is inside. It is deep. The boy fears sleep more and more. He starts to flee from it. Certain nights it's Emma who wakes up with a start, and the boy is standing at the foot of the bed, immobile, watching her. Silhouette floating in the shadows, half-outlined or half-erased by the short, copper-colored flame that illuminates from below. The young woman cannot suppress a shiver. Is it really her that he sees? She doesn't know. She fears his absences. It happens to him even when he's awake: suddenly the boy's gaze freezes and she understands that he's gone, he's somewhere else, distant, in a place where she can neither follow nor meet him.

Certain nights he is no longer there. His place in the bed is deserted. He has gone out. He walks in the city. He moves with a rapid, regular pace, his mechanics hardly slowed by his slight limp—like a worm with eleven feet. It's not the gait of a pedestrian, not the unsteady gait of a loopy drunkard, not that of a nocturnal flâneur. No hesitation. No trace of nonchalance. He moves. It's the determined gait of someone who has a precise location to get to. Who knows how. Who knows why. Seeing him, no one would suspect that chance alone guides him. The boy has no established itinerary, he has no place, no goal to reach. What matters is the movement. Move. Do not stop. Leave thought aside, only the body, the arms, the legs, the body only—Somme, Ardennes, Argonne, Champagne! It's the uncontrollable urge of a traveling fugue that moves him. He could walk in place, like a mouse, like a laboratory rat, he could indefinitely spin the wheel under the soles of his feet without advancing an inch. He would be totally incapable of retracing his steps and yet he never gets lost.

He returns with the day—like those creatures that feast on blood and know the secret to immortality. Emma has not gone back to bed. She waits. She keeps watch. When she hears the noise of the door, she gets out of bed and goes to meet him, she crosses the apartment barefoot and opens her arms wide to him. He brings in the fresh breath of the night, she envelops him with the damp heat of the duvet. They stand there for a long time, enshrouded on the threshold.

The winter is harsh. There is talk of a shortage. There is rationing. They practice restraint. There is less sugar, less bread, less oil, meat, coal. Less for who? In the stores people start to complain. The housewives grumble. Life costs so much, they say. Emma cannot listen to this, not when it's all about their mouths, about money and food. Their stomachs, their purses: Is that all they take into consideration to assess the cost of existence? If she is lacking something, it's not this. "I would eat the leather of my shoes for each meal," she says, "as long as you were at the table with me!" She thinks this. She believes it. Who knows? She squeezes the boy's hands in her own and brings them to her lips and kisses his fingers. Never has she ever loved him so dearly. Life costs a great deal, it's true: it's high time we took notice.

They hibernate. Apart from the boy's nocturnal wanderings, apart from a few necessary errands, they remain hidden away in the shelter of the apartment. Them. Just the two of them. Piano and reading and long hours spent simply lying next to each other, in silence, simply smelling, odor, heat, simply listening to each other breathe. They also take baths together. It's a habit they started the first night of the new year, without planning it—Emma was soaking in the bath, the boy appeared, he watched her for a moment, then he got undressed and joined her—which they enjoyed and redo at every opportunity. The bathroom on those days is a sauna. The water smokes, the steam escaping in slow curls, like hot springs that erupt along the fault lines in volcanic rock, lacquering the walls, giving the tiles a new shine, a brilliant gloss. Emma traverses this steamy scene and gets in first. She stands for a moment, the time to assess the temperature, her long legs in turn lifting and then plunging in, like the feet of a flamingo moving cautiously in the flat water of a pond. And her skin is tinted the same pale pink as the bird. Finally she sits down, leaning against the enamel with one of those sighs provoked by delicious sufferings. She doesn't move anymore. The water, agitated for a moment, calms. The lapping dies down along the curved walls, and beneath the clear surface, the slack body of the young woman looks like it's beneath a gigantic magnifying glass. See: the bottom of oceans, where the human odyssey began, wasn't it based on the same model? There is everything: a shore of white sand, a jumble of brown algae at the hollow of which is hidden the coral-red of a shell, and the long sides, splayed, the abyssal arches, and the soft side that climbs towards the peaks, already half emerged, the fertile domes, the twin islands, round, full, nourishing, bursting the watery pockets of their erect points to indicate the sky, the air, the air to devour, the air in the lungs, the breath to take, the first. Everything is there. Everything there is. Emma breathes, peacefully, and the tiny waves around her breasts follow the same movement, adopt the same rhythm. A sea spray affixes and shines on one of the blackcurrant-colored buds. Then she turns towards the boy and his eyes, through the veil, flash almost feverishly, and her gaze invites him, accompanied by a slight mysterious smile outlined on her lips. The boy steps into the bathtub. He moves between the thighs of the young woman, wedges in, back against her stomach and his head on her chest. She wraps her arms around him, places her chin on the top of his head. They are cramped, but it's better. She would like for them to be even more crowded, tighter, closer. She would like him inside of her, in her belly. The cold grips them gradually. They let it come. They do nothing else. She tells herself sometimes that they could die like this, together, their bodies set in ice, their youth forever preserved. Centuries later people would still be talking about it.

At night, in bed, she reads him the most beautiful pages devoted to what they call the cursed lovers. A compendium of thwarted love, of unjust separations, of tragically convergent destinies, of blazes, of flashes, of stars and meteors that explode in flight, shaking the universe under the impact of their encounter and their debris forever falling as a fine golden dust over the land of men. Stories too vast for a restricted world. The heroes are beautiful. Their feelings are noble and pure. Often they are chaste—matters of the soul first.

Lying nestled against each other under the thick white quilt, they appear buried under a tombstone covered by snow.

The armoire in the bedroom, however, where the scandalous, forbidden books lie on a shelf, remains closed. Eros blacklisted. Those damned books, they don't read them anymore. Hell, for them, has closed.

IT'S NOT UNTIL APRIL that they poke their heads outdoors again. The air stings, but there are large swaths of blue in the quilted cloth of the clouds. And in the light, a promise.

It's been a long time since they've walked those streets together. They are both bareheaded. They walk holding hands, with timid, hesitant steps, and looking around them, at things and people, with intrigued, anxious, nearly fearful glances. They could easily be taken for two strangers discovering the city, or two earthlings let loose on another planet. It's a bit like that. But in reality their state of mind is closer to that of two ancestors returning to the remnants of their past, and not recognizing anything. But they are not very old. And Paris has not changed so much, nor has their absence been so long. Where, then, does this impression stem from, of no longer being a part of the décor, the scenery, of having passed, in a way, from the stage to the pit, from actors to spectators—at a spectacle they hardly comprehend?

They are two, but who are they?

What are they?

Where are they going?

Lost, that's all there is to it. The old wheels don't work anymore. The idols come crashing down. Hugo, Liszt, overrun. Mazeppa, the hour of your fall has perhaps arrived, beaten in your mad race by an even madder competitor, this Dadaism that some have started to straddle. But, you know that if you fall, she falls with you. She cannot *ad vitam aeternam* carry you on her own. She cannot fish you out each time. If you sink, she sinks. But isn't that what you're already doing? Grasping, clinging to each other, lost in this city that you thought you knew, thought was familiar. What's wrong? Where is reality? Is yours still happening? What is it worth? You throw these glances around like you're on the alert and you don't really understand what you see, you can't manage to absorb it. There is a gap. A fracture. A fault—in which you risk losing yourself. And you are far from the shore. You are alone. Yes, the wind has turned. Today, the old reality is fading, its face like an ancient, acrimonious sorcerer. It is obsolete, reality. It has expired. And it does need to die, the bitch, we must be rid of it—no hard feelings?—in order to make room for something more— bigger, more exciting, more exhilarating. Today surrealism is born. Youth sprouts. It presages. It's spring. Tabula rasa. Do you finally feel it, the breeze? If not, it's as they say: you don't have the new spirit. Or perhaps, deep down, you have too much of it.

Surrealism: it is April and while many women walk on the Champ-de-Mars, Mars is unleashed on the Chemin des Dames. The American troops arrive at the California Plateau, in Aisne. Wilson is cleared of his debt to the Marquis de La Fayette.

Surrealism: it is April and while the cannons thunder, Paris sparkles. The champagne glasses overflow. Life is in full swing, ebullient, hectic, moving to the rhythm of the Hotchkisses, death gets fatter, the cadavers hurry to the Champs Élysées, the terraces fill and the trenches empty.

Surrealism: it is April and next month the great Fair will begin. While ephemeral shacks spring up on the cobblestones, in the countryside secular farms disappear, Hurtebise, Royère, Malval, and simple tents stand where entire villages have been wiped from the surface of the Earth, Ailles, Courtecon, Beaulne-et-Chivy, Vallée-Foulon. But, pretty May, do what you will. The Boches are a disease. The Boches are dirty fleas. Poincaré knows how to handle a pair of shears, cutting ribbons as quickly as he awards medals. Applause. Trumpets all around. From the front row to the loges, people jostle each other. Mobs invade the esplanade, and suddenly Invalides is swarming, they come from everywhere. It's joyous, it's joyous. There's a good soldier!

Surrealism: all these serenades under the hand grenades, these courtiers beneath the mortars.

Surrealism: Poincaré is not *rond*.

Surrealism: it's April and the artists enter the fray. Theater of the greatest battles. Cocteau, Satie, Diaghilev, Massine, Picasso: French, Russians, and Spanish—the triple entente in one parade. Ballet. We dance. They play well together! Châtelet is set ablaze, worse than the Caverne du Dragon. Fortin. Bastion. Critics throw red balls at the assailants. The battle rages on. The *avant garde* fights. To hell with decorum! To hell with reason! While others are skinned alive for plots of arable land, they tear each other to pieces for the Mamelles de Tirésias.

Surrealism: it is April and we must change our lives, we must transform the world. Rimbaud and Marc united under the same banner. Liberty! Melancholy. Down with the enemy, whether he be a military man or a bureaucrat, tsar or Kaiser, heir, functionary, head of the family, landowner, bookkeeper, bourgeois, or aristocrat. From now until autumn we will hear the tune of rebellion. "The Song of Craonne" echoes *The Songs of Maldoror*. The revolt simmers. The mischievous are examined with a fine-tooth comb—Fire!—like in the case of Madame Margaretha Geertruida Zelle, called Lady MacLeod, called agent H21, called Mata Hari. Strip it off, you bitch! Strip, you dogs! Dreams take shape beneath French cloche hats and Adrian helmets. Dreams are born under Russian *ushankas*. Blood! Blood! The red dawn, in Vincennes, in Petrograd, in Oulches, in Panama. Bouquets of white lilies and scarlet roses are thrown at their feet. And the fighting continues. While forces devastate the land of Picardie, big-band cymbals reverberate in the capital. Louise Michel? No, better: Louis Mitchell's Jazz Kings. A musical revolution! It's rocking in no-man's-land. It's swinging between the barbed wire. They speak of two hundred thousand dead in three months on the French side. They speak of three million seven hundred thousand francs profit in the Casino de Paris. They speak of defeat, they speak of triumph. Feat, defeat. They call it a show-stopping performance. Surrealism!

It's April and they walk hand in hand, Emma and the boy, looking around them at this changing life, this transforming world. And it's then something occurs that is perhaps the greatest testament to a reality in the midst of disappearing, the farewell sign of a phantomlike silhouette dissipating in the haze. It happens in an instant. Here it is:

They have just passed the Café de Flore when the boy feels a tap on his shoulder. He reflexively jumps away from Emma, turns around, grabbing at his hip at the same time, searching for the handle of his machete—but not finding it. He turns around, his body tense, ready to fight.

"Hola, Mazeppa! Easy now! . . . At ease, old boy."

The man has a big smile on his face. Head thrown backwards, chin lifted, which gives him an air of defiance. There's still a cigarette in his mouth. His gray-green eyes shine through the thin smoke.

"Is that how you greet your corporal?" he says.

The boy slowly recovers his bearing. His lips open. His eyelids blink. Looking at his stupefied expression, the corporal lets out a brief laugh—two silent hiccups.

"Surprised? I didn't expect to see you either . . . So, you made it out, you bastard! That makes me damn happy."

The boy scrutinizes him, examines him from top to bottom, not yet certain that it's not one of his ghosts playing a dirty trick on him. Skinny, emaciated, the corporal is wearing a fedora on his head and an old dark blue, wool coat with a velvet collar on his back. Not so different from a soldier's greatcoat. Worn, moth-eaten clothes. The unusual appearance of a vagrant rendered celestial by his eyes.

He raises his right arm towards the boy. The sleeve floats, hangs, like a broken wing.

"We never did find it . . ."

His smile slims, takes on nuance. His absent arm falls back down.

Emma approaches the boy. She slides a hand under his elbow and presses herself against him. A gesture, an attitude that is at once possessive and protective. She looks over the stranger without graciousness. She doesn't like him. Out of instinct. There is something about this man that repulses her.

Her little stunt does not escape the corporal. Until now his eyes had merely grazed the young woman's face, but now they settle on it. For a few seconds his gaze, intense, penetrating, probes her. Then:

"It's you," he says.

It's not a question.

"Me?" asks Emma.

The corporal nods his head.

"I often wondered what was hiding behind that initial, 'E.' Mysterious . . . E as in Ernestine? As in Eulalie? Éléanore? Émérentienne? Églantine? . . ."

"Emma," says Emma.

She lets it out in a sigh, reluctantly, a bit like a confession that had been extracted from her. She regrets it already but it's too late. She curses her own tongue.

"Emma," repeats the corporal. "Of course . . ."

The corner of his mouth lifts, his cigarette with it. With a nod of the chin he signals to the boy.

"I'm sure he hasn't told you," he says, "but this bastard saved my life. If he hadn't been there . . ."

This time Emma keeps her lips closed, pinched. The man rapidly glances at the boy and then back at her.

"A brave soul," he says. "Bravest of the brave. And a fucking bastard too—forgive me, mademoiselle . . . A fucking goddamned bastard! Like all of us who were there."

He nods his head again.

"An abomination, this thing," he says. "The worst. But we had to be there. It was our place, Mazeppa's, mine. The realm of the poets is there, in action!"

He's been drinking. Emma suddenly realizes. Not enough to be drunk, but enough to have brought a luster to his eyes—unless this radiance has another source. But he's still smiling. His cigarette burns. Emma squeezes the boy's arm a little tighter. All three of them are stopped in the middle of the sidewalk. The passersby walk around them. A wave of people.

"If it were anyone else," continues the corporal, addressing the boy, "I would have suggested we go throw one back to celebrate our reunion. But we're not those kinds of people, are we? . . . And I have something better than that, my boy!"

He plunges his hand into the pocket of his coat. Emma expects to see him pull out a flask of alcohol, or a necklace stolen from a queen, or a revolver. She expects nearly anything except for what appears: a book. A thin white pamphlet.

"You're lucky," says the corporal, "it's my last copy. In fact I was just about to bring it to a friend, but no one will appreciate it as much as you, I'm sure of it . . . Go on, take it!"

He hands it to the boy. Cigarette ash falls onto his chest as he does. The boy grabs the pamphlet. The corporal turns towards Emma.

"It might not be as worthy as your prose, Mademoiselle E, but I ask for a bit of indulgence: it was written with my left hand!"

A wink. Emma feels herself blush. Her cheeks cook. She is mad at herself for this weakness.

"I'm counting on you to read it to him," says the corporal, indicating the boy. "All the parts!"

Then he points his working hand to the sky.

"Adieu, Mazeppa!"

He takes a step back.

"And hang in there! . . . Don't forget about life, Mazeppa! Life!"

A flash of a smile and he pivots on his heels and blends into the crowd and quickly the current carries him away.

A long moment passes and the two of them are still standing there, immobile, eyes glued to the empty space that he's left behind. Who knows what each of them sees. Emma still feels the sting, the slight burning on her skin, and a gnawing anger in her chest. She abruptly snatches the pamphlet that's hanging from the end of the boy's arm. The title jumps up at her, printed in large black capital letters:

THE WAR

IN

LUXEMBOURG

She doesn't need any more. A nasty grimace comes to her lips. Of disgust. Of contempt.

"The war! . . ." she spits.

Really spits. She wipes her mouth and throws the work to the pavement, like a peel, a piece of trash. She takes the boy's hand again.

"Come," she says.

For a moment the boy stares at the booklet that's opened in its fall. The white sheets, turned over, facing the ground. Emma squeezes his hand. The boy lets himself be led. He starts to walk again.

It's the beginning of the final act.

NOVEMBER 9, 1918, a memorable date: Wilhelm surrenders.

Our own Wilhelm, Apollinaire, also surrenders—to death.

On November 11 of the same year, during a secret pastoral meeting, at dawn, in a dining car, in the middle of a forest (surrealism?), an armistice is signed.

Fire ceases. Bells sound. Hearts exalt.

To think that all it took was a few signatures at the bottom of a page. Peace.

Peace to bodies and souls.

On November 13 the trepanned poet is led to his final home. On the way to Père-Lachaise the funeral procession crosses a delirious crowd tirelessly celebrating the end of hostilities. Joy! Joy! The roads are teeming. The hearse is surrounded on all sides. They laugh, they dance, they embrace. Happy people. And as clumps of earth rain on the coffin, the jubilant pack ridicules the vanquished emperor, bellowing at the top of their lungs: "No, don't go, Guillaume! No! Don't go! . . ." (surrealism?). Then the gates of the cemetery close and silence falls again.

Adieu.

> *On earth we'll see no more of each other*
> *Fragrance of time, sprig of heather*
> *Remember I wait for you forever.*

It's over.

Is it, really, the realm of poets?

Of everyone.

But let's not deny ourselves the pleasure. As luck would have it, the Kaiser is alive. His son the Kronprinz, too. Fortunately, Ludendorff is in good shape. And von Bülow. And von Hindenburg, von Kluck, von Tirpitz, von Heeringen. Thank God President Poincaré is in perfect health. Foch, too. And Pétain. Like Nivelle. Praise God twice over that Marshal Joffre is not only safe and sound but will also accede to immortality when two months later the Académie Française welcomes him into its ranks (an admirable institution that always knows how to recognize its own). May God be definitively praised!

Peace and justice reign.

Alas, there is another scourge that hasn't ceased:

On the morning of November 15, Emma doesn't get up. She feels weak, a bit feverish. The beginning of a headache, heavy limbs, sore muscles (like the ones she sometimes felt after certain exploits on the rug. But it's something else today). Over the hours her temperature rises, reaches the low hundreds, surpasses them. She sweats abundantly, then, suddenly gripped by long shivers, she shudders. An immense fatigue exhausts her body.

It lasts three days. Feverish peaks give way to glacial descents. She doesn't leave her bed. During this time the boy remains at her side. He doesn't know what to do. The situation is unprecedented: it's him, normally, who lies there, and she who takes care of him. He paces the bedroom, tormented, powerless. He walks around the bed. He places a damp towel on the young woman's forehead. He makes her drink sugared water. He holds her hand. Is it his fault? Is it because of him?

On the fourth day, at the end of the morning, its grip loosens. The fever breaks. Emma breathes easier. She manages to get out of bed. She washes up, puts on a nightshirt and a dressing gown. She swallows a bowl of soup in the kitchen. Then she sits in the armchair in the living room. They spend the afternoon there. The boy regularly brings her tea. After which he sits back down at the foot of the sofa next to her and leans over her and looks at her. In his black eyes there is worry and apprehension. Emma smiles at him, weakly. Outside it's raining.

Night falls and the darkness gently erases their features, then their contours. Emma stands to go turn on the light. After a few steps her legs buckle, she collapses. The boy hurries to her. He lifts her, one arm beneath her thighs, the other beneath her shoulders, he carries her to the bedroom. She lets him, body abandoned, drained of strength. He can feel the acrid, burning breath exhaled through her nostrils. He places her on the bed once again, folds the duvet back over her.

From this point the illness quickly worsens. Her temperature climbs again. Profuse sweat covers the young woman in successive waves, like backwash playing with bits of flotsam. The vise tightens on her skull. An enormous mass settles on her chest and weighs, weighs more and more, constricts her thorax, her ribs, her lungs, crushes her bones. Sometimes Emma seems to struggle, fight against this invisible and formidable monster, sometimes she appears utterly motionless, eyes closed. And gradually as her pain intensifies, so does the boy's anguish. A sort of panic takes over. He has begun his meager caregiving all over again. He makes endless trips to the bathroom and wets the towel and passes it over his patient's face, her temples, her neck. Several times he tries to get her to drink, warm tea, cold water, she swallows nothing, the liquid streams down her chin, he wipes it, he places her gently back on the pillow, he takes her hand, keeps it in his own, caresses it, frightened by the heat that her skin gives off and he gets up and goes back to the bathroom.

Around midnight the wheezing begins. The air becomes scarce in Emma's lungs, her breathing even more painful and difficult. At one point she turns towards the boy, her eyes shining with fever. Her lips move: she wants to talk to him. The boy leans over the pillow to hear her. In a murmur she says: "Maman . . ." This word makes the boy shiver. He recoils and looks at her. Has he understood correctly? Is delirium taking over? He cannot guess at the obscure path of Emma's thoughts: in the whistles now escaping from her obstructed bronchial tubes she has recognized the final symptoms of the illness that took her mother. She is wrong; the tuberculosis that Laure Van Ecke suffered from is not of the same nature as this flu (not the Spanish flu, no matter what they say) that has taken possession of her. But no matter, in her clouded mind the connection has been made. For her, there is no more doubt: the time has come to reap what she has sown. Her lips continue to move, and when the boy leans over again, she says: "I am going to die, my love . . ." This time he jumps. Standing near the bed he shakes his head forcefully, squeezes his fists. No. No. What about their trips? What about Italy? Rome, Venice, Parma, the islands, the dolphins, the sirens? What about their life as entertainers and their flock of child prodigies? Their grand adventure? Grand, grand, always grand! A promise is a promise. She cannot die. The boy shakes his head no. No. Emma slowly bats her eyelids. Then she starts to spit up a kind of reddish-brown foam, like prune juice.

The agony goes on and on. Between the wheezes, the coughing, the trembling. The phases of extreme agitation alternate with those of total stupor. And it's almost the same for the boy, who suffers with her, is agitated with her, trembles with her, who instinctually gathers vast breaths of air when he sees that she's missing them, breathes, inhales deeply as if this could fill her own lungs with oxygen, and who scampers to the sink to rinse the basin and cool the towel, and who brings them back into the bedroom, and who places them at the edge of the bed and gives her his hand.

Just before dawn there is a respite. Emma is lying on her side; her breathing continues to whistle but the spasms have stopped. She looks like she's dozing. Only her eyelashes quiver, like the wings of a butterfly. The boy observes her. He doesn't dare move. As the sun continues its slow ascent beyond the horizon, hope rises in him. He cannot help himself. But it's a trick—like any other.

The calm lasts only a little while. Suddenly Emma is seized by a terrible coughing fit, her entire body jostled, rocked: a rag doll in the fist of a sharp-tempered little girl. Her fingers tighten over the duvet. The brown juice spurts between her lips, staining the sheet. The crisis leaves her panting. At the cost of an immense effort she returns to her back. She remains still for a moment with her eyelids closed, her mouth open, trying to regain the breath that is inexorably diminishing. Then she suddenly opens her eyes again, and they seem excessively large and luminous in the middle of this face with its ashen pallor. In her eyes shine the final flames. She stares at the boy. Her blue lips move once more. The boy leans over. She murmurs his name in his ear, the name that she gave to him. She says: "Félix my brother . . ." She swallows. She says: "Félix my child . . ." And it's hardly a trickle of air. She says: "Félix my love . . . My love forevermore . . ." And then her heart stops beating, for her and for him.

The sun rises.

THE BOY LIES NEXT TO HER without moving for two days and two nights. Death doesn't take him. Not yet.

Then he wanders through the apartment, lost, dazed, shaky, he walks through all of the rooms and corridors.

Then he returns to the bedroom and stands in the doorway. Leaning against the frame, he stares at her. The princess. The gypsy. Sleeping Beauty. His gaze falls to the little writing desk, near the window. On the desk are ink in a well, three quills, blotting paper, a stack of cream-colored paper. It's here, with these tools, that she would write her poems. It's here that she would write her letters. My love, she would say.

The boy walks towards the desk. He lifts the cap off the ink and plunges his index finger inside. He traces a long convex line on the wall of the bedroom, a gentle slope in the middle. Then its twin in a reflection. It makes an ellipsoidal figure that could just as easily represent an almond eye, positioned vertically, or a vulva. God knows what in reality.

The boy continues his work. He traces other lines, other features, designs other forms and objects, perhaps symbols, obscure, enigmatic, ending on the dividing wall by composing what looks like a vast erotic-cosmic fresco, evoking the decorations of the cavern that they used to visit—the sepulchral bedroom overlooking the river.

His testament and his contribution.

The ink has run out. He lets the inkwell fall. A few drops splash the tip of his shoe.

After that the boy returns to the bed and stares at the young woman once again. For a long moment. Then he approaches her, he lifts her and carries her in his arms into the music room. He sits her on the blue velvet chair. He covers her from her feet to her chin with a tartan rug that had belonged to Gustave, their father. He looks at her again. Then he sits on the piano bench and starts to play. He plays for her. For them. He plays gently at first, slowly, pressing down on the keys one by one, with a single finger—his China ink fingerprint inscribed on the pale ivory. Then he adds other fingers. The entire hand. Then two hands. And he presses harder and harder, producing dissonant chords, disharmonious, disjointed. What he hears in his head has nothing in common with what reverberates in the room. The notes, the keys blend together, all the more so as tears now blur his vision. And then he starts to hit with his flat hand, with his palm, his fist, his fists, he hits the keyboard with big blows, he strikes, he hammers the ivory as the blacksmith does molten metal, and this is the only funeral march that he is capable of performing, this is all he can offer her. For she is dead. And with her, love. And with her, art. And with her, music. And with her, romance. All of it dead. The boy abruptly stands up, tipping over the bench, and with a grand gesture he brushes aside the sheet music placed on the music stand. Then he grabs the stand with both hands and shakes it and breaks it apart. Then he does the same with the lid of the keyboard, splintering it in his hands, then using it as a cudgel to attack the instrument. He strikes, he strikes, an obsessive lumberjack, and the keys crumble, come dislodged, spurt, spit like teeth from a jaw. Then he attacks the body of the piano, which he thrashes with all his strength. Under the blows the wood gives way, cracks, splits, and in the depths of the Érard the chords vibrate, its metallic guts give rise to deep, lugubrious sounds, similar to the distant echo of a bumblebee, of a tolling bell. The boy keeps at it until the lid breaks between his hands. Then he grabs the oboe in its case and demolishes it. Then he grabs the drawing, his own—the house, the sun, the garden, the woman—and thrashes it too, and the wooden frame and the glass pane smash to pieces. His hands are bloody. He doesn't feel it. What does he feel? His eyes are red. He looks haggard. On his face mix tears and sweat and mucus. He turns his head from left to right searching for whatever is left to destroy. He squats down and gathers the notebooks of sheet music and tears them up, the ballads, the sonatas, the preludes, the scherzos, the transcendent études soon litter the ground like large hideous confetti. This inspires him, it seems, because he then leaves the room and heads straight for the living room, towards the shelves holding their library, and he takes an armful of books that he then spills over the shreds of sheet music. He makes several such trips, as many as necessary to empty the shelves and leave nothing but dust, carrying, transferring, trip after trip, the piles of books, novels, treaties, essays, and the heavy encyclopedias in dozens of volumes, throwing them higgledy-piggledy onto the floor. To finish he goes into the bedroom and opens the armoire and he relieves the shelves of the precious collection of erotic volumes that they had secretly, patiently, amorously amassed, she and him. For it is said that nothing shall be spared. Hell itself razed.

After the final trip he stops. The books lie in a heap in front of the vestiges of the piano. There's debris everywhere, splinters of wood, of glass, of ivory scales, of crumpled paper. Everything is ready for the auto-da-fé. The boy, standing, shoulders stooping, stares at the pile. Now he seems emptied. Dazed. He sways slightly on his legs. At his feet lies a forsaken piece of paper that must have come unattached from one of the books: an illustration of an apple in a cross-section view.

The boy turns towards Emma. He kneels near the chair. He takes the young woman's hand, kisses it, then places it back on the tartan rug, softly.

He looks at her.

My love, she would say.

Then the boy gets up, and with shuffling steps goes to the kitchen to look for matches.

♥

THERE, THE ESSENTIAL HAS BEEN SAID.

Although he still has another twenty years to live, these will not amount to anything in the end but the unique and final diluted stanza of his autumn song.

The boy gets back on the road. The end of the trip he does on his own, footloose (the axle, remember, is broken), or, in other words: floating in the ill wind, which carries him.

Over the course of those first years he is seen in Eure, in Pacy, in Vernon. He is seen in Elbeuf. He is seen in Rouen. Following the twists and turns of a river, it seems. He is seen in Havre and in that grand old city, Montivilliers. Then he goes back down. He is seen in Lisieux. He is seen in Argentan. He is seen further down in Chartres. He is seen in Mans. Not to mention the less important cities, villages, hamlets, and solitary arid regions, those countrysides absolutely lacking in souls. He sleeps under the stars. He is later seen in Orléans, in Blois, in Tours. At the whims of another river. He sleeps beneath the bridges. He is seen in cathedral squares, in the shadows of Gothic or Romanesque portals, beneath the arches and the vaults and all those mammoth loose stones, crushing.

. . . Here, there. Like the . . .

In truth, he is not seen—and it's not because of camouflage this time. It's that the population of wretched men is vast. It already was, but the war made it even bigger. He among them, among so many, a vagrant. Nothing distinguishes him. He lives, as they say, by his wits. He begs. He steals. Petty thefts, frugal pillaging, just enough not to die of hunger. During harvest season he lends his muscles to

430

the farmhands who aren't too disgusted by his appearance or his face. He gathers, he collects, in exchange for which they give him room and board and something to eat. He sleeps on the straw, in the barn. He eats soup and bread. He doesn't aspire to more. If in his great generosity the farmer gives him a handful of francs, the boy saves them for the less prosperous days: in an inn he will have another bowl of soup, or hot wine to fight the cold.

He is found in Châtellerault. He is found in Poitiers. In Niort. In Limoges. He crosses the land of Auvergne, which knew sulfur and lava in antediluvian times, eruption and chaos, and which is today a peaceful vacation destination where the well-behaved volcanoes sleep. In Clermont-Ferrand he is arrested for a vagrancy offense. He has no passport, cannot produce any identity document or good moral credentials, cannot even be identified by a third party, no vicar, citizen, anyone whose word would serve as support. They lock him up for a month, in a cell of four men, where he spends time with two other wretches and a lazy bum, a part-time thief. These are his companions in chance and misery, brothers-in-arms—it's crazy, however, how much they resemble each other. They don't become friends. He is released. He takes off again.

The misadventure soon repeats itself in Brive-la-Gaillarde. Jail again. This stay is longer: ten weeks. The trade-off is the guarantee of a roof over one's head and a pittance in the stomach. He doesn't protest. He sleeps on a bench. When his nightmares take him he paces the ten feet that separate the steel door from the barred window a thousand times over.

His sentence completed, they free him. When they open the cell he doesn't fly away swiftly: his flight is feeble. He is worn out. Outside, inside, inside, outside: What's the difference? What does it matter? Only as much importance as we accord to it. He has already seen a lot of things. He has lost a great deal. Innocence and frivolity and desire and joy and . . . Better not to make a tally. What has he gained?

Habits are tenacious but one is not obliged to live, we can settle for being alive.

It's been ages since his clothes have fit him properly. They float around his carcass. His cheeks are gaunt, his hair and his beard have grown like wild grass—brown crab grass with the first threads of silver. He looks sixty; he's not even thirty.

He is in Aurillac. He is on the windy Causses of Lozère. He is in Mende, in La Canourgue, in Florac. He might have returned to his starting point, near the mouth of the Rhône, if a representative of the German nation hadn't once again crossed his path. What they call a twist of fate.

The episode took place in 1921 in a seedy joint in Alès, in the Gard. The boy was sitting at a table in the back. For the two pennies he had left they give him a bowl of beef broth. The yellowish stew steams beneath his nose. It tastes vaguely of pepper. Swimming in it is a marrowbone without any marrow. But the little room is heated. There are four other customers. Three are locals, regulars. They're at the counter. Leaning on their elbows and yet turned towards the fourth, who is seated at a table on which rest two bottles, one empty and one half-empty. He looks like a regular too, but he is not a local. Of the four it's undoubtedly he who has the strongest mastery of the French language, yet his accent betrays him: he comes from across the Rhine. A Boche. The bushy eyebrows, the parboiled complexion. He is also the drunkest of them all. The three others take advantage. They heckle him, titillate him, looking for trouble from him, speaking to him as if to the village idiot whose flights of fancy have always pro-voked hilarity. They take turns and keep questioning him, extracting answers that they already know, pushing him to recount his story that he's recounted to them a hundred times and which always makes them laugh out loud. And the guy is caught in their game, between two glasses, he replies. He says that he's not just anybody. He introduces himself as a musician. A musician from Bremen! he specifies, index

finger brandished. "Bremen the lemon!" says one of the three, the
three laugh. And when they ask him what he plays, the guy responds
that he plays violin and the string bow, and, he says, "I am at least
as good as that damned Niccolò!" And one of the three compatriots
repeats: Nicolo! Nicolo! And another does a little dance step imitating
a joyous violinist, and the three laugh. The guy swears that one day
he was summoned by the empress herself—a great lady—to play in
her private chamber, for she had heard him boast of his talent and
she absolutely wanted to hear his playing with her own ears. "Hoho!"
exclaims one of the three. "I hope you stroked your instrument for
her, the baroness!" And the three laugh.

They don't speak, they bellow. The guy's voice and his German
accent in particular assault the boy, working at his nerves. He doesn't
lift his head. Elbows spread, forehead lowered, he blows on his soup.
He drinks in little sips. But he cannot entirely escape.

"And what about us, are you going to play us a little tune?" says
one of the three. And the two others: "Go on! A little tune!" And they
demand and they insist, begging the guy to give them a glimpse of his
immense talent, but the guy knocks back his drink and sets the glass
down and gestures with his empty hands and he replies that he has
been sadly forced to trade his instrument for a plate of lentils and a
tranche of smoked lard in order not to die of hunger. "My violin!" he
says. "My dear violin! A marvel made by the great Austrian master
Jakobus Stainer!" "Jakobus the nimbus?" asks one of the three, and
the three laugh. And the guy says that that work of art that he used
to possess had been worth, in his time, double that of any other
rattle that came from the workshops of Amati or Stradivari. "On the
potty!" adds one of the three. "I want my mommy!" outdoes another,
and the three laugh. And the guy laments that it was with a heavy
heart that he had to give up this jewel, a rare pearl, for a mouthful of
bread! "Make up your mind," says one of the three, "was it bread or
lard?" And the guy hits his fist on the table and says that all of this is

because of Versailles, it's Clemenceau's fault, it's France's fault. "It's your fault!" he says.

That's when things start to take a turn for the worse. The wine turns sour. The laughs become fake. In the back of the room the boy's hands start to tremble slightly.

"Versailles!" the guy repeats. And he says that what France wants with the cursed treaty is to crush his country, humiliate it, strangle it, bleed it dry! "That's what France wants. And what are they going to leave for the Germans? Nothing. Nichts! French pigs!" he says. "Hoho!" says one of the three waving his hand. "Keep it down, Fritz! This isn't Berlin!" one of the three says. And there's only one person laughing now. "Nichts! Nichts!" repeats the guy. And he says that he would prefer to be in his own country a thousand times over, that he had had to leave because the French pigs had left nothing in it, nothing to drink, nothing to eat, he says that now, in his dear and beautiful country, you have to pay a billion marks for a glass of beer. "A billion!" he says, index finger brandished. "That's no reason to come siphon off our cheap wine!" says one of the three, and it's the same one who laughs again. "And a violin," says the guy, "a splendor signed Jakobus Stainer, is not worth anything now but a fucking sausage! French pigs!" he repeats. "Sausage or lard?" says one of the three. "You know where you can shove it, your sausage?" says another. "You want to know how many we skewered, sausages like you, when we were over there in Crouy?" says the third. "Whole chains of them! Filthy Boche meat threaded on the bayonet! Ha! Ha! They made a nice brochette!"

And that's when things utterly deteriorate. The guy stands up, face lobster-red. The three thieves aren't laughing anymore. In the back of the room the boy stares at the marrowbone floating in his bowl. The tempest isn't passing. His hands tremble.

"Bastard!" yells the guy in an explosion of spit. "Dirty Bastard!" And he tells them that they wouldn't be putting on such airs if the Americans hadn't come flying to their aid. "The big mama hen," he says, "come from America to brood the poor little French chicks and take them beneath her wing." "Shut your mouth!" says one of the three. "Help, Mama Hen!" says the guy in a high-pitched voice and a grimace meant to imitate the expression of a terrified chicken. "You were fucked! Squashed!" He says without the Yanks, this would be his home. He says that he wouldn't be forced to drink that disgusting cheap wine and that he would be savoring a nice blond beer in a glass, for one mark. "You'll shut your mouth!" yells one of the three. And the owner asks if it's his wine that he's calling cheap. And the guy talks about revenge. He says that the time will come. And the owner says that a Kraut like him wouldn't even be able to tell the difference between barley wine and grape wine. And the guy says that the mama hen won't always be there and they'll just see how many little chicks will end up on the spit. "Shut up!" says one of the three. "Swine!" says another. "Not even chicks, says the guy, just eggs. Broken eggs. We'll gobble you up in an omelet!" And he continues to bitch like this, and the three threaten him, insult him, then end up leaving the counter to go over to him, rebuking him, and they push him, jostle him, the chair falls, and the guy defends himself, he gesticulates, he whines, "Schweine! Schweine!" he says, and suddenly, right in the middle of that tussle, a hand grabs one of the empty bottles by the neck and crashes it down on the guy's temple, and that hand is the boy's. And before the guy collapses, the boy has enough time to break the bottle on the edge of the table and sink a shard into his eye.

And that's where things stop.

When the gendarmes arrive, the three rascals have taken off. In the room they find only the owner, behind the counter, a hunting rifle in his hand, the guy sprawled on the ground and pissing blood, and the boy, seated at the table, finishing his broth.

THE GUY DOES NOT DIE but he loses an eye. He will never see straight again.

The circuit court in Gard condemns the boy to twelve years of forced labor. Not long ago they would have decorated him with a medal, now he gets twelve years of penal servitude—for a German he didn't even kill. Times change, and values with them.

He spends six days in the local prison, after which he's transferred to the prison of La Rochelle, where he spends one night. The next day, on a little steamboat, he goes to the penitentiary on the island of Ré. He stays there four months, waiting for the next convoy to Guyana. His hair is cropped short and his beard shaved off.

On the day of the departure there are about four hundred serious criminals and two hundred repeat offenders assembled in columns in the courtyard of the compound. He among them. They do roll call. One by one. Everyone is present. They are given gear. They are given registration numbers. Then, escorted by guards, gendarmes, military supervisors and a company of snipers, the group of condemned men starts marching to the port, and from there sets off on a boat from the Nantes Navigation Society, *La Martinière*, an old ship from the German fleet that has been converted to a galley.

The sea.

The other shore.

He will see, he will understand, finally.

The boy doesn't see much of the ocean, as it turns out, shut in as he is, heaped up with a hundred others in a dark stinking cage, at the bottom of the bottom of a hold. They roll, they pitch. Here, there . . .

The sun doesn't dazzle them. They barely see the white flashes of albatrosses' stomachs between the bars.

After fourteen days of crossing, the cargo ship enters the mouth of the Maroni river. Two hours later they land at Saint-Laurent-du-Maroni.

They have arrived.

The welcoming committee is made up mostly of poor bums in rags, skin and bones, amassed along the jetty like so many Crusoes watching the first ship materialize, the first sign of civilization after a quarter century of isolation. Shipwrecked? Not really. Wrecked? No doubt. They are, however, in theory, the luckiest. They are freed. These men have paid their debts, these men have made it to the end of their sentences, but a perverse and unjust system forces them to remain in place, with hardly any rights, without work, without resources, without hope of return. A mirror for the newcomers—a visionary reflection. Here you are warned upfront, comrades: in the event that your conduct is exemplary, in the event that death doesn't come to shorten (soften?) your stay, here, before your eyes, is the best-case scenario for you.

These unhappy souls are ready to fight among themselves to be able to unload the boat for a pittance. Only some will be chosen.

The penal colony.

They have arrived.

There will be no spectacular adventures, no tragic or fantastic escapes, only the sordid, miserable quotidian, seven thousand convicts under the control of an idiotic and corrupt penitentiary administration, in the middle of a hostile environment, in the heavy, hot, humid climate of the tropics.

The boy is first assigned to a forest work site, in the middle of the savanna. From five in the morning to noon he cuts down and chops up trees. He makes steres: cubic yards of logs carefully piled to present to the surveyor at the specified hour. Day after day for three years he fulfills this wooden chore.

He is then sent to Cayenne where he is tasked with taking care of the shitter. It's a promotion. The city has no sewers. There are a dozen of them who go around to the dwellings to collect the contents of the toilets every morning. They gather the shit and fill a cistern and go to empty the cistern in a swamp a little ways away. The task is deemed sufficiently trying that they are released from any other activity. At the end of the morning the convicts are free. Free in the penal colony. They can see to their hobbies. For the majority this consists in making junk. They make baskets, rugs, canes, pipes, jewelry. They weave, they cut, they sculpt, they carve coconuts, they paint tortoise shells. Artists and artisans. They offload these trinkets onto civilians or onto the families of the watchmen in order to add to their coffers. A few francs gleaned here and there, with which they will be able to pay for supplemental rations of food or hooch, or better treatment, or such and such service, such and such product of some sort or nature of any kind. Here as elsewhere, everything is bought, and everything is sold. Here more than elsewhere. Everyone is involved. The rules forbid the convicts from having money on them, and yet they all do. Not on them: in them. Cash stashed in little zinc tubes shoved up their rectums. It's the only way. Piggy bank in the slop and castles in the sky, one might say. Beyond the tiny advantages that these savings might bring them, their reserves serve above all to maintain dreams. They talk of escape. Clearing out. Breaking free. It's only with a nest egg, saved penny by penny, that they might be able to one day grease the right palm, procure the right accomplice, the right guide, the right boat and everything else needed to flee, to get the fuck out of here with only a hint of a chance of success. One day, yes. One day. Taking off comes at a high price. All of their hope lies there, at the bottom of their intestines.

The boy does none of this. No junk, no trifles, no resourcefulness, no nest egg. Outside of the chore of emptying the shitters imposed on him, he doesn't work. He doesn't traffic. He doesn't dream of saving nor even of gaining money. He doesn't think about escaping. He doesn't think of the future.

The boy doesn't dream.

After five years of this routine they send him to Saint-Laurent where he is tasked with cleaning the city. He sweeps the streets, pulls out the weeds, cleans the stables, that kind of task. During this period, he develops a friendship with another convict. Or rather something that looks, from a distance, like a semblance of friendship. The guy is named Charles Lautrain. They call him Piaf. He's a tiny little man, almost a dwarf. He's speckled with lesions. His cheeks, his forehead, his arms, his hands are constellated with pustules similar to badly healed burns. They are sand fly stigmata—leishmaniasis. Despite this and everything else, the man has a joyous air, often a smile on his lips, and when he laughs, a curiously coquettish reflex makes him bring his hand in front of his toothless mouth. Piaf is an old-timer. He's sixty-four years old. He was condemned to twenty years for poisoning his wife. When the boy meets him, he's already served sixteen. At least that's what he says.

The man speaks easily. He likes to chat. Perhaps that's why he had his heart set on the boy. The boy is an audience that is not only captive but docile, patient. He won't interrupt or contradict him, he keeps quiet and he listens: the ideal interlocutor in the eyes of the old man. They are often seen together. The old man does not miss an occasion to unload, whether that be during the day, in the city, broom in hand, or at night, lying in his hammock. Four years straight he recounts his adventures, his experiences, sometimes his lessons, to the boy.

Charles Honoré Lautrain, called Piaf, registration number 38744, died at the age of exactly seventy years, after having spent twenty in detention and two in forced exile. They will find his decapitated cadaver seated at the foot of a mango tree, his head placed on his knees and his eyes devoured by red ants.

The boy won't be there to mourn him.

On June 6, 1933, he is freed.

HE ENDURED MALNUTRITION and bullying. He resisted chiggers and maggots. He avoided typhus, scurvy, beriberi, dysentery, hookworm, leprosy, cholera, tuberculosis, yellow fever, sharks, stabbings.

Now, he can die.

They give him his exit uniform: a three-piece suit, a shirt, a hat, shoes. They give him his pay—a derisory sum. That's all.

He is free.

He is not permitted to leave the territory. He is not permitted to practice most professions. He is not permitted to enter into most establishments. He is not permitted to sit on a public bench. He is not permitted to walk on the grass. He is not permitted to flee.

He is free.

He dawdles for a little while through the city. During the day along large roads, rue Mélinon, rue de la République, avenue des Cocotiers, during the night in the narrow, dirty alleyways, impassable after the rain, in the Chinese quarter or that of the freed. This is the zone. With a floor made of trash, puddles of stagnant water that spawn fetid odors and whistling toads. Around the shacks, the shanties, the wobbly dumps fixed up with rotten planks and rusty scrap metal. Signs of all kinds. Businesses. Hovels. Did you want something picturesque? You've got grime. Everything here is authentic, in the cesspits, in the backrooms of Asian gambling dens where the former convicts with tattooed skin play, and lose, and argue, and kill one another, where in front of sticky bars the blacks come from neighboring Suriname, with skin like soot, with sarongs in tatters, to drink the gold they've just won to their last dime. Rum. Punch. Tafia. It's poured. Drunks

everywhere. Floundering bodies and souls everywhere. The large
bakery in the center is called *Au bon acceuil*. Europeans pass it in their
immaculate clothes, negresses in garish calico, Martiniquans in mul-
ticolored robes, proud and nonchalant mestizos, Guyanese dressed up
like junk-shop dolls, scruffy Vietnamese, half-nude Indians covered
in pendants and amulets. All these people swarming about.

And he among them.

Because that's how men live.

Two weeks, three weeks go by. The boy wanders. He sleeps in a
shelter on a cot among ex-convicts and rats. He sleeps on the ground
under the fluttering canvas roof of the covered market. At dawn he
wakes up surrounded by a group of vultures dancing around him,
the slow swagger of scavengers. He eats the least expensive things.
Fried food, rocky beans, tough pieces of rancid beef, tips of hooves
in quick broth. Once he's given slivers of fried cassava wrapped up
in a newspaper. He eats the cassava. When he goes to get rid of the
greasy piece of paper, his eyes catch on a photo. It's the first page of
Paris-Soir, dated from six months ago, and the photo shows a brown-
haired pale man with a narrow mustache. He's already seen this face.
He racks his memory. Then he remembers: the little dog, the river, the
German soldier in front of his easel, a paintbrush in his hand. The
painter. The war. The past.

He crumples the sheet of paper in his fist and throws it on the
ground.

His savings are gone.

One night he goes to sit on the bank of the Maroni. The moon is
full and pale. It's beautiful. On the opposite shore shine timid little
lights. It's the city of Albina. Surinam. Dutch Guyana.

The boy watches a couple of macaws cross the border. Then a band
of skunks swim away.

In the distance, in the bush, the red colobus monkeys cry.

Two hours later he crosses the bend of the river on a leper's boat.

HE IS A PORTER IN PARAMARIBO. He is a shoe shiner in Georgetown. He is a sugar cane harvester in the plantation of Demerara. He is a butterfly chaser in Bartica. He is a sawyer in Marlborough. He works for gas companies in Venezuela, on the banks of the Maracaibo lakes. He taps chicle trees. He digs into the rock in the emerald mines of Colombia, in Muzo, in Chivor, in Montecristo, in Gachalá, and the men who surround him are all thieves and assassins and fugitives. He loads and unloads cargo holds in the port of Curaçao. He is a factotum on the schooner of a Syrian merchant who sells fabric and opium. They go along the coast to Macapa and the Amazon estuary, then from Macapa to Belém, from Belém to Fortaleza, from Fortaleza to Recife, from Recife to Salvador. That's where he gets off. He picks cocoa beans in the fazendas of Bahia. He harvests coffee in the Minas Gerais.

Then he goes inland.

He is nearly naked, skin cooked and tanned. A machete on his hip, a canvas bag on his shoulder carrying a handful of Brazil nuts and two coconuts and a half-pound of dried beef and one pound of black beans and three boxes of matches. That's all his provisions.

He eats the beans.

He eats the nuts.

He kills a twenty-foot boa and guts it and finds four big eggs with beige shells in its entrails.

He eats the eggs.

He eats the boa's flesh.

In the savanna of high Tombador he wounds a wild pig and doesn't have the time to finish it off before the entire hoard charges him and he has to take refuge in a tree and stay there for a full day before the pigs leave him and abandon him to his fate.

He spends a season among an indigenous population on the edge of Rio Vermelho. It's a village. A dozen shanties, sixty inhabitants. They were in the thousands a hundred years earlier, but progress could not be stopped. The men are nude apart from straw pouches covering their penises. They are red, bodies tinted from head to food with urucú seed. Their noses are pierced with a bar and their lips with a labret. They're happy. They're jovial. The women wear cotton sarongs and belts made of bark. On patches of cleared land they grow sweet potatoes, cassava, tobacco, corn. They have parrots and macaws in their yards. The boy gardens with them. He fishes with them. He learns to carve bows and arrows. He hunts the toucan. He hunts the anteater. He hunts the porcupine. He hunts the hare. With them he learns to recognize the edible roots, the berries, the mushrooms. He learns to unearth, in rotting tree trunks, big pale larvae called *koro* that melt on the tongue like butter and that taste like coconut milk. He makes pendants with the claws of the large armadillo. And jewelry from monkey teeth. And headdresses from egret feathers. The Indians sing all night long. They dance in front of the fire, their giant shadows projected onto a mural of kapok trees, and these shadows could be the very spirits their litanies are about. Theater and pantheon. The boy attends their masses. There is the coryphaeus who keeps the rhythm with a calabash rattle filled with gravel. He wears a diadem of vermillion feathers. He is the ibis-man. Another, tall and well-built, assumes the posture of a wild animal, lips reared, teeth bared. A cape of ocelot skin thrown on his back. He is the jaguar-man. They smoke cigarettes rolled in the leaves of dried corn. This lasts until dawn. They sleep until midday. The boy has his reserved spot in a shack with a palm-leaf roof. He shares it with the sorcerer and an old widowed woman who sings her numerous losses. She has had three husbands and three sons, and they all died. One by one she placed their remains in a pit until their flesh was putrefied, then she washed their bones, she painted them and decorated them with feathers and submerged them in a basket at the bottom of the *rio*. By water or by fire everything ends up disappearing. The boy doesn't understand her language, but he knows what she's singing. The old woman has two paralyzed legs. She drags herself around on the beaten earth. She is the caterpillar-woman.

One morning he leaves again. He brings a bow, arrows in his quiver, and a bit of poisonous paste in a bamboo tube.

He is in the vicinity of Cuiabá, where men are desperately looking for gold. They wait for rain. After the rainfall the whole tribe throws itself into the riverbeds and plunges balls of wax into the current, waiting for the precious specks to stick to them.

He hunts egrets with two Corsican cousins.

He mines diamonds in a *garimpeiro* encampment near Poxoréu, and the men around him are all thieves and assassins and fugitives. Diamonds: the Virgin Mother's teardrops in the hands of these bandits. It's not safe passage, however, that they'll buy with them. Their personal liturgy is founded on the rule of the three Cs: "Cemitério, cadeia, cachaça." Cemetery, cellblock, cachaça. One of these bandits spreads his jewels on the table in a hostel and pushes one towards the boy, saying that he wants his bow. The boy refuses. That night three of them surprise him and beat him up, rob him and leave him for dead in the mud.

He gets up.

He crosses the state of Mato Grosso, massive like the distant land of France. A territory ravaged six months of the year by the deluges and the other six months by absolute drought. He follows the path of a four-hundred-mile-long telegraph line across the desert, constructed by Marshal Rondon forty years earlier and proven to be obsolete as soon as it was finished. A trail that was crudely cut through the brush and the bushes and the cacti and the thorns. The telegraph poles like bare trunks, sterile, with neither sap nor branches nor foliage nor buds and often eaten by termites or knocked down by lightning, and never repaired or replaced. For what purpose? Morse code is dead. Hardly one message per day transmitted from a lost post to another lost post just to mutually assure that everyone is continuing to die a slow death. Between each pair, the line snakes in the dust.

In the middle of this desolation the boy once again encounters a few members of a primitive and nomadic tribe and he wanders with them for a bit. On their backs, the women carry large bamboo baskets that contain all their possessions. Little tamed monkeys cling to their hair. Scrawny dogs trot between their legs. Together they all march hunched over or stooped, searching the crust of arid cracked earth and the dry grass for their pittance. They eat locusts. They eat spiders. They eat lizards, snakes, rats. They eat tubers and seeds. At night they throw spears towards the skies to kill evil spirits. They know that the souls of dead men embody jaguars and the souls of women and children disappear into the void. They sleep right on the ground tight against each other to shield themselves from the cold and the boy sleeps with them. One day they offer him a little girl who is not even two years old as a spouse. The boy refuses. They insist. He refuses. Their paths diverge.

He picks the telegraph line back up and stops at each post. Each one at a distance of fifty miles or more, each one isolated and cut off from everything, each one maintained by a man or a couple or a family and half, if not all of them, completely crazy.

At the Juruena station he is housed in a hovel owned by three Jesuit priests: a Dutch, a Brazilian, a Hungarian. They have come to civilize the savages. In a mixed jargon they speak to him of remission and redemption and damnation. They speak to him of salvation. They try to lure him with the promise of the existence of a kingdom governed by a just and good king. But the boy has already played the Exalted One and he won't do it again.

He leaves the missionaries to preach in the desert and continues on the road north. Under his bare feet the grass grows back and turns green again.

He harvests rubber in the province of Manaus on the edge of the Rio Madeira. For two straight months he gets up at dawn to bleed the trees of their latex alongside a handful of *seringueiros* whose only wealth is the air they breathe and their only future the debts they incur. The owner of the plot is hardly better off. He's a tall beanpole of a man that no one has ever seen without his gun—an old Winchester .44 caliber rifle. They say he sleeps with it. They say that he was a colonel in the army and one of the main instigators in the 1930 revolution and that he's hiding here out of fear of reprisals. As his concubine he has a mammoth mestizo that he apparently kidnapped from a brothel in Trinidad. They have twin sons named Euclid and Archimedes who are twelve years old.

The boy earns just enough here to pay for passage in a dinghy owned by a Lebanese merchant who sells canned food and weapons. The next day the merchant drops him on the shores of the river of creation, and soon the boy plunges into the depths of the fertile jungle.

Amazon! Amazon!

This is it.

He roams virgin territories. Uncultivated lands. A jungle dense with fig and rubber trees, with jatobas, with courbarils, with copaibas. Entire acres covered in brambles and intertwined with cat scratches. Between the trunks and the trees. Between the roots and the foliage. Between the endless vines of the strangler fig tree and the high stilts of the walker palm tree. Amazon! Amazon! Nature explodes. Sap abounds. Corollas, cupolas, sepals, orchids sparkle here, hibiscuses there, and everywhere on the trees and the bushes ripen fruits and berries. He eats soursops, he eats guavas. He eats wild honey. He eats birds and saki monkeys. Amazon! Amazon! At every height unknown flowers, yellow, red, white, mauve, orange, purple, they upholster the walls and the arches. For him. He is the only one in this domain. He moves through the diffuse light. He discovers. He sees what no one has seen. He unknowingly walks along the equator. Zero latitude. No degree. He is in the middle of the world. Amazon! Amazon! He eats tarantulas. He eats iguanas. He eats pineapples that taste like raspberries. He eats hearts of palm and acerola cherries. He eats the fruit of the araca boi and that of the açai. He eats tortoise and uakari monkey. Amazon! Amazon! He roams. Far from any path. Far from any known road forged by anyone of his species. Pioneer of these lands, it seems. If there were predecessors, they're dead, they've been in exile for so long that even the memory of their existence has been erased. A nude conquistador. He explores. He climbs. Christens the smells just like the tapir or the anteater. A beast among beasts. Marking his path, the only essentials are rest, food, and water.

Amazon!

At the end of this long journey he ends up on the banks of the Rio Pastaza, near the Peruvian border. It's started to rain. The boy watches the gray waters of the river flow. The drops lash his skin. His hair drips. Towards the east a layer of haze floats. He's been there for less than five minutes when suddenly four men fall from trees or from the sky. Indigenous peoples. They surround him from a distance. Revolve around him slowly, immense blowpipes in their mouths, pointed in his direction. They are cautious. They are wary. They don't know what he is. What sort of creature. A man? An animal? A demon? A spirit of the forest?

Does he know himself?

His machete hangs from the end of his arm. He drops it. It's all he has. He raises his hands.

He remains in their village for as long as the rainy season lasts. He sleeps a lot. The Indians are distressed by his nightmares. Every time he wakes with a start, as if in a trance, it provokes endless debates among them. There are hardly more than thirty individuals. The leader of the tribe is particularly loquacious. He seems to find pleasure in the boy's company. Often he talks to him for long stretches of time punctuated with great bursts of laughter. Around his neck hangs the shrunken head of a valiant enemy. There is another, also, who seems to appreciate the boy's presence. A young Indian girl, barely pubescent. She makes eyes at him. She prepares and brings him a cassava and hot pepper fritter that she's thickened with her own saliva. She traces the contours of the scars on his torso with her fingers. With her flower crown and her painted forehead she reminds him of the icon that had watched over his sleep in the home of Joseph and his son Louis-Paul: La Diosa Centeotl. The first goddess he had ever come across. That was a long time ago.

When he leaves one morning, at daybreak, the young Indian is there. A thin and humble smile stretches across her lips. With her scepter of corn she makes a sign that could be a blessing or a banishment. And this near-goddess will be the last human being the boy will see.

Faith may abandon us, said Joseph, solitude remains.

THAT YEAR GERMANY ANNEXES AUSTRIA.

That year in Spain the Republican forces, opposed to Franco's nationalist insurgents, capture the city of Teruel.

That year in China the nationalist troops of Chiang Kai-shek, opposed to the Imperial Japanese Army of Hirohito, blow up the dykes of the Yellow River, causing the deaths of between five hundred thousand and nine hundred thousand people, according to sources.

That year in Munich, the chancellor Adolf Hitler, Il Duce Benito Mussolini, the French prime minister Édouard Daladier, and the British prime minister Arthur Neville Chamberlain sign an agreement on the status of Czechoslovakia. Upon his return to France, Daladier is roundly praised for having saved the peace. Upon his return to England, Chamberlain is welcomed as a hero and called the Peacemaker.

That year the film *Snow White and the Seven Dwarfs* is projected for the first time on French, Belgian, and Canadian screens.

That year the Francoist troops, opposed to the Republican forces, take back the city of Teruel.

That year Juan Carlos I is born, future King of Spain.

In Romania, King Charles II abolishes the parliamentary regime to install a royal dictatorship.

In Glasgow, Scotland, the Queen of England christens the ocean liner *Queen Elizabeth*, the biggest and most beautiful in the world, and naturally unsinkable.

That year in France, the National Society of French Railroads, Société nationale des chemins de fer français (SNCF), is officially established.

That year in France, the prime minister Édouard Daladier breaks with the communists, announcing the de facto end of the Popular Front.

That year in France, the statutory law authorizes Daladier to call for the house arrest and internment of foreigners susceptible to public harm, as well as the opening of special centers to facilitate their permanent surveillance.

That year in France, the Bíró brothers, having fled the anti-Jewish laws of Hungary, file a patent for the invention of the ballpoint pen.

In Italy, the racial laws, founded on scientific hypotheses intended to prove the existence of the Italian race and its belonging to the group of Aryan races, are ratified by the leader of the government Benito Mussolini and promulgated by King Victor Emmanuel III.

In Germany, Heinrich Himmler issues a decree addressing the need to "combat the gypsy nuisance."

In the United States, Samuel Gensberg, son of Jewish immigrants from Poland, invents the first pinball machine.

In Moscow, the Soviet Union opens a third large trial, over the course of which twenty-one former Bolsheviks accused of espionage and of a plot to assassinate Stalin are judged. All confess. All but three are condemned to death and executed.

The journal *Pravda*, which means "Truth," reports that the verdict is greeted by large displays of widespread joy.

That year Léon Trotsky, exiled, creates the Fourth International.

That year Kanō Jigorō, founder of judo, which means "gentle way," dies.

That year in the little village of Kaio, Japan, a young man of twenty-one years named Mutsuo Toi decapitates his grandmother and kills twenty-eight other inhabitants with the aid of an ax, a katana, and a Remington M11, before killing himself.

In Basel, Switzerland, the Sandoz laboratory synthesizes lysergic acid diethylamide more commonly known as LSD.

In the United States, the director Orson Welles adapts the science-fiction novel *War of the Worlds* for radio and terrorizes a large number of listeners who actually believe an alien invasion is taking place.

In Germany, the forces of the Third Reich engage in a pogrom against the Jewish community. Over the course of this incredible feat, baptized Kristallnacht, Crystal Night, two hundred synagogues are destroyed, thousands of businesses and companies vandalized, a hundred Jewish people assassinated, and nearly thirty thousand deported to the camps.

In the United States, Jerry Siegel and Joe Shuster, two sons of Jewish immigrants, create a character called Superman.

In France, the character Spirou is born in the eponymous journal.

In Brazil, the most celebrated of the *cangaceiros*, Virgulino Ferreira da Silva, called Lampião, dies.

That year in Germany, the chancellor Adolf Hitler unveils the Volkswagen factory, which produces the new car of the people: a vehicle that will be known internationally under the name Beetle, and designed by engineer Ferdinand Porsche, member of the Nazi party and also creator of the Tiger tank.

That year at Yankee Stadium in New York in the United States, the black American boxer Joe Louis defeats the German champion Max Schmeling by knockout at two minutes and four seconds in the first round.

That year the Vatican recognizes the nationalist government of Franco.

That year the Italian football team wins the World Cup, presumably encouraged by the message sent by Il Duce, Mussolini: "Win or die."

That year Germany annexes the Sudetenland.

That year the writer Georges Bernanos publishes *The Great Cemeteries Under the Moon*.

That year off the African coast, a fisherman hauls in a fish identified as a coelacanth, unseen for around seventy million years. What some call a "Lazarus taxon," it was the resurrection of a species thought to be definitively extinct.

AND THEN? When all the paths have been marked and followed? And after that, long after, when the sun is nothing more than a white dwarf?

Time narrows. An old man appears. His own ancestor.

Have to reach the end.

Sea, sea, she had said to him. But he saw one shore of the sea and he saw the other shore and he found nothing. The two edges of the horizon and he found nothing. What fabulous trip was she dreaming of? Peaceful and warm. Golden and light.

If it's not down here then maybe it's up above.

The boy lifts his eyes. In front of him are the first foothills of a great mountain range. The Andes. Like a gigantic telluric caprice, a monumental dread constructed by powers whose very existence exceeds us. Ramparts and towers and precipices. In the distance the immaculate scree of a volcano. Snow that never melts.

The boy begins his ascent.

He climbs.

Who knows how many hours and how many days and how many nights. Who knows?

He climbs.

And little by little the incline becomes steeper, the slope more abrupt. The plants disappear. Grass, moss, lichen. The barren rock. The rock stripped down to the bone. And same with the boy. His memories come and then they go. One by one. Layer after layer, stratum after stratum they surge and then vanish. Images, sounds, sentiments. What to retain? Nothing. Make room! Make room! Make room for the void. As he climbs everything detaches from him. Or is it he who detaches from them? All those things and all those beings. The humble and sweet smile of the young Indian girl. A pink dolphin in the mauve waters of a rio. The metallic blue wings of a morpho butterfly, large like fig leaves. And the melted ears and nose and lips of a leper in a dugout canoe. The infant cry of a howler monkey. The cry of a gull on the deck of a cargo ship. The cry of Private Wachfeld calling to his mother. The red hand of the corporal sprouting from the mud. The white envelopes in the corporal's hand. The big black flies on the eyelashes of the gelding. The rats. The worms. The fields of cadavers. The stench of decomposing flesh. And the supple flesh, the tender flesh, the warm flesh, the living flesh of Emma. Emma's breasts. Emma's hips. Emma's mouth. My love, she would say. My love. Emma's eyes. Emma's voice. Emma's words. My love. And the pearls of sun hanging from the willow's branches. Their tree. Their dear tree. And the verses of the poet. And the song of the oboe player. The warm gaze of Gustave beneath his heavy eyelids. And Brabek in his cask bath, beneath the stars. The enormous laugh of the ogre. His enormous feet. His enormous hands. His enormous heart. And the bronze horse. And the silver horses. The trembling ground. Kazoo dancing, his grace, his chaos, his dog-like caresses. And Jesus in his cradle. And Joseph the wise man. The oak-man. His roots in the earth and his mind in the clouds.

All of his memories, as many as there are, they come and then they go. They run through the boy's head and then grow distant, fade, the multitude, all of humanity. His humanity. Little by little he rids himself of them.

He climbs.

As long and as high as he can, he climbs.

Then he stops.

Now it's the crude mountain. Everywhere, all around. The rock rugged and stark. The skeleton. Now they have all gone. All those beings, and all those invisible and immaterial things that have a name while he has none.

See: there is nothing left.

The boy sits on a flat rock that juts out. For a moment he thinks he can smell the odor of his mother again. Her aroma of saltpeter and ash. Then that vanishes like the rest. He lies on his back, facing the sky. He is alone.

He spends the last three days of his life watching the condors swirl.

ABOUT THE AUTHOR

MARCUS MALTE was born in 1967 in La Seyne-sur-Mer, a small harbor city in the south of France, along the coast of the Mediterranean Sea. As a child, Malte immersed himself in literature, discovering the novels of John Steinbeck, Albert Cohen, Louis-Ferdinand Céline and Jean Giono. He began writing in elementary school and chose to major in film studies after graduating from high school. At twenty-three, Malte became a projectionist in La Seyne's historical movie theater and soon wrote his first short stories. Later in the 1990s he began reaching a broader audience with a series of novels, a couple of hard-boiled detective stories in which Malte created the recurrent character of Mister, a jazz pianist.

Marcus Malte's fiction includes *Garden of Love* (rewarded with a dozen literary prizes, including the Grand prix des lectrices de *Elle*, crime fiction, 2008); *Les Harmoniques* (Prix Mystère de la Critique, 2012); and more recently *Le Garçon* (*The Boy*) for which he received the famous Prix Femina (2016). *The Boy* is his first novel to be translated into English.

ABOUT THE TRANSLATORS

EMMA RAMADAN is a literary translator based in Providence, RI where she is the co-owner of Riffraff bookstore and bar. She is the recipient of a PEN/Heim grant, an NEA translation grant, and a Fulbright fellowship for her translation work.

TOM ROBERGE is co-owner of Riffraff bookstore and bar in Providence, Rhode Island. He learned French as a Peace Corps volunteer in Madagascar and was formerly the Deputy Director of Albertine Books, a French language bookstore in New York.

ABOUT THE INTRODUCER

JULIE ORRINGER is the author of the novel *The Invisible Bridge* and the award-winning short-story collection *How to Breathe Underwater*, which was a *New York Times* Notable Book. She is the winner of the *Paris Review*'s Plimpton Prize for Fiction and the recipient of fellowships from the National Endowment for the Arts, Stanford University, and the Dorothy and Lewis B. Cullman Center for Scholars and Writers at the New York Public Library. She lives in Brooklyn.

RESTLESS BOOKS is an independent, nonprofit publisher devoted to championing essential voices from around the world, whose stories speak to us across linguistic and cultural borders. We seek extraordinary international literature that feeds our restlessness: our hunger for new perspectives, passion for other cultures and languages, and eagerness to explore beyond the confines of the familiar. Our books—fiction, narrative nonfiction, journalism, memoirs, travel writing, and young people's literature—offer readers an expanded understanding of a changing world.

Visit us at restlessbooks.org